Additional titles by t

Handbook for Touring Bicyclists
Strike Three! Take Your Base
An Extreme Encounter: Antarctica
Bicycling Around the World: Tire Tracks for Your Imagination
Motorcycle Adventure to Alaska: Into the Wind
Losing Your Best Friend: Vacancies of the Heart
Rafting the Rolling Thunder: A Journey Through
The Grand Canyon
How to Deal With 21st Century American Women:
Co-creating a Successful Relationship
Bicycling the Continental Divide: Slice of Heaven,
Taste of Hell
How to Live a Life of Adventure: The Art of
Exploring the World
America on the Brink: The Next Added 100
Million Americans
Living Your Spectacular Life
Old Men Bicycling Across America: A Journey
Beyond Old Age
Zen Between Two Bicycle Wheels: Eat, Pedal, Sleep
America's Overpopulation Predicament:
Blindsiding Future Generations

THE KICKSTAND CHRONICLES: THE MIRACULOUS, FUNNY, SUBLIME, AND DOWNRIGHT TERRIFYING

INEVITABLE MOMENTS OF THE JOURNEY—BICYCLING ACROSS SIX CONTINENTS, 45 YEARS, 150,000 MILES

Frosty Wooldridge

Author's Tranquility Press
MARIETTA, GEORGIA

Frosty Wooldridge /Author's Tranquility Press
2706 Station Club Drive SW
Marietta, GA 30060
www.authorstranquilitypress.com

Ordering Information:
Quantity sales. Special discounts are available on quantity purchases by corporations, associations, and others. For details, contact the "Special Sales Department" at the address above.

The Kickstand Chronicles/ Frosty Wooldridge.
Paperback: 978-1-957208-73-2
eBook: 978-1-957208-74-9

Dedicated to:

My brother Rex Wooldridge for his intrepid spirit, adventures around the world, and for his steadfast belief in the power of self-confidence. When he walks into a room, he inspires others to attain their highest and best. When it comes to adventure, he sets his mind into gear, his soul on fire, and his heart toward the vast expanses of the planet. Together, we've shared some great adventures around this amazing globe. To him, more exploits, more friends, more laughter, and more of all life has to offer.

Acknowledgments:

Special thanks to Sandi Lynn for brilliant copy editing along with ideas for creating a compelling and motivational piece of literature. Thanks to my fabulous wife Sandi for her treasured ideas and daily support.

The Spirit of Adventure

"If the roar of a wave crashes beyond your campsite, you might call that adventure. When coyotes howl outside your tent—that may be an adventure. While you're sweating like a horse in a climb over a 12,000-foot pass, that's an adventure. When a howling headwind presses your lips against your teeth, you're facing a mighty challenge. If you're pushing through a howling rainstorm, you're soaked in adventure. But that's not what makes an adventure. It's your willingness to struggle through it, to present yourself at the doorstep of Nature. That decision creates the experience. No greater joy can come from life than to live inside the 'moment' of an adventure. It may be a momentary 'high', a stranger that changes your life, an animal that delights you or frightens you, a struggle where you triumphed, or even failed, yet you braved the challenge. Those moments present you with uncommon experiences that give your life eternal expectation. That's adventure!"

Frosty Wooldridge

Table of Contents

Introduction

Movement constitutes the lifeblood of bicycling. Much like stallions galloping across wide-open plains, I understand their sheer delight in movement. They glide through tall grasses—graceful, strong, kicking, playing—showing off for no one, save their own delight. I, too, "gallop" on a bicycle with an endless ecstasy of motion coursing through my body.

In my youth, my parent's military careers kept us changing bases every two years. By fifteen, I had traveled throughout the USA and abroad. Every "adventure," as dad called them, carried us into the wilderness. We camped because we were too poor to rent a motel.

That may have been an excuse because my parents loved the wilds. A stream, lake or ocean beach provided their quiet time. We pitched a tent every night in the perfect spot. "Perfect" because it was located in the woods.

It gets into your blood—traveling and camping. For me, those formative years brought a clarion call to explore. The movement creates the potential for growth. One improves through the input of experiences and each one offers a better grasp of understanding. The end result equates to wisdom—along with a sense of harmony with all creatures and life on this planet.

While I grew up, a bicycle became my wings. It carried me down dirt roads and through the woods. Each morning, like a workhorse, it carried me on my paper route with a load of news and comics. I had no idea that it was preparing me for a life of two-wheeled adventures around the world.

While traveling one summer, I met two guys on touring bicycles at the Arctic Circle on the Dalton Highway in Alaska. They sounded reverently enthusiastic about bike adventuring. They said, "We live on the edge of wonder every day." Voila! A smooth mesh of spokes and gray matter clicked in my brain.

In the summer of 1975, I set out to cross the United States coast-to-coast. On a bike, my days on the road exceeded my wildest dreams. I felt a treble-hook latch onto my soul. Life flowed into simple, peaceful rhythms. While I pedaled up steep mountain grades or through barren deserts—big events meant nothing, and the little things became important. Food, water and a campsite turned into my daily concerns. Something new might happen around every bend in the road and "anticipation" made each day exciting. Constant aerobic activity released body drugs called "endorphins." That MUST be why I've enjoyed a love affair with bicycle touring over the years.

Along with the "happy high" of bicycle adventuring, I've discovered that life is not a solitary journey. Cycling teaches lessons. Animals, plants and insects share their wisdom. I am thankful for their taking the time to teach me. In this book, you will meet them. One other creature teaches, too, and has delighted me through the years. It's the human being on his or her path. For that journey, no guidebooks exist, except for the rising sun. It lights whichever chosen path.

This book shares a few of the most profound experiences of my past 45 years on the road—sometimes three months and at other times, a full year. Happily, each of us carries panniers full of dreams. It's up to us to fill them with each stroke of the pedals. Out on the road, it is as much a spiritual journey as it is physical. Hopefully, you too become addicted to the art of bicycle adventuring. As the Hobbit said, "There's a whole lot of adventure outside your front door."

You might enjoy another quote by an intrepid traveler named Jean Luc Picard of the Starship Enterprise. He and Commander Riker sifted through a broken ship that had crashed before its time. They talked about "time" passing.

Captain Picard said, "Someone once said that "time" is a predator that stalks us all our lives. But I rather believe that time is a companion that goes with us on a journey. It reminds us to cherish each moment, because it will never come again. What we leave behind is not as important as how we have lived."

Essentially, this book offers you "miraculous… funny…sublime… and downright terrifying" moments across six continents of bicycle travel over four decades. Each one of those "moments" touched me deeply whether physically, mentally or spiritually.

Additionally, I've been told that bicycle touring equates to 90 percent of drudgery and only 10 percent of excitement. I beg to differ. Bicycle travel engages your mind, body and spirit 100 percent of the time. It also elevates you into the realm of an "uncommon man or woman." It places you in that rare air of Captain Cook who sailed around the world, or Marco Polo who walked and rode a horse across Asia, or John Muir who walked thousands of miles across North America, or Nellie Bly who traveled everywhere, or Amelia Erhardt who flew solo across the Atlantic and attempted to fly around the world.

You might look up Heinz Stucke who has bicycled around the globe in 190 countries over the past 60 years. Another modern-day explorer, Dutch woman Hera Van Willick has ridden across six continents. She's featured in a video "Pedal" by vimeo.com. It's outstanding!

She said, "I put my cycling into these categories—learning, growth, teaching, love, contact and exploration. I don't just pass through a country. I live where I ride."

As You Travel Across the Globe

A new country, a new culture, a new language, and new opportunities for enthralling experiences await you around this planet. Each cyclist crosses world boundaries to discover the varieties of humanity on an intimate level at 12-15 miles per hour. We don't fly in, pay for a bus trip around the city, eat at elegant restaurants, and/or sleep in fancy hotels. We don't wear pressed pants and fancy shirts. Women cyclists lack makeup, frilly dresses and high heels that boast a cosmopolitan slant.

We don't carry an 'air' of attitude, wealth or privilege. When a long-distance touring cyclist reaches across a new country's border, he or she becomes an ambassador of peace, friendship and inspiration. One of the great gifts of bicycle travel manifests in each cyclist's extraordinary ability to bring his or her understanding, patience and humility to each new country visited. In many ways, a cyclist becomes the finest ambassador for his or her country, because the citizens of countries around the world enjoy the bare-bones freedom as well as commonality of humanity within cyclists and within each of us.

The Nastiness of Life: Raw Adventure Takes Guts, Gumption and True Grit

Raw adventure takes guts, gumption and true grit. You choose to get off the couch and power your way into the sheer nastiness of life! Yeah, it might be nice one day, and it could be okay another day—but life might throw you a tornado or a howling rainstorm to test your resolve. You must bring your courage to life. You must dig your feet into the day. You must bring your club to the game of life and intend to take charge. As for a reality check, you carry your body and mind into unknown danger. You could get killed at any moment with thousands of automobiles racing past you at 60 miles per hour. Especially if they are "texting" on their smartphone! At the same time, you marshal all your senses to discover your finest qualities of spirit.

While the rest of humanity lives from day to day, you relish physical, mental, emotional and spiritual challenges. What is life all about? Will you read a book by some philosopher to find out? The heck with that! Get your butt out there into the wind, the rain, the storm, and the tempest! Imprint a living book of your experiences into your own mind-body. Take your sheer guts and face the grit of life speeding toward you. Spit into the wind. Take a dare with life! What's normal? One wealthy friend of mine said, "Normal isn't all it's cracked up to be."

Become anything but normal! My dad said, "Kick butt and take names later!" Another more euphemistic way of saying it, is by Richard Bach, "The perfect speed Jonathan is not the speed of light or speed of a butterfly. The perfect speed is...being there."

Are you facing the Great Plains of America on your bike? What about the Atacama Desert in Chile? Ever cooked in the heat of the Outback? Have you faced 130 degrees Fahrenheit crossing Death Valley? What about climbing into the Himalaya or the Andes? Ever busted into the Swiss Alps? The tougher the ride, the greater the stories.

So, get out there, whatever you love doing, and rock it! Express yourself in paintings, photographs, playing guitar under the stars, climbing, rafting, kayaking, backpacking, bicycling and/or whatever pulls at your heartstrings. It's your life! Live it to the max!

What Dream Has Your Name on It?

As a veteran touring rider, and also a day rider—when I travel on my bike, I may stop at an overlook, sit by a river...or simply rest on a pile of rocks. I may lay on my back in the grass and look up at the clouds skidding across the sky. They make me dream!

Especially when I'm on tour, dozens of people yell, "You're living my dream!" Some say, "Wish I could do what you're doing." One guy said, "I wish I would have done what you're doing when I was young...I'm too old now."

First of all, I am a farm boy from LeRoy, Michigan. Nothing special. I rode my bike five miles to school each day. Milked cows and baled hay, cultivated corn, and fed the chickens. No big deal. My 10th-grade teacher said, "I never thought that you would amount to much of anything."

My dad who served in the United States Marines bequeathed in me a sense of self-confidence. Probably, that proved his greatest gift to his kids.

After graduation from college, I decided I wanted to bicycle all seven continents. I took a teaching job that afforded three months off every summer. And yes, I've written numerous books and articles.

Mostly though, I'd like to see everyone living their own dreams while they enjoy this "singularly amazing moment of life" on this planet.

So, here are some ideas for you to consider:

Most people stumble through their teens, stagger through their twenties and meander into their thirties.

By forty, they suffer a mid-life crisis before bumping into the big "50".

From 50, they face the last third of their lives with a sense of a downhill slide. Most never lived any "epic" moments or vanquished any dragons let alone navigated a great sailing ship called the Black Pearl like Captain Jack Sparrow. None took off through space like Star Trek with the Next Generation on the Starship Enterprise.

Most Americans enjoy two-week vacations with scant time to climb Mt. Everest or raft the Amazon. Others feel so locked into their jobs that nothing or no one can change their fate.

What if teens and twenties changed the course of their existence by co-creating their lives with a greater power, a higher understanding and a plan to enjoy their chosen way of life? Remember that quote by Jean Luc Picard, "...What we leave behind is not as important as how we lived."

Breathe that statement into your spirit. Incorporate it into your mind. Engage it with your curiosity and passions.

What turns you on in your daily existence? What moves you to action? What appeals to you?

For every human being on Earth, a little engine inside calls for "something" to activate a life purpose. How do you discover which path calls you?

What heroes do you follow? Why? What great moments in history move you? How do you feel when you study a certain subject? What books engage your interest? What famous movie role inspires you?

It's my contention that you discover your life path by following the slightest thread of your desires. From there, you make your intentions.

One such young lady wanted to fly an airplane. As she grew up, she used a doll for her co-pilot, which she placed next to her in her "airplane" with two seats in her room. As she grew older, she kept the doll next to her and carried it with her when she attended college. After college, she worked at an airport, but couldn't afford flying lessons. Nonetheless, she made friends with pilots and trainers alike. At all times, she kept her doll with her to remind her of her dream to fly.

As fate entered the picture, she became an assistant to a veteran airline pilot trainer. She worked hard, showed up on time, stayed late and kept the books in order. After a year of watching her, he offered her some time in a flight simulator. Soon, she showed her adept skills as a pilot which impressed the trainer. He offered to take her up in a single-engine plane for flight training. She earned, scraped and saved money for flying lessons. After two years, she gained her pilot's license. At all times, her doll sat with her in the cockpit.

Soon, she learned how to pilot a twin-engine plane. She flew clients all over the country. With that money, she learned to pilot a 747 with the same trainer who started her out years before. When she received her license to pilot a 747, she earned a job with a major airline.

Today, as an international 747 airline pilot, she visits places all over the world. Along with her, that same doll, that same dream that same intention rides in the cockpit beside her. In fact, she is a friend of mine and wrote a book: **A Chick in the Cockpit: My Life Up In The Air** by Erika Armstrong.

Ask yourself: What dream has your name on it?

On this long journey of your life, you must co-create your life path with the creative energy within you. You possess all the tools and all the ingenious energy to engage in a positive, useful, purposeful and happy life.

Open to possibilities daily, engage the flow, and receive the favors of the universe. Finally, weave your story toward co-creating your dynamic life. Take action toward your chosen destiny.

You Can Be Young and You Can Be Old

My Irish friend Dave tips the scale at 71 years. Yet, he thinks he's 21. He relates his story on bicycle adventure: So, having been cycling for the past 27 years, here are my personal thoughts and observations on some aspects of cycling long distances.

Cycling brings you a pure exclusive and overwhelming joy. It's a great feeling of freedom and well-being as your legs propel you across long distances and to new destinations. The soft "hum" of your tires on the road, the pleasure of taking a sip of drink on a really hot day. The small beads of salty sweat make their way through your bandana and roll down to the tip of your nose and onto your top tube. You've got to love that moment you reach the summit of a really hard climb and you click into a slightly higher gear the second you reach the top.

The uplifting feeling you get when a tailwind picks you up and you are propelled effortlessly forward at great speed. Knowing that the burning muscular pain of a long hard climb will be instantly forgotten on the descent and the next day. The expectation of cycling around an uncharted bend not knowing what is around the corner!

Hearing heavy rain on the outside of your tent, knowing you're safe and dry. Fixing a puncture and immediately finding somewhere to wash your hands. The smell of a new inner tube. Knowing that you can cycle over 80 miles day after day after day. Meeting new people, be it other cyclists, other travelers or just folks you just meet along the way. Having a shower and a cold beer after a long day in the saddle. Finding out what is making that annoying "clicking" noise on your bike and eliminating it.

I'm in my seventy-first year now and as I write this, I am preparing for a cycle across Asia. I can't wait. That's what cycling does to you; it becomes part of your life, your heart and your soul. Once mounted and riding your bicycle, you become one with yourself, the world and with a little bit of imagination, the universe.

The Way of the Long Distance Cyclist

"I want to see the world. Follow a map to its edges and keep going. Forgo the plans. Trust my instincts. Let curiosity be my guide. I want to change hemispheres. Sleep with unfamiliar stars. And let the journey unfold before me." Iohan Gueorguiev displayed his handwritten manifesto on his handlebars

This book comprises more than 45 years and 150,000 miles of travel across six continents. It includes 15 trips coast-to-coast across America and Canada to Mexico. The stories herein comprise the wildest, craziest, funniest, most provocative and most dangerous moments of my life on the road. The chapters are arranged in sequences that integrate the characters, events, dramas, humor and philosophies of this book in a coherent and complimentary style.

SECTION I: TOURING THE UNITED STATES

Chapter 1—Teeth, Claws and Antlers

"The hard life that never knows harness, The wilds where the caribou call. The freshness, the freedom, the farness— Oh God! How I'm stuck on it all."

—Robert Service "Spell of the Yukon"

Ramshackle buildings with wooden boardwalks lined the streets as we pedaled into Dawson City, Yukon on a hot July day. Stooped-shouldered, craggy-faced prospectors shuffled along in the dirt without giving us a nod. Bowie knives hung from their belts and they gripped rifles in their hands as easily as a Chicago businessman carries a briefcase. Their faces reflected the rough life that hadn't changed since the days of Jack London.

Ever an optimist, I didn't know how anyone could live in that place where the winter winds bit like driven nails.

My brother Rex purchased a gold pan and caught up with me at the Klondike Grocery Store. I crammed apples into my panniers.

"Ready to camp?" Rex asked. "I'm itchin' to hit the stream for some gold panning."

"The storekeeper said we could find a place a mile from here on a tributary of the Yukon," I said.

"This buckaroo is gonna make the big strike," Rex said, joking.

We pedaled our fully loaded mountain bikes out of town to an abandoned path overgrown with bushes. The rutted trail led through deep woods and several times, we got off the bikes to hoist them over fallen trees. We followed the path down a ravine until it stopped at a wide, shallow stream. A sandbar stood in the middle of the slowly gliding current. It was one of those places where tranquility kept a vigil and only the whisper of the wind broke the silence.

"This is the perfect place to start the next Klondike gold rush," Rex said, slapping his pan. "You want first chance?"

"Go ahead," I said. "I'll set up the tents."

Rex took off his shoes and waded into the water. I pulled the panniers from our bikes, pitched the tents, and had camp set up in 30 minutes. After starting a fire with deadwood, I boiled some water for tea.

With a steaming cup in one hand, I grabbed my journal and walked down to the river's edge. Sitting against a rock with my socks off, I wasn't paying much attention to my gold-panning brother. Overhead, white clouds skidded across the sky and a cool wind whispered through the pine trees. We camped in a serene setting—the dark soil, the rocks, and a pine-scented forest—and beyond, a river that crawled between sandy banks like escaped quicksilver.

"You rich yet?" I yelled at Rex as he dumped another panfull of muddy water.

"Any minute now," he said, standing up to rub his back. "This gold panning hurts my back."

Rex continued his task while I wrote a few lines in my notebook. That journal had been a part of my bicycling travels for many years, but every time I began scribbling, I still wondered what to write. That shatteringly beautiful waterfall we had seen last night, turned to molten gold by the sun? The slow dark glide of that bald eagle on his dinner patrol. The salmon lashing upstream toward birth and death?

So absorbed was I in my thoughts, I only partially heard the harsh crackling of nearby brush and breaking limbs from across the stream. But what happened next brought me leaping to my feet and turned my blood to ice. The journal fell from my hands.

Terrifying roars and bellows filled the air, and sounds of snapping limbs echoed across the river. Whatever it was, it was BIG—and the battle was being joined.

"What the hell was that?" Rex shouted, dropping his pan and scrambling out of the water.

"I'm not sure," I said, as he stopped beside me, breathing hard.

"I don't think we should wait around," Rex said—and at that moment a bull moose stumbled into view, head erect and blood blackening on his torn shoulder. He lowered his rack, as an enormous grizzly rushed at him and swatted the antlers aside. The grizzly charged with his thick neck lowered and extended, and his jaws opened wide as he lunged for the moose's throat. Somehow, the moose avoided the grizzly's teeth, and dug in his haunches so that the muscles in his legs were cable tight. He countered with a lunge at the bear's chest. Horn ripped through his brown hide, hit bone—and the grizzly roared, but the killing lust was on him.

In its charged again, half-rearing on his hind legs, both paws swatting at the moose like a boxer, staggering the animal. The moose bellowed, gave ground, and came back again— and suddenly both animals reared, hooves to fangs, one desperate to live, the other intent on killing.

"Let's get out of here," I whispered. "Leave the gear. We'll get it later. This is not the time to worry about the small stuff."

Rex needed no urging, and although every nerve in my body—and probably Rex's—screamed at me to run like hell, I forced myself to walk my bike into the tree line. There, back in the shadows, we watched the brutal drama unfolding on nature's stage.

The moose suffered the worst of things, yet he battled gallantly, keeping his antlered head low and catching the grizzly each time it charged. But the bear was the size of a VW Beetle, almost as heavy and as solid as the moose. He towered higher when he stood—so that he could strike downward with his razor-sharp claws, ripping his prey's shoulders like a toreador lancing the forequarters of a bull to weaken it—and make it lower its head for the matador's sword thrust.

A bull moose weighs 1,200 pounds and a grizzly can reach 1,100 pounds. These two seemed evenly matched in size—which meant that the bear, with his four-inch claws and two-inch teeth, enjoyed an advantage. Barring some stupid move, like allowing his jugular to be pierced by an antler, the grizzly's victory was a certainty.

From our hidden vantage point, looking out between the limbs of trees, we saw bright rivulets of blood running down the bear's chest. The moose was now a pitiful sight, staggering with weariness, back into the shallows where the water was turning reddish brown, and a large piece of antler was broken off by one mighty blow from the grizzly's paw. In came the bear again, roaring so fiercely it was almost a scream, and the exhausted moose grunted back its defiance.

Now, however, the battle's balance had shifted. The bear's sharp claws ripped into the moose's ribs, laying them bare. Then the bear's teeth sank into the neck, and only by a supreme effort was the moose able to shake him off again.

I didn't want to watch anymore, yet my fascinated eyes were ready for the final drama. After five minutes that seemed like hours, the bear made one last head-down charge—and sent the moose sprawling into the river. The moose made a final bellow, a last exhausted attempt to rise, but it was hopeless. The grizzly had him by the throat, and the moose thrashed erratically for a minute, then died.

"Oh, my God," Rex whispered, gripping my arm.

The bear held his grip until the moose stopped quivering. Then, raising his massive anvil-shaped head, he let out a roar that shivered the forest air, and began feeding.

I felt as Rex did, as any human being would—it had been a frightening scene. Savage violence was unleashed beside a beautiful stream in the wilderness. Yet no one had committed a crime. Life sustains life.

The grizzly, blood mixed with froth lathering his jaw, raised his head and looked right at us. Whether the wind had shifted or not, we were leaving.

"Come on," I whispered. "Let's get back to town, not that anyone there is going to believe what we saw."

In the morning, we rode back to find our gear still intact, but on the sandbar, a partly devoured moose carcass was the only indication of the battle.

In silence, we folded the tents and packed our gear.

"I guess you're out of a gold pan," I said.

"I don't care," Rex said. "Money can't buy what we saw yesterday."

We pedaled our way out of the woods. The gravel road wound through the mountains like a lazy serpent, bending and slithering its way along the Yukon River. We pedaled our bikes up a long grade to the "Top of the World Highway." No telling what lay ahead. That's the way it's been for my bicycle and me—always the promise of a new adventure around the next bend in the road...

Robert Service known as the "Poet of the Yukon" said it this way:

The summer no sweeter than ever,
The sunshiny woods all a thrill.
The grayling a leap in the river,
The bighorn asleep on the hill.

It's that great big, broad land way up yonder,
It's the forests where silence has lease.
It's the beauty that thrills me with wonder,
It's the stillness that fills me with peace.

The strong life that never knows harness,
The wilds where the caribou call.
The freshness, the freedom, the farness—
Oh God! How I'm stuck on it all.

(This grizzly looked back at us as we carefully fled the scene.)

Chapter 2—Walking Across America on His Hands

> ***"Courage is one thing. A sense of purpose another. When you put them together in one human being, the world can be changed."***
>
> ***—John Brown***

That first summer, I pedaled through heavy traffic for the beginning of my coast-to-coast bicycle adventure. The Los Angeles smog-choked me for 100 miles into the Mojave Desert. After crossing the Colorado River, I breathed easier when the brown cloud flowed south toward Phoenix. I pedaled into cleaner air in the mountains. Climbing steep grades took half the day while coasting down the backside took only 45 minutes.

In New Mexico, I crossed the continental divide and descended into the desert on Route 380. With a blazing sun overhead, I struggled along the two-lane pavement. Sweat dripped from my face and arms. Every breath crowded my mouth with air as dry and hot as cotton balls. Heat waves rippled over the pavement as I descended further into the barren landscape. The thermometer hit 103 degrees by the time I was ten miles out of Roswell, New Mexico.

Ahead, I noticed a lone figure walking along the left side of the road. It was hard imagining how anyone could be walking down the highway in that torrid heat.

"I wonder what that guy's doing walking in this heat?" I muttered to myself. "Looks like he's got a dog with him, too."

"That isn't a dog," I gasped seconds later, doubting my eyes, and straining harder to make out what I saw.

It was another man walking in his hands. Within a few seconds, I found out why. His legs were missing.

Less than forty yards away, the lone figure was a man reading a book, walking beside another man walking on his hands. A camper van was parked on the shoulder a half mile ahead. I rode up even with them. Something inside just made me stop and lay my bike in the gravel.

I couldn't help crossing the road, knowing that whoever this man was, he possessed inconceivable courage. What was he doing out here walking on his hands in the desert? He saw me and stopped. He lowered his body down to the ground, resting it on a leather pad that covered his two severed legs just below the groin. His Paul Bunyan upper arms led down to his hands, which grasped two rubber pads. Sweat soaked his T-shirt. His sandy-brown hair framed a tanned, round face punctuated by a pair of clear eyes. He flashed a beautiful smile.

"Hi, how ya doin'?" I said, approaching with my hand extended. "My name is Frosty."

"Glad to meet you," he said shaking my hand. "I'm Bob Wieland. This is my friend Alex who helps me on this journey."

"Pleasure to meet you both," I said. "I gotta tell you Bob, I'm more than a bit curious seeing you out here in the desert."

"The same could be said about you," he said. "What are you doing out here?"

"I'm riding my bicycle across America."

"That makes two of us," Bob added. "I'm walking across. I'd bike but my legs are too short for the pedals."

I laughed. His humor was natural. We bantered a few minutes about the weather. Bob gave me a short history of his journey. He started at Knott's Berry Farm on the coast of California and intended to reach Washington DC. It would eventually take him 4,900,000 'steps'. His friend fixed meals, but often, people asked them into their homes for the night. If no one offered a night's lodging, both men slept in the back of the camper pickup. His friend drove the vehicle ahead and came back to walk with him. His companion read a book while guiding Bob down the left side of the highway. Bob lost his legs in combat. I asked him when he had started.

"I've been out 19 months and have completed 980 miles," he said. "At my speed, I can finish this adventure in three more years, maybe less."

"Why are you doing it?" I asked.

"There's a lot of adventure out here on the road. I suppose I could sit back and get fat watching TV for the next fifty years, but I want to do something with my life. I want to make a difference. I have to make do with what I have left. You know the saying; you only go around once."

"You have my greatest admiration," I said, shaking his hand again.

It was one of those moments where you don't quite know what to do or say. I just met the most incredibly courageous man in my whole life who was looking up at me from the pavement. His legs were gone. He was a man, but he stood only three feet high. His hands had become his feet. That gray leather pad was belted to his bottom like a baby diaper. Those rubber pads on his hands were his wheel tread on his arduous journey. I gasped inside myself at the enormity of his quest.

"Guess I better get moving," I said, reluctantly.

"Take care," Bob said. "Have a good ride. I'll get there one of these days."

"There's no doubt that you will reach the Atlantic Ocean," I said.

While turning away from that amazing human being, tears filled my eyes. I started crying halfway across the road. What he was attempting staggered my imagination. My friends thought I was nuts taking a transcontinental bicycle trip, but they had no understanding of how easy I had it compared to Bob Wieland.

Miles and years down the road that moment colors my mind as vividly as the day it happened.

Most human beings have handicaps in one way or the other—physical or psychological. What's important is how they handle their limitations. He concentrated on what he could do, not on what he couldn't do. Instead of giving up, Bob pushed forward into the unknown not only determined to succeed, but expecting to succeed.

George Bernard Shaw celebrated people like Wieland when he wrote, "This is the true joy of living, spending your years for a purpose recognized by yourself as a right one...to be used up when they throw you on the scrap heap of life. To have been a force of nature instead of a selfish little clod of ailments and grievances complaining that the world will not devote itself to making you happy."

Bob Wieland pushed himself through 3,500 miles of hardship that few people could comprehend. He gutted his way up mountains, sweated his way across deserts, and fought through raging storms. Every labored breath drew him closer to his goal.

Two years later, I was listening to NPR radio while eating breakfast one morning. Bob Wieland reached Washington DC thus succeeding in his quest to walk on his hands, coast to coast across America.

I sat at the breakfast table crying like a baby because that man had given me the courage to face my own struggles from that one meeting in the New Mexico desert. I'm sure he touched thousands more on his remarkable journey across America. Here's to you, Bob Wieland, to your courage, your humor, your passion and your life.

As a special note: Wieland completed his walk across America in three years, eight months, and six days...4,900,000 steps with his hands. He went on to own four world weightlifting records. He ran and completed endless marathons...New York

Marathon, Boston Marathon, Chicago Marathon, Marine Corps Marathon and many more. Get this...he hand-cycled across America three times! In 1996, Wieland was named the Most Courageous Man in America by the NFL Players Association and Jim Thorpe Foundation. In 1994, People Magazine recognized him as one of the six most amazing Americans in the past 20 years.

"It's basically impossible to stop a person with a big heart," said the only double amputee to complete the Hawaii-based Ironman Triathlon without a wheelchair.

Of special note, I called his organization to speak with his secretary. I asked her to relay a message from the cyclist in 1984 who stopped to talk with him on Route 380 south of Socorro, New Mexico. She wrote back that he remembered that day vividly and wished me well.

People ask me why I'm always upbeat and enthusiastic. I tell them, "I met Bob Wieland."

(Frosty crossing into the New Mexico desert where he met Bob Wieland.)

Chapter 3—Arrested for Having Too Much Fun!

> ***"I can't help myself. Even if I have seen the mountain ranges dozens of times, the undulating roads that lead to the horizon, I cannot help it. They continue to make me fall in love. This is my happiness: having fun like a child, losing track of time, enjoying the road, not counting the kilometers, stopping to take pictures here and having a snack there, changing destination on the fly, feeling connected to nature, just stopping to look and breathe. This is the meaning of cycling for me."***
>
> ***—Natalie Allegra***

Outside Vicksburg, Mississippi, on Route 80, my brother Rex and I cranked east through the afternoon heat. Sweat dripped from our noses and splashed onto the top tubes. It ran down our spines like tiny rivulets. It burned our eyes from beads running down our foreheads. Salt stained our black riding tights like the colors of a Zebra.

Rex and I were on the last month of a coast-to-coast touring adventure. Our legs glistened with sweat as our muscles labored under the constant down-stroke on the pedals.

Up ahead, heat waves rippled off the summer pavement, while a blazing sun baked the weeds along the two-lane highway. Trees lined the road, and crows and sparrows scattered in all directions as we passed. One crow struggled to escape from three sparrows darting in on him. They pecked at his feathers—attempting to drive him away. After each attack, he spun wildly in midair to avoid them.

"Those guys are giving that big fella' a hard time," Rex said, pointing. "I never have figured out why they attack a crow like that."

"Sparrows drive away crows because crows will eat the young of smaller birds," I said, remembering a natural science class from school. "They're protecting their nests."

Rex, dripping in a sweat-soaked T-shirt, cranked ahead of me, pulling his water bottle and spitting as he took the lead. "We should make Vicksburg pretty soon. You want to stop at a salad bar and clean 'em out?"

"Good idea."

Riding in the South during the heat of the summer months could be compared to pedaling in a steam sauna. Heat and sweat were our constant companions.

Howard and I left a trail of droplets from our perspiration-soaked bodies. No matter. We looked forward to seeing the Civil War monuments in Vicksburg. We waved at passing cars. The Deep South was laid back and moved at a snail's pace. People seemed to get a kick out of our riding cross-country through their towns. They took pictures of us—sometimes having family members gather around our bikes.

We pedaled fully loaded mountain expedition bicycles. Condor, my bike, was named for an experience I had while touring in South America where two curious condors swooped down upon me while I crossed a 15,500-foot pass in the Andes. With 12-foot wingspans, they soared 20 feet off my handlebars, while they eyed me as either a piece of meat or as someone who was invading their airspace. Rex's bike, Bilbo, was his pride and joy. As always, our orange flags (one six feet up on a fiberglass rod and the other 2 feet into the traffic side) flapped in the breeze. They let all traffic know our location. Those flags had saved our lives numerous times.

With so much attention, we had a lot to talk about after leaving a photo session. People said the darnedest things about long-distance touring riders. They kept us laughing because they thought we were either courageous or crazy. We were talking about the comments from a family that had stopped their car to take our pictures when a black-and-white police cruiser passed us traveling westbound. We waved at him. He waved back but did not smile.

I routinely wave to police officers out of respect or fear—I'm not sure which. I know they can give me a ticket for speeding. But, on a bicycle, they can't, so I never give them much thought. I watched him go by in my rearview mirror. A few seconds later, he flipped his car around and turned on his flashing red lights.

"That cop turned around," Rex said, sucking on his water bottle.

"Maybe he got a call for an emergency back down the road," I said, glancing back.

I expected the cruiser to fly past us. But it didn't. The police officer pulled in behind us. I looked in my rear mirror to see him pointing his finger for us to pull to the side.

"That cop is pulling us over," I said.

"Probably for speeding," Rex joked. "Maybe he's going to give us a ticket for going too slow. Now wouldn't that be a good one? No! I've got it. He's going to give us tickets for not having licenses to drive bicycles."

We pulled our bikes to a stop. A rotund, middle-aged officer in a blue uniform got out of his cruiser. He sported a chin like a bullfrog's during mating season. We stood astride our bikes, looking back, not sure why he had stopped us. "Afternoon boys," he said, walking up to us.

"Afternoon boys," he said, walking up to us.

"How are you, sir?" I asked.

"I'm fine," he spoke in a raspy voice. "When I passed you boys, I noticed you were smiling and laughing."

"Yes, sir," Rex said. "We're having a great day. We love it here in Louisiana. In fact, we're hoping to meet Huckleberry Finn when we cross the Mississippi River."

"How far you goin'?" the officer asked brusquely.

"We're on our way from California to Georgia," I said. "Pacific to the Atlantic."

"You boys ever had your heads examined for mental righteousness?"

"Beg your pardon?" Rex said.

"You know," he said, "Common sense. Anyone in their right mind wouldn't ride a bicycle across the country."

"Our mom told us we were crazy to ride our bikes across America," Rex said. "But, so far, the craziness hasn't killed us."

The officer looked over our packs as if he might be looking for drugs.

Right then, I didn't like this guy's demeanor. My dad always told us to be polite and keep smiling at a police officer. We should always say "Yes, sir" or "No, sir," to a man with a badge. This was one of those times to be extra polite.

"Have you had a good time in Louisiana?" he asked in a stern voice.

"Yes, sir," I said. "We've had a real fine time, and we're looking forward to Mississippi."

"Right now, you're in my jurisdiction," he said. "When I drove by you, it looked like you were having a lot of fun."

"Yes, sir, you could say that," Rex said, with a puzzled look sweeping across his eyes.

"Would you say you're having TOO much fun?" the trooper asked, straight-faced.

"TOO much fun?" I said. "Well, err, yes sir, we're probably having too much fun, right, Rex?"

"YES, SIR, that's right, we're having too much fun."

The officer stepped closer. He looked serious. Maybe I had seen too many movies depicting stereotypical redneck cops hassling people. Nonetheless, I was concerned. He looked the part—thick neck, crew cut, short fat fingers, belly hanging over his belt, and boots that hadn't been polished in a coon's age.

"I hate to say this boys, but there's an ordinance in this county for having too much fun. Because I'm an officer of the law, I'm sworn to uphold that ordinance. I'm gonna have to write ya'll a citation. May I see some form of identification?"

"Sure, officer," we replied, giving him our driver's licenses.

"A law against having too much fun?" Rex said, with a hint of indignation.

"That's right, boys," he said. "I see you're brothers. You wait here while I write you up."

"Yes, sir," I said.

"I'll be right back in a few minutes," he said, walking away.

"This is crazy," Rex said. "This guy is out to lunch. He's only got one oar in the water. He's 51 cards short of a full deck. This guy's a lighthouse with no light on!"

"Don't say that too loud," I muttered. "He's got a badge and a gun."

"He can't give us a ticket for having too much fun," Rex complained. "That does it! I'm going right into the county courthouse and demand a jury trial on this one. I mean, this is nuts! We can't take this lying down. I'll get the ACLU if I have to. Too much fun, right!"

"I thought he was kidding," I said. "But, he's not kidding."

While we waited, I drank a quart of water and switched my bottles on the down tube to have a full one ready. It was warm water but quenched my thirst. Darned if I could figure out what we had done to get this cop upset. But I had learned never to argue with a police officer. They commanded absolute authority. Minutes later, he walked up to us with two tickets in hand.

"I know ya'll think this is out of line," he said. "But I don't make the laws... I just enforce them. By the way, I like riding bicycles, too. How come you boys are riding mountain bikes with drop bars?"

"They're more durable, and we don't get many flat tires," I said. "They give a smoother ride. Plus, we have three positions for our hands with drop bars. Straight bars fatigue our hands by keeping them in one position."

"I'll have to remember that," he said. "By the way, I live in Vicksburg. Are you boys hungry?"

"Yes, sir," we replied, not understanding why he was so friendly when he had just given us tickets.

"There's a nice restaurant called 'Aunt Dorothy's' with an all-you-can-eat salad right after you cross the Mississippi River. You can't miss it," he said, walking back to his car.

He drove toward Vicksburg. I stood there looking at Rex who was just as incredulous as I was.

"What in the hell just happened to us?" I asked.

Rex looked down at his ticket and started laughing.

"What's so funny?" I asked.

"Read it," Rex said, chuckling and slapping his thigh.

On the ticket in long-hand, it read, "This is a citation to the Wooldridge brothers for having too much fun on their bicycle trip across America. You can either pay a large fine down at the county courthouse, or you can come over to my house (directions below) and take showers plus eat my wife's great cooking. You're welcome to stay overnight. My kids would love to hear about some of your experiences. It would be an honor and a pleasure to have you visit us."

"I'll be damned," I muttered.

After riding into town that evening, we followed Officer Buford Jackson's directions to his house. We leaned our touring bikes against the white railing on the front porch of a traditional Southern home where a couple of rockers awaited the evening sunset and friendly conversation.

I knocked.

When the door opened, I had never seen a wider smile, a bigger grin, a larger heart, nor a face as full of mirth and mischief as I saw on Buford Jackson at that moment. Behind him, two girls and a boy must have been told that Ricky Martin and Tom Cruise were coming to dinner because their faces displayed a youthful expectation that something special was about to happen in their lives.

Buford showed us the guest bedroom and hot showers. "Give me all your dirty clothes," he said. "Adeline will have them washed and dried by morning."

"Ask the boys if they like summer squash, green beans and garden tomatoes?" Adeline called from the kitchen.

"We like everything," Rex said.

Buford smiled, "These boys can eat a whole hog and a bucket of mashed potatoes with coleslaw."

"Don't forget the pumpkin pie," Rex said, laughing.

"She just made a fresh blueberry pie for tonight," Buford said.

"Break my heart," I said, my mouth already watering at the thought of my favorite pie.

Before we could protest about his washing our clothes, Buford gathered our sweaty shorts, shirts and other dirty clothes and walked off to the laundry room.

That evening, we ate a dinner fit for kings. Adeline Jackson, in a long cotton dress and just a touch of make-up, couldn't have been kinder.

At the table, she sat Rex between the two girls and Zac next to me. I hate to admit this, but my brother is good looking which left the two girls giddy with excitement.

Buford grasped his son's and daughter's hands. Rex and I completed the circle when Buford spoke, "Dear Lord, bless this food..."

After grace, we plowed into the food dishes being passed around the table. Rex struck up the conversation with our starting and finishing point of the ride.

Shirley, nearly 14 with a blonde ponytail, asked the first question, "What does San Francisco look like?" Later, Paula, 12 with pigtails, asked, "How many miles do you ride in one day?" Zac, all 8 years old with a crewcut, asked, "Where do you go number two if you live in a tent?"

Once they heard about the basics of bicycle adventure, they asked about our favorite moments on the tour. Rex described crossing the Golden Gate Bridge with the sparkling blue waters below and watching the two-masted sailboats plying the waters of the bay. He spoke about our ride into Yosemite where we watched a 'moonbow' (rainbow caused by moonlight) at the base of Bridal Veil Falls. I talked about our ride through Death Valley with 116 degrees of heat that felt like riding inside an oven. Later, we pedaled our way to the rim of the Grand Canyon and looked down a mile below to the Colorado River.

Zac's eyes grew wide with wonder as Rex described the Painted Desert and the Petrified Forest. Paula and Shirley could hardly contain themselves before asking the next question.

"You know," Rex said, after answering the last question. "It's not the adventures that count as much as it is the friends we've made along the way. Your daddy and mama are the best story, of this trip and you kids, are the best, ever! My brother and I are so thankful we ran into your dad."

Rex glanced with a sly smile over at Buford. I added my own 'look'. We weren't THAT amused when he had given us the tickets for having 'too much fun'.

Buford shrugged innocently. Then he asked with a grin, "What'd you fellers think after I handed you those tickets?"

"Would 'bewildered' seem to fit?" Rex said. "At first, you were so serious, we didn't know what to think. After you walked back to your cruiser, I was ready to..."

"You don't want to hear Rex's words," I said. "Needless to say, we thought we might be in a Hitchcock movie."

"Just thought I'd put a little humor into your day," Buford said.

"He's a good cop," Adeline said, "but he's a practical joker, too, and he has a heart of gold. We're real glad you boys came over for dinner. Aren't we children?"

At that moment, Shirley, Paula and Zac's faces lit up. They nodded.

"What made you think of giving us tickets?" I asked.

"You know," he said, "it came out of the blue. I guess I wanted my kids to see a bit of the world through some strangers' eyes."

"We have more stories," Rex said.

"They've heard enough. It's time for bed."

"No, daddy, please..." they pleaded.

"You heard me," Buford said.

"This dinner conversation has been great for our kids," Adeline said. You boys have given them an appreciation for geography, highways, mountains, camping, and most of all, a sense of what's out there."

"Have any of you read 'The Hobbit?" Rex asked Shirley.

She nodded and said her teacher had read it to the class.

"Well," Rex spoke. "Bilbo Baggins said, 'There's a whole lot of adventure outside your door. That's why I named my bike after him.'"

"That's right," I said. "It's out there waiting for you when you choose to travel."

Shirley gleamed and followed her siblings to the bathroom to brush her teeth. Who knows what kind of adventure path her life would take? It might be on a bicycle.

The next morning, as we pedaled onto the highway, I was reminded again, as I had been hundreds of times in the past that people are full of surprises.

In the case of Buford and Adeline, my world became richer thanks to their unexpected hospitality. Shirley, Paula and Zac bring a smile to my heart and mind whenever I think back on the magic of that evening.

Bless the Jacksons for their love, generosity, sense of humor, and their children with big, bright eyes filled with expectation. I am thankful that most of the world is filled with Buford's and Adeline's, and because it is, we are all blessed with joy at surprising moments in our lives.

In my lifetime, I hope to get arrested many more times for having too much fun.

(Most nights, we camp out in the wilds. This night, a lady invited us to camp in her flower garden.)

Chapter 4—Talons from the Sky: Coiled Scales on the Ground

"The mystique of bicycle travel fascinates modern Americans. Why would anyone endure the pains of providing their own locomotion via pedaling rather than the comfort and speed of a car, boat, plane or train? The answer lies in the antiquity of 'pedaling bliss.' It thrives in the meshing of your energy with the energy of the universe. It rushes into the secret corners of your mind to explore the world on your own terms. Too much comfort leads to tedium or the indolence of life. Once you swing your leg over the saddle of a bicycle, a whole new mental, physical and spiritual dimension opens to every cell in your body. You 'fly' at the 'perfect speed' with a comet's tail of memories following you into eternity."

—Frosty and Sandi Wooldridge

Heading eastbound across southern California, the sun set low in the sky. We looked for a campsite in the rocky terrain east of Joshua Tree National Monument.

"We better find a spot soon," Sandi said.

"I'm looking, dear," I said.

Up ahead, we noticed a fluttering hawk, holding his position as the sky effervesced into pink-white thunderheads in the twilight. Very still! Very quiet!

We pedaled the bikes toward the hawk on that lonely highway. The bird continued fluttering like a helicopter holding position in order to land. We pedaled closer, closer—until we rode up to the perfect camp spot 100 feet off the highway behind some big rocks.

"I'm going to check out that hawk," I told Sandi.

"I'll get the tent set up," she said. "You want pasta for dinner?"

"Sounds great," I said. "I've got Pesto in my pack."

Quietly excited, I crept over several 20-ton boulders on my way to get under the hawk. He kept fluttering until, suddenly, he dove straight down.

I hurried over boulders and dirt until I crept up to where I figured he landed. Before me, not 20 feet away, in a dirt arena surrounded by rocks, the hawk stood in front of a transfixed rattlesnake. The hawk hopped into the air as it dared the rattler to strike. And yes, the rattler complied by lunging at the bird. The hawk hopped backwards. Quickly, the snake recoiled into a striking position.

The hawk, using his wings and talons, jumped back into the sky toward the head of the snake, toying with him, daring him to strike. The rattler struck again, but the hawk danced out of the way. For the next 10 minutes, the hawk danced into the air toward the rattler but avoided the snake's deadly fangs.

They pirouetted the dance of life and death. One looked for dinner while the other looked for life. One dared death while the other lunged for its life.

I crouched in the rocks transfixed with wonder. Sometimes, I cannot help but thank the Bicycle Gods for their gifts to me as I travel around this planet on Condor, my iron steed. Who could serve up a moment like this? Who could dream it? Who could imagine it? Each time, I feel tremendous gratitude for this sublime journey on a bicycle.

Before me, the snake struck and then recoiled. The hawk hopped up to dare the reptile to strike. Each time, the snake grew wearier and more fatigued. Until, as the last rays of the sun slipped below the horizon, the snake made one last strike for its life, but the hawk seized it by the head with his talons. Seconds later, he pecked it on the head until it died in his clutches.

Moments later, the great hawk flapped his mighty wings with the snake securely gripped in his talons. The hawk took to the sky with dinner for his family. One life lost to give life to another. I watched the mighty hawk fly into the sunset for a memory that sticks with me through the years.

This enchanting moment visits me often when I move into Nature. Without a doubt, Condor carries me into exquisite life-moments that render poetic beauty, life and death struggles, mountain heroics and storms that fulfill my spirit.

Such moments cause me to write this about the Power of Adventure:

> ***"Adventure offers every human being the ability to live 'the' moment of his or her most passionate idea, fantasy or pursuit. It may take form in the arts, acting, sports, travel or other creative endeavors. Once engaged, a person enjoys 'satori' or the perfect moment. That instant may last seconds or a lifetime. The key to adventure whether it involves painting, dancing, sports, or travel: throw yourself into it with rambunctious enthusiasm and zealous energy—which leads toward an uncommon passion for living. By following that path, you will attract an amazing life that will imbue your spirit and fulfill your destiny as defined by you alone. In the end, you will savor the sweet taste of life pursuing goals that make you happy, rewarded and complete. As a bonus, you may share your life experiences with other bold and uncommon human beings that laugh at life, compare themselves with no one and enjoy a whale of a ride!"***

—Frosty Wooldridge

(Sandi and Frosty on tour across America.)

Chapter 5—What's in an Empty Pizza Box?

> ***"Life is like a box of chocolates. You never know what's in that box of chocolates, Forrest."***
>
> ***—Forrest Gump's mother***

After riding over 4,000 miles on the Northern Tier of America from Astoria, Oregon to Bar Harbor, I pedaled on the tail-end of our coast-to-coast bicycle adventure by a bunch of 70-year old's. When I was young, I didn't think much about it during my first crossing in 1975, but now that I'm a senior citizen, every day grows more precious and the adventure more meaningful.

As I cruised into Vermont on the tail-end of our bicycle adventure, I lagged behind my friends Gerry and Don by an hour. We pedaled over hills, hills and more hills. Because I take a lot of pictures, I often fell back several miles.

It took me 15 minutes to get a great shot of a muskrat paddling across a glass-still pond. Nothing like wildlife going about their daily business. He created a V-wake behind him that cut across the pond. Two diving ducks created circles. When the V-wake intersected with the rippling circles, it created a great photograph. I love the creativity of Mother Nature.

As for the speed of my bicycle, I call it the "pleasure pace" which means I enjoy every mile. Some call it "Eudemonia," "Satori," or "The Perfect Speed." It's the connection of mind, body, and spirit coming together to form a natural "high" or "total happiness." When you pedal a bicycle through such beauty for eight hours a day, it transforms you and becomes a winsome dance. I've discovered over the years that bicycling pertains more to a spiritual experience than a physical one. No, I'm not saying it's a picnic busting over a 12,000-foot pass in the Rocky Mountains, but then, the views more than compensate. As you can see from the picture, I'd choose the mountains seven days a week.

Like all the New England states, Vermont provided such beauty, but suddenly, my rear tire suffered a flat. "Dang," I muttered to myself. "Those guys will be drinking beers and eating dinner by the time I catch up to them."

No matter, I stopped near a cable guardrail. As you can see from the load on my bike "Condor," I had to pull a lot of gear off the back to get to the wheel. Just as I pulled the axle from the dropouts, an SUV passed me and honked. I waved.

As with all flat tires, I peeled the tire off the rim with my plastic levers. I checked the tube, found the glass chard that cut it, and patched it. I checked the rim tape for problems, then checked the tire for any other foreign objects and replaced it back onto the rim. After pumping it up, I dropped my solid axle back into the dropouts, replaced the nuts and aligned it. Then, I replaced the cables on the cantilever brakes. All in all, I spent 45 to 50 minutes.

After making sure the bike was roadworthy, I replaced my heavy pack (80 pounds) and bungee—corded it all back onto the rack. At that moment, I pulled out my water bottle for a swig to quench my thirst. As I sat on the piling of the guard rail, that same SUV rolled to a stop across the highway. A kid jumped out with a pizza box and two cans of lemonade. He ran across the highway toward me.

"My dad said you might like some refreshments," he said. "He remembers when he rode his bicycle across the country after finishing college. He still talks about it. It was the best time of his life. He's got an 8"x10" photo of him and his buddies celebrating on the Atlantic Ocean right on his desk. Every day he sees it, that photo, it lights him up."

"Well, thank you," I said as I waved to the entire family. "Good for your dad! I bet he's got lots of stories to tell."

"Yes sir," the boy said. "He tells them around the campfire when we go camping. Somehow, he always comes up with a new one that makes us laugh."

The boy crossed back over the road. Everyone in the car smiled. "Safe travels," the father said. I waved, "Back at you!"

They drove off. I sat there realizing that my two buddies were eating dinner and drinking beers up ahead. I sat there munching on the MOST incredible and best-tasting pizza of my life, to this day, it will be the greatest pizza that I ever ate. Why? Because it was given to me on a very hot day in Vermont on a very lonely road. It rewarded me for fixing my flat tire. It tingled my taste buds like no other pizza because of the kindness of other human beings. It was given with love, trust and a sense of connectedness that all of us humans carry in our hearts.

When I finished, I placed the empty pizza box on top of my pack. With the last gulp of lemonade, I flattened the two cans to be recycled when I reached the next town. I remounted my bike Condor and pedaled east with a big smile across my face and an even bigger one across my spirit.

"Darn," I muttered to myself. "Sometimes, flat tires are a good thing!"

"Unexpected kindness is the most powerful, least costly, and most underrated agent of human change." – *Bob Kerrey*

With that reality, over the years, I have always passed "kindness" forward. I compliment the store clerk about her necklace or earrings. I thank the waitress for her exemplary service with an extra-large tip. I salute the passing police officer because he works a dangerous job that maintains our society. I slap a $5 bill into a homeless person's hand at some intersection. Why? But for the grace of God, that homeless person could be me. I thank a military person for his or her service to our country. I've picked up a million pieces of trash across six continents to

make the Natural World more beautiful. It takes almost nothing to smile at anyone passing or giving a kind word.

It's wrapped up in this quote: "Love and kindness are never wasted. They always make a difference. They bless the one who receives them, and they bless you, the giver."

– Barbara De Angelis

(My touring bike, loaded with gear and an empty pizza box filled with kindness and memories of the goodness of folks around the world.)

Chapter 6—Riding Below Sea Level

"I'm so dry I can't spit."

—Doug Armstrong

Death Valley, California in the summer pops the mercury at over 130 degrees Fahrenheit. Ground temperatures reach 200 degrees. A sane cyclist would not attempt such an arduous journey. But who said anyone bicycle touring was sensible?

My partner Doug and I headed north on a border-to-border, Mexico-to-Canada ride in early April. At that time of the year, moderate temperatures make bicycle riding a pleasure. It rarely exceeds 90 degrees in the desert.

We reached the cutoff of the Henry Wade exit at the southern end of the valley on Route 127. We had a choice of a downward inclined dirt, gravel, and sandy road into the south end of the park—or we could stay on the pavement and climb three passes of 2,200 feet, 3,100 feet, and 1,800 feet to get to the side entrance of the valley. We opted for the shortcut on gravel.

Henry Wade, a miner, escaped death in the valley by taking this route in 1849. He saved his family.

It was a wonder how anyone could take a team of horses over sand and washouts. The heat bore down on us. I imagined Henry Wade driving his team over this desolate land. How he made it in the scorching heat proved a miracle. We checked our four gallons of water and figured we could make it to the paved road 30 miles north of us. Late in the afternoon, we decided to camp so we could get an early start in the morning.

At dawn, we prepared ourselves for the ordeal awaiting us. We each carried four gallons of water. We felt we could reach the main road where we could flag a motorist if needed. At 7:00 a.m., we headed into Death Valley. We began the ride in cool air, but that quickly turned hot, dusty and dry. In the first hour, we experienced a terrible time pushing our mountain bikes through the sand. We rode into it, got stuck, and had to push the bikes out. At times, the sand swallowed the tires up to the spoke nipples. We might as well have been riding over a sticky topping of cheese pizza—still basking in the oven.

"Man, I wasn't expecting this kind of heat," Doug said.

"I feel like I'm a tray of chocolate chip cookies in a 450-degree oven," I complained.

"Tough it out, dude," Doug said. "We just have to make it to the asphalt where it'll be a cakewalk to Furnace Creek."

In the next two hours, the heat intensified. On the east and west of us, the Black Mountains and the Panamint Range serrated the sky. Erosion gullies cut the summits into vertical lines. Telescope Peak on our left rose to a snowcapped 11,049 feet. Colors abounded throughout the valley. Brown and black sedimentary rock swept down in front of us. Purple canyons accented with yellow layers of rock streamers contrasted with the white salt flats of the ancient dry lake-bed on the valley floor. Sage brushes dotted the terrain along the road.

By noon, I struggled, and the heat had climbed to over one hundred degrees. The ruts beat-up my butt. When I cranked on the smooth road, it was too soft. Where it was hard, ripples pounded me. Fatigue gripped my body. I rode on a treadmill, not going anywhere, no matter how much I cranked the pedals. The landscape changed but it was like someone came over to my house to show pictures of their trip into the desert, but each picture was an exact copy of the last. After seeing five hours of the same picture, I wondered what the point was. I got weaker and weaker. I yelled at my bike to stay up in the sand. I yelled at the road. The coyotes, if they were listening, heard a lot of bad languages that day. Not only that, I gulped warm water at an alarming rate.

"How much water do you have left?" Doug asked.

"About a gallon," I said. "It can't be that much further to the pavement."

"Probably not," he said. "I swear it must be over a hundred and ten degrees right now. It's just sucking the moisture right out of my body. I can't feel myself sweating, but I know I'm losing water fast. My mouth feels like I'm chewing cotton. My tongue sticks to the top of my mouth. My teeth are even dry! My water is almost too hot to drink and I'm still thirsty after I drink."

"Someone's coming toward us," I said. "Let's flag them down and ask for water."

We watched a dust cloud approaching from the north. Minutes later, a man and woman from Alaska stopped to chat.

"Do you guys have any idea how hot it is?" the lady asked as she rolled down her window.

"We figure it must be over a hundred degrees and zero humidity," Doug answered.

"It's a hundred and ten and supposed to go up to a hundred and sixteen," she said. "It's the hottest April on record."

"What's the chance you have some water?" I asked. "We're getting low."

"Sure," the man said, grabbing a five-gallon jug. "You guys must be pretty courageous or pretty nuts to be bicycling on a day like this."

"We didn't plan on being in a heat wave," Doug said.

The couple talked about their experiences in Alaska when the temperature hit 60 below zero for a week. The man said his spit froze before it hit the ground. They didn't like this heat.

"Would you boys like something cold and wet?" she asked.

"You don't need to ask twice," Doug said.

"Here's a couple of cold pears from our cooler," she said. "That ought to keep you going for a few more miles."

"Thanks," I said.

They left in a cloud of dust.

"Can you believe it, Doug?" I said, munching on my cold pear. "Here we are in the middle of the hottest spot on earth, the lowest place in the Western hemisphere, and on the hottest day on record in April—and we're eating cold pears."

"I'm glad they came by with water, or we could be in trouble," Doug said. "Let's get moving. We still have more than 50 miles to Furnace Creek."

We pounded the pedals into the relentless heat. My hands ached from gripping the bars. The road bashed my butt. It's times like this that misery describes the ordeal. It was miserable. Heat waves shimmered across the salt flats below us as we pedaled our way deeper into the Death Valley.

We finally hit the black top. What a relief, except it was two o'clock and getting hotter. More heat waves rose off the pavement, and the mountains changed texture as the sun dropped in the west. The Black Mountains reached into the sky like piles of coal while the Panamint Range waxed into blue mist.

The road wound around an alluvial washout on the eastern side of the valley. We kept pedaling downhill past Desolation Canyon. Hunger caught up with us at the Ashford Mill. It featured a mud building in the middle of the valley, which once processed gold ore from the Golden Mine near there. We parked our bikes by one of the picnic tables near the site. As we prepared lunch, we sat in a blistering hot wind, with nothing but rock and sand surrounding us for miles. We might as well have landed on the moon.

We prepared our usual fare of wheat bread, tomatoes, green peppers, avocados and mustard. By the time we had cut everything up and made a sandwich, the slices of bread had turned into crackers. Doug bit into his sandwich.

"My bread is dry," he said. "The heat is turning my sandwich into crust and instant 'heat dried' food. I can't believe how hot it is."

"I feel like I'm in a microwave oven," I said. "Let's get out of here."

"Where do you think we're going to go with any great speed?" Doug asked.

We finished our lunch, including our tepid water. What I wouldn't give for a gallon of ice-cold orange juice!

We headed up the valley still riding below sea level. A few bushes grew and some grasses, but it was desolation for 12 miles across the valley. We rode along the salt flat basin of what was once the 90-mile-long Lake Manley. By 4:00 p.m., we neared the lowest point in the Western Hemisphere at 282 feet below sea level. It's called Badwater, and a shallow pond shimmered in the breeze under the torrid heat. We wondered why the water wasn't sucked into the sky from evaporation. Being spring fed, it maintained a constant depth even on the hottest days of the summer.

It was scorching, ungodly hot. I sometimes wonder why I put myself in such miserable conditions. It was so hot I could barely breathe. My skin was caked with salt and my mouth felt so dry I couldn't spit. My butt was sore, and my hands were fatigued from the dirt road. My bottles were full of hot water and the sun bore down with no mercy. As if that wasn't enough, the temperature kept rising. It was a hundred and sixteen degrees. Yet, I put myself there because that is the nature of adventure. No matter what the price of the physical discomfort, I knew I would be fine. The heat was not going to kill me, but it was going to give me a reference point for comfort. I was sweaty and dirty, but only for a short time. The price that day was the feeling of being in the fires of hell. The heat waves licked at my body and there was no escape.

But with these terrible conditions, the other side of the coin was the emerging moment; a time when I could move through this one place on earth and be a part of it. I could see snow on Telescope Peak 12 miles away and 11,000 feet up. That valley may be a prisoner to the sun and heat, but it also offered majestic, eerie scenery—something I couldn't touch, feel or smell unless I was there. Was it worth it? Only one answer—give me my bike and the open road.

"Frosty," Doug yelled. "Come over here. This lady has a nice cold Orange Crush for us."

"Thanks a million," I said, walking up to her van. "You can't imagine how much I've dreamed of a cold drink for this entire day."

"Yeah, I can," she said. "I've biked across America in the heat of the summer."

By now we had drunk four gallons of water, but we hadn't urinated once. Back on the bikes, we talked about the 116 degrees of heat and how great the soda pop tasted. We headed north, cranking hard with a good tailwind. We passed the Devil's Golf Course, Artist's Drive, the Natural Bridge and Mushroom Rock. The snaking highway wound along the side of Death Valley up and down shallow grades until we reached an oasis at Furnace Creek. In the middle of this valley of scorching heat, date palms! A pool! Cold orange juice! I drank nearly a half-gallon of juice without lifting my lips from the jug. This was paradise on the other side of agony.

As I dove into the pool, the whole day's journey washed away into pleasure.

Furnace Creek featured an oasis created by 2,000 gallons of water per minute flowing out of a rock fissure in the mountains above the valley. We visited the Borax Museum, the mining implements exhibit, and Harmony Borax Works. A day of rest and sightseeing refreshed us.

A day later, we awoke at 6:00 a.m. but didn't get started for two hours. Heat waves shimmered across the asphalt. The black pavement meandered along the valley floor, always vanishing over the next alluvial fan. Lots of washes and rocks dotted the ground around us. In twenty miles, we passed large sand dunes and passed the Devil's Cornstalks, an area where bushes survive the heat by bunching up together to conserve their water. Nature is an odd force. It creates deadly, horrid conditions and then allows plants and animals to evolve in that area to live precariously. Nature encourages life but tries to make it die of thirst or starvation at the same time.

At Stovepipe Wells, we reached five feet above sea level and began climbing. We crossed a large alluvial fan at 1,000 feet of elevation. The road snaked higher, with a steeper grade of 2,000 feet. We wound our way along dry washouts until the road narrowed into a single canyon making its way up and out of Death Valley. In Granny gear, we cranked up that incline on our way to 6,000 feet. With the altitude, the temperature released its grip as if we had walked out of an oven and into an air-conditioned restaurant. Near dusk, we camped on a rock ledge at 5,200 feet. We saw the final grade ahead of us, but we were content because the temperature dropped to a cool 60 degrees.

Behind us, Death Valley stretched out in shadows moving across the canyons and a half-moon cut its quiet splendor into the darkening sky. A coyote howled. Our campfire crackled in the hushed evening air while rice, lentils and vegetables steamed on the flames. We camped on a high plateau away from civilization. Doug and I sat out in the middle of nowhere.

Yes, a nice place to be.

(Sand dunes across Death Valley where the temperature reaches 134 degrees Fahrenheit in the summer.)

Chapter 7—High Speed Chase

> ***"I pity the man in his car who drives across the great southwestern desert, and thinks it's boring."***
>
> ***—Pamela Gilbert***

On Route 72, near Parker, Arizona, I headed east into the twilight. It had been a blistering hot day and my body felt like a dishrag that had cleaned out a pot of greasy spaghetti and hung over the top tube to dry. My chances of finding a stream for a bath equaled zero!

Nonetheless, it had been a good day. Red flowering cacti filled the air with their sweet scent while pink cloud streaks sliced the heavens into sections while lighting up billowing thunderheads that boiled toward the sunlight. Their tails faded into the eastern darkness. Saucer-like clouds skidded across the sky to the south of me.

Nearing Bouse, I stopped at a closed gas station and parked my bike against the side of the cracked, plaster wall of the building.

"Might as well check the spigot to see if I can get a bath," I said, kneeling by the pumps. "I'll be darned! Water!"

I grabbed my soap, razor and towel. The water shot out of the faucet full blast. I soaked myself down—clothes and all. After soaping up my shirt, shorts and socks, I shaved my face. As usual, my neck resembled a bloody dogfight after the razor had done its business. No matter what the ads say about shavers, they can rip a man's neck to ribbons. Nevertheless, my body tingled at the newfound clean feeling on my skin. After rinsing away the soap from my shorts and jersey, I stepped into clean clothes. I hung my wet tights, socks and jersey onto the back of my pack for quick drying and loaded my water bottles.

Bouse featured ramshackle buildings on flat desert sands. I cranked into the cool evening air. A mile out of town, I scanned the road for a campsite. My tires made the only sound as stillness crept over the land. A few crows flew over the sagebrush and the thunderheads had darkened with the fading light.

I don't like being on the road at twilight. Too dangerous!

"Come on, where's a place to camp?" I complained out loud. "I'm out in the middle of nowhere and need to find a place to sleep for heaven's sake."

In the distance, not more than a hundred yards, I saw an old barn.

"Bingo!" I said. "That looks like home tonight."

In minutes, I would have my tent pitched behind the building and be cooking dinner. This deserted highway meant a quiet night's sleep.

Just then, a coyote loped along the highway off to my right 30 yards away. He looked intent on something that had caught his eye. I pressed harder on the pedals. He continued loping along, not noticing me. He ran ghostlike in the twilight shadows. He was as quiet as the air.

As I followed him, he veered toward the high side of the shoulder near a bush. When he approached it, a jackrabbit shot out of the cover and headed straight down the side of the pavement. The coyote changed from loping gear to Warp Factor two. Every muscle in his body coiled. The stillness was broken by a cloud of dust from his feet and the race was on. The rabbit did a three-step hoppity, hoppity, hoppity hop, then ran four strides like a dog, then three more short half steps, and back to running like a dog. At the same time, the coyote, with his nose cutting into the air like an F-16 jet and his tail streaming behind him, edged closer and closer. About the second the coyote was about to open his mouth and grab the rabbit, the speedster turned on a dime and shot left across the highway in front of me. Mr. Coyote pulled his teeth back into his mouth and executed a 90-degree turn. From a dead stop of zero, the coyote accelerated again to high speed. Again, the rabbit raced ten yards along the highway and did another right turn. Mr. Coyote closed quickly.

On the right side of the road again, the rabbit, followed less than a few steps behind by the coyote, leaped across a shallow culvert. Big mistake! As he sailed over the ditch, the dark figure of the coyote leaped faster and higher through the air, like a heat-seeking missile homing in on its prey. In midair, the coyote's teeth reached down and clamped onto the rabbit. When they fell to earth, the rabbit screamed a death cry. Silence.

When I pedaled up to the spot, I saw the coyote, with the rabbit in his mouth, become part of the darkness.

(What it looks like riding over the endless spaces of America's West. The road points straight toward the horizon.)

Chapter 8—Tomorrow is Dark on the Horizon

> ***"Just as a white summer cloud, in harmony with heaven and earth, freely floats in the blue sky from horizon to horizon following the breath of the atmosphere—In the same way the pilgrim abandons himself to the greater life that...leads him beyond the farthest horizons to an aim which is already present in him, though yet hidden from his sight."***
>
> *—Lama Govinda*

Remember your school days when your friends were prone to do screwball stunts that you knew were insane at the time, but you did them anyway? Afterward, you may have regretted your actions, but in the process, you learned a few things about yourself. On one of my journeys across the USA, I rode with three wild and crazy guys—itching to break out of the mold.

It was no one's idea, then everyone's—so we decided to do it. Ride 200 miles in one day on loaded touring bikes? That IS crazy! We sat at a restaurant on Route 380 near Socorro, New Mexico, making our plans for the assault on what would be the toughest physical challenge of our lives. A hundred-mile day on loaded mountain bikes proved a challenge even on the flats. Two hundred miles with hills thrown in and unpredictable weather might be an impossible dream. It could be a nightmare. John, Mike, Kevin, and I put our hands together over the dinner table that night and made a commitment to ride 200 miles in one day.

We had talked about the mythical 200-mile day for weeks as we powered our way over the New Mexico Rocky Mountains.

The "moment" arrived. A couple at the restaurant offered their trailer for a bunkhouse. We accepted.

As we walked out the doors, our stomachs bursting with food, I contemplated the 200-mile day only hours away. I was going to do it, ready or not, because three of my friends had answered the challenge. The group energy carried me. I was in control of myself but had no control over what was coming.

Wait! I wanted to make that ride. I wanted to confront my mind and body. It intrigued me, and I wanted to follow the idea to its conclusion. If I never attempted it, I wouldn't know success or failure. In such an endeavor, I had a 50-50 chance of success if I tried. If I gave no effort, I had a zero chance of knowing the outcome.

How can I explain something comparable to riding a loaded mountain bike on a double century? It would be like forcing someone to run up and down the Rose Bowl steps all day with a whip at his or her legs. In my case, my mind was a self-applied motivator, not a whip. It was interesting what my mind could do. Anyone's mind can create extreme athletes and superhuman efforts. One's mind is more powerful than a whip.

We took a shower in the trailer and bedded down. I slept fitfully, hearing John rise for a visit to the bathroom. At 3:05 a.m., I awoke again to hear the wind blowing outside and my bicycle flag flapping against the trailer. I got up and strapped down my bike flag. Stars sprinkled the night sky like diamonds on black velvet. A 10-mile-per-hour breeze blew eastward. I chuckled thinking how easy it would be to ride 200 miles with a tail wind blowing us down the highway. Minutes later, I returned to my bed.

"Bleep, bleep, bleep," the alarm sounded at 4:30 a.m.

My brain staggered awake. I gobbled my cereal. In minutes, I dragged my panniers out and hitched them to the racks. Everyone staggered around the trailer getting their gear ready.

Outside, I noticed the wind had died. It was dead still with the first hint of dawn cracking the dark morning horizon. The stars vanished with the coming light. With a full belly and sense of purpose, I slipped into the pedal straps at 5:05. No one followed, as they were busy with their own preparations. I figured every second was going to count that day, and the last of it was going to exact a price from my body. Thinking about it gave me butterflies, but that was okay, as long as they were flying in formation.

I stopped at three gas stations for air, but none had anything over 50 pounds of pressure. I needed more and could inflate my tires in another town. My muscles warmed up with each stroke on the cranks as I rode along the main road leading out of town. Streetlamps triggered by photoelectric cells, popped off with the growing sunlight. A bearded fellow in a green VW asked me where I had started.

"San Francisco to Savannah, Georgia," I answered.

"That's great. Have a good time. Good luck."

The edge of town welcomed me into the desert. Several run-down houses offered an ugly display of junk in their front yards. Two dogs gave chase. I stepped on the pedals and revved my bike to higher speeds. I clicked into the high end of the middle chain ring. In seconds, the dogs trailed behind me. I hit 18th gear going down a slight grade.

"Come on suckers," I yelled. "Keep chasing me."

The road leveled out, into a valley, with a long climb ahead of me. I pressed on the pedals and hoped my Achilles tendon would take the pressure. It was recovering from the mountainous ride behind us. It was a bit disconcerting knowing that I might hurt myself further by doing 200 miles of hard cycling. Somehow, I would succeed. Bob Wieland's inspiration came to mind as I cranked over the Pecos River. My thoughts focused on success.

Sweat beaded on my arms as the sun broke free of the hill in front of me. I pressed my legs into the rising land. Kevin rode up behind and passed, yelling, "Ninety miles to the Texas line and I'm cracking twenty."

"You'll burn yourself out at that speed," I hollered.

I knew he wouldn't last. It would come down to riding a pace line and working together. I crested a quarter-mile climb only to face another. After the second one, flat plains stretched to the horizon. I slipped into high gear and cranked a steady cadence. Kevin was a mile ahead. John and Michael brought up the rear.

Originally, I didn't want a group ride because I could not keep up with John. To try would kill me because he possessed incredible endurance. That's why he was known as "Mad Dog John Brown." His bulldog tenacity had served him well over the years. Within ten minutes, Mike and John were on my tail. We stopped for a bathroom break.

"We gotta' ride in a pace line to make it today," I said. "It's the only way we're going to pull this thing off."

"You're not wrong, mate," my Australian friend said.

We slipped back into the toe-clips. That was the last time my feet hit the ground for three hours. We caught and held Kevin with us. Our pace line jelled, and it was comfortable. Each of us pulled for five minutes, plowing through the air, pushing ourselves, then dropped back to drink and munch on a piece of fruit. We clipped along at 20-miles-per-hour. No wind. No hills. No traffic. No problems.

Each time I faded to the rear of the pack; I felt a change in my attitude. In the back, the pack pulled me along in its draft. I cranked at 70 percent of my normal effort, which proved relaxing. My view consisted of rumps and legs pounding the pedals, along with side flags and vertical flags flapping. Sweat dripped from their arms. They spit off to the side. Each of us rode 12 inches off the rear tire of the man in front, in perfect cadence and harmony. I rode at the tail end of a living machine that possessed one purpose—grinding out 200 miles.

I kept a constant eye on my rear view mirror. If a tractor-trailer rolled up, I called out, "Bogie 6." (Which meant they were at 6 o'clock behind us. At 12 o'clock, they were in front of us) If two big trucks were going to pass us at the same time, they passed each other, I called, "Bogie 6 and 12." We exited the highway.

When the lead changed again, I moved up to the third slot. Everything was much the same, but I had to keep my place behind the number two rider. I couldn't slack off because the man behind me depended on my consistency. I had to concentrate every second. If I didn't, my front tire would rub the forward bike and cause an accident. I didn't look at the landscape but down at the spinning tire in front of me. I enjoyed pedaling more when I was behind John. I felt a greater sense of emotional well-being behind John because we were close friends. Kevin and Mike were casual buddies. John and I shared a kindred spirit, born of age, and similar spiritual appreciations. Being closer to him made my ride easier. Over the years, we'd pulled each other along in many ways.

Moving into the number two position, I felt more wind resistance. I drank water, knowing that I couldn't falter at the point position. I watched for traffic. I gathered myself for the next shift. In minutes, John pulled left and dropped to the rear.

"Good pull John, way to go," Kevin said.

I was in the lead again, pressing against the wind, cranking at 100 percent power at a steady cadence. My legs worked harder. I lathered up with the extra effort. When a truck passed, I was hit hardest by the draft, but I kept a firm hold on the bars. In my determination to maintain speed, I dropped down on the lowest part of the bars. Several times, I downshifted to maintain speed. When the land leveled off, I shifted up. With a slight downhill grade, I kept a constant speed and only increased it gradually. If I wasn't in harmony with the group's speed needs, they let me know with verbal abuse. A complete rotation turned every twenty minutes.

Cap Rock, New Mexico, flew by with the only hint of the population being a lone black dog rushing out to chase us.

“I'll feed him a Zefal sandwich,” Kevin said, brandishing his air pump.

The dog didn't reach us in time as we sped past his territory. He pulled up short, barking his disapproval of our momentary encroachment. Beyond Cap Rock, we rode over flat, grassy plains as we pressed into a side wind.

At the end of three hours, we stopped for a break. My rear end was hurting, and everyone made a few butt jokes. We watered up and stuffed ourselves with apples, bananas, and tomato sandwiches.

Back on the highway, our pace line formed up. It became our salvation, but Mike became a nagging spur of the moment. At the end of his lead pull, he dropped back and kept dropping back. He was a strong rider who could pound the pedals at any pace, but his mind wasn't into it. He was a confirmed pessimist.

After the next break, Kevin took the lead followed by John, Mike and me. We called Kevin “Revvin' Kevin” because he spun his crank at high revolutions. When he hit the lead, he got into it and pedaled us into the ground. He was like a lead Husky on a dog sled, and he wasn't about to slow down for anyone. We battled to slow Kevin down and speed Mike up. Later, we stopped and asked Mike if he wanted to make the run for the 200.

“I reckon you better go ahead,” he said. “I'll meet up with you tomorrow.”

At the Texas State line, we pulled away from Mike for good. It brought a load off our minds, but I knew John felt sad about leaving his countryman. Once the pack meshed into a determined team of three, the miles flew past. At 12:55 p.m., we completed the first 100 miles. They seemed like nothing because I knew it was the second 100 that would kill us. On the good side, my feet felt good. No pain. My body loved the power output. Talk about a natural high! Those feisty endorphins (the body's natural drugs) released into every cell of my body. My whole being buzzed crossing the endless fields of red soil in west Texas. Thousands of plowed furrows in perfect rows stretched to the horizon. It looked like the farmers were driving their tractors off the ends of the earth. It looked like they might be swallowed by the red dirt ocean that rippled toward the blue sky.

At Brownfield, we drank water and orange juice. Hunger seemed to engulf us as we stuffed our faces with sandwiches and fruits. We inflated our tires, filled our water bottles and oiled the chains. Everyone complained about their butts. Mine didn't feel too bad. Maybe endorphins were keeping my cells deliriously happy. Maybe I was crazy!

We slowly pedaled out of town but soon revved it up. Out of Brownfield, we hit a six-mile stretch of gravel road. It pounded us. John lost a screw from his rack and took ten minutes to replace it. We ate dust from passing cars, which caked on to our arms and legs. Dirt got into our chains and the breeze changed into a head wind.

At Tokio, Texas under a darkening sky, we had completed 167 miles by 8:00 p.m. We cranked eastward into a storm front gathering from the south. My body ran on empty as we brought our goal down to twenty-three miles. We had attached flashing lights to our arms for safety and wore reflective vests. A chameleon sky swirled overhead. I kept stuffing raisins and nuts into my mouth as the wind picked up. A passing car driver stopped us to ask what we were doing.

"Don't you know there's a tornado watch?" he asked.

"No, but we do now," I told him.

"Be careful," he yelled, driving away.

At that point, a rush of wind crashed into our bodies. Lightning crackled on the horizon. To make it even stranger, a pumpkin-colored full moon broke from the horizon, only to vanish into the clouds minutes later.

John looked over at me, "What are they going to throw at us next?"

"Rain," I joked. "But I'm not stopping now."

"How about you, John?" Kevin asked, his eyes blazing.

"If you Yanks are that crazy," John said. "The Australian representative of this mad dash will equal anything you mates throw at him."

"It's settled," I said. "Let's see how miserable we can make ourselves."

The wind blew hard into our faces at that point. We busted into it with the determination of an American battleship flying an Australian flag. I'm sure people in passing cars considered us crazy. I rolled into another world as my body answered the call. I felt tired, weary, bonking, and ready to quit—but my mind wouldn't let me. My mental whip drove my body onward. John and Kevin held the same resolve as they maintained the pace. Nothing short of an erupting volcano could stop us now. Each of us was determined to cross the finish line. At 10:30 p.m., we entered Post, Texas, only to find out that we had several miles more to go before completing 200 miles. We turned back with the wind and raced out of town, then turned back once again into its fury. At 11:30, we watched the meter on Kevin's bike turn over 200 miles. We had ridden for 17 1/2 hours. Our energy consumption exceeded 14,500 calories each.

We opted for a motel at the end of town. I walked into the room in a state of utter exhaustion, endorphin euphoria, and mental weariness. My pulse dropped. I fell onto the bed, waiting for the others to finish their showers. I had never felt that way before, nor have I since. When I stepped into the shower, I sighed in ecstasy with warm water cascading down my body. I toweled off. When I returned to the room, John and Kevin snored peacefully. Seconds later, I joined them.

Tomorrow was dark on the horizon.

(Texas is big! It took us eight days to cross from west to east.)

Chapter 9—A Man Named Joe

> ***"I never told my own religion nor scrutinized that of another. I never attempted to make a convert, nor wished to change another's creed. I am satisfied that yours must be an excellent religion to have produced a life of such exemplary virtue and correctness. For it is in our lives, and not from our words, that our religion must be judged."***
>
> ***—Thomas Jefferson***

A hill descends into St. Johns, Arizona, on Route 180, at the eastern end of the state. Entirely unaware that a torture chamber of hell awaited my friends and me. My traveling companions John, Mike, and Kevin rolled ahead because I had stopped to fix a flat tire.

On our coast-to-coast, we had toured the Petrified Forest near Holbrook, and had ridden east across the arid prairie. A full-blown western sunset with a multicolored light-show stretched to the horizon. Majestic thunderheads piled up in the heavens above us. We planned to pick up Route 380 east into New Mexico. While coasting to the bottom of the hill, I saw my friends talking with a middle-aged, portly man in a blue Chevy Nova.

"How's it going mates?" I asked, pulling to a stop.

"I want you to meet my new friend, Joe," John said.

"Hi Joe," I said, looking at a man who looked like the local school custodian.

"Joe has asked us over to his house for showers and dinner," John said. "We can camp in his back yard."

"Sounds great," I said, noticing Kevin giving me odd eye signals.

“You boys can follow me,” Joe said. “My house is two miles from here.”

We hopped on the bikes for a quick ride to his place. Kevin rode alongside me.

“What a good deal, huh! Showers and a hot meal,” I said.

“I think it's going to cost us a bit of religious conversion,” Kevin said. “I tried to talk John out of this but he didn't seem to understand.”

“John's an innocent child,” I said. “But we can handle it.”

“I'm not so sure.”

“Don't worry about it.”

Famous last words of General Custer. Four sweaty bicycle riders following a middle-aged man to his home in the suburbs! That’s innocent enough. We rode up his driveway and withstood the glare of his wife who stood on the porch like the wicked witch of the North. She swept the porch, but I swear she could take the broom and fly.

I knew things weren't right when this oversized Army drill sergeant’s wife named Hazel grabbed him by the arm as he walked up the porch steps.

“What do you mean bringing home a bunch of strangers again,” she demanded, talking through her clenched teeth. “Wasn't last week's batch enough for you? You haven't cleaned up after them, YET! This time, you clean up! Do you hear me, HUSBAND?”

Joe wilted under her barrage. Kevin faded back. I was ready to punt. John and Mike stood there smiling like two kids in a Norman Rockwell painting. Then she turned her fury toward us. I cringed. We stood there looking into the face of Medusa.

“You boys are welcome to stay the night since my “loyal” husband has already invited you, but you have to realize the problems my husband gets us into. He can't cook, can't vacuum, won't take out the trash, won't wash dishes, won’t mow the lawn, can’t tend a garden, never walks the dog, does nothing around the house, and KEEPS inviting strangers into our place like it's a haven for stray dogs. The kitchen is a disaster area from the last episode. But since you're here, you can camp out back and come in for showers. Just don't waste my hot water."

"Yes, ma'am," John said in a mouse-like whisper.

"You Australian?" she asked.

"Yes, ma'am."

"Welcome to America!"

At that moment, I wanted to crawl back to the road like a cowardly mutt and find a campsite in a peaceful meadow outside of town. But to my dismay, John walked his bike toward the backyard. He did not understand our predicament.

The wicked witch of the North swirled around on her black heels and stomped back into the house, probably to file her fangs and polish her claws. I was ready to split that second and Kevin would be on my tail. But Joe regained himself and herded the rest of us to the backyard, where he made sure we pitched our tents.

"I'm going to take care of you boys. Make yourselves at home," he said. "The bathroom is on the left inside the house. I'm going to make some mountain food for you. There are clean towels in the washroom. I have some interesting reading for you, too."

I showered quickly. My plan was to excuse myself and slip into my tent to avoid the sermon about to be given. But Joe proved a master at shepherding his newly found sinners. He was going to save us. He tagged me with dishes and silverware before I could get outside. He put Kevin in charge of stirring the gravy. Joe knew we were like two racehorses ready to bolt. John and Mike hadn't experienced his brand of evangelism, so they were like gerbils in a glass tank. I gave into Joe because he would haul me out of the tent anyway.

The fact is, I'm a sinner, but sometimes, I don't think the little sins add up to all that much in the eyes of the Creator.

Heck, everybody lies a little. We all have done something we don't want others to know about. We can't be perfect. I don't want to be perfect. I like my foibles. They give me character flaws that others find interesting. The world would be a dull place if everybody lived perfect lives. Because, if they were, we'd have no one to talk about. Look how exciting Monica Lewinski made our lives for an entire year! What about Clinton's peccadilloes? What about Madonna's kissing Brittany on stage in front of millions? What about Janet Jackson's costume malfunction? What's up with the latest on Britney Spears? How about Brad Pitt's latest date after the Angelina Jolie fiasco? It's fun to talk about those characters. As it is, we're all a bunch of folks going down the road of life doing the best we can. Some of us fail.

But most of us don't want to be reminded that we're "bad." Because, at times, being bad is good. I mean, it is fun to be bad because it feels so good, so how can it be so bad? Then, to have Joel Osteen tell me I'm going to fry in the chambers of hell takes away all the fun of being bad. Besides, if I was really good, I'd probably go to heaven and live on the same street as Oral Roberts, Pat Robertson, Reverend Schuler, the Pope and Billy Graham. To think that I'd have to listen to them every day for the rest of eternity would drive me crazy. I'd be the first man to commit a crime in heaven and be sent to hell.

Anyway, as Joe cooked the food, we set out the dishes. Soon the table filled with steaming food, rolls and ice water. We sat down to a large spread fit for a king. His mountain food consisted of boiled vegetables in gravy. Joe opened quarts of homemade apricots and applesauce. He added seven-grain bread for sopping up the juices on our plates. Hazel stayed in the next room, presumably combing the snakes on her head and watching Pat Sajak mesmerize his audience with "Wheel of Fortune."

Not long into the meal, Joe passed around cards that explained his faith. I nodded politely along with Kevin. We had heard the spiel before. It's not that I didn't respect his right to his beliefs, but I hated having them jammed down my throat. With a break in the conversation, I excused myself and escaped to my tent. Kevin followed.

We expressed our relief at having made it out alive. Better that John and Mike catch the thrust of Joe's crusade. It was new to them. As I sat in the middle of my tent, writing in my journal, I felt relieved. Suddenly, my zipper ripped upwards under its own power. In a moment, I was staring into Joe's savior-like brown eyes.

"Hi, I thought you might need some important information that you can read in your spare time," he said, handing me a book.

"Thanks, Joe," I said.

"You're welcome," he said. "I hope I didn't disturb your writing. Good night."

Seconds later, he repeated the same lines to Kevin. That was it. I was leaving at dawn. When Joe returned to the house, I whispered to Kevin.

"I'm making like the Pony Express at daybreak," I said.

"I'm making like the Union-Pacific before daybreak," Kevin shot back.

"Deal."

Sleep came swiftly. I couldn't wait to get out of there.

With the first bird's chirp before dawn, Kevin and I packed our gear for the escape. Not a word was spoken. I didn't tell John because he was such a good-natured friend, and he might talk us into staying. No way did I want to chance that. Like ghosts, Kevin and I vanished into the morning darkness. We would never see Hazel and her Medusa again. When we reached the end of the block, we started laughing and talking about John and Mike's fate.

"Those poor guys are in for a sermon," Kevin said. "He'll chain them to the pews. We may never see them again. They're going to answer the call and become missionaries."

"Can you believe that guy broke into my tent?" I said.

"Yeah, but as soon as I heard him talking with you, I blew out my candle, so he would figure I was asleep," Kevin said. "But he had seen my light on while talking with you, so he took it upon himself to open my tent and shine a flashlight on me while he told me about his book."

"Yeah, well, we're safe now. Let's ride."

We cranked down the street with light streaking across the sky. Near the edge of town, we found an all-you-can-eat pancake house. We couldn't pass it up. We parked the bikes against the glass.

A waitress took our order. Minutes later, she brought us two plates loaded with buttermilk pancakes. We slapped on butter and poured syrup over the stacks. Halfway through my pancakes, I felt nature calling.

"I've got to go, Kevin," I said. "Order me another stack."

"Okay," he said, his mouth stuffed with pancakes.

I walked around the outside of the building to the bathroom. The lock was broken on the door, but it was so early that I didn't figure anyone would see me from the street if the door was opened. A few minutes later, I washed my hands and headed back for the pancakes. Rounding the corner of the building, I choked at the sight of Joe standing over Kevin, cajoling him. Kevin's eyes rose to the top of his head as he stuffed a fork full of pancakes into his mouth.

"Oh my God, Joe is coming after me," I said to myself.

I ran back to the bathroom but remembered it wouldn't lock. I'll fool him. The girl's bathroom...that's it. I'll hide in there. In a panic, I bolted for the lady's bathroom. It was unlocked. I walked in, closed the door, and punched the button on the doorknob lock. It was a shoe-box bathroom with no partition for the toilet. From my nervousness, I had to go again, so I walked over and sat down on the toilet. I felt safe.

Like a scene out of a horror movie, I heard a key slip into the tumbler and the ping of the doorknob lock release. That's all I needed—a little old lady finding me sitting on her toilet. Or worse yet, a gorgeous blond coming in to fix her panty hose. I sat there paralyzed. What else could I do? The worst that would happen would be when she saw me, she would shut the door in embarrassment. I would be embarrassed too, but she wouldn't know me from Adam, so it wouldn't be a big deal. I sat there holding the toilet paper roll in my hand awaiting the stranger at the door.

"Hi," Joe said, sticking his head into my chamber.

I looked up at him, feeling my skin crawl, and my emotions smoldering into anger. But I kept calm. Joe did not understand his rudeness.

"Your friend promised me that you guys would come back for breakfast," he said. "I'll be expecting you in a few minutes. You don't want to waste my breakfast goodies."

"Yes Joe," I said. "Is it okay if I finish my business?"

"Oh, don't mind me," he said, closing the door.

Back with Kevin, my pancakes had cooled off. I was upset.

"Do you believe that guy walked in on me in the girl's bathroom?" I told Kevin.

"He asked me where you were, so I told him I thought you went to the bathroom," Kevin said. "Then he grabbed the keys off the hooks after he got done talking with me. He's a man with a mission. He's trying to save us from ourselves."

"I don't want to be saved," I said. "He told me you agreed to come back to his house for breakfast."

"Are you kidding?"

"That's it, dude! We're gettin' outta' Dodge after these pancakes are in my belly. I can't take it anymore."

Five minutes later, we sat in the saddle, cranking hard. We broke free of the city limits—heading for wide-open spaces. In my mind, the New Mexico border would save us. We would be out of his jurisdiction, and as like outlaws pursued, we urged our iron steeds ever faster through the cactus-covered badlands. Ten miles out of the town we relaxed.

"We're cool now," Kevin said, looking down at his computer. "He's probably got Mike and John chained inside his house..."

At that moment, a man driving a blue Chevy Nova roared past us, pulled off the highway and slammed on the brakes. The door swung open. The driver leaped out with his hands spread like an eagle holding his prey to the ground.

"Joe!" I gasped, my spirit dribbling down into the soles of my shoes.

"You didn't come back for breakfast!" he complained. "Listen, if you need food, or shelter, I can get you into one of our churches in the next city."

That did it. Joe pushed me over the edge. Kevin and I stood astride our bikes being pandered by this poor lost soul.

"Joe," I said. "Hold your horses for a minute and let me speak. You're a nice guy, and you've shown our friends American hospitality. But your price was too high. You've bombarded us with your philosophy from the first moment we met. Do you know my name or my friend's here?"

He stammered.

"Do you even remember my Aussie friends' names?"

He looked down, shuffling his feet.

"You don't even care about our names," I said. "You just want to save us, but you haven't even considered that we might have our own philosophies. Did you know there are thousands of religions in this world? Why not respect everyone's religion and leave them be. How would you like me barging into your life, pushing my religion on you? There are two things I never try to change in another person—their religion or politics. It's a waste of time. I'm not going to change yours, or anyone's, so I just let people be.

"The next time you ask people into your home, ask them about their adventures. I'll bet you will learn more than you ever dreamed possible. Travelers have some of the greatest stories in the world, never seen on television, because they are people experiencing the world. No gloss, no glitter, just reality. Can you do that the next time? If you do, you won't infringe on their personal philosophies, and everyone will have a great time visiting you. Most of all, you will enjoy them, for what they are and what they believe, and you will learn to respect everyone's personal choices. There is no single answer to God. In fact, God comes to everyone with a slightly different color, size, feeling and angle. You need to respect that."

"He's right, Joe," Kevin said. "We tried to escape because you made us uncomfortable by pushing your beliefs on us. I'm 24 and I don't mind a discussion on beliefs, but I don't like religion jammed down my throat. I don't care what you believe as long as your religion fulfills your spiritual life. Religion is a personal thing. Our friends were being polite, but you've made it bad for us."

"You're right," Joe said, standing there like a small child. "I've been harping on your friends all morning about joining my church."

"You tell them that we'll be up the road riding slowly so they can catch up," I said.

"If you need anything, money, food..." Joe started in again.

"JOE!" I exclaimed, cutting him off. "We need your respect, nothing more."

"You're right. I'm sorry."

"Thank Hazel for her home-canned apricots and applesauce," Kevin said.

"I will."

Kevin and I slipped our feet onto the pedals. We waved at Joe as he slid into his Nova. He turned his car around and seconds later, vanished from our rearview mirrors.

"Boy, life's a big adventure, isn't it?" Kevin said, rolling his eyes. "That poor guy. I feel sorry for him. I think he's lonely."

"It's too bad we can't get him on a bicycle tour," Kevin said. "It would give him new perspectives."

"True, but he'd quit on the first climb."

"Guess you're right."

John and Mike caught up to us in New Mexico on a hill climb. Mike didn't care about our splitting, but John was none too happy about it. At first, he rode by us, not speaking, even after we said, "Hello." I knew he was upset, which made me angry over the whole Joe episode. A short time later, John stopped alongside a guardrail and parked his bike. I didn't know what to expect from my dear friend, but he was reasonable, so I felt confident that we would work it out. He stood there waiting for us, his arms folded and a serious look on his face.

"John, I'm sorry about this whole mess," I said, riding up.

"You boys have all day to explain your abandonment of your mates," he said, with a slight smile slipping into his serious demeanor.

Once we explained our position, John understood the whole story. He started laughing. We started laughing. Even Mike laughed. Then he looked down at his back tire. Flat tire number six! We laughed some more. It was agreed. We blamed the whole day on a man named Joe.

(Taking a break on a guardrail in the middle of the day.)

Chapter 10—We're Doomed Buffalo Breath

"Somebody asked me: Why are you doing this? I couldn't come up with an answer. But I love every kilometer of it. The highs and the lows. The sunshine and the storms. The solitude, the unknown and the absurdity of it all. I like it that things will always work out in the end or maybe one day they won't. Until then, my goal is to see the world. My motivation: the kindness of strangers and the beauty of the wild. And my home is on the open road."

—Iohan Gueorguieo, cycling around the world

I camp in the wilds. It's peaceful, aesthetic and spiritual. It is a communion with nature. Whether it's the desert or mountains, I prefer the smell of the wilds.

But wilderness camping features precarious moments.

Sandi and I cranked our way toward Alaska, laboring up mountain grades in the Sawtooth Range of Idaho on Route 75. Late in the day, we came to a river intersecting the highway.

"Let's follow that dirt path down along the river," she said. "I bet we find a good camp spot."

"Could be good for a bath and campfire," I added. "Let's do it."

"I need to adjust my rear derailleur," Sandi said. "Could you give me a hand with it?"

"If you'll fix dinner."

"You rat."

"I'll do the dishes."

"Deal."

We followed the trail that looked as if it would reach the river, yet be out of sight of the road. Two minutes later, we found ourselves at the perfect campsite. Someone had built a rock fire spit in a clearing with a sandy beach on the river twenty feet away. Plenty of firewood lay around the area.

"I'll grab some wood and start the fire," I said. "I can check your derailleur before it gets dark."

"Okay, I'm taking a bath."

Even with a warm night in June, mosquitoes didn't seem to be out in force. Sandi washed up while I started a fire. In a few minutes, flames licked the evening air, lighting up the surrounding trees. We had 15 minutes before darkness. I pitched the tent and set-up the air mattresses and sleeping bags. I stripped the panniers off the bikes and set them inside. With my tool bag in hand, I bent down to check out Sandi's derailleur. The stretched cable had caused it to be out of line with the free wheel. I tightened it and adjusted the derailleur.

"She'll shift like greased lightning tomorrow," I said to Sandi as she returned to camp.

"The water is lovely," she said. "Hurry up and get a bath before it gets dark. This spot is beautiful."

"Sure is," I said as I grabbed my towel and bottle of biodegradable soap.

"I'm making spaghetti, so hurry up. It'll be ready in fifteen minutes."

By the time I returned from the river, the steaming pot of spaghetti wafted through the evening air. The flames danced light around the entire area. Sandi poured tomato sauce into a second pan. Minutes later, we gorged ourselves.

"That's it for me," I said, "My tummy's busting at the seams."

"We better wash the pans."

"I'll do it in the morning," I said, getting up.

"What about raccoons?"

"Don't worry about them."

"Okay, if you say so."

We doused the fire and crawled into the tent. One thing about touring through the mountains—my legs felt weary. I fell asleep in seconds.

The next morning, the sky brightened on the eastern horizon. One of those layered, surging, blazing red sunrises raged across the stratus clouds low to the horizon. Bursting through the heavens, it brought color to our world. It burned red on the rippling waters of the river, and contrasted with the lush verdant foliage of the trees.

"Frosty, wake up," Sandi said, nudging me. "You smell anything?"

"Yeah, it smells like...oh no, it's...a skunk," I said, squeezing my nose.

"Look outside the flaps," Sandi said.

"What do you mean me...why me?"

"You're closer."

"You and your weird logic," I groaned, looking out the flap. "You guessed it... we've got a big, fat, stinky skunk checking out our campsite. He's waddling around the bikes...now he's headed for the river...now he's climbing up to the bikes again...whoops, now he's sniffing the fire pit... now he's into the saucepan."

"I told you to wash that thing out."

"You're right. I screwed up.... oh good, we're cool. There he goes back to the river...ah good, he's going into the... oh, oh, oh no, he's headed over here. He's less than twenty feet away and still coming. I'm gonna be sick. He's coming right for our front door."

"Quick, close the flap," Sandi whispered.

"If that black and white stink bomb lifts his tail, we're done. We can kiss off this trip for the next month. We won't be able to ride or buy groceries or anything," I said. "Nobody will be able to stand us up for a month of Sundays. I think we're doomed."

"We picked a great spot all right," Sandi added. "That skunk smells like something died inside of a garbage can. Stinking stink bomb anyway. How did we ever get into this one?"

"Dirty dishes," I admitted. "But how we gonna get out of here?"

"See where he is now," Sandi said.

"What is it with you?" I asked. "Do I look like I have F-O-O-L painted across my forehead?"

"Oh, take a peek."

"I'm always the one who..." I grumbled, pulling back the flap. "Ohhoooo."

I was nose-to-nose with the skunk. I froze. I couldn't speak. I held my breath. Sandi remained motionless in the back of me. The skunk's beady eyes looked through the netting right into mine. If it had been Valentine's Day, we could have kissed. All the while, her glossy black nose kept sniffing the netting, leaving drool marks across it. Fright paralyzed me as I slowly lowered the flap.

"I saw my life pass before my eyes," I whispered to Sandi.

"You look as if you saw a ghost."

"I'm amazed she didn't unload on me."

"Maybe she got a whiff of your morning buffalo breath and knew she was bested."

"You're so kind to me, Sandi."

"Look out now. See what's happening."

"Oh no, not me, nope, it's your turn."

"Okay, let me see," Sandi said, lifting the tent flap. "I think he's gone...nope, he's over there by the bikes again...oh, there he goes down along the river....he's headed along the bank, away from us."

We waited another five minutes until the waddling stink bomb vanished into the woods. His essence lay in the air like a barnyard full of chickens. I looked over at Sandi.

"Let's get our gear packed, and get out of here," I said.

"Does that mean you're not gonna wash dishes?" she said, smirking.

She was right. I had broken the rules of the wilderness, and we both nearly paid a heavy price for it. It's important to clean dishes and remove all food in a wilderness camp setting. In bear country, food must be hung in a plastic bag 100 yards from camp. It's even important to wash our faces and brush our teeth to remove food odor.

We flash-packed the bikes and tore out of there as if possessed with something akin to "fear." But there's something different about that kind of feeling. We didn't fear for our lives, but we were afraid of being stunk to high heaven. Reaching the highway, we laughed in relief.

"What was it you said about me having 'buffalo breath'?" I asked Sandi.

"Just kidding," she said.

We headed north into the Sawtooth Range. We pedaled into a lovely day for bicycling through the fresh air of the mountains. Now, every time I smell a skunk, I remember that morning by the river.

Still can't figure out how Sandi knows what a buffalo's breath smells like...

(You can show a sad face or a happy face. More fun to show a happy face on your bicycle tours.)

Chapter 11—Leap for Life

> ***"There is nothing like cycling for appreciating a country. I cycled coast to coast across America at 68 years of age. I was amazed at the experience, the stunning scenery and people along the way. I believe I wouldn't have been able to appreciate it or enjoy it as much on any other mode of transportation."***
>
> ***—John Edwards***

Heading east on Route 92 out of Provo, Utah, Sandi and I cranked hard through the afternoon. Above us, craggy 10,000-foot peaks poked into a cloudy sky. With the temperature over 100, we dripped our way through deep canyons. We stopped for a rest area at a turnout.

"Sure, it is a lot different than the salt flats," Sandi said, sucking on her water bottle.

"My legs are feeling this hill," I added, with a sweat bead ready to drop off my nose. "Guess they forgot about climbing after so long on the flats."

"It's prettier up here."

"Sure is," I said. "These mountains inspire me."

A few minutes later, we coasted down a steep incline, only to climb again. I hate losing altitude, only to climb again, but it's useless to fight it. We coasted through endless curves. Ahead of us, on the crest of a climb, a large boulder had fallen onto the road. I decided to move it off the road so it wouldn't smash a car's undercarriage to bits.

"Give me a minute Sandi," I said, laying my bike on the side of the road. "I'm gonna get this rock off the road. Could get somebody killed."

"I need a rest anyway," she said.

At that moment, another small rock cracked down from the overhead. It bounced across the road before slamming into the guardrail.

"Looks like we're under some falling rock," I said, hoisting the boulder to the side of the road.

"LOOK OUT!" Sandi yelled.

A shower of small rocks bounced across the road. I looked up to see where it was coming from.

"Look at that," I said, pointing upward.

"It's a Bighorn sheep," Sandi said. "He's knocking those rocks down on us. He looks like he's in a tight spot."

About 100 feet above us, a Bighorn stood on a ledge, stuck where he stood because the path ended. His massive, curled horns swept back from the top of his head. He looked a bit pensive as he nearly leaped forward but stopped.

"He's gonna jump, but there's no place to go," Sandi said.

"Unless it's that ledge above him."

"That's gotta be more than 15 feet away and higher!"

"Maybe that's why he's hesitating."

Without a second pause, the ram coiled his body before launching himself up and out to the ledge above him. His trajectory rose upward but not quite high enough to reach the higher rock. Instead, his two front feet slid like skids on a flat rock, and one rear leg caught the edge of the ledge. He was about to fall 100 feet to his death before our eyes. But in a split second, with his one leg locked onto the ledge, he threw his front legs upward and thrust his head back. He kicked with his one back leg to launch himself upside down, his hooves pointed to the sky, back toward his original ledge. While in the middle of his flight back, he twisted his body like a cat before landing. But again, only his front legs made the lower ledge, and his one back hoof reached the rock. His front legs skidded onto the ledge again, but his rear end was not going to make it. With only a split second left before he slipped off the ledge, he bellowed as he kicked hard with his one back leg that had made the ledge. That thrust kicked the back of his body upward and with the momentum of the leap, spun his rump around until he fell sideways onto the ledge. He lay there stunned. Seconds later, he stood up, and walked back the other way.

"My God," said gasped.

"I felt that," I said.

John Muir, America's first environmentalist and creator of our national parks systems said it best: "How many hearts with warm red blood in them are beating under the cover of the woods, and how many teeth and eyes are shining? A multitude of animal people, intimately related to us, but whose lives we know almost nothing, are as busy about their own lives as we about ours."

While bicycling, I roll quietly into the last of the silence. It allows me to peek into their lives—often.

(During a bike tour, you get to see nature up close and personal.)

Chapter 12—Stan the Nomadic Road Warrior

> ***"The bicycle is no longer a beast of steel...no, it is a friend. It is a faithful and powerful ally against one's worst enemies. It is stronger than anxiety, stronger than sadness. It has all the power of hope."***
>
> ***—Maurice Leblanc, French novelist***

Through the years, I've picked up pedal partners during my travels around the world. They've pedaled through 50 states with me for a glimpse of one of the wealthiest societies on the planet. Sometimes, they discover different aspects of the United States of America than what they expected.

Heading east on Route 64, my Australian friend John Brown and I had coasted more than ten miles off the plateau leading out of Grand Canyon National Park. We stopped at the Chevron gas station where Route 64 intersects Route 89. We exhausted our water supply from camping in the desert the night before, so we filled our bottles out of the station spigot. I pumped air into my tires when John said, "Hey dude, let's hit the road. I'm hot sitting here."

A few seconds later, I replaced the air hose, but nature called.

"Gotta' hit the bathroom," I said as I hopped off and leaned my bike against the station wall.

When I returned, John showed a puzzled look on his face. He twisted around with one leg swung over the top tube and looked down the road. He clicked his brake handles by pressing them and releasing them in rapid succession.

"What are you looking at?" I asked.

"Don't know," he said. "I barely got a glimpse of a guy riding by on a mountain bike, at least, I think it was a mountain bike. I don't know because he had gone by when I looked up from my map. It was the strangest bike setup I've ever seen."

"Let's catch up to him and find out," I said.

We headed north on Route 89 into a blustery wind. The highway swooped down a long incline into a valley. On the west side of the highway, a metal bridge spanned a canyon, but it looked out of place because it didn't have a road leading up to it or away from it.

"That bridge has no purpose," John said.

"Another pork barrel project by some politician," I said. Beyond the useless bridge, multicolored buttes and mesas slipped by us with sand swirling through the sagebrush alongside the road. Minutes later, we spotted orange flags flapping from the back of what looked like a small vehicle moving slowly in the breakdown lane.

Up closer, we saw a bicycle loaded like a gypsy wagon. Two dark blue mountain backpacks hung vertically stacked (in place of panniers) over the back wheel like saddlebags on a horse. A tent, sleeping bag and mattress filled the middle section over the rack. A wooden stick crossed in the back where two orange flags hung out on the traffic side. In the middle, like the back bumper on an old Cadillac, a spare tire hung from a horizontal stick.

Pulling alongside the rider, I saw two blue front panniers under a plastic beige milk crate, which the owner steel hose-clamped to his old-style flared Schwinn handlebars. Two one-gallon white Clorox bottles hung from the handlebars, on both sides of the gooseneck. The second set of Clorox bottles hung to both backpacks behind the rider's rear end. With four gallons filled with water, the rider carried an extra 32 pounds of weight. Sitting up in the milk crate and with its head poked out of a six-inch round hole in the cardboard cover, a black cat stared at me. He appeared to be the navigator of this two-wheeled road-ship.

I slowed to 10 miles per hour, to match the speed of a wrinkled old man spinning a low gear. He wore blue work pants, high-top leather work boots, a red nylon windbreaker, leather work gloves and an orange stocking cap. His weatherworn face and thin, wiry frame cast a tall shadow under the morning sun.

John and I introduced ourselves to the fifty-nine-year-old man who called himself "Stan." I asked him what kind of gear cluster he cranked. He said it was a 24-front chain ring "granny" to a 34-toothed rear end low gear. That explained why he rolled so slowly. He acted reserved, but as the miles unfolded, so did his astonishing story.

"Thirteen years ago, my life lacked purpose, so I pressed the eject button on the plastic world. I sold my computer company—bid farewell to what was left of my family and took off on my bicycle. I'd worn out three other bikes until I came across this mountain bike. I'll wear it out too, but so far, it's the best of the lot. I've customized it over the years so it's able to carry the 200 pounds of gear I pack on it."

"200 pounds!" I gasped.

"That's right," Stan said. "This is my home. I never thought I would be on the road so long, but I know I will never go back. I live on my investments. My wife died of cancer and my kids don't give a damn about anything. If I had stayed in my job or tried to keep caring about things they didn't care about, I'd have gone nuts. Instead, I decided to be happy."

Our group rolled further into the desert as John and I probed Stan for more of his background. Thirteen years on the road from Alaska, the Yukon Territory, through the USA, Mexico, Central America and to the bottom of South America in Ushuaia. Never the same road twice! With that many years on adventure highway, he possessed the stuff of legends. While he shared some of his experiences, the cat issued a "Meow." Stan smiled.

"This is my best friend Little Chum. Life has had its disappointments, but Little Chum never lets me down. He's a great company and never complains. He's cycled with me from Canada to Argentina with never an argument. He sleeps during the day and prowls around my campsite at night. We communicate, unlike any two creatures. Little Chum knows my mind."

"Don't you ever get homesick for friends?" I asked.

"No point in returning. Life is today. Anything else doesn't mean squat. I don't look back, nor do I have any false aspirations. I rarely think of home. They are busy with their lives. It's no longer my problem. My philosophy deals with this instant. Stan's Law states that wherever you are right now, bets are you're better off than you will be this time tomorrow."

"What about expectations?" John asked.

"No disappointments with my law," Stan replied. "You won't see me straining my neck around the next bend in the road or even talking about next week. I keep a diary, but when it's full, I throw it in the fire."

"What?" I gasped, nearly wavering into his packs.

"What's in the past is done. Besides, can you imagine carrying around 13 years of diaries? I'm already too heavy. No! I never ride the same road twice and I don't think about yesterday. I don't care about yesterday."

Stan sat erect in the saddle. His smooth cadence complimented the millions of pedal strokes his legs pounded out over the years. Deep lines on his face showed a comfortable acceptance of life—as he chose it. Stan proved himself a road warrior.

"Twenty-five miles is my daily target," he continued. "If I don't make it, so what? On the flats, I average 8 to 10 miles an hour. I figure I do a million-foot pounds of work a year. But I'm in no hurry. Isn't that right Little Chum?"

A faint meow came from inside the crate as Stan's legs spun their way through time. I thought about my load of 70 pounds and my own travels that paled in contrast to Stan's. What single event sent that intriguing human being toward his extraordinary destiny? My amazement increased as Stan revealed a few episodes from his bicycle sojourn...

"Hell, I've got enough roads to keep me busy 'til I die. I never think about how far I've gone or how far I'll go. I stay in the Americas because there are sufficient experiences here."

"Any funny ones?" I asked.

"Hundreds," he said. "The one I cherish the most happened a few years back in the Yucatan of Mexico. I was camped out one night in a stand of scrub trees. As usual, I put Little Chum out for his nightly prowl. I put my dentures in my coffee cup outside the tent. I got tired of knocking them over at night and getting water on the floor. The next morning, my teeth were missing, so I called Little Chum. He sniffed the cup and followed his nose to a burrow about 20 feet away from camp and started digging. I helped him. I pulled out sticks, fur balls and rodent skeletons before I got 10 inches into a pack rat's den. Wouldn't you know it, there were my teeth, smiling up at me. I rinsed 'em off and popped 'em back in my mouth. I tell you breakfast wouldn't have been the same that day without my teeth."

We laughed before John asked, "Any dangerous times?"

"My worst experience was in the Peruvian Andes when soldiers slashed through my tent with their bayonets cutting my shoulder at the same time. They hauled me away to jail. They interrogated me just like you see in the movies. Bastards anyway! I wrote letters to the U.S. Embassy until I got some attention. My educational background and innocence got through to them. A sergeant befriended me and even discussed Mark Twain while my tent was being repaired. Two weeks later, I was released on a weekend, but since I didn't have any money until the banks opened on Monday, they let me stay in prison for two more days. I can tell you that Americans don't have any idea of how lucky they are to live in a free country. The kids growing up today take too much for granted.

"Another time I camped out in a bad spot, but it was my fault. I was tired and didn't think about where I set the tent down. It was in a dry wash. That night, a desert rainstorm drenched the area. I woke up to water seeping into my tent. I kept picking the floor up until a flood of water was pulling at every corner of my tent. I looked out the flaps to see Little Chum standing on high ground with each lightning flash. I was in the middle of a flood. I leaped out of the tent as a wave of water swept it downstream. For the next couple of hours, I sat in the rain, talking to myself about how stupid I was to set up the tent in such a bad place. Little Chum was soaked to the bone and shivering. In the morning, I tracked downstream and found my tent snagged on a tree. I was lucky to recover everything."

John and I kept trading places in order to hear Stan. He proved a remarkable character. I felt like a polliwog and he was the big daddy, the one who had gone before—who knew the ways of the world. His philosophy intrigued me even though I couldn't begin to live like that. I carried great expectations for each new day on a bicycle adventure.

But that proved the key to his unusual life path. That's the one thing about living and being human. It's a miracle on this single green planet somewhere out in the black void of space. It gives a beginning and a lifetime later, it ends. What we do in the interim becomes our choice. We're given certain abilities and intelligence, but for those of us born in a free country—we can decide our life choices. What's more important, we can change our decisions at any time.

As for me, I am a cloud watcher. Clouds do not hurry. They change so slowly that most people never notice, and never look up. But each of us CAN look! That's what Stan does. He's out there tonight under the stars, filling his days with living. Stan doesn't complain, nor does he live in desperation. He allows the wind to caress his cheeks and shoulders. Its stormy fingers play in his hair, and the rain cleanses his spirit. The stars, moon and sun have shared sweet secrets with him in the morning dew. He makes love with nature on his bicycle. Stan celebrates the moment.

Ahead of us in the afternoon a crossroads appeared. Stan pedaled through it without looking back as we turned east.

"Take care guys," he said.

We watched his orange flags vanish over the hill. John and I continued our trans-continental trek with new ideas about life. The one thing that dismayed us, was Stan's disregard for the diaries he tossed into the fire. But that was Stan. If it weren't for the way he lived, we would never have known about his teeth smiling up from the bottom of a pack rat's hideout.

(Bikes stacked up against the wall of a restaurant. If it's an all-you-can-eat joint, we eat them out of house and home.)

Chapter 13—I'll Hang Myself First

> ***"It has been said that the influences surrounding the first four years of life command the future directions of the child in its life to come. Had I been raised in bleak urban surroundings; I am certain my life would have been vastly different...all children deserve contact with Nature as a part of their heritage. This is not, unfortunately, the general pattern of civilization. Untold millions are doomed to live in insufficiency because of failure to realize the importance of experience with the Natural World.***
>
> ***Generations to come will suffer for our embezzlement of resources, practical and spiritual, that were my heritage. The more our children see and know the Natural World, the better equipped they will be to face the basic realities of life and realize the noble potentials of existence this planet has to offer."***
>
> ***—Ansel Adams, photographer***

My friend Pam and I pedaled through Wyoming on our way to Alaska one summer when we rode into the jaws of danger. If you're headed for disaster, preparation is nine-tenths of survival in the wilderness.

Yellowstone is the father of our national parks system. The Grand Teton Mountains, just south of Yellowstone, puncture the sky like broken shards of glass. Old Faithful vents itself on the hour. Bear, elk, coyotes, moose and bison roam the landscape, while majestic eagles soar through endless skies overhead. This region features one of America's famous wilderness sanctuaries.

Pam and I heard a story late in the afternoon from a camper-van couple as we pedaled north on the Rockefeller Memorial Parkway leading into Yellowstone. Outlandish! Their story was too impossible to happen. Because of it, a bear ran loose in Yellowstone that had tasted human blood.

I had heard of people doing stupid things like walking up to a female moose with two calves to take a picture. Their lives were in danger, and they were lucky not to have been stomped to death. Some had been. A fellow bicyclist in Alaska wanted to see a grizzly up close. He left a fresh salmon carcass on the ground outside his tent. Nature granted his wish with a 900-pound grizzly. That bicyclist wouldn't forget his meeting with a bear. The beast mauled him.

One night in a camping area in Yosemite, I woke up with Pam clamping on my arm with fingernails like vice grips. She had heard a bear outside our tent. We looked out the nylon flaps to the campsite next to ours. A bear commenced licking a dirty pan on the picnic table.

"Do you think he's going to come over to our tent?" Pam whispered.

"Naw," I reassured her. "Our food is in a metal box. We're safe."

"Look at him," she said, her fingernails clamping into my arm again. "He's sniffing their tent."

"He's clawing their tent," I said.

The bear stood up on his legs and ripped a long slash into our neighbor's tent. We heard a muffled scream. Seconds later, two children followed by their parents sprinted toward their car. The bear waded into their tent, ripping and grunting as he tore everything to shreds.

"What if he comes over to our tent?" Pam said.

"We can run over to our bikes and jump in the back seat," I joked.

"Great," she groaned. "You're so comforting."

The bear sauntered into the woods after he found his prize. The next morning, we found out one of the kids had left a Hostess Cupcake Bon Bon half-eaten in his pocket. The bear sniffed it out. In the process, he shredded a thousand dollars worth of camping gear.

But the story the camper-van couple told us topped anything I had ever heard. Many foreigners had seen American cartoons, and Yogi Bear and Boo Boo in "Jellystone Park" were funny characters in the 1960s. But bears in Yellowstone were no laughing matter. They were hungry and ate anything. An Asian family was visiting Yellowstone with their five-year-old child. At a point not far north of us, they had stepped out of their car and approached a bear that was trying to cross the highway. People snapped pictures from every angle, blocking his path. The couple thought the bear was cute, so the husband walked across the road followed by the mother carrying a camera. The beast stood still while the father walked up and placed the boy on the bear's shoulders. The kid grabbed the animal's ears. The father backed up while the mother took a picture.

The child suddenly pulled on the bear's ears. A second later, the bear shook the kid off its neck and mauled it. The parents screamed. The bear chased them. The woman reached the car first and jumped into the back seat slamming the door behind her. The husband wasn't as quick. Sliding into the front driver's side, he didn't get the door closed fast enough. The bear ripped a few creases into the man's shoulder. At that point, a brave person in another car rescued the child. Mayhem broke loose with people screaming and the parents in shock as they sat in their car crying in pain and anguish over their child.

The confused bear ran wild until he made his way back into the woods, not knowing why horns were honking and people were yelling at him.

After that story, we were uneasy about camping. We had no choice because no vacancies existed in the park. The rangers would not let us camp unless it was in a regulation spot. We were frightened as darkness surrounded us like a movie theater just before a "SCREAM I" film was about to roll. For one of the few times in my life, I was nervous—no—I was scared.

That's when my best wilderness instincts came into play. Pam and I pulled our bicycles into the bush about 100 yards off the highway. We smelled sulfur nearby and headed toward it. Even with a quiet breeze whispering through a dense mantle of pine trees, sulfur gasses permeated our surroundings. With a darkening sky, we pitched camp by a steaming fumarole. The air smelled like a dozen drunks, who had smoked a carton of cigarettes, drank ten cups of coffee and eaten double helpings of rotten boiled eggs for breakfast. It was dank, disgusting, odious and downright sickening—just the way I wanted it, so not even a bear would come sniffing around our camp.

I strung 50 feet of my nylon parachute cord two feet off the ground around our campsite. Having picked up a tin can from the highway, I filled it with rocks and set it up to fall when the rope was tripped. That would give us a signal that the bear was heading our way. After we had locked the bikes up, we retired to the tent. I wasn't through with our escape plans.

"You have your knife?" I asked Pam.

"Yes."

"Open the blade and leave it in your riding gloves."

"What for?"

"If that bear comes around, we may have to cut our way out of this tent and run for a tree."

"Won't he climb after us?"

"They won't climb trees under five inches in diameter, so pick out a skinny one."

"Great," Pam lamented, not too excited about our prospects for a good night's sleep. "How could those people be so stupid?"

"Don't ask me."

"What's that rope for?" Pam asked, spying two six-foot-long pieces of nylon next to me.

"One's for you."

"What for?"

"If that bear comes, I want you to slash the side of the tent and make a run for the trees. Make sure you take this piece of rope with you."

"Why?"

"Well, that bear's going to go after one of us," I said. "Let's run in opposite directions. If you shinny up a tree, you should be safe."

"But what's the rope for?" she asked again.

"Just in case the bear comes after me, I want to be prepared."

"What do you mean?"

"If he climbs up the tree after me, I'm going to be a dead man. He'll grab my legs first and yank me down out of the tree and eat me. To save myself from going through that kind of pain, I'm going to use this rope to hang myself first. That way, I won't know what happens."

"Great idea," Pam said. "I suppose you want me to do the same."

"It's your option."

"You're so romantic..."

The next morning, we woke up relieved to be alive. We packed our bikes and pedaled to the Old Faithful attraction. The famous geyser blasted into the summer morning with a plume of steam. To the relief of everyone, park rangers had captured the bear.

As we look back on that night, we laugh at the events of the evening, especially the two 6-foot pieces of rope.

I would have hung myself before that bear got me!

Over the years, I have placed myself in danger, not on purpose, but it came with the territory. I chuckle at all the people who try to make their lives so safe, when, in reality, a 'bear' situation could take them out at any moment. They essentially will never camp next to a 'steam vent' or worry about being eaten by a mountain lion. And that's okay, because we all get to choose our levels of involvement in life's game.

But for me, I like what Helen Keller said, "Life is either a daring adventure or nothing. Security is mostly a superstition. It does not exist in nature."

And so, it is—one moment in the future, another bear will be waiting for me.

I'll be ready with my six feet of rope...

(Standing in the middle of our campsite in the middle of Montana on the Lewis & Clark Trail.)

Chapter 14—I'm Happy Being Ugly

"You got to be crazy to ride your bicycle across the country," a man at a convenience store said as we parked the bikes for a rest break. "You're insane," said a college coed on an overlook of the Big Sur. "Why don't you get a horse or something that will carry you?" a cowboy said to me in Montana. "You couldn't get me to ride a bike across America if you put a Smith and Wesson to my head," said one Texan in Amarillo. "I'd be too scared to do something that crazy,"

—an old lady said, on Route 66. FHW

Heading toward Glacier National Park in Montana, I had camped out at Flathead Lake on Route 93 the night before. I felt the northern latitude cool sleeping in late July. The day warmed up as I headed into Kalispell. I spent an hour in town picking up a new tube and chain oil. The past two weeks had been terrible flat-tire luck. Every thorn in Montana decided to claim my rear tire as the perfect resting place for its sharp personality. My spare tube had so many patches it resembled the suction cups on an octopus' tentacles

After loading up on bananas, apples and a Persian melon, I prepared myself for the 20-mile climb into Glacier Park. Before getting started, I gobbled two bananas. That made me hungry for the melon, so I cut it into sections and ate them. People walking past laughed as I hung the banana skins on top of my rear pack under a bungee cord. It looked like a fresh kill of bananas. One couple with their teenage daughter asked a lot of questions as to how much I ate. I told them on a 100-mile day on the flats; I burned around 7,000 calories. But my daily distance averaged more like 60 to 70 miles. In the mountains, I averaged 50 miles per day but still burned a lot of calories because of the foot pounds exerted in the climbs. The highest mountain I ever climbed was a pass in Bolivia at 15,500 feet on a gravel road. That burned a lot of calories in the thin air. But the craziest day of my life happened when my friends talked me into an insane 200-mile day in New Mexico and Texas. My friends and I calculated that we each burned a total of 14,500 calories in 17 hours of riding.

While I talked, the girl's spirit brightened, and I could see a sparkle in her eyes. I may have inspired her to try world bicycle touring. As they walked away, she tugged on her mom for permission to go on a tour someday. I heard the mother reply, "That's for people with wanderlust, not you dear."

I wanted to catch them and correct the parent by telling her that I had met dozens of women bicycle touring in countries around the world. I wanted to say that everyone has that "wanderlust" and all they have to do is act on their dreams before they are convinced by their friends or parents to do what's normal. What's normal usually means settling down and getting a job. I was told when I was a teen to "Do it while you're young because once you settle down, you've got to take care of responsibilities." Whoever made that statement was right. I wish everyone could reserve their 20s for world travel to give them a greater perspective on people and conditions around the globe. They would come home richer in spirit and understanding. They would have a greater environmental appreciation for our fragile planet. Furthermore, anyone can ride a bicycle around the world if they choose to do it. However, long ago, I decided the best thing I could do was keep quiet and let people make their own choices. I have a secret wish for that girl: follow your thoughts and live your dreams.

After gorging myself with melon, I looked three months pregnant. I waddled over to my bicycle. Moments later, sweat poured from me as I climbed a hill out of town. I was excited to make Glacier by nightfall.

Up ahead, right in the middle of a side road, I saw a man waving his cowboy hat at cars. As I drew closer, his thin features were covered in a red plaid shirt, worn jeans, and pointed boots topped off with a ten-gallon, black Stetson.

"You," he yelled, waving his hat at me. "Come over here."

"What's the problem?" I asked, not wanting to be hassled.

"Why in tarnation ain't you ridin' a horse, or drivin' a car, or anything besides that Thar' bicycle?" he drawled, drunk as a skunk.

"I like to go slow, and I don't have to feed my bike or put gas into it," I said, stopping in front of him.

"Well, I'll be damned," he said, scratching his scruffy black beard, peppered with gray. "Ain't nothin' like it used to be. Well, I'll tell you what young fella'. I'm gonna buy you a drink."

"I don't drink, sir."

"You don't drink?"

"Nope."

"Well, sir, would you set down at that bar over yonder and tell the Ugliest Man in Montana why you ride a bicycle instead of a horse?

"Who is the ugliest man in Montana?"

"You're lookin' at 'em and I'll prove it."

Even though he was drunk, he seemed interesting enough, so I walked my bike over to the bar he had mentioned. We walked into a log cabin that had stuffed animal heads on the walls, including grizzly bears, elk, moose, badgers, trout and geese. Traps, guns, along with bows and arrows rounded out the artillery that decorated the back of the bar. I wanted to sit down in one of the wooden booths, but he was intent on leading me to the bar. I quickly understood why. Up over the cash register was a large picture of a man with a rifle walking out of the woods dragging a bear. It was titled: "The Ugliest Man in Montana." My newfound friend happened to be ugly!

"That's you, isn't it?"

He cocked his head as he rubbed the hairs growing off the top of his nose, “Sure nuff, it's me, that bear was one of the toughest fights of my life.”

“You fought a grizzly?”

“It wasn't but a few years back when I had to battle the meanest and hungriest bear in Montana. He was so big, that my ole friend Paul Bunyan wouldn't even come to help me.”

“No kidding,” I said, realizing that I was about to hear a story.

“Yep,” he said. “I was cuttin' timber one day, usin' a ten pound ax, when this varmint comes into our camp and headed for the cook’s tent.

Well sir, the lumberjacks scattered for fear of their mangy lives. Not me 'cuz that bear made me mad... by the way, do you want to buy me a beer? My mouth is awful dry.”

“Bartender, give us a beer and a sarsaparilla,” I said, ready to pay a couple of bucks to hear this man's story. He appealed to my inner child. Even in his drunken state, he showed spunk.

“As I was sayin’, that bear had me upset because he ate my chicken and dumplins which didn't bother me none, but then that critter gulped down my blueberry pie. Now that got me all fired mad. Nobody eats my blueberry pie and gets away with it.”

“I can't blame you,” I said, chuckling to myself as this old coot relived his story by swinging his arms and raising the beer to his lips for a swallow.

“There he was slurpin' down my pie when I charged into camp. Soon as he saw me, he knew he was in trouble 'cuz he ceased slurpin’.”

“What'd you do?”

“Why, I done what any self-respectin’ lumberjack woulda' done,” he said, sweeping the hair out of his face. “I ran over ta where he was standin' and grabbed ahold of his tail and bounced 'em betweenst a couple of trees. I thrashed 'em and I bashed 'em and then I thrashed 'em some more.”

"What was the bear doing during this bashing?" I asked.

"Whall, he was so ah scared for his life that he crawled out of his skin and ran off into the woods and nobody done ever heard of him again."

"You must have been a bit sore after the fight, weren't you?"

"Whall now, I had a few calluses on my hands, but nuthin' to speak of... o'course, there was another time when I was face to face with this killer..."

"That's okay, Ugly," I said, seeing his empty beer glass, which meant the next round was coming out of my pocket. "I've got to be getting down the road."

"I guess you're right sonny."

"By the way, what's your real name?"

"You can call me Ugly," he said. "It don't matter what you do in this life, as long as you're happy. I'm happy bein' Ugly."

A mile out of town, I chuckled to myself over Ugly. I never could understand what makes an alcoholic, but in this case, he had brightened my day with his bravado. In my travels, I've seen rich people, poor people, regular people—and what Ugly said is true—the bottom line in life is being happy.

It's more important than anything else.

(This is "Ugly" the "Ugliest Man in Montana" winner for that year. It's an annual event so everybody gets a chance to become the "ugliest man" in Big Sky Country.)

Chapter 15—It's All Downhill, 'Cept What's Up

> ***"Travel enriches and teaches; it is a teacher of life. The bicycle is a faithful friend who can take you wherever you want to go. Travelling by bike is full of strong emotions: the challenges and fatigue are at first discouraging, disappointing and upsetting. But then, if you have an indomitable spirit, you don't let yourself be defeated by the inertia and routine, since following the road reveals our emotions, which is the only way we possess of truly living."***
>
> ***—Gillian Willman***

Climbing! It's hard work having fun. My legs pay a price in the mountains. I never complain because mountains provide beauty not found on the flats. Many times, pedaling becomes incidental because my eyes gaze at a distant canyon. At other moments, I may crest a pass that offers a 50-mile view across cloud-shrouded summits. With every climb, a descent becomes inevitable. I go from hard work to fun. After cranking for hours on a steep grade, at the top, pedaling becomes easier. I shift into a higher gear, and seconds later, my gravity-motor takes over. No more pedaling. I get to glide down the other side. It's a sheer delight after a long climb.

Yet, with mountain touring, it's in the back of my mind that whatever I lose in elevation on a descent, the road will make me pay with another climb.

That's the way the snaking road treated me on Route 89 heading into Jerome, Arizona. What made it even more maddening was the incessant up and down—all that morning.

By the time I reached the town's cobbled streets, I felt exhausted.

"I'm hot, sweaty and sticky from all this climbing," I muttered to myself. "Got to get a shower one of these days."

I stopped at a small park.

Jerome is perched on the side of a mountain, overlooking the Red Rocks of Sedona 20 miles across the valley. After leaning my bike against a table, I spotted a bench waiting for me to rest my weary body. It was quite a view. Sitting there, relaxing my legs, I looked up and down the street. I stared into a ghost town. The well-maintained storefronts were built in the 1800s. Hotel Connor (1898) stood on the corner of the main street. Jerome had prospered during a copper strike but was abandoned when the ore ran out. Over 6,000 miners called that mountaintop home for the duration of the King Copper Mine. They mined over $1 billion from the ore before it petered out in 1953.

Because of all the bars, brawls, bordellos and shootouts—historians called it "The Wickedest Town in the West."

I could imagine horses and wagons, along with cowboys riding up and down the streets. I sat there wondering how the horses pulled heavy wagons up 2,000-foot grades from the valley.

I munched on my third banana and was about to peel an orange when I noticed two riders coming up the street below me. They rode mountain bikes. One appeared younger and the second was much older. They kept cranking until they spotted my bike. The older lady turned toward me. She dripped sweat from her face and arms. Her jersey was soaked.

"How are you doing this morning?" I said, greeting her. "Looks like you've been working overtime."

"Ah," she smirked. "It's all downhill from here, 'cept what's up."

"I guess you could look at it that way," I said, noting her rather odd statement. "Where you coming from?"

"We just busted our tails riding up from the valley," she answered. "I'm training for a tour around Europe for three months this summer. I want to be in shape for the Alps. I'm doing another 3,000 feet yet today."

"You're a glutton for punishment," I said. "These up and downs are killing me."

"I've been living in these mountains my entire life," she said. "It's a matter of attitude, and you won't find anyone with a better attitude than mine."

"I like you," I said. "My name's Frosty."

"Katie Lee," she said, gripping my hand. "This is my friend Paula. I like your bike. It's a beauty. You sure have it loaded. I like that orange flag out to the side and the one on top."

"I like drivers to see me long before they pass," I said.

"Smart boy," she said. "I think I'll do the same for my trip."

"I recommend it."

We talked and talked some more. At 65, going on 25, this lady proved herself a walking dynamo. Her energy exceeded most people one third her age. She had been a dancer, cowgirl, bartender, guitarist, mother, waitress, bookkeeper, saleswoman, farmer, mountain guide, horsewoman, and was currently a singer in a country band.

As we talked into the morning about touring. The conversation turned to people. She thought many folks had given up their lives to television and cars.

"Damned smartphones," she said. "They've damn well ruined the youth of this country. They think their problems should be solved in one hour. They think they can have something for nothing. When they can't have it, they fall apart. You ever notice how lazy everyone one is today? I mean, they drive the shiniest cars while their bodies go to hell in a handbasket. Not me by God. I'm going to make a hundred, and give 'em hell all the way."

Katie talked my ears off. Her spunk rubbed off on me. I loved her spirit. She didn't know everything, but she knew how to live. Her life force touched me. She picked me up that day. She raised my consciousness. She had been through tough times, but never sat around feeling sorry for herself. I promised myself that when I grew older, I would remember her, and I would be like her. A special note: at the age of 80, she undressed herself at the top of the town and got on her mountain bike to ride along Main Street town in the nude. She said, "We need to shake things up around here." If you visit Jerome, there is a story about her riding past a bar...the patrons gasped as she rode past the window. One guy said, "What was that?" The bartender said, "I don't know, but it looks like it could use an iron to get out the wrinkles."

Everyone fell on the floor laughing.

Katie Lee became only the 175th European to traverse both the upper and lower ends of the Grand Canyon, and one of the first women. On later trips alongside two pioneering river runners, Frank Wright and Tad Nichols, she helped name many of the side canyons along the Glen, which was submerged beginning in 1956, when the Colorado River was dammed to create Lake Powell. In the driveway of Lee's small blue house in Jerome was a silver Prius decorated with bumper stickers—**Restore Glen Canyon** and the **Road to Hell is paved with Politicians**—and a vanity plate. It read: **Dam Dam.**

She said, "The Grand was immense and powerful. Awe-inspiring. Loud! You went down there, and you could see how the earth was put together."

She was also known as "Our Lady of Glen Canyon." She tried to stop the damming of that beautiful canyon, which rivaled the Grand Canyon, but failed. She reached the ripe old age of 98 before passing away in her sleep in 2017. I called her before she passed. She remembered our conversation distinctly.

In the afternoon, I coasted down a long curving highway to the floor of the valley.

Free ride. It was fun, but at Camp Verde on Route 279, the road climbed. Soon, trees replaced the cactus and the road meandered toward the sky. It carried me toward Strawberry Hill. I burned my legs cranking up a steady incline. Twenty miles later and I was still busting my butt wondering if that Queen Medusa of a mountain had a backside.

My legs exploded with blood. I guzzled quarts of water. A monsoon of sweat from my body splashed onto the pavement. I munched slices of bread, inhaled apples and swallowed chunks of banana like a street-sweeping vacuum cleaner at Disneyland. Into the late afternoon, the mountain still climbed ahead of me. I looked around each bend with high expectations that it would be the crest. Forget it. This road was taking me to heaven while putting me through hell.

In the early evening, golden sky banners waved across the horizon, lit by a fiery sun. Just when I was about to call it quits and accept my fate of no bath again that night, I hit the top. Shifting into higher gears, I rolled along easier, then faster. I leveled off in high gear, going down, slowly at first, then faster. My whole attitude changed. From a grinding struggle to ultimate success. A mile later, a campground with a shower came into view. Katie popped into my consciousness. She had said, "All you have to do is keep pedaling." She was right.

"It's all downhill from here, 'cept what's up," her voice whispered in my ears.

(Standing in a field of wildflowers in the Rocky Mountains.)

Chapter 16—The Voluptuousness of Living

> ***"Riding a bicycle is a way to harmonize life with time and space: it is to go and to stay in measures still human."***
>
> ***—Sergio Zavoli***

Riding east on Route 155, we neared a pass through the Greenhorn Mountains of the Sierras. Flat terrain near Delano, California, gave way to peaks that cut the sky into wrinkled shapes at the horizon.

Wildflowers bloomed along our route and grows steeper with every crank of the pedals.

John, Mike, Kevin and I biked on a cross-continent journey. John, hailing from the coastal town of Kiama near Sydney, Australia, was a charmer. His voice and wit were the keys to our having been invited into three families' homes within the last week. The night before, we had sat in a restaurant devouring the "all-you-can-eat" salad bar when a couple overheard John talking about the southern California climate. Before we knew it, John, who could be as charming as a Koala bear in one of those airline ads, had us invited into Larry and Valerie Johnson's house for the evening. Our hosts couldn't do enough for us, and they loved to hear about our experiences. It's as if the price of admission was sharing our lives.

Being invited into complete strangers' homes may seem awkward, even unheard of by most travelers, but we'd been asked into peoples' homes often during our tours. It may be the vulnerability of a bicycle rider. People feel we're honest, sometimes giving us the keys to their homes and cars.

On one tour, a man stopped me on the highway and invited me to his home. He tossed me his house keys before driving off to a ball game. When I arrived at his home a half hour later, there were two bags of fruits and vegetables on the table and a note saying, "Help yourself."

I'm not sure why people think a touring bicyclist is trustworthy. Maybe they believe it takes a depth of character for someone to pedal a bike for long distances—that someone who earns every mile with hard work and sweat could not be dishonest.

Anyone with less character would never ride a bicycle because it's not a free ride. It takes guts to pound the pedals mile after mile, mountain pass after mountain pass. My legs burn and I'm always hungry. I'm soaked in sweat, and I'm exhausted at the end of the day. It's not for those with weak physical resolve. Age makes no difference because I've met men and women in their seventies on world bicycle tours. It's their attitude.

Being asked into homes also has to do with a cheery disposition and the sparkle in their eyes as well as my own. Some folks get a kick out of living and they can spot it in others. They enjoy connecting with another life-force person who returns the energy. For that and other reasons, I've enjoyed many memorable evenings in peoples' homes around the world.

But that day, the heat and the climb hit me. John proved a ferocious climber. Mike stayed with him. Kevin and I followed them. From flats to hills, to bigger hills, to mountains. I pushed my bicycle into the Sierras. By the afternoon, I had climbed 1,000, 2,000, and 3,000 and was headed for 4,000 feet. Even with my 22 to 34 gearing, my legs took a beating. The constant power strokes with no rest kept my muscles pumped and full of lactic acid. Kevin wasn't faring much better. The grade caused me to sweat profusely, so I stopped to drink often. Each time, the cool afternoon air-dried me quickly. Minutes later, more sweat moistened the dried salt. Passing cars threw dust on me, which locked onto the sweat. At the next water stop, it dried again, leaving me feeling like a mud-covered dirtball.

When I reached 5,000 feet, darkness crept over the mountains. A gray mist slipped down from the summit, cutting visibility. By that time, we labored through tighter curves that hugged the mountainside. I was ready to call it quits.

"John is probably at the top of the pass right now," I grumbled.

"I wouldn't doubt it," he said.

"It's another 1,000 feet, but we'll have to do it in the dark for the next half hour," I said. "I'm blown out right now. You wanna keep riding?"

"My knee is acting up," Kevin said. "But I can do another fifteen minutes."

Kevin and I slipped our feet into the toe clips and shoved our bikes into motion. We continued upward into the mist. Sweat-soaked my shirt. A few minutes later, a car passed us going downhill. I didn't think much of it until the car swung around and slowed beside us. The electric window slipped down.

"Good evening, mates," John Brown said. "How would you boys like a nice hot shower and dinner compliments of my new friend Ross?!"

"Only if you promise never to drag me up a mountain again," I said.

"But you wouldn't be getting a hot shower," John said. "So why would you be upset?"

"Because you dragged us up this mountain all day and I'm going to die," I said.

"If we hadn't gotten this far, we wouldn't have met Ross and his nice shower," John said.

"You're right John," Kevin broke in. "We'll just bend your spokes after the shower!"

"Fair enough boys," John said. "Follow me another half mile."

"All the hot water you want, too," Ross said from the far side of the car.

"I'm going to live for it," I said as my body continued lathering up with mud-laden sweat.

Ross and John drove away. I felt weary and caked with dust, but the thought of a hot shower kept me going. I dreamed about it as I pedaled the last two miles up the dark, winding highway. Even though I was tired, that single thought kept me going. It seemed to make the next fifteen minutes go faster because I imagined the soothing, hot droplets massaging my skin. The cranking seemed easier. Kevin started talking about the shower. Sweating like two horses and steaming in the cool night air, we reached the guest ranch sign John had mentioned.

Ross operated a summer kid's ranch. He gave us kitchen privileges. He led us to a row of six shower heads.

"Plenty of hot water," he said.

"God," I said, "is going to give you an A."

John, Kevin, Mike and I slipped off our shoes and walked into the showers. After adjusting the temperature, we walked under them with our socks, shorts, shirts and gloves on. I've never heard so much groaning and laughing. Everyone soaped up.

Hot water streamed over my aching muscles. As the first rush of water doused my head, it cascaded over my face and streamed down my shoulders. I tore off my shirt and slapped it down on the tile. I peeled off my socks and shorts. The water ran down my body in waves, taking away the dirt and grime. Soothing steam filled my nostrils. I grabbed a bar of soap and lathered up my hair.

The soap and water did more than clean me. The whole day's hardship vanished in moments. I was in the middle of one of the greatest showers of my life. I had felt so worn out coming up the mountain, but now I felt tingling in every cell. As I stood there, transformed in the spray, I was aware of my friends' shouts at our good fortune at having this hot shower at the end of a tough day. From those gut-busting power cranks on the pedals to this ecstasy.

My mind slipped back to when I read Aldous Huxley's "BRAVE NEW WORLD." The protagonist was born in a test tube, and his fellow human beings lived in a bubble-covered city, where everything was perfect. He broke out of the city into the forbidden zone, which was a wilderness where he had to hunt for his food and had to protect himself from mosquitoes and animals. He held his own life in his hands. He became vulnerable to the normal consequences of life. The "savage" said he wanted to know love, hurt, pain, joy, hunger, heat, cold...

That book changed my life. I decided I didn't want to be so comfortable that living became too easy. I didn't want to go from my air-conditioned house to my climate-controlled car to an office complex where everyone wears the same suits and thinks the same way as they claw their way up the corporate ladder with accompanying stress levels and ulcers. Too much comfort and success kill the spirit. I wanted to know the differences—because in the opposites, came perspective and appreciation. I have never been a spectator. I can either live life, or watch others participate. The result of my decision becomes more precious with each passing year.

Life sweeps along swiftly enough without spending precious hours and days on useless routines or inactivity. I've figured out many answers to life's problems while riding my bike. I've embraced life's ups and downs, even mosquitoes biting me. I don't put myself at extreme risk, but neither do I want to become bored or work a job that doesn't enrich me. In that mode, life would pass by mundanely. In a twinkling, I would be on my deathbed wondering where it all went so fast.

We have 70-odd years to fill up our lives, and I want to fill them up with the voluptuousness of living. Especially on a touring bicycle. It is being aware of pain, of joy, of potential within myself—of being excited for every leaf on a tree as it flutters in the wind or watching a hawk rip down from the sky to grab a mouse, or the delight of discovering a ladybug on my leg in the early spring, or gazing upon a mountain as it pierces the clouds.

It leads me to a kind of rage too, which is the blood sister of love—because the people of this world make it a charming, insane, exciting and confusing place. I want to maintain the ability to deal with them, with my mind, and spirit—at full bore. To see is to know, and to know is to fall in love with what is known.

What's this?!? My shower just turned cold. The hot water ran out. I jumped back. The cold water shocked my skin. My four friends and I headed for the towels. We dried our bodies and gathered our belongings. Dinner steamed on the stove.

The next day, we loaded our bikes with food and water. We thanked our host. Within seconds, sweat glistened on our bodies. Was it a lot of hard work? Not really. It was another day of glorious adventure across America on two wheels.

Have I made the right choice after reading Huxley's book? Is it worth the agony and sweat of climbing a 6,000-foot pass or one at 15,000 feet through a blizzard in Bolivia? You betcha! I want to fill up my life with living. Even when I'm home working a five-day week, I make every day a positive experience. Daily life provides adventure choices. Weekends are a grand adventure. Each sustains the balance.

One night while sitting around a campfire, John and I, both being teachers, invented the A.B.C. Concept. It fits our philosophies for happy living. The message is a simple attitude that anyone can choose to follow. With any life activity, a person can "go for it" and enjoy it before/during/after. That's the strategy of the ABC concept:

A. AIM—take aim at life-like Terry Fox who had cancer and ran on one leg across Canada to attract attention to the disease before he died. Fight for what you believe in like David Brower or John Muir when they brought their environmental message to Americans long before it was in vogue. Diane Fossey tried to save the gorillas. Ann Kanabe rode her bicycle trans-Americas. Anyone with a passion can work toward fulfilling his or her dream.

B. BUOYANCY—keep buoyant in the troubled waters of living. Maintain motivation with a positive attitude. Keep lighthearted against heavy odds. Lightness travels well and long. Bob Wieland, in his walking across America on his hands, epitomizes buoyancy. He didn't stop at that success, either. Later, he—completed the Boston Marathon. When hand-cycles came out, he hand-cycled across the USA three times!

C. CELEBRATE—jump up and shout about being alive. Celebrate life. Don't be afraid to be counted. Show your energy and excitement. Jump into a cold stream when you want a bath. Laugh at the hill you are about to climb. Remember that riding through the mountains is like a dance. Let the mountain lead and you follow. Blow up that special photograph and hang it on your wall. Relish your excitement. Reach beyond your boundaries. Finally, you need not be afraid of failing, for that fear can prevent you from ever being fully alive. Failure can lead to success if you never give up.

Winston Churchill said it best: “Success is going from failure to failure without loss of enthusiasm.”

Chapter 17—We Turned Up a Dirt Road Today

> ***"When you see a dreamy cyclist, don't trust his/her inoffensive and benevolent look: he/she is preparing to conquer the world."***
>
> ***—Didier Tronchet***

Doug and I woke up beside placid waters with a gray mist hanging low over the mountains. Slender wisps of moisture played upon the mirror images of trees while Canada geese, grebes and mallards trumpeted their morning songs.

After breaking camp, we pedaled down a logging highway in northern California. Monstrous trucks frightened us when they rumbled past. Their first draft blew us off the road and seconds later, threatened to suck us back into their rear dual wheels. It didn't make for peaceful riding. A glance at the map gave us an alternative.

We turned up a dirt road heading in a similar direction. It got rougher on a route less traveled. Because of the corrugated gravel, our hands took pounding for hours. Nonetheless, it was worth getting away from the trucks. Our chances of seeing wildlife grew tenfold. Going into the wilderness was like looking at the surface of the ocean—nothing on top, but just below the water, a parade of creatures' swims in those depths. The woods, too, has an array of creatures living in their branches, on the forest floor, over the meadows and in the lakes.

"This sure beat those logging trucks," said Doug.

"Can't argue with you on that point," I said. "I'll take a dirt road any day."

Another thing along a dirt road: the peacefulness. Not quite like silence, but a quiet away from machinery—where the wind purrs through the trees on its unhurried journey up a mountainside. I hear birds chirping, squawking, arguing and flapping their wings everywhere in the forest. A woodpecker rat-a-tat-tats against a dead tree trunk while chickadees fly loop-d-loops in the meadow. Insects, too, inhabit the woods; butterflies flutter from wildflower to wildflower. Crickets chirp a symphony of sound whenever I pass by a bog. Bullfrogs add their low notes. The admission to this grand performance—only the price of my pedaling efforts.

The colors keep me enthralled. Pine green means pointy and leaf green offers softness. Cattail green means long and white moss green means spongy. Yellow flowers dot the green along with white, purple and orange petals chiming in for contrast. Tree bark colors add their own special flavor.

This dirt road measured more than fifty miles in the middle of northern California snaking its way toward Mount Shasta. Not far along the dirt, we stopped by a lake with a dozen islands in the middle—loaded with birds and ducks. It provided a sanctuary for raising families. A variety of calls echoed across the water.

We rode up to a clearing where four antelope bounded across the road, saw us, then hastily ran back into the woods, their white patched butts bouncing like pogo sticks until they vanished. Off to the side, a muskrat paddled its way across a pond where several ducks fed on grubs.

The woods grew thick, sometimes thin, and rose or fell depending on the terrain. A group of mule deer hopped across a ridge. The road led down into a valley with Mount Shasta on the horizon and a pink sunset coloring long white clouds outlining the sky.

Our campfire flickered beneath a stand of pine trees that seemed to be in the midst of a whole mountainside of lava rocks.

It was as if the rocks had exploded from somewhere up the mountain. This region was near the Ring of Fire, where volcanic mountains dominate the Cascade Range. As we sat there, a pack of coyotes howled at a crescent moon.

In the morning, the sun rose through the mist lighting up 14,179 foot Mount Shasta that dwarfed four other peaks around it. We soon enjoyed a clear sky and a view of the snow-covered cone of the dormant volcano.

With a nip in the air, we began our continued slow descent on a two percent grade through thinning trees as we dropped to 3,300 feet. A wide valley stretched before us. We continued on hard-packed dirt. A half dozen gray squirrels darted across the road, and we heard birds chirping in the woods.

Out of the trees, we rolled through farmland. Off to our right, a flat field of short grass had not been cultivated for more than a year. Above the field, a red-tailed hawk fluttered in midair. Suddenly, it dropped like a dagger and skimmed three feet off the ground at high speed.

"It's looking for food," Doug said.

"Yeah, but they usually look for it way up high."

"That's right," he said. "That bird is too close to the ground to do anything even if it saw something. It would be going too fast to stop."

Five seconds later, the hawk back flapped its wings and in a cloud of dust, crashed into the ground much like a shortstop diving for a line drive, and when it caught a rodent, rolled over with the prize clutched in its talons facing the sky. Abruptly, flapping its wings, the bird righted itself. There was no fight, no death struggle, and no sound. Seconds later, the hawk lifted into the sky with a field mouse in its talons.

"My God, that was incredible!" Doug said.

"Did you see how fast she stopped?" I added.

"On a dime with a nickel's change," he said.

"What a way to start a morning ride," I said.

As if nature was trying to show off its best efforts, another show was in the making. We pedaled past a pond near the highway. Because of our silence, animals become startled after we're already on top of them. At the pond's edge, six Canada geese suddenly sprinted across the water, wings flapping wildly, trying to break free of the surface. We saw their foot marks in the water as they ran across the pond. Within seconds, their black and white colors exploded out of the water with a flurry of wings climbing into the sky. Once airborne, they flew into Mount Shasta's snowfields.

"Who are we supposed to pay for this morning's show?" Doug asked.

"Maybe we'll have to pull a ten-mile 14 percent uphill grade," I said.

Another five minutes along the way, we crested a ridge. Three volcanic peaks thrust into the sky before us. Mount Lassen, Cinder Cone, and Shasta poked through cloudbanks. Maybe California didn't want us to leave. It had already shown us Yosemite, the Yuba Valley, the 49er trail, and now this.

Fifteen minutes down the road, five mule deer ran up a ridge on our right, and out of sight.

"Bet those guys are long gone," I said.

"They weren't waiting around for us... hey, look!" Doug yelled.

Five deer crossed the road, not twenty yards in front of us. They jumped over a fence. They leaped like a jack-in-the-box on four legs at once. One by one, they glided over the fence and vanished behind the hill.

"I can't take this kind of nature overload so early in the morning," I said. "It can't get any better than this."

We cranked along until we crossed through the middle of a marsh. Again, nature jumped up in the form of wings everywhere. Canada honkers poked their heads out from tall grasses, while mallards rushed into a flight when we startled them. Grebes hugged their hiding places in the deep grass. Blackbirds, sparrows, and birds of every color and description lived in the marsh. Each possessed a different song and flew with a variety of wing beats.

"You know," Doug said. "We're so lucky to see these wild wings on parade."

"You got that right," I said.

At the Route 299 intersection, we met a toy maker and his wife. While we talked, more than five hundred heads of cattle bolted up the road behind us. A few cowboys on horseback drove the herd toward pastureland higher up the valley. We didn't think much about it as they passed, but that was the direction we were headed. Five minutes later, we said goodbye to the toy maker and began climbing out of the valley.

Have you ever followed a herd of 500 cows on a bicycle? Neither had we, until that morning. At first it was funny seeing how the males peed as they walked, leaving watery S trails in the road. When the females peed, they stopped and made a large splash. The big problem was how they did their morning constitutional.

The road was filled with land mines in the form of cow pies. It got so thick at times; we couldn't avoid it. At first, we navigated around the splash piles by steering in circle eights. Except the more we pedaled, the thicker the minefield became, until cow poop squeezed up from our tires into our brake pads. At one tight juncture in the road, I was turning hard to miss one cow pie. It was one of those pies where the cow took the time to stand in one place and build up a large green mound. I swerved to avoid it, but my front tire, already mired in green goosh, lost traction. Down I went, left hand out-stretched, headed for the steaming green cow pie. Splat! My hand made a perfect five-fingered landing right into the middle of a rather warm, squishy, pile of poop. My bike and panniers fell into two other piles near the one where my hand was now implanted.

"Nothing like getting close to the good green earth," Doug said, as he pulled up next to me. "You always were one to get your hands into everything."

"That's not funny," I said, pulling my hand from the cow pie.

We laughed. I poured my water bottle all over my arm and hand. I grabbed my paper towel roll out of my day pack and began wiping the stuff from between my fingers, off my arm and off the panniers. Next, I squirted my water bottles over my hand to clean the remaining poop away.

We mounted the bikes and rode through the remaining mile of "natural obstacles." Soon, we cranked up a 1,500-foot grade out of the valley. As we neared the top, the view from where we had come to where we were was filled with memories.

Our experiences reminded me of what Henry David Thoreau once wrote: "We need the tonic of the wilderness, to wade sometimes in the marsh where the bitten and meadow hen lurk and hear the booming of the snipe; to smell the whispering sedge where only some wilder and more solitary fowl builds her nest, and the mink crawls with its belly close to the ground."

We turned up a dirt road today, and it was more than worth it.

(Lake Moraine and the Seven Sisters, Alberta, Canada. Pure wilderness!)

Chapter 18—Eat Dessert First; Life is Uncertain

> ***"It is generous with the cyclist because he/she cuts through so much air, in every time of the year and with every temperature, that he is in a good mood and energy, that he is cleaned from the stress. It starts thoughts, like a physical law, it makes them drip one by one: plik, plik, plik. It's like they sound in his/her head, forming stalactites. Bicycling requires essentiality, efficiency, simplicity, even in clothing. It is outside fashion but has and inspires a personal style in who uses it on a daily basis. It is enchantment in the mornings and magic in the evenings..."***
>
> ***—Emilio Rigatti***

Couldn't have found a more perfect spot among tall pines and a needle soft floor to pitch my tent on this day which I shall remember for the rest of my life. Birds are chirping above me as the light fades from the sky and a cool wind whisper through the trees making them creak as they sway back and forth. The campfire chases away the darkness in a small circle surrounded by towering redwoods.

Sunshine blessed us today as we rode the 49_{er} Trail toward Sonora, California. Flowers bloomed along the road like a bouquet from a child's coloring book. But something happened today that fills my heart with sorrow.

When Doug and I awoke this morning, the sun had broken through the cloud cover, revealing immense forests shrouded in gray mist. A green mantle of pines swept towards towering peaks of the High Sierra. The mist swirled like giant pinwheels above the treetops while we ate our breakfast.

Doug and I eat foods that give us top performance. While touring, we buy seven-grain cereal and mix it with sunflower seeds, raisins, and fresh fruit. A loaf of wheat bread hangs off our packs, and we spread peanut butter over each slice. Water is the simplest liquid to keep and pour over the cereal. Because bicycling utilizes so much energy, we top breakfast off with an apple or an orange. We eat our food from the same stainless steel pots used for cooking and washing dishes. After breakfast, we break camp and push the bikes out of the woods to the highway.

We had descended from a snowstorm at 6,000 feet out of Yosemite National Park. The rolling highway led us away from Yosemite through tall trees, high mountain beauty and spring colors. The dripping wet color of pine green glistened along every mile on the road. We dropped another 1,000 feet before stopping for lunch on a grassy spot near the road. Doug grabbed his food pack, and I followed him with mine.

Our lunch ritual was the same every day. We bought groceries for two days of riding. Complex carbohydrates in the form of fruits and vegetables, rice and lentils were our main staples. We celebrated lunch because hunger constantly stalks a cyclist. We sat in the shade, spread our towels and prepared sandwiches. I'll admit it—Doug eats more than me. No, let me clarify that statement. He inhales more food than a humpback whale. He makes a shark look tame when it comes to appetite. To give you an idea of how much Doug eats at a sitting, I'd lay bets on him in a pie-eating contest against the Pittsburgh Steelers. Doug would eat them under the table. If there was a word to describe how much food he consumes, it hasn't been invented yet. That's Doug, all 6'4" of him. Yet, through the modern miracle of bicycling, he's lean and clean.

He sat with his legs stretched out in a V. He laid out eight slices of bread, along with a bag of vegetables. He carries a cutting board which he washed off with his water bottle. Within minutes, he cut everything into slices. He stacked tomatoes, cucumbers and green peppers on top of each other before topping his sandwiches with mustard. His eyes lit up as his tongue licked his lips in anticipation of the coming feast. Not to be outdone, I too, chopped with vigor. Hunger stalks riders on a bicycle adventure because we love to eat, and food dazzles our taste buds. Thirty minutes later, we polished off four bananas for dessert.

We were ready to go when I held us up for another minute because I had to take a bathroom break. Back on the road, we cranked up a hill with sweat dripping from our bodies. Not five minutes later, we saw a bicyclist coming the other way as we rolled into a valley. At the bottom, he coasted to a stop. Doug and I slowed to a stop.

I was looking at the bike rider when I noticed he was carrying a black puppy on a platform on his rear rack. I smiled, "What a nice..." I began to say. Before I could finish my sentence, the puppy bounded off the platform and ran across the pavement toward us. I heard a vehicle coming, but before the driver or anyone could bat an eyelash, the puppy yelped in a death cry after being crushed by two sets of wheels from a pickup truck going 50 miles per hour.

From a happy disposition with blue sky and sunshine overhead, I was jerked into pain and bewilderment. My first thought was for the fellow across the road who had seen his puppy crushed to death before his eyes.

Blood gushed out from the dog's body.

"Oh no, oh no," I said in a withered voice.

It shocked my senses from a lovely day to a terrible moment that happened with no rhyme or reason. Only that moment. Had we eaten lunch for 30 seconds longer, or had I waited to relieve myself, the exact meeting of that fellow bicyclist would have saved the puppy. I felt sick.

The rider got off his bike. He walked across the road, picked up the dog and walked up to us.

"I'm so sorry," I said with grief in my voice.

"Nothing you could do. It wasn't anyone's fault," he said.

The driver stopped and ran back, "I'm sorry," he said. "I couldn't stop."

"There's nothing you could have done sir," the bicyclist said. "Thanks for stopping."

"I'm sorry son," the driver said as he walked away.

"I'm so sorry," I repeated. "Is there anything I can do?"

"No," he said. "I need to take Sierra for a walk in the woods."

As he carried the pup away toward the trees, I stood there, my heart crushed with pain. He had lost a special friend, one he had run through the high country with, one who had sat by campfires with him.

A half-hour passed before I walked up to where he was burying Sierra. I introduced myself. His name was Bob, and he began crying. I walked up and embraced him. His pain moved into me. I wept with tears running down my face onto his shirt, soaking a small circle into it. I held him tight. He talked with his face on my shoulders, sniffling through his nose, convulsing with gasps of air. Minutes later, we picked up rocks and finished covering Sierra's body. Bob and I walked back toward the road. Bob didn't look back, but his whole being was torn. I sensed the anguish ripping at his foundations.

"I don't understand why this happened," he said.

Doug nor I said anything. What could we say? What could we do?

Nothing.

Bob decided to continue south. He wanted to figure out why this happened. I gave him one last hug. Doug did, too. Bob walked across the road, picked up his bike and rode off.

"Do you know only one car has ridden by us in the last 45minutes?" Doug said.

"This just blows me away."

"Eat dessert first."

"What?"

"I read it on one of those climber's T-shirts in Yosemite, it said, 'Eat dessert first, life is uncertain.'"

"No kidding," I lamented. "Let's get going."

I pulled my bike up from the gravel shoulder and grasped the bars with both hands. Looking down, I slipped my right foot into the pedal strap. I pressed hard. The wheels gleamed as they advanced. For the first time in my life, I noticed that the spokes go forward, and go backward simultaneously. They rotate up as well as down while the bike travels along the road. There is no power stroke for the spokes. They merely carry the load placed upon them. On the end of the spokes, the wheel rolls around. Just like this planet revolves in space. No reason, other than that's the way it is. I don't know why Sierra died. No reason. I fell in behind Doug, watching his freewheel spin forward, staring at his derailleur as it dropped the chain into lower gears when we began climbing out of the valley. For the rest of the day, I watched his spinning back wheel.

Sitting here in this tent, the light has faded, and the last bird has ruffled its feathers in silence. The mountain air is hushed, and my candle flame flickers quietly. I shall never forget this day, nor its message—eat dessert first, for life is uncertain. Take it all in daily—joy and sorrow, good and bad times, confidence and uncertainty, smiles and tears, love and heartbreak—because this is the best moment of life—present living. Nothing is guaranteed even five minutes into the future. At no time are any of us immune to misfortune no matter what our situation in life.

You can be rich, famous, handsome and happy. It makes no difference. You can look at Princess Di, John F. Kennedy, John Kennedy Jr., Derrick Thomas, Elvis Presley, Martin Luther King, Marilyn Monroe, Jane Mansfield, Amelia Earhart, James Dean and countless others. The grand parade of life marches on with or without you.

I eat dessert first; make the most of your life daily.

(Life on a dirt road leads to many different adventures. You never know who you will meet on the highway ahead.)

Chapter 19—Hey! There's an Outhouse

> ***"Let's cage ourselves and let the animals run free. Let's tear down our egocentric structures and build anew. Let's find new stars and new songs to follow. And finally, as Thoreau suggests, let's build some new foundations under our dreams. For if we have the prowess to destroy the earth, then we can surely save it."***
>
> ***—Steve Van Matre***

Riding a bicycle around America offers intimate glimpses into our history. While cranking the pedals at the lightning speed of 12 miles per hour, I am able to keep a sharp eye out for old relics of the past that pop up in hay fields, ravines and woods. Old combines, model T cars and manure spreaders are a few artifacts—rotting, rusting and sinking into oblivion.

But one of America's more interesting antiques is in the distance, hidden in the trees, a solitary wood structure with a door and a small window. Grass grows tall around its sides with flowers enhancing its sun-bleached boards. Among many facets that are disappearing in our modern society is the often-shunned outhouse. Many cyclists plug their noses or choose to wait a little longer when faced with the unpleasant prospect of entering these smelly, bug-infested domains.

Although not wanting you to question my taste, I've ridden past hundreds of these bucolic treasures and found each shack quite interesting and a definite factor of our American heritage. These relics yield humor, memories, and yes, even beauty. They lie about the countryside in mute testimony of our ever changing society and humbleness in the scheme of nature. Now you see them, someday you won't.

While touring through the hills near Cadillac, Michigan on old Route 131, I discovered a yellow painted outhouse that featured two doors. On the outside, a poet wrote the following words: "Two swinging doors, on a little old shack, that sets all alone, somewhere out in the back. Two words on the doors that let you get in: one says, 'Woman,' and the other says, 'Men.' You've got your old TP wound tight on the roll, but when you step in, there's only one hole."

On a ride through Smuggler's Notch, Vermont one autumn day, we stopped by a dilapidated shed. Two of us had to go, but it seemed that we were out of toilet paper. There in this rickety outhouse, beside a quiet stream was an old "used" form of TP. Again, graffiti told the story: "Next to the stool, on a sawed-in-two log, sits a brand-new copy of a Sears catalog. A thousand and one items, at which you can gaze, but the book's only good, for a hundred and one days."

Outhouses come in a variety of shapes, sizes, and materials. Although predominantly made of wood and shingle roofs, many in different parts of the country exhibit creative genius. I saw one once replete with a wind indicator. It informed the owner when it was safe to use or when it was deadly. Another outhouse sported a bird feeder with plenty of perching pegs. The owner was a music nature lover, which made his or her morning constitutional a symphony of chirping.

As a child growing up on the farm, we had an outhouse for emergencies. That might have been the best thing that ever happened to me. While riding my bicycle around the front yard, I remember having to get off the bike, run to the outhouse, hold my breath and step inside. It was a race to see how long my lungs could hold out. If I didn't make it, I rationalized that a small lung full of foul air wouldn't kill me. I exhaled and breathed a bit to sustain myself—but not too much. Seconds later, I burst out the door, gasping for air while zipping up my shorts.

Why is an outhouse one of the best things that ever happened to me? Perspective! Call it what you will, but I began life with basic living, basic needs, and basic understandings. Those values haven't changed no matter how far technology advances this society. No matter how fast we charge helter-skelter into the future, it's the basics of our lives that sustain us. Every time I'm on the road pedaling, the sight of an outhouse carries me back, and when I use it, the memories overwhelm me... it stinks like hell! Many years later, I hold my breath and hope I make it out before breathing that horrible air. I still fumble at the door, gasping. Seconds later, I jumped on my bike and rode away.

One evening in Colorado, on Route 24 north of Leadville, my riding friends and I stopped to camp near a river. I climbed the tailings of an abandoned mine, about 10,000 feet high in the Rockies. Near the entrance, a ramshackle outhouse stood out from the mountain. I couldn't have asked for a more beautiful view from an outhouse. The old coot who built that one possessed an eye for the aesthetic. It stood on the mountainside facing west, into the wind, with a million-dollar view. He must have enjoyed the sunsets from his perch. A mantle of pines led skyward to magnificent snowcapped peaks. I sat there that evening after a hard day's ride pounding over two passes.

The summer breeze cooled me while my friends built a roaring fire below. The river swept past like a black, watery conveyer belt. The bicycles were propped against a few pines while everyone's excited voices chattered about the day's ride. Soon, the sky began its dramatic color show, announcing the day's final curtain. Yellow-golds splashed against black mountain profiles. This was a place for keeping in touch with perspective.

The next morning, we packed our bicycles for the ride south. After throwing my leg over the bike, I glanced at that outhouse...

"Hey Frosty, you coming?" my friend Gary hollered.

"Just giving that old outhouse one last look," I answered.

"If you've seen one, you've seen 'em all."

"It all depends on your perspective," I muttered to myself.

In seconds, my feet pressed the pedals, my heart raced, and the asphalt passed beneath my wheels.

Outhouses and bicycling—they provide a sense of balance in the scheme of things.

(Stopping along the Columbia River Gorge where Lewis & Clark traveled in 1804-06.)

Chapter 20—What is in a Campsite?

Have you wandered in the wilderness?
The sagebrush desolation,
The bunch-grass levels where the cattle graze?
Have you whistled bits of rag-time at the end?
Of all creation, and learned to know the desert's little ways?
Have you camped upon the foothills, have you galloped o'er the ranges?
Have you roamed the arid sun-lands through and through?
Have you chummed up with the mesa? Do you know its moods and changes?
Then listen to the Wild—it's calling you.

—Robert Service

Doug and I rolled hard today. We pushed on the pedals through a hundred curves. Climbed high and rode slow! Good riding and has no flats. Late in the afternoon, we sailed into an expansive valley in northern Idaho. Lovely country—lakes everywhere and abundant animal life. Fish leaped out of the water for a hatch of mayflies. A mantle of pines swept up the mountains like the beard on Santa Clause. Highlighting this scenery, a raging, colorful bouquet of spring flowers bloomed along the road. Every curve felt like turning the pages in a child's coloring book. Route 97 heading toward Coeur d'Alene exceeded our expectations.

Throughout the day, Doug and I chattered about the sights. At times, we rode in tandem, talking about anything and nothing. We had bicycled through so many parts of the world that we found ourselves comparing other continents that had similar terrain. We never ran out of things to talk about. After a certain topic slipped by with the miles, we fell silent. Then something would catch our attention and we launched into a new topic.

"Looks like a camping spot up there," he said, spotting a trail that led down to a lake.

"You got enough water?" I asked. "I'm a bit low. Should have filled up at that last town."

"No worries," he said. "I've got enough for both of us."

"You always cover me."

"You had the extra seam sealer for me last week."

"Yeah, I guess you're right."

We turned into the wilderness. In minutes, the path led us to a spot on the water. I looked out across the lake. With a dip of my finger, I could tell it would be a cold bath. That's the price we pay for not paying any price. Before I knew it, Doug had his tent pitched and walked around gathering wood for a campfire. I looked up to see pine needles gently waving in front of the sky. Below me, brown pine needles covered the ground. Something about it—being in the woods—hearing a bird chirp, a tree creaking the breeze, a squirrel dart across the forest floor, the constant whisper of the wind through the branches, and the hum of mosquitoes.

I pitched my tent as the sky changed from streaks of pink to gray and then black. I love building my nylon shelter in the woods. My neighbors are the pines that silhouette against the last splashes of light. When I look up, a clear, black sky cradles a million friends of mine—the stars.

In minutes, Doug built a blazing campfire. It threw light into the woods. I tossed the last of my panniers into the tent, along with my food pack. I unscrewed my self-inflating air mattress, pulled out my sleeping bag, and spread it out. My candle lantern, flashlight, knife, book and journal were in place. I like to come into an organized tent and have everything where I can grab it without going nuts trying to find it. With my tent ready, I slipped into the icy water of the lake. Doug did the same. We shrieked at the cold water, but the bottom line—being clean.

After drying off and putting my tights on, I grabbed my pot and food pack. Doug already had his rice, lentils and vegetables cooking on the corner of the fire. I pulled up a rock for a seat. Out on the lake, a crescent moon rose. An armada of Canadian geese swam across the moonlight line on the water. An owl hooted through the darkness.

"Hey, Doug, look over there in that tree," I said, pointing to the edge of the camp.

"What?"

"That hoot owl," I said. "He's looking at us. See his big yellow eyes?"

"Oh yeah, he's a big one," Doug said, cutting up an apple into his fruit salad.

In a short time, my pot full of rice, lentils and veggies was steamed at the side of the fire.

"Nice ride today," I said.

"Yeah, good climbs, lots of animals," Doug added. "The weather is warming as we ride north. Must be spring is kicking in around here. I'm amazed at the number of birds flying north. We're in the middle of the migration season. Did you ever see so many flowers?"

"Yeah, and so many colors," I said.

In time, we dug into our food pots and ate with a vengeance. Food is not a habit for us; it's a celebration and we talk about it a lot. The taste and smell of it in our mouths are heightened by our pedaling. Our bodies burn extraordinary amounts of energy on the road.

After dinner, we stared into the campfire. Doug started writing in his journal, and I sat there, mindless, fixating on the embers jumping around in the coals. They popped and glowed, never stopping until they vanished. At intervals, the wood hissed when its moisture turned to steam. When the logs burned down, we threw on a few more pieces.

I'm tired at the end of a day's ride. My whole body feels limp. My leg muscles are tight from being pumped with blood but relax an hour after I stop. The effects are good because my quad muscles bounce around under my skin like steel coils.

Before stepping into my tent, I walked out to the lake. The moon rose higher into the night sky. It reflected off the glass smooth surface of the lake. The stars were thrown against the black curtain of the evening sky. All was well in my part of the world. I headed for the tent.

I lit my candle lantern. My tent brightened. I pulled out my journal and wrote about the events and people of the day's ride. When I get to the end of my writing, I add a section under "Reflections of This Day." That night I wrote: "I like the way the pedals move over the ground when I watch Doug in front of me. I watch his footfall below his panniers in a steady rhythm. His foot drops down but never touches the earth—only for a second does it skim over the pavement, then moves upward again for its power stroke. He walks over the earth, never quite touching yet always in contact. He's sitting, yet standing, but walking at a running speed and moving forward. It brings pleasure to my senses to watch the motion. The day becomes a moving picture with animals, people, clouds, trees, and mountains a part of the setting. Often, it's mindless, which is okay, because it's peaceful motion. It keeps me in the 'here and now' of living."

I like the pulse of the pedals.

(View from our campsite along the Colorado River near Arches National Park.)

Chapter 21—More Important than Panniers

> ***Does the road wind uphill all the way? Yes, to the very end. Will the journey take the whole long day? From morn to night, my friend.***
>
> ***—Christina Rossetti***

Bicycling. I like it for the movement. I don't know if it's poetry in motion, but it is poetry in me. The crank-set equates to the engine of my travels and the wheels turn with every stroke of my legs. Each day is an experience of movement like the reels of a movie slowly unwinding into scenes of cities, mountains, deserts, jungles and/or clouds gathering in the sky.

I like moving slowly, under my own power, being inside this living motion picture. No cameras are trained on me, no orchestra plays music, yet whole symphonies echo from canyons, mountains, and deserts. Birds provide piccolos and flutes. Thunder rocks the heavens with base. The wind vibrates like a hundred violins singing in the trees—and lightning crackles like a golden harp strung across the sky.

I ride through the day dazzled by nature's artistry. I move at my own speed, savoring each unfolding vista—a river valley, rocky seashore, or a mountain range bearded with evergreens. Animals, birds, and insects add their special design to the tapestry around me. Sunsets and sunrises roll across the sky like avalanches of fire, taking my breath away and enhancing my spirituality and closeness to the universe. Their beauty gives me much food for thought as I eat my simple meal by a campfire.

And yet, there is another thing that would make this perfection more enjoyable. Man is a social animal, not meant to spend long intervals alone. There is this conflict, this dichotomy between the self that sustains me and the adventure—versus the person who loves home and hearth. But then, there are never easy choices. Yin and Yang govern us at every turn; there is the active wanderer or the passive stay-at-home person, and they wrestle at every turn of the wheels.

Still, I must admit that almost anything is better if shared with another person. Were it not true, it is unlikely humanity would exist. Because we are such changeable animals, the struggle is our destiny—whether I grind up a steep mountain with panniers bulging and muscles straining, or coast easily down the other side. I would rather do this, and all things, with a friend.

Bicycle touring, like going to the movies, is more fun when shared with another person. Who else are you going to nudge when the good guy jumps off a cliff in a harrowing escape from the villains? Who else can you reach over for a handful of popcorn or sip his or her drink? A friend.

Friendship. It's more important than panniers. It's more important than what I own or what I carry. Such companionship energizes me. It comes from the natural chemistry of two people who enjoy each other's company. A friend is one who shares your spirit. You can be yourself because he or she makes no judgments upon your behavior and likes you the way you are—and you like the way they are. It's a mutual plateau of peacefulness that enhances the journey with laughter, trust, and affection—and shares its problems and joys.

I've traveled many roads around this planet, many times alone. I would rather have done it with someone, but I must face the fact that most men and women are not suited for being bicycle gypsies—their eyes focus on a different prize.

I have witnessed amazing beauty, and incomparable ugliness. I have seen the horror of hundreds of miles of blackened rainforests and sunsets worth a million dollars in gold. If I had that much, I would have given it up to share those experiences with a friend.

How much delight can the armchair traveler or weekend tourist gain from a quick flight over the Grand Canyon or a two-hour exposure to the Great Wall of China? There is no substitute for time, and that's the one thing a bicycle traveler enjoys. It is why I will be able to tell my grandchildren that I saw the rainforests being destroyed; walked for miles on the Great Wall of China while listening to the ancient dead who built it—and it is why I will go to my grave a satisfied man, for I will have done what so many people only dream about.

I think that is what drives me on, what causes me to punish my body when I work hard to earn money for my adventures. It may be why I have never married, preferring to put that off until a time when I feel I've seen as much of this planet as I am destined to see. I'm only going around once and want to see as much as I can. I embrace the labor necessary to make that possible. The planning is hard, the preparation is rigorous, and even the journey is maximum exertion—comparable to the pioneers with their Conestoga wagons crossing the plains. It is—I admit—a mixture of heaven and hell, and while it may be a demon that drives me, it is the angels I see in the clouds above the Andes, and the presence of the Creator, the emerging creative force, everywhere the turning wheels of life take me.

Bicycle traveling as a way of living creates many experiences "normal" people rarely enjoy. It comes from moving out of the realm of routine security into the unknown world of chance. It is a bit frightening—yet exhilarating—something like leaving home for the first time as a teenager. It takes courage to abandon the nest, leave town, and break away from safe reference points.

The first time I found myself 1,000 miles from home, with my life dependent on a simple metal frame, panniers holding all my possessions, and two rubber tires, I wept. I am sure much of it was from loneliness, amplified by a 100-mile day. A strange ache throbbed in my mind. All my friends lay behind me, secure in their homes, enjoying dinner and watching a show on television. Here I was on a cold mountaintop, with the wind moaning through my bicycle spokes, unpacking my tent and sleeping bag. There wasn't another soul within a hundred miles. I was alone, a solitary man on a solitary journey. Damn right I missed home! At that moment, I would have given all I owned for the sound of a human voice and the sight, coming through the dusk, of another human being. That's when the tears poured down my cheeks.

With my heart heavy as an anvil, I pulled my food pack out of my panniers, along with my stove, and began cooking dinner. Somehow, the act of working, of taking care of needs, became like a balm soothing my soul. Just then, a silvery moon peeped above the distant mountain as the sky turned cobalt blue. It was like all the golden chariot wheels of creation paraded across the sky—elevating my mood.

I listened to the song of the escaping steam, to the birds chirping and the whispering wind, and looked up as the starlight sky became the ceiling of my kitchen. Then I half-shouted, "For God's sake man, get real! This is living life. Accept it and quit feeling sorry for yourself. Enjoy it, damn it!"

I have been lonely since, but never like that—and always, the thrill of being on a bicycle, miles and miles into a strange land, overcame any melancholy moments I had upon remembering friends and home.

It's never been simple, but it does get easier. As a departure date creeps up on me, waves of tension grip my stomach. A strange ache throbs in my mind: Do I really want this? But the greater stimulations of the world touch my soul, and I'm off on another grand exploration. Who knows, they may even last a lifetime.

Once in Australia's outback to my incredulous disbelief, I met Bob and Sarah Wilson in their late 70s. They too, were bicycling around the world, and I was overwhelmed by their courage—until they laughingly assured me that it was fun, a wondrous adventure they had dreamed of as they raised their children and now, they were free of obligations. “We'll be on tour till we die,” vowed Sarah. I believe they will and may good fortune be with them.

In preparing for a journey, my mind changes to a traveling mode. If I'm going alone, it gears up for the loneliness I will experience. But with each adventure into the unknown, I encountered others like me. They are out there—and it's always a joy to be with them. We meet as equals, no questions asked—so a lot of BS is quickly dispensed with.

Our mutual reference points are places we've been and the places we're headed for—discussions no others can understand unless they have escaped their daily orbits and flung themselves into this supreme adventure. Meeting others of like persuasion is one of the great joys of traveling adventure's highway. I met John Brown, an Aussie on the Princess Highway south of Sydney that way.

“Where you from, mate?” he asked after we shook hands.

“Colorado, USA.”

“Nice push-bike.”

“It's a pretty good ride and really dependable.”

“That's good,” he said. “This one’s been a bit of a booger, but it's held up pretty well considering I rode across Europe and my country with it.”

We've ridden together since and have become close friends.

Traveling through different cultures, I have gained perspective on my own country. One of America's saddest afflictions, as I see it, is the possessions that have made us materially rich but spiritually poor. Think about it. When have you ever read or heard that wealth made great men, made historical heroes, or created men of courage and vision? My reading in religion, philosophy, and novels by great writers has shown me that the pioneering spirit that builds nations and a lack of it breaks them down. We see it everywhere in the destruction of our planet and in rampant overpopulation.

Living today is even more frustrating. We own so many possessions, but we can't buy love or friendship, so we starve to death in the lonely vacancies of our hearts. Yet, we make our choices, and too often, they are big cars, status homes, and more excess.

Curiously, our homes are poorly designed energy-wasters. The Indians of the plains had the best home, the tipi, warm in the winter and cool in the summer. Its cone-shaped design remains one of the greatest architectural marvels, considering it came from a "primitive" source.

Those who bicycle tour understand how little is needed for comfort and survival. Once, high in the Andes, I pedaled through a blizzard and was on the verge of freezing to death. It wasn't a fine mansion with a huge fireplace that saved me. It was a simple tent, known since the dawn of time. When mankind first discovered how to take animals and cure their skins, he also discovered what nature had given the beasts of the field, could also keep them warm and dry. It's a simple equation—but it escapes most of us. Tepees were made of buffalo hides. Animal skins made beds. No plastics need to be applied.

Each of us makes choices in our lives, and I know for a fact that mine have cost me a wife or enduring sweetheart. Women, for the most part, are nesters more than wanderers—and that can create problems that may never be resolved. I am a prisoner of my wanderlust. I would love to have a sweetheart go with me on every world journey. But I know that is a forlorn hope—so I go myself. Something drives me to see another sunset, or one more mountain range, even if I must see it in solitude. But in the final analysis, I long for someone to share the journey—someone to accompany me down the byroads of my soul.

Wendell Berny wrote: "The world cannot be discovered by a journey of miles, no matter how long, but only by a spiritual journey, a journey of one inch, very arduous, humbling and joyful, by which we arrive at the ground at our feet and learn to be at home."

My home is the world. I'd prefer sharing it with someone.

Friendship. It's more important than panniers.

(Biking friends Gerry, Frank and Don, riding the Lewis & Clark Trail.)

Chapter 22—Temporarily Full

> ***"I began to feel that myself plus the bicycle equaled myself plus the world, upon whose spinning wheel we must all learn to ride or fall into the sluiceways of oblivion and despair. That which made me succeed with the bicycle was precisely what had gained me a measure of success in life—it was the hardihood of spirit that led me to begin, the persistence of will that held me to my task, and the patience that was willing to begin again when the last stroke had failed. And so, I found high moral uses in the bicycle and can commend it as a teacher without pulpit or creed. She who succeeds in gaining the mastery of the bicycle will gain the mastery of life."***
>
> ***~ Frances E. Willard How I Learned To Ride The Bicycle. 1895***

Sin City, Nevada. Route 16 led us down the primrose path of moral destruction. Las Vegas draws people from around the world. It features entertainment with stars strutting their stuff across the stages. In addition, it offers the finest food spread anywhere in the West. My Australian friends John, Mike, Kevin and I hit the glittering lights after a hard day's ride out of the California desert.

After finding a motel, we headed to the nearest hotel with an all-you-can-eat salad bar. I had visited Vegas before, so I knew about the elegant buffets offered at the casinos. My two Aussie friends had no idea what to expect. After the day's ride, we ran on empty.

Usually, we stash food into our packs before dinner in the bush. By the time the sun sets, our hunger pangs grab us by the throats. We cook our food while munching on bread, nuts, fruits, crackers, carrots, and sunflower seeds—impatiently waiting for the main course.

I start gobbling anything I can get into my hands while I'm sitting in my tent. I feel like a giraffe with the stomach of a humpback whale.

That night, we walked into the Garden Buffet of a large Mirage Hotel. Lights flashed everywhere and people stood at rows of one-armed bandits, pulling the levers with no purpose other than passing time.

We paid the cashier $5.19 to enter the dining area. John's face grew in amazement at the rows of steaming foods offered at the entree area. Succulent aromas from meats, fish and poultry wafted through the air. Everything from pork chops to breaded veal awaited patrons. Choices included ham, prime rib, sausages, bacon, filet mignon, roasts, and ribs. They featured swordfish, snapper, cod, halibut, perch, bass, trout and squid. Baked, broiled and fried chicken, duck or turkey was available. For those who love those little snails, a sautéed pan full of the crawly creatures awaited distinguished pallets.

Huge bowls featured garden salads, speckled with carrot slices, radishes, cucumbers, zucchini, olives, mushrooms and sunflower seeds. A half dozen dressings completed the color scheme. Mixed salads with potatoes, carrots, beans, Jell-O, and pasta dotted crushed ice bins. Fruit selections included bananas, apples, prunes, oranges, grapefruits, cherries, cantaloupes, tangerines, watermelon, honeydew melon, Kiwi fruit, pears, grapes, strawberries, raspberries, blueberries and peaches.

Cheese sauces awaited those who wanted to make Mexican tacos or dip their baked potatoes into the fondues. From there, hot loaves of bread under glass were offered such as banana nut, garlic, date, multigrain, to pure white French bread. Many dishes filled with cashews, almonds, filberts and pecans were out for the taking. Each line led up to a drink station that offered coffee, beer, wines, champagne and soda pop. Once customers stuffed themselves with food, they were drawn to the dessert bar, which in a word was deliciously decadent. If you weren't overweight when you arrived, you would be at the end of your dinner.

They offered ten pies—apple, banana, lemon meringue, pecan, pumpkin, tapioca, rhubarb, Boston cream, chocolate and cherry. Cakes—German chocolate, white, angel food, cheese, lemon, coffee, Carmel swirl and black. Every kind of cookie was offered including chocolate chip, oatmeal, date, cream filled and more. Five fabulous ice creams begged to be tasted—mocha chocolate, French vanilla, chocolate cherry, rainbow and strawberry swirl. You could finish your ice cream off with a big scoop of hot fudge being melted by a candle.

"What do you think John?" I asked as we headed toward the main food station.

"This place is mine, mate," he said, his eyes glazed over with wonder.

For the next one and a half hours, John inhaled nine plates of food, Mike ate seven, I consumed six, and Kevin gobbled five. We ate ourselves sick. Our stomachs ached from being stretched to the bursting point. When we stood up to leave, each of us looked five months pregnant.

"I ate so much, I'm going to die," I told John. "How about you?"

"Well mate," John said, puffing out his stomach. "It looks like you yanks have to take back seats to your kangaroo mates."

"Why's that John?"

"It was a nice feed, but I'm only temporarily full."

(How much can one man eat in one meal? If you're riding a bike on tour, you can eat everything in sight!)

Chapter 23—The Coffin Man

> ***"I have learned this, at least, by my experiment; that if one advances confidently in the direction of his/her dreams, and endeavors to live the life which he has imagined, he will meet with success unexpected in common hours. He will pass through invisible boundaries. He will engage new and liberal laws. And, he will live with the license of a higher order of beings."***
>
> ***—Henry David Thoreau***

Bicycle touring becomes even more special with all the interesting people met along the way. They approach me at every stop. Curious and full of questions, they make my day with their homespun hospitality. They advise me about local events and interesting places to visit. I'm invited over for a hot shower and dinner. But it's those rare, eccentric characters who cross my path that intrigued my imagination. They express infinite possibilities for the human spirit.

Most of us have a chance to fill up our lives with seventy to eighty years of living, and we can use them as we see fit. Some of us do it in highly imaginative ways. For a few, travel is the ultimate freedom of expression. It brings the unknown into focus. Traveling east toward Vermont on Route 373, I stood on the dock waiting for the ferry to take me across Lake Champlain. Spring colors decorated upstate New York. The boat wasn't due for another hour, so I pedaled around the parking lot until I found a spot to write in my journal. I'm usually the center of attention with flags flying and a half-dozen bananas hanging off my rear packs. Not that day. Another traveler commanded MY attention.

In the corner of the parking lot, a buckboard wagon right out of a John Wayne movie was parked in the shade. It had a shortened harness on the front, along with a blue and white cotton surrey top. Pots and pans hung from the sides along with a fold-out table and bench. Heavy rubber covered large spoked wheels. A series of plastic-covered news clips were tacked to the sides of the frame. The most curious aspect of this contraption wasn't evident until I rode closer. A gold-trimmed black coffin cradled itself onto the main frame of the wagon. The news clips were printed in many different languages.

Off to the side, a man who looked in his late fifties stood talking with tourists. Long silver hair flowed from under his cap and he sported a goatee. His eyes matched the sky. He related to those tourists about some experiences in Australia.

I looked at the news clips until I found one in English from the London Times. This guy had traveled through 85 countries on five continents. They called him “The Coffin Man.”

Backing up, I grabbed my camera for a shot.

“Hold it, sonny,” he said. “Please read my sign before you take a picture.”

“What sign?” I asked.

“Right here,” he said, pointing.

I moved closer to the rear of the wagon. It read, “If you are going to take a photograph, I ask that you donate $1.00 and I will stand in the picture with you. This is the way I make a living for my travels.”

“Sounds fair enough to me,” I said, handing him a buck.

After the shot, I asked him how long and why he had been traveling with his buckboard.

“It's been twenty years this coming May,” he said, stroking his goatee. “It dawned on me when I was forty-five that my life was passing me by. My kids were grown, and my wife died of breast cancer. I was broke but in good health. I worked for a year to save up money to travel around the world. Within ten months, I was broke again. But by that time, I had the travel bug. I figured I wanted to see every place on this planet in my lifetime. I itched to get back on the road. That's when I thought up this idea to make money while I traveled. It's the cheapest way to go, and I make a decent buck along the way."

"Where's the horse?" I asked.

"You're looking at him," he said, slapping his sinewy thighs.

"You pull that wagon?!" I gasped. "How do you get it up the mountains?"

"I've cut out any extra weight, so it's pretty light," he said. "Here, you can pick up a corner to see how light it is. You'll be surprised."

I pressed my kickstand down to park the bike. After picking up a corner of the wagon, it felt like 250 pounds, maybe more, but I could see that a strong person could pull it up a six percent mountain grade.

"So, where do you sleep?" I asked.

"Sonny, it don't take an Einstein to figure that one out," he said.

I looked up at the wagon.

"No," I said.

"Yes," he said.

"I'll be damned," I said.

"Hey, you guys! My wife and I would like to take a picture of you two crazy people," a man said. "After that, we'd like to take you out to lunch, if you don't mind."

"You don't have any idea how much I eat," I told him.

"No, you won't believe how much I eat," the Coffin Man said.

The couple snapped our pictures before taking us to lunch. They asked more questions than a reporter. They were fascinated by our different modes of travel. Late into the afternoon, we finished a long discussion of world politics, people and countries around the world. I had missed the ferry, but could catch it in the morning.

I asked the Coffin Man what was one of his favorite adventures in his travels.

“It's hard to pick out one favorite moment out of hundreds,” he said. “But once, I was caught in a monsoon rain on a muddy road in India. I had given up hope of getting out of there for the rest of the day. As luck would have it, three guys rode by on their own modes of transportation.

“What was that?” I asked.

“Elephants,” he said. “They hitched up one of those beasts with a rope to my wagon and then motioned me to hop on board with them. Hell, I didn't know how to get up on one of those things, so they motioned me to the front of the beast. I stood there when the elephant got up close to me and rolled out its tusk in front of my foot. I stepped into his curled snout, and that elephant hoisted me up to his back. It was the most exciting elevator ride to the second floor of any building I've ever taken.”

That night, we camped together. We both agreed that we had an incurable love for travel. I crawled into my tent and looked out the netting to see the Coffin Man climbing into his bed. I don't mind saying that it was a strange feeling watching this man who was so much alive and who was living such an incredible life—casually climb into his coffin and close the lid behind him.

Our discussions that day excited my passion for travel, and reminded me of a piece written by John Steinbeck in his book, **Travels with Charley.**

“When I was very young and the urge to be someplace else was on me, I was assured by mature people that maturity would cure this itch. When years described me as mature, the remedy prescribed was middle age. In middle age, I was assured that greater age would calm my fever and now that I am fifty-eight perhaps senility will do the job. Nothing has worked. Four hoarse blasts of a ship's whistle still raise the hair on my neck and set my feet to tapping. The sound of a jet, an engine warming up, even the clopping of shod hooves on pavement brings on the ancient shudder, the dry mouth and vacant eye, the hot palms and the churn of stomach high up under the rib cage... I fear the disease is incurable."

Reclining there on my back, with a million stars twinkling in the night sky, I smiled realizing that the disease had infected me... as I smiled at the universe.

(Yes, travel affliction is an incurable disease. It causes cyclists to ride into wondrous places, raise their hands in triumph and celebrate the moment with indescribable joy.)

Chapter 24—Mouthwatering Strawberry Sunsets

"What I have lived, he has also lived. In this silence, we are close, so intimate. Any other words would only be a distraction. This is not a celebration. We both know that it is not the goal that matters but what we have created, how we have shaped ourselves and adapted to the world. We have joked, and we have cried, we have contemplated the wonders of Mother Earth, we have suffered, and we have shared. We have lived every day. This is the most important celebration: the celebration, at every moment, of the Life that has been given to us."

—Kim and Flippo Graglia, at the end of their bicycle ride from North Africa to Cape Town, Africa, and A Taubabou on the Horizon

They descend upon us at the enchanting hour of the day—sunsets—when the minutes wind down like the hands on a grandfather clock. With seconds ticking off, shimmering gold streaked across the heavens offering a final curtain for the day's ride.

Sunsets come in many shapes and sizes for a bicyclist. I ride into them, away from them or to the side of them. I might be pedaling over hills, up a mountain or through a desert. They cause sunlit peaks, dark canyons, and mystical shadows. Their most precious gift is color.

Australian Sunset

While cycling south along the East Coast of Australia in New South Wales, I was at the tail end of an extraordinary day. Riding along the Princess Highway through the towering eucalyptus trees of the Royal National Park, I swooped down steep grades but remained 500 feet above the ocean. The sky stretched robin's egg blue to the horizon. Near sunset, a kangaroo popped out of the bush and nearly got hit by a car. That hastened my desire to find a campsite.

With the sky beginning its fade from daylight to darkness, I searched for a spot in the woods along the beach. A dirt trail caught my attention, so I followed it through the brush. A path opened onto a knoll jutting into the surf about 50 yards. With waves crashing 60 feet below me, I pitched my tent as the moon appeared over the eastern horizon. The Southern Cross punctuated the evening sky. The sun settled into the horizon. A sun-line stretched up the beach and radiated liquid gold across the crashing waves. A fine mist swept shoreward with each onslaught of surf boiling into the sand. Gold colored the evening. The sun settled in the nap of two mountains and profiled a lone eucalyptus tree.

When the sun reached the horizon, it grew bigger, with reflections working off its face. I looked directly into its searing beauty without burning my eyes. Sitting there, propped against a rock, I watched the cirrus clouds splash golden. When the sun dipped behind the mountains, the water turned black. The eastern sky grew dark, with stars appearing one by one million. Golden hues followed the sun on his journey to the other side of the world. My ears perked to the crashing waves and the smell of salt wafted on the cool evening breezes.

New Zealand Sunset

Sunsets in the mountains create visual phenomena rarely possible otherwise. Distant terrain silhouettes against the sky. It was in such a setting as Beautiful Valley, New Zealand where my riding partner Doug and I witnessed a sunset of colors, shadows and movement. We crested a ridge on a valley rising toward gentle mountains in the west near Mt. Cook National Park. The valley ran smoothly as a golf putting green. That's what we saw under the ebbing rays of the sun. Sheep paddocks sectioned the land into a lush patchwork—punctuated by trees and fences.

We rolled southwest toward the mountains. Soon, we climbed steep grades.

"This is the first hill that made me shift all day," Doug said, clattering into low gear.

"That makes two of us," I added. "Have you noticed how green it is here?"

"Yup, but the sun's going down, so we better find a campsite," Doug said. "Those shadows across the mountains keep getting longer."

The valleys in the distance revealed smooth pastures with sheep grazing for as far as we could see. Their nibbling caused perfection seen only on golf courses. As we crested a high ridge, a rancher's house was situated 300 yards below us. To the left and right, a valley narrowed toward the plain. Directly west, paddocks aproned up against the tree-covered mountainside. As we stood there, two dogs gathered 500 sheep and squeezed them through a pasture gate. We heard the whistles and calls of the owners directing the operation. Once through the gate, the woolly critters expanded out of their wedge shape when the dogs circled—yipping and nipping. Half the sheep were sheared and white, while the remainder were unsheared and dark. The contrast created a polka-dot effect within the mass of animals moving across the field.

Further off in another paddock, where this bunch was headed, 1,000 sheep grazed. The dogs corralled the near bunch and headed them toward the higher section.

During this time, the man and two boys stood watching. The dogs knew what to do and pushed the reticent sheep into a wedge, which forced the first few through the gates. Once the animals moved in mass, an hourglass shape evolved through the gate. The black and white sheep became grains of time. They moved through and the figure vanished into an oval which, in mass, moved toward the opposite side of the field. The dogs returned to their owners. Soon, the sheep scattered, some toward their fellow critters in the next field, and the rest grazed toward all corners of the paddock.

We stood astride our bikes, mesmerized by the entire scene while the sun slipped beneath the mountains. Once the direct light vanished, the shadows ceased, leaving thousands of sheep fading into the twilight.

American Sunset

The prettiest sunsets occur over water. On a Mexico to Canada cross-country journey through the Sierras one spring, my friend Doug and I had pushed hard through the mountains of northern California. We had pounded the pedals through hundreds of valleys at 3,000 to 4,000 feet of rise and fall. The cool springtime had us sweating up the hills and freezing on the way down. We grabbed a hot shower at a trailer camp on Route 89. After the showers, we headed north on Route 147 but stopped on the shore of Lake Almanor when the sky fractured with boiling cloud formations over a pine-covered mountain across the lake.

Yellows, oranges and pinks played over the waters and bounced off the clouds. Vapor expansions in the mist, constantly moving into and out of each other created sublime pastels in changing shapes, much like one of those kaleidoscopes we rotated around our eye sockets as kids. This was one that was high in the heavens. In the distance, further across the lake, snow-covered summits peeked out of the clouds.

As we stood there, pitching our tents in between scenes of the light show, a squadron of 50 Canada geese circled once, then lowered their wings for a final splashdown. After landing, their honking quieted as they paddled to a secluded spot along the shore. In front of us, black grebes swam back and forth across the glass-quiet waters of the lake. As they paddled, a thin ripple wake stretched out in a V shape behind them. Sometimes another grebe crossed their path, intersecting the V wake, which then created triangles and off-angled boxes on the water's surface.

"Man, this is too incredible," blurted Doug.

"It's almost like a jigsaw puzzle of angles," I said.

Colors played pink on the lake until "plop," the grebes dove underwater, leaving circular ripples expanding outward. Seconds later, they popped to the surface like little feathered corks where they created another circle of ripples that intersected the first circles. It was a magical collection of rings and lines highlighted by the sun. Around the lake, elegant pines pointed skyward. Mountains stood robed in white. A chameleon sky rushed everywhere at once going nowhere at all—and those ducks kept paddling across the pastel waters.

I'll admit it, sometimes when I see beauty like this; I am filled with wonder. My ears perk to the sublime poetry of the flapping of wings making their final descent from the sky. It's silent in the wilderness, but not the kind of silence you might expect. I hear nature. Once the ebbing rays of the sun settle below the edge of the world, wild creatures give their own greeting to the night. Fish jump upward, grabbing an insect, then drop back into the black depths with a splash. On a distant hill, a coyote, called a song dog by the Indians, pokes its nose toward the sky and follows with a melodious yipping and howling. At the water's edge, a raccoon washes its food. Canada geese rise up out of the water, flapping their wings and protesting vocally at nothing in particular. Crows squawk from their night perches, while chickadees chirp incessantly until the last ray of light quiets their enthusiasm.

Elk bugles their call to the wild that shatters the stillness at the end of the day. Along with those voices, an evening breeze blows through the trees, causing a fluttering of the leaves and creaking of the branches. Fireflies flicker their tiny lights like Tinker Bell's pixie dust sprinkled along the shoreline. Not to be denied, mosquitoes hum through the air. Above this wonder, a canopy of stars twinkles in the ink-black sky. The only disturbance is the momentary flash of a shooting star as it streaks across the heavens as if to place an exclamation point on a perfect day.

One of the most extravagant sunsets I've ever seen was on the coast of Oregon in the summer after a rainstorm. We camped above the roaring surf with huge rocks standing out in the water—when one of those mouth-watering strawberry-red sunsets worked its magic across the water and sky. With two tents up and four bicycles propped, Jeff, Mary, Laurie and I sat by a roaring driftwood campfire.

If it hadn't been for Laurie looking backward, we might never have seen a perfect rainbow arcing across the misty sky behind us. We sat between a rainbow and a sunset as the waves rolled into the beach every few seconds. All was calm—but the SKY blazed red against the cloudbanks. What a problem we faced! Five precious minutes to view the magic. Our heads flipped back and forth trying to see every moment of the show.

The fiery globe boiled into the Pacific, leaving a red path stretching right up to the shoreline. Then, poof, it vanished—and with it, the rainbow. But the extravaganza wasn't over for a half-hour because the sky turned every shade of purple, crimson, and red.

We sat by the fire reflected in the sky overhead. The day ended as it had begun, full of light. Being there with my companions made it even more precious. My dear friend Duncan Littlefair has a poem that I read often. Like the fire reflected in the sky, his words reflect the gift of life:

"This is indeed a beautiful day. Let us rejoice in it, and be glad, and let us count our many blessings. Let us be grateful for the capacity to see, feel, hear and understand. Let us be especially grateful for the ties of love that bind us together giving dignity, meaning, worth and joy to all our days."

(Sun setting over the steaming waters of a small stream in Montana at the end of the day.)

Chapter 25—It is Not Your Age That Counts

"You suffered crotch rot, hot days, sweat dripping down your back and off your nose that splashed on the top tube, sweaty body, voracious appetite and other challenges. You 'soared' across a continent with blue skies, cycling buddies and incredible characters who enriched your life. Each day on a bike becomes a 'moment'. While those moments abound on a bicycle adventure, the new day beckons you onward, not to tarry with yesterday—and, for you, another possibility for a unique 'moment' that will live in your body, mind and heart for the rest of your life."

—FHW

Touring through Hobart, Indiana, one summer, I heard about a triathlon being run the next day. I decided to enter if they allowed same-day registration. The swim, bike and run event takes place worldwide, with a large following of people from many walks of life. I had run in several dozen myself and it was a great way to meet people who enjoyed physical fitness.

Even while touring, I like to run and swim at every opportunity along the route. I swim in rivers, lakes, pools and oceans. Running is easy to do in the mornings before breaking camp. Bicycling is easy for me as I crank the pedals 70 miles a day, which includes a handicap of 70 pounds of gear. It would be fun to test my mettle in a triathlon.

The next morning, officials allowed me to register when several competitors didn't show up. After stashing my bags and camping gear with a family from Indianapolis who came to race, I surveyed the course. It included a mile swim, a 46-mile bike ride and finished with a six-mile run.

They set the race in age group waves. More than 600 triathletes lined up on the beach. They ranged in age from 18 to

71. The oldest woman was 71 and the oldest man was 69. Knowing how tough a sport it is, I was amazed at the number of older people lining up for the swim.

When the gun fired, the first wave of triathletes dove in with arms flying through the water. When my age group came up, I stepped up to the line. I felt nervous and full of expectations. I knew the next four-plus hours were going to be tough. I couldn't help myself. I would push my body to its limits during the race.

In seconds, I pulled handfuls of water past my body as I swam toward the distant marker. Some guys cruised past me, and I passed others. I swam in the thick of it. Rounding the marker 15 minutes later, I felt good as my strokes felt strong. I cruised into the beach with a good time.

After changing my clothes, I jumped on my bike and flew down the road. Several people glanced at me on my mountain bike as if I was pretty strange compared to those sleek racers, but I didn't mind. My legs made up for a lot of their equipment. I kept picking them off, one by one. For the next hour, I hammered on them at 24 miles per hour, sometimes faster as I gained surges of strength. By the time I came into the transition area, I placed in the top ten of my age group. A quick change of shoes and I rushed onto the running course.

The run proved tougher because I hadn't been training, so I wasn't picking anyone off, but I wasn't losing places either. I ran into the chute in the top third of the racers and ninth place for my age group. It felt good to have been at full throttle for four hours.

Everyone stood around, cheering the racers as they came in from the run. Even though it was a race, everyone loved to see every competitor finish. Most of us congregated around the fruit, bagel and drink tent. I ate 30 pieces of cut-up orange slices, watermelon and grapes. An hour later, most people finished the race course. Race sponsors announced the awards ceremony would be held in fifteen minutes.

People gathered around the platform while the times and awards were given out. By the time they were nearly finished, it was more than four hours since the start of the race. Many people were walking to their cars when the sponsor made a special announcement.

"Friends, you're not going to believe this, but two racers are still out on the course, and they're battling for second to last place," he said. "Right now, 69 years old John Haglan is leading 71 years old Martha Gingrich. They're a half mile out, so if you would like to cheer them at the finish, let's line the race course."

In seconds, more than 500 people lined both sides of the course leading toward the finish. With 100 yards to go after the turn off the main road, the two triathletes rounded the corner not five yards apart. They were in a race for their lives, as it was apparent that neither wanted to be last. John Haglan was limping but still holding on to the lead—while Martha gained on him. The crowd, caught up in the drama, screamed support for the two racers.

With 50 yards to go, Martha grabbed the lead from John. At that point, the aging triathlete seemed to lose his legs, but kept fighting to sustain his stride. The crowd cheered wildly and gave them high fives as they raced down the chute. Martha was going to win by 10 yards when just before the finish line, she stopped, turned around, and waved to John to hurry up. When he reached her, she joined hands with him and they both ran across the finish in a tie. The crowd went wild.

There wasn't a dry eye at the race.

Two hours later, everyone was gone except the cleanup crews. I loaded my bike and filled my water bottles. That day was one of the greatest sports events I have ever witnessed. Martha and John showed everyone in that race that youth is a matter of attitude.

Samuel Ullman wrote: Youth is not a time of life; it is a state of mind; it is not a matter of rosy cheeks, red lips and supple knees; it is a matter of will, a quality of imagination, a vigor of the emotions; it is the freshness of the deep springs of life.

Youth means a temperamental predominance of courage over timidity, of the appetite for adventure over the love of ease. This often exists in a man of 60 more than in a boy of 20. Nobody grows old merely by living a number of years. We grow old by deserting our ideals. Years may wrinkle the skin, but to give up enthusiasm wrinkles the soul. Worry, fear, self-doubt bows the heart and turns the spirit back to dust.

Whether 60 or 16, there is in every human being's heart the lure of wonder, the unfailing childlike curiosity of what's next, and the joy of the game of living. In the center of your heart and mine, there is a wireless station; so long as it receives messages of beauty, hope, cheer and courage, you are young.

When the antennas are down, and your spirit is covered with the snows of cynicism and ice of pessimism, then you have grown old, even at 20. But so long as your antennas are up, to catch the optimism and create enthusiasm, there is hope you may die YOUNG at 80.

John and Martha's enthusiasm generated more power and excitement than the winners of the race. In fact, in Latin, the word 'enthusiasm' means 'eon theo' which means 'with God.' When we look at the emerging creative energy of the Great Spirit, then it means that anyone with 'enthusiasm' is continually renewing and creating energy and moving with the energies of life. They are, quite literally, forever young—until their very last breath on Earth.

Thank you, Martha and John, for your living proof of living with 'enthusiasm', because in the end, age doesn't count.

(Bikes decorated fences, store fronts and towns across America.)

Chapter 26—No Motor, No Fun

"Bicycle adventure creates surprises. They arrive in endless forms. Some delight you and others scare the pants off you. One moment you're riding along and the next, a kangaroo bounds across the road in front of you. At another point, a box turtle makes its way across the road while you ride through the redwoods along the Avenue of the Giants. You stop in amazement at the glory of such a tiny, slow-moving creature amongst giants having lived since the days of the Roman Empire.

The wonder of the encounter thrills your spirit, your mind and most of all, your heart. How about the surprise with meeting someone who inspires, encourages and applauds your journey? Remember that evening ride where the sun shone brightly in the west while your shadow danced 50 feet across the highway and played on the meadow? The surprises continue as long as you keep pedaling. And, how about that huge canine racing out of the driveway to chew off a piece of your leg? We can all do without that surprise!"

—FHW

When Jack Frost stretches his icy fingers across northern Michigan in late September, he sets the stage for one of the most spectacular parades Mother Nature ever created. Beginning in the far north, a runaway color fire of visual excitement soon spreads out of control. No amount of sunshine or warm weather can extinguish the blaze once this annual phenomenon ignites.

Autumn tantalizes our eyes with brilliant colors that look like millions of tiny brush strokes painted across a crisp blue sky. Trees dress in scintillating coats of burnished gold, fiery reds, blazing yellows, sensual crimsons, and radiant oranges. With each passing day, leaves drift down, enchanting us, yet we cannot help but feel a sad note at summer's passing.

The first week of October is perfect for touring. I love taking advantage of autumn's final pleasure. Cool evenings surrender to sunny days as Indian summer stands as the last bastion against winter. Even with moderate temperatures, I wear wool tights and a warm sweater.

Additionally, the bewitching month beckons ghosts and hobgoblins, along with black-garbed cackling old women on broomsticks silhouetted against the full moon. Autumn is a time of celebration, a time for tart apple cider, pumpkin faces, and warming our hands over campfires.

As the change of season gathers strength, we see our breath on a chilly morning. Birds gather in great masses as they begin their retreat to warmer climes, and the haunting cry of the loon echoes across placid waters from lakes deep in the wilderness.

Northern Michigan like much of North America, is blessed with extraordinary natural wonders. Lake Superior is one of the largest freshwater lakes in the world. Mountains rise to a height of 1,900 feet, which makes for exciting bicycle touring, especially when riding at the peak of the color season in autumn. But while visiting most natural wonders in the USA, Americans travel by automobile. Even if they fly, they always end up in a car. It is a glass, metal and vinyl compartment that obscures nature's finest moments, especially on a dirt road, deep in the forest.

That's why Doug and I prefer traveling via bicycle. With that in mind, we started out from White Fish Point, Michigan on October 1st. It heralded the peak of the color leaf change. We stood near the point known as the Graveyard of the Great Lakes where the Edmond Fitzgerald, an ore ship, sank in a gale. Gordon Lightfoot eulogized the incident in a ballad.

Leaving White Fish Point, we pointed our bikes west on Route 123, and headed for Pictured Rocks National Lakeshore. The map indicated a gravel road through old-growth hardwood forest, mainly beech, maple, and oak. The route traced the shoreline of Lake Superior. It showed waterfalls, cliffs, ghost forests and Grand Banks. Few people know about this national park because of its obscurity, and even fewer of them want to drive its gravel road or camp in its primitive campsites.

Dark skies greeted us as we headed into a brisk wind toward Tahquamenon Falls. Soon, cold rains swept over the trees.

"You told me this was Indian summer, Doug," I said as we pedaled into the rain. "We're gonna freeze our butts off."

"Don't worry, the weather report said this week's going to be warm and sunny," Doug replied. "We just have to get through this rough spot today."

I wondered why we had launched ourselves into this storm front, but soon, I warmed up with the aerobic activity and pedaled through water-soaked leaves glistening with colors like fresh paint on a new canvas. A couple of bluebirds winged their way across the highway and perched in a tree near us. Their chirping delighted us. Above, a squadron of Canada geese flew south through cold gray skies. Soon, we made our way to the lower falls, which were ringed with golds, reds and yellows from the maples that lined the riverbanks. Fifty thousand gallons of water pour over the falls per second, and in the autumn, many leaves fall from the trees simultaneously.

We camped in an abandoned house along the road. In the morning, ice coated the leaves. The day promised happy riding when a warm sun rose through the treetops.

It took us the whole day to reach Gitche Gumee, "The Great One," named by the early Indians. Camping on Lake Superior was like camping on an ocean without waves. At dusk, Canada geese dropped out of the sky, honking until they settled into silence with the darkness.

Gravel road. It began the next day, and it's what a mountain bike is all about. Fat tires, low gearing, and muscle. We pedaled our way into Grand Marais Bay and plucked apples from trees alongside the road.

Heading west again, we made our way around colorful tree-lined curves, down hills through glades and meadows with flowers along every mile of our path. We entered Pictured Rocks National Lakeshore under a canopy of autumn magic. The trees made the road more like a tunnel painted from an artist's palette.

At Hurricane Campground, we walked on the beach toward two old steamers that had been caught in storms and run aground at the turn of the century. Waves lapped at the broken wooden spiked hulls. Nature can be as kind as a calm day or rise up with 120-mile-per-hour winds and cause havoc with everything in its path.

We returned to the bikes. I stood hard on the pedals and grimaced as I cranked up a sandy incline from the beach. When I reached the parking lot, two fishermen watched as Doug and I labored under our 60 pounds of gear strapped to the bikes.

"Looks like a whole lot of work," one of them said.

"It's a whole lot of fun," I answered as I pulled past him.

"No motor, no fun," the other guy shot back, chuckling as if he had made the smartest statement of his life. "Ain't no way you'd get me on something that ain't got a motor."

At that moment, I thought about defending my point of view. But I said, "Good for you!"

I cranked through some heavy sand out to the firmer surface of the road. Doug followed close behind.

"What was that all about?" he asked when he caught up with me.

"Those guys think that the only way to have fun is to have a motor-driven vehicle," I replied.

"Little do they know that we've ridden these bikes around the world," Doug said. "I tell you, we don't get no respect."

Several miles down the road, I thought about the no motor, no fun comment. Leaves fell like colored raindrops. The dirt road hugged the coastline of Lake Superior providing peaceful vistas of birch, maple, and cedar trees backed by the lake's clear waters. A redheaded woodpecker belted out his own song as he rat-a-tat-tatted against a tree. Adding to the display, two squirrels chased each other through the branches, chattering at one another more in jest than confrontation. A bumble bee zipped by on its way through the woods. Not far from the road, a chipmunk rustled through the leaves as it scurried over the forest floor.

A special music plays in the wilderness. No way can a person hear that magic on a motor-driven machine! You have to stop and listen in the woods. Sublime music plays in the breezes. The grand orchestration creates rhythms that can only be heard in silence, like when you walk or ride a bicycle.

Those two fishermen drove their pickup into these beautiful woods without hearing, seeing, touching, or sensing nature. They jumped out of their truck only to fire up their powerboat to roar to a fishing hole across the water. When they arrived, their radio drowned out any wildlife experience. I've seen it many times in my rides through other national parks where hikers screw their smartphones into their ears, becoming oblivious to any natural experience around them. They miss the essence of nature for which they came in the first place. Many campers arrive in their motorhomes complete with large TV antennas and sit inside, around the television at night—instead of sitting by a campfire, swatting mosquitoes and listening to the night sounds.

Maybe I was lucky my parents never had a TV in the house while we kids grew up. I missed the no motor, no fun concept. Dad and mom took us camping on weekends. We gathered wood for the fire and pitched the big tent together. Dad got into conversations with fellow travelers. We fished lakes and climbed mountains, catching glimpses of animals, which fired our thirst for the natural world. That's why I jumped onto my one-speed in the first place. After my paper route, it carried me into adventures in the woods. Advantages? Self-determination, for one. Satisfaction was another benefit. Worn out at the end of the day from so much physical activity, I slept like a rock. Riding that first bike gave me an appreciation for up-hills and downhills. Each is necessary. A balanced outlook prevails when dealing with life's trials.

"Looks like a steep climb coming at us," Doug said, interrupting my thoughts.

"I can feel my sweat pores opening up right now," I said, laughing.

"Hey, look out, those no motor, no fun guys are coming up behind us," Doug said.

Sure enough, those guys were speeding toward us, with a dust cloud billowing behind their truck. As they approached, the woods became captive to the roar of their engine. The next sound we heard was a car horn. Then "Whoosh!" They sped past us in a cloud of dust. We smelled dirty exhaust from their tailpipe and tobacco smoke from their cigarettes. As if to punctuate their philosophy, they tossed a beer can out the window after passing.

Moments later, serenity returned to the woods. A crow squawked from a distant tree. Mosquitoes circled our heads. A hummingbird buzzed across the road but hovered a moment to look at us. A covey of white-winged butterflies danced over the last wildflowers of autumn. Maple leaves fluttered their golden colors in the trees. I knew that before the day was out, we would see a deer slipping across the road and into the woods, his white tail flashing through the fall colors.

As Doug and I mounted the bikes once again, he looked at me grinning, "Like the man said, 'No motor, no fun.'"

"Yeah, I guess you can't argue with logic like that," I said. "Let's get on with our own insufferable misery."

We reached Miner's Castle at the western end of the park. The view from the cliffs provides one of Michigan's premiere natural attractions. The castle is actually a rock formation created by wind, water and waves. Anyone looking out over Lake Superior can't help but feel a sense of peace from deep down in his or her spirit. I think it comes from the silence, the waterfalls, and the pace of life in the wilderness.

Henry David Thoreau wrote: "We need the tonic of the wilderness, to wade sometimes in the marsh where the bittern and meadow hen lurks, where the deer play and where we can hear the booming of the snipe; to smell the whispering sedge where only some wilder and more solitary fowl builds her nest, and the mink crawls with its belly close to the ground."

(Frank Cauthorn riding through the woods may be one of the most spiritual joys.)

Chapter 27—Not for a Million Dollars

"Doctor Sarvis, laboring on his bicycle up the long grade of Ninth South toward his home on 23rd East, was not unaware of the pressure of the traffic accumulating in his rear, the clamor of horns pounded by impatient fists, the motorized hatred fermenting at his back. But he thought, "Screw 'em. Let 'em wait. Let 'em fester. Let 'em walk. Let 'em ride a bike like me, would do me and them and everybody a world of good. Cleanse our city's air, reinvigorate the blood, tone up the muscles, strengthen the heart, burn up that surplus fat, stave off arteriosclerosis, cut down on bypass operations, eliminate transplants, lower the cholesterol count, and prolong healthier lives. Yes, and reduce oil consumption, slow down the waste of steel, rubber, copper and glass, free human labor and engineering skills for important work -- anything bad for the auto industry and bad for the oil industry is bound to be good for America, good for human beings, and good for the land."

—Edward Abbey

Route 180 headed into the shoebox town of Roby, Texas. We traveled through cowboy country, where men either rode a horse or drove a pickup. They worked on a ranch or an oil rig. John, Mike, Kevin, and I stopped at a grocery store to fill our food packs and water bottles. One of us stayed outside to watch the bikes while the other three stepped inside to shop. John volunteered for guard duty. Several people had gathered around the bikes asking him questions. They caught his Australian accent, which created a whole new conversation.

I grabbed a cart and walked into the store. At the produce section, I picked up tomatoes, avocados, and green peppers for sandwiches. A melon completed my dessert needs. I grabbed a loaf of wheat bread on my way to the orange juice cooler. It felt so hot I decided to treat myself to a half-gallon. I picked up a small container. For my dinner, I picked up a box of Rice Pilaf with lentils.

At the checkout counter, Mike and Kevin were nearly through with their purchases. I threw my food down onto the conveyer belt.

"Looks like you eat healthy," the cashier said.

"Yes, ma'am," I said. "I pound those pedals, so I need to eat high-energy foods."

"Wish I could get my husband to eat right," she complained. "He's got high cholesterol. The doctor told him to lose weight and stop eating red meat, but he won't listen. He eats salt like sugar. I need to get a mule to kick some sense into him."

"Yes, ma'am, I know it's hard to change a person's diet when they've been at it for a lifetime," I said. "Try to feed him more chicken and fish."

"Thank you for the help."

"You're welcome."

By the time I walked out of the store, a dozen people had gathered around John. But one string bean Texan with a ten-gallon hat dominated the conversation.

"Why would you come all the way over from...where was it you said you was from?" he drawled.

"Australia," John answered.

"Yeah, Australia, and ride yore bicycle across Texas?" he asked.

"Across America," John corrected him.

"Across America," he repeated. "Why would you ride a bicycle? Why not take a car?"

"It's the best way for meeting people," John said. "I go 20 kilometers per hour...."

"How fast?" the Texan asked.

"Make that 12 miles per hour on the flats," John said. "I get to see the country up close. Besides, it doesn't cost me anything but my food."

"It's a lot of work," the Texan said, wiping his brow with a bandanna.

"Yeah, but I keep in great shape," John retorted. "Maybe you ought to try it."

"ME?" the Texan gasped.

"Why not?" John pressed him.

"Oh no, not me," the man said. "You couldn't get me to ride one of them bicycles across America for a million dollars."

"You wouldn't do it for a million dollars?"

"No sir, not for a million dollars."

"Well," John said, rubbing his chin. "Would you ride my push-bike to that stop sign at the end of the street for a million dollars if I could hand it over in cash right now?"

"Just to the sign?"

"That's right."

"Maybe for a million dollars, I could do it."

"Well then," John said. "If you could make it to the sign, could you ride my bike to the end of town for a million dollars?"

"For a million dollars, I could do it."

"If you can ride to the edge of town, you could make it to the next town for a million dollars."

The Texan pondered the distance and money, then said, "Yeah, I could make it over to Boyds, 'coz it's not more than fifteen miles."

"Now, if you could make it over to Boyds, I bet you could make it to the next city, and then the next state, and then across the country."

The Texan scrunched up his brow, pulled his hat down over his head, and slapped his thigh. He pondered the whole idea with a crowd of ten onlookers waiting for his reply. He slapped his thigh again, "NOPE! Not for a million dollars. No sir, you wouldn't get me to ride a bicycle across America for a million dollars. Everybody would figure I was nuts."

Everyone laughed. Moments later, the crowd dispersed. John bought his groceries, and we pedaled off minutes later. As we rode out of town into the Texas plains, John rode alongside of me.

"Frosty," he said.

"Yeah, John."

"Now I know why you Americans have that saying about horses."

"Which one is that?"

"You can lead a horse to water, but you can't make him drink."

(Does bicycle touring make you happy?)

Chapter 28—Sweating is Fun

"While bicycling down the West Coast, travelers enjoy majestic moments of Washington and Oregon's coastlines. They watch Gray Whales spouting great steam clouds when they surface. They see otters playing in the lagoons. They watch seals frolicking in the surf. Endless pelicans and other seabirds fly in formations across the waves. Beachcombers walk the eternal sands. Life thrives along the shoreline of the Pacific.

Once you hit California, a whole new experience awaits: the Redwoods and the Sequoia trees. So, what is so special to place your hand on a redwood? Well, you're touching a living being that has thrived since the time of the Roman Empire. It's been growing since Leif Erickson touched his sailing ship down on the shores of North America. That 350-foot-tall tree, weighing 120 tons, and 25 feet across at the base has been growing long before Captain Cook sailed around the world or Robert Falcon Scott pitched his tent on the South Pole along with Roald Amundsen."

—FHW

"You must be crazy!" a rotund, aging man said at a corner stoplight in Tucson, Arizona. "It's hot enough to kill a camel. Why do you want to sweat to death on a bicycle on a day like this?"

"I don't know," I replied, wiping my brow, with sweat splashing onto the handlebars. "It's fun, I guess."

"What's fun?"

"Sweating...sweating is fun."

The light changed. I slid back onto the saddle, slipped my feet into the straps and pressed my heavily loaded bike, Condor, into the torrid afternoon. It WAS a scorchingly hot day, and I was soaked. The mercury topped 104 degrees, but still, I smiled. I waved at the man as I headed down the street.

"You gotta love it," I yelled, glancing back.

He shook his head, throwing his hand down as if to push my attitude away from his mind. Guess he didn't or couldn't understand what I meant.

While I'm on tour, many waiting moments at stoplights in cities provoke cryptic comments and bits of humor from motorists and pedestrians. Did you know that 80 percent of conversations with strangers begin by talking about the weather? When I ride a bicycle on a sultry day, that's the first topic at every stop—whether it is a fruit stand, convenience store, or picnic area. It matters little whether I'm touring or not, but often when I'm exploring the world on two wheels, folks love making comments as to my mental viability.

"Ya gotta be nuts..."

"What made you so crazy...?"

"I feel sorry for you fella'..."

What do I get out of sweating when riding my bike? It messes up my nice shorts with salt stains, soaks my socks and makes for an odorful jersey. Salt stains appear everywhere, and I get sticky when the sweat dries. Unwashed long enough, I begin to ripen—smelling like a Tasmanian mongoose that crawled away from a fight with a Mongolian skunk somewhere in the dregs of Siberia. Even copious amounts of deodorant can't cover up the real me. Does that mean I should give up bicycle touring? Hardly!

But transcontinental adventuring does have a few discomforts. One day on a ride across the southwest, my partner and I suffered a few consequences. We rolled our way across 200 miles of open desert from Joshua Tree National Monument, California following Route 62 toward the Arizona border. Few living human souls reside between those two places. My riding partner Julie and I carried three gallons of water each to combat the 105-degree-plus temperatures.

Before we reached the Colorado River, our last night in the tent nearly killed both of us. When I took off my shoes, the fetid air rising betwixt my toes caused Julie's eyes to roll to the top of her head, while she struggled to raise her hand to pinch off her (she didn't make it), and then quietly succumbed—falling limply onto her air mattress. The heat, ammonia and ripe toes overwhelmed her. Henceforth, if we couldn't take a bath at a campground, we bought a shower bag to give us nightly hygiene.

Sweating has its positive side. We have more fun sweating—while working hard at playing. Julie did recover from the odor attack in the tent. The next day, we leaped into the Colorado River. Nothing beats the feeling of clean rapids caressing our bodies after sweating. We immersed ourselves for an hour, appreciating the cool water swirling around us.

On a ride in Australia, south of Sydney, I befriended a bicycling nut named John Brown, who lives to sweat. He trains for triathlons by riding up the awesome Macquarie Pass near his home in Kiama. John took me for a ride up this path of 'bitumen' that led through Eucalyptus trees, rain forest, huge boulders and waterfalls. It winds around with more curves than a plate of spaghetti. As we cranked up the pass, John kept talking.

"Isn't this fun, mate?" he asked.

"Oh yeah, just great," I said as I looked up more than 1,000 feet over our heads to the top.

"You'll be right mate," John says, his chain clattering in a lower gear.

"Ya gotta love it," I said.

From my middle chain ring, I quickly dropped into Granny's gear. My legs, already accustomed to intense aerobics, powered into the rising land. Sweat beads appeared on my forehead—then melted into each other, forming water tracks that ran down my cheeks, over my nose, along my neck, through the hairs on my arms—ultimately reaching a dripping-off point, where they launched themselves. Splish, splash—onto the pavement—a steady torrent dripped from my neck, nose, down my stomach and from my ears. Water sloshed back and forth on the bottom edge of my sunglasses.

As the climb steepened, my heart raced, my muscles gorged with blood and my lungs gobbled air to feed the furnace. My riding gloves darkened into interesting patterns as the sweat soaked through. My jersey dripped water around my abdomen, then seeped down into my riding shorts. My legs glistened with moisture.

I grabbed a bottle off the down tube. A cool steady stream of water caressed my mouth, down my throat and into my stomach. Water never tasted better. Up we climbed into the clean, fresh air—our bodies uniting with the bikes—our spirits soaring... we neared the top. A big smile crossed our faces. Sweating IS fun, even in Australia. Perspiration is an international sport.

Pedaling in New Zealand, the summer heat betrays the frigid winds of winter in much of the USA. Kiwi-land has its summer during North America's winter. With New Zealand's undulating mountainous terrain on the South Island, sweating is a joy. Every kilometer is geared for ultimate cycling enjoyment. Many of the 21 million sheep fixed their eyes on us as we rolled by. We enjoyed being the starring attraction to their day. Seals along the coast stopped their frolic in the cold Pacific waters to watch us. Penguins stared at us from their beach nests. Further inland, Mount Cook at 12,500 feet with its brilliant white peak and imposing glaciers whispered to our spirits. When we sweated our way into the rain forests of the West Coast, the wind was so clean, we gulped great vats of air just for the pleasure of bringing it into our bodies.

Yes, sweating is more than fun. It's an attitude and a journey. It's an awareness of living, of doing, and of participating. Each second I crank the pedals, whether it be in the wilderness of the world, or down my own city block, sweating is fun. It matters not what my intentions are, or where I'm going. The spokes will carry me.

For each of us who pedals two wheels, perhaps our fondest memories are those times when we crest a hill and glide into the valley below. The wind cools the sweat, and our body relaxes from the climb. The flowers offer their treasures while horses in nearby pastures prance along the fences—as if they too, would like to share in our freedom. For a bicyclist, the road that leads past our house, connects with all the highways of the world. Sweating is the process; it's the joy; which is more than fun, it is living.

(Frank and Frosty at the Golden Gate Bridge.)

Chapter 29—Pedaling Rain Song Blues

> ***"This grand show is eternal. It is always sunrise somewhere; dew is never all dried at once; a shower is forever falling; vapor is ever rising. Eternal sunrise, eternal sunset, eternal dawn and gloaming, on sea and continents and islands, each in turn, as the round earth rolls."***
>
> ***—John Muir***

We traveled west through the farm country near central Ohio when we saw it. Ominous black clouds boiled across the horizon. A rush of wind pressed against our faces—cool and threatening. A chill descended upon the land. The animals ceased their activity—sometimes gazing toward the approaching fury. The horizon changed from light to gray, then to darkness. Distant lightning fingers probed the land followed by thunderclaps.

Goose bumps popped onto my skin as I drew nearer to this spring storm. The clouds resembled gray giants who beckoned us into their mansion of rain and fury. Did they mean to chill us to the bone, soak our bodies and frighten us with their thunder? The wind stilled as a momentary calm left us breathing fresher air. The first drops fell lightly, splatting against the pavement. We faced the sheets of rain advancing toward us. The first heavy downpour splashed against our bodies, glasses and helmets. Soon, dancing droplets soaked the pavement, drained to the highway shoulder, and vanished into the ground. Water seeped into the gear, ran up the tire treads, and washed outward from our tires. It trickled onto our riding shoes, finally advancing indiscriminately down our backs, and settled in our crotches.

I've heard some riders complain about, and others accept—the rain. But no matter what, while riding a bicycle, the rain becomes my intimate partner. When I've resigned myself to being wet, other appreciations begin. It's a silent splendor at first, but while riding in the rain, my eyes are my passport to a different world. I have a rain jacket to stop the drumming on my back, but past that, the rain offers excitement—often overlooked by those who complain.

As the storm engulfed us in early spring, we accepted the soaking with passive tolerance. At first, we pedaled into a calm rain, but as we pedaled a mile into a wide expanse of open space, the rain became nasty—hailstones pelted us from the sky. At first, we thought it was cute because the peewee marble-sized ice balls bounced on the pavement, off our helmets, gloves, and backs. No big deal, until someone up there decided to go bowling for dollars. A thunderclap shook the ground under us, while delivering a severe warning of our impending doom. There we were, in wide open spaces, when golf ball-sized hail hit us with its version of Rocky II.

With this meteor shower pelting us, four cyclists pedaled for a lone patch of trees a quarter mile ahead. We dragged our bikes through heavy grass, while defending ourselves as best we could against the pounding hail. Once out of danger, we checked for casualties. Nothing severe.

We weren't the only ones under those maple trees. Six Guernsey cows swished their tails while standing protected against nature's dart game. Other creatures had taken refuge too. Above us, situated in the branches, blackbirds and sparrows along with two-morning doves clutched quietly to their own protection. There we sat, fully sheltered against one hellacious bunch of violence pounding down on the fields around us. When it ceased ten minutes later, nature decided that one last reminder would be good for our appreciation of its powers. A morning dove dropped its own bomb on my head—splat! Then one of the cows decided to add her own shower to the rain by peeing near us.

Riding in the rain can be a pastoral experience when the setting is right. In Michigan, on a summer ride near Cadillac on Route 131, the rain had been falling for several hours when we spied a pond in the woods near the road. A large maple tree stood near the water, which would provide us with a large umbrella of protection. There is something about a pond in the woods, away from civilization, closer to the essence of life. What stopped us was a silver sheen created on the surface by the raindrops plunking down. The mini-splashes jumped up, reflecting the gray sky.

We parked the bikes in tandem against a maple tree, then sat quietly for a few minutes. From the far cattail-covered shoreline, a muskrat swam across the pond with a branch in its mouth, leaving a V wake behind it. Not ten minutes later, three white-tailed deer walked down to the water's edge for a drink. They sported sleek spring fur coats and looked ready to bind away from danger with the snapping of a twig or a silent scent on the wind. We sat quietly, our bicycles glistening with the raindrops.

In my travels, I have experienced every kind of rain-song blues. But even at the wettest of times, I know that rain makes the grasses grow and flowers bloom. When I'm lucky at the end of a storm, a rainbow arcs across the sky.

Speaking of these sky bouquets, what a special gift for the touring rider. Once the rain departs, the sun comes out, spreading warmth across the land. For a moment in time, a magnificent color band arcs across the rain-soaked sky. Purple, orange, yellow, green and red splash with dazzling intensity against the sunlit clouds. What's at the end of a rainbow? Some say a pot of gold. Others wish for something more than they have. I keep pedaling, often finding more than wishes. The grass turns lushly green. The fence posts begin to dry. The pavement sheds its watery sheen. Birds chirp from every tree. As I press the pedals into the rising land, my legs move me forward into a storm, through the rain, into the sunshine.

As a final note, however, let's face it, if it's raining while you're bicycle touring, it sucks, big time!

(Riding in the rain on the Lewis & Clark Trail along the Columbia River.)

Chapter 30—Grief is Circular: On The Long Ride

"I feel like I am an artist, and my bicycle is my brush."

—Scott Stoll

Have you ever felt the energy of joy? What about winning that soccer game, tennis match or racquetball tournament? What about a triathlon? Maybe a mountain bike race like the Leadville 100? Incredible how every cell in your body 'rises' to such euphoric heights! You feel good down into the deepest reaches of your heart, mind and body. You explode with something that only you can explain...sheer ecstasy!

Wouldn't it be wonderful if the entire human race could feel joy and ultimately, daily happiness every day of the year?

On a long bicycle ride, you feel that joy once you reach the top of a mountain pass, from the grind-up Independence Pass at 12,100 feet in Colorado...to the road leveling off, and then gravity propels you downhill. You feel elated. Or, ride along a rushing whitewater river...where the water imbues your cells with energy, joy, and happiness. Or, how about sitting by a campfire with the embers throbbing with an indescribable beauty? Every cell in your body dances with peaceful energy...spiritual energy. Your entire being feels right with the world.

That's a taste of the good times on long-distance bicycle tours. For months, in 2021, I followed Canadian Arie Hoogerbrugge across Canada, America and now into Mexico. I followed senior citizen Lee Rogowski on his journey from Key

West, Florida to the northernmost part of Maine. One man is young and vibrant. The other is old, overweight, with a heart condition and used an E-bike to cover thousands of miles.

Both men shared that certain courage that it takes to strike out across the planet on a bicycle no less...much like Marco Polo, Captain Cook, John Muir, my lifelong friend Doug Armstrong (all 7 continents on a bicycle), Heinz Stucke (over 50 years across 196 countries) and dozens more. On the female side, Tahnee Seagrave, Finoa Kolbinger, Sanne Cant, Juliet Elliot, Jenny Graham, my friend Bonnie Gagnon and dozens of others. It's certainly been an honor to have met some of them and ridden with them.

What do they all possess in common? Answer: a certain mental, emotional and physical courage to reach outside of themselves for greater wonder, with true grit and pluck beyond the ordinary person. As they live their lives, they inspire the rest of us mortal human beings.

Heinz Stucke said, "It's the unknown around the corner that turns my wheels."

That's not only in bicycling, but all endeavors whether it be Simone Biles, Michael Phelps, Caleb Dressel, Tamyara M. Mensah or Sydney McLaughlin. Some become famous for a moment or a lifetime...yet all face their inner demons...just like you do!

For this long-distance rider, I've enjoyed the great 'highs' in life. It's been a good journey over the years. But I've also discovered the 'lows'... those times when I was so lonely or depressed, that when I looked up...all I could see was the bottom.

I lost my Dad when I was a teenager. One lousy heart attack that hit my Dad at 46 years of age... completely changed the trajectory of my life. Pain, hurt, anger, frustration, meaninglessness and rage. One minute he's there umpiring a baseball game, and the next, he's falling over the catcher and died on the home plate. How do you process that 'event' as a young kid with dreams of a college athletic career? I simply staggered into each day for several years until the pain slipped into my rearview mirrors. I kept going because that's what my dad taught me, "Keep going son, no matter what... and you'll get there...whatever your goal."

But these years later, on long-distance rides across Europe, America's Great Plains, the Continental Divide, Alaska's wilderness endless expanse, the Atacama Desert, the Outback, China, India...I've found that grief is circular.

That grief tumbles around in your mind like clothes in a front-loading dryer. It's amazing how one's mind repeats tragic events just like memories of pleasant events. While on the bike, the miles pile up as the good and bad moments make their mark on your psyche. For me, such subconscious meanderings give me perspective. Since I'm alive, I choose positive thoughts and actions. No sense in wasting time with all the negatives in the world. Like my friend Scott Stoll, who cycled around the world for five years, said, "I feel like I am an artist. My bicycle is the brush."

The Broad Strokes of the Brush of Your Imagination

While riding, my dad visits me. Sometimes, he rides along with me, sits on a ski chairlift, or swims a lap with me. Sometimes, I spot him in a crowded mall only to wake up from a dream. At other times, he's laughing with his buddies on an old 8mm movie. Seeing it immediately brings an instant Niagara of tears. All of the time, his 8"x10" picture hangs in my office. His picture remains in my wallet on every journey. He's with me...he shaped me, he molded me into a man that he wanted to be proud of. Sometimes, I burst out crying because I can't talk to him. I can't hug him, and he can't hug me for assurance.

All I've got are memories, pictures and those 'moments' when he rides with me via my imagination.

For the millions of you who lost your father or mother at an early age, or any age, we share a circular grief that others don't know, cannot understand and won't be able to relate to. I remember that the Spirit of St. Louis flyer Charles Lindbergh said, "Death is the last great adventure."

When I go on THAT adventure, I know my dad will be there straddling his bike with his hands on my bike. We will ride together once again.

(Standing on Lolo Pass where Lewis & Clark camped.)

Chapter 31—Forks in the Road, Stop Signs, Cul De Sacs and Dead Ends on the Highway of Life

> ***"While bicycle adventure-touring turns from days into weeks and weeks into months, you turn a corner in your mind, your heart and your spirit. You tap into a wellspring of eternal emotional bliss. You push two pedals that give your body renewed energy with every stroke. You see things differently while gaining whole new perspectives. You transform from one person into a whole new individual every day. Ironically, no psychologist can figure it out. But you know! The energy of the universe charges through every cell in your body to create pure magic."***
>
> ***—FHW***

While taking a ride down a country road near dusk in my teens, an old farmer, plodding along with his walking stick, abruptly stopped me.

His wrinkled-weathered skin did not diminish the energy in his clear blue eyes. Silver locks flowed from his wide-brimmed hat while his peppered beard gave him a majestic air of wisdom.

"Where you goin' sonny?" he asked.

"Just taking a ride to catch a few fire-flies when the night settles in on us," I said. "They seem to show their magic just as the sun goes down, but before the stars come out. I like the way they turn the long grass into streetlamps, but none of the city noise to go with it."

"Should be a lot of them out this evening as soon as the red-winged blackbirds fall silent," he said. "So, if you don't mind my asking, where are you going with your life?"

"My mom wants me to go to college," I said. "She said it will give me a leg-up on living as well as make me a better-educated man."

"Good for you," he said. "But what do you want to do with your life?"

"After I graduate from college," I said, "I want to travel the world before settling down for a job. I want to figure out some things about this life."

"Do you mind a bit of advice?" he asked.

"My dad told me to listen to my elders to learn their wisdom," I said.

"The path to your destiny has 'forks in road' that require the imperfect ability to discern the difference between opportunity and pitfalls," he said. "You will make mistakes in judgment. You will fail often. But remember to make those failures into stepping-stones toward your ultimate success. Never get down on yourself. None of it comes easy, but it gets easier as you travel the path with a good attitude, application by work and your ingenuity."

"My dad said something like that," I said.

"Smart dad," he said. "In addition to 'forks' there will be 'cul de sac's ' or 'dead ends' where you rest and re-evaluate the route you have taken. Everyone comes to these markers at some point. You will become wiser. Experience is the best teacher. So, if you find yourself going down the wrong road, or the route isn't working for you, turn around and go back. When you return to your original location, strike out in a new direction with the wisdom you learned while you traveled along the wrong road."

"That works for me," I said.

"As a young man, you are heading toward your 'destiny,' he said. "To me, the term 'destiny' implies a pre-ordained purpose by some higher power. This implies a personal belief in that higher power. That may or may not work for you. It also implies that one's 'destiny' answers the question, 'Why am I here?' You will find out on your journey."

"Another thing," he said. "Your mom is right... choose your friends carefully. You will adopt some of their characteristics into your personality. When you hang with the smarter, more responsible folks in your school, you become more like them and succeed like them."

"Additionally, memories of your experiences are what come to you in those future quiet times with yourself. Make sure you accept yourself at all times. Even if you are not sure, assume a sense of confidence in your own talents whatever they might be or come to be."

"Some memories will be filled with regret, and some will be joyous. You will have both in your life. You get to choose the number of each by the way you live. And one final thought from my days of meditation on hay bales and sitting beside a quiet pond with dragonflies, turtles, snakes and muskrats: everything you become, you chose. And everything you chose, you wanted."

As the fireflies lit the long grass, the old man tipped his hat before continuing on into the gathering darkness.

"Thank you, sir," I said, as I rode into the magic of fireflies and stars twinkling in the sky.

(The Grand Tetons in Grand Teton National Park, Wyoming.)

Chapter 32—Savage Moment in Yellowstone National Park

> ***"There's something overwhelming about being in raw nature. It's got an aura about it is that is really kind of majestic and spiritual."***
>
> ***—Christopher Lloyd***

On my solo journey from Mexico to Canada on the Continental Divide, I hooked up with two Irishmen for a week, but they cut west after viewing Old Faithful.

When Gerry and Dave pedaled westward, I felt my heart grow sad. At the gate entrance of Madison Junction campground, I paid my bill for the "Hike-biker" section. No laughter tonight around the campfire. I pitched my tent in silence. I aired up my mattress and fluffed up my sleeping bag. I set up my cooking gear and snugged up my miner's lamp around my head. Darkness crept in silently. I cooked my dinner in silence. I wrote my notes quietly. Loneliness made its way into my soul.

"Loneliness is the human condition. Cultivate it. The way it tunnels into you allows your soul room to grow. Never expect to outgrow loneliness. Never hope to find people who will understand you, someone to fill that space. An intelligent, sensitive person is the exception, the very great exception. If you expect to find people who will understand you, you will grow murderous with disappointment. The best you'll ever do is to understand yourself, know what it is that you want, and not let the cattle stand in your way."—Janet Fitch, White Oleander

Thankfully, I like the kind of person I am. I've made my parents proud. As I said at the beginning of this adventure, I broadcast "high vibrational energy" wherever I go. I've heard that, if you radiate friendly vibrations, friends naturally gravitate toward you. If you give love, you will receive love in return. Better to share with Gerry and Dave for a week than not at all. They became another thread in the tapestry of my life. I feel rich, funny and more blessed by having spent such a grand time with two Irishman. I count my blessings.

The next day, I pulled down my tent and pedaled onto the highway by 6:30 a.m. I rolled along the Gibbon River to pass by a steaming pond on the opposite side of the road. Very quiet. No traffic. I sensed nature's rhythms pulsing through the early morning hour. Soon, I viewed 60 feet of descent and the white water of Gibbon Falls. It resembled a bride's veil. Still no traffic.

Back on the road, I stopped on a bridge with the Gibbon River crossing underneath me. I took a few shots of the rising sun sparkling on the waters. So peaceful.

Once again, I made the adventure my companion. I delighted in the sheer beauty all around me. I felt my spirit renewing again on my wondrous journey.

I pedaled with vigor into the clear, crisp morning air, through deep forests and along the Gibbon River about 30 yards away on the west side of the highway. Above the river, a red tail hawk followed the current southward, probably on his breakfast patrol. A big fat buffalo munched grass on the east side of the river. Still no traffic. On my left, on the far side of the river, I noticed a cow elk bending down to take a drink. I love seeing majestic elk, moose and deer. They soothe my soul.

Without warning, I barely caught the big, hairy figure of... oh my God, a grizzly bear... as he crept along the deep grass on the far side of the river until he got within 30 feet of the elk... from out of the grass cover, he charged the elk...she saw him and stood up, startled, and started to bolt backward away from the river... but within seconds, the 700-pound grizzly ran right into the cow elk and grabbed it by the shoulders with his three-inch claws... in a moment, he chewed into the bottom of the elk's neck and twisted his huge anvil head... almost like poetry in motion, his enormous body rode the elk down to the ground... where he held her until she could no longer struggle... she stopped... fell limp... life feeds on life and death feeds life.

"Holy crap," I exclaimed as I stopped Condor in stunned amazement.

While I probably should have been scared to death, it happened so fast that I just stopped and stared. I stood across the river and 40 yards away from the bear. The grizzly could care less about me. His breakfast lay in a bloody mess in front of him. I ripped out my camera to take pictures. He began feeding on the carcass. He ripped open the belly and took out his favorite parts. His bloody muzzle turned bright red.

I stood behind a tree, but still astride Condor just in case I had to ride like the wind. I even pointed Condor downstream to give me more speed, quickly, should the grizzly notice me and figure me for dessert. Of course, at 185 pounds, I didn't mean much to his main course of 1,000 pounds of elk meat.

My God! I am blessed with this moment," I muttered to myself.

Within a half hour, a dozen cars stopped to see why I kept snapping pictures. Soon, a whole slew of cars emptied and folks with 1000 mm lenses snapped pictures off fancy tripods. Shortly, three bald eagles landed by the carcass. The bear walked off a distance and snoozed. The eagles closed in for early morning snacks. Then, Mr. Grizzly woke up in 10 minutes and returned to feeding. Amazingly, he jumped into the river to swat at fish or something. His actions appeared comical from where I stood. Within the next hour, more tourists arrived.

I figured I'd seen the best show of the day and turned Condor northward to seek my fortune around the next bend in the road. I've experienced some amazing moments on Condor, and this one rides up there with the top 10 of my life. As I said in my quote about bicycle touring, “The long-distance bicyclist carries an insatiable desire to interact with possibilities that may emerge around the next bend in the road. The bicyclist lives in that moment and then pedals forward to the next moment, always advancing, never in retreat.”

As John Muir said, “How many hearts with warm red blood in them are beating under cover of the woods, and how many teeth and eyes are shining? A multitude of animal people, intimately related to us, but whose lives we know almost nothing, are as busy about their own affairs as we are about ours.”

To that quote, I say, “Holy catfish, what the hell of a start to this day! It doesn’t get any better than this.”

(Grizzly sitting by his morning meal, taking a rest from eating.)

Chapter 33—Oracle Of The Soul: Discovering Gems of Understanding

> ***"Mankind has invested more than four million years of evolution in the attempt to avoid physical exertion. Now a group of backward-thinking atavists mounted on foot-powered pairs of Hula-Hoops would have us pumping our legs, gritting our teeth, and searing our lungs as though we were being chased across the Pleistocene savanna by saber-toothed tigers. Think of the hopes, the dreams, the effort, the brilliance, the pure force of will that, over the eons, has gone into the creation of the Cadillac Coupe de Ville. Bicycle riders would have us throw all this on the ash heap of history."***
>
> *—P.J. O'Rourke*

On a bike ride through Tennessee, I happened to stop by a Warm Showers host. That night, in his backyard, we sat around a campfire with four other cyclists who had pitched their tents on his green lawn. Of course, his warm shower was appreciated!

The Warm Showers concept interests me because I think it creates international goodwill and friendships. I've hosted dozens of international visitors from China, Japan, India, Holland, Norway, Italy, France, Sweden, Germany, Austria, Mexico, Africa and more—at my home in Golden, CO. Sandi and I live on Route 40, the main drag from San Francisco to the East Coast. We're the last stop as you exit the Rocky Mountains to enter the Great Plains.

It's really special when you meet people with an interest in exploring our planet on bicycles. Last fall, we enjoyed dinner with Sue and Pete Reah from Great Britain. They cycled across America coast-to-coast last summer. We still keep in touch. We met Lars and Maud bicycling the Continental Divide; they hailed from Holland as they stayed for several days. Lovely couples.

That night in the hills of Tennessee, our host told us a story about the "Gems of Understanding" he had learned on his travels around the world.

As the embers burned and the smoke curled into the night sky, he related about a special sage in a king's court in medieval times:

"As you grew up, you experienced different lessons along your life-path. You discovered a hot stove hurt when you touched it. A candle flame caused pain when you passed your finger over it. A rosebush thorn made your finger bleed. A bee sting caused you terrible agony," he said. "From those experiences, you avoided the obvious in your daily meanderings. Marching into your teens, you discovered friendship, jealousy and betrayal. A bully beat you up. A girlfriend undermined you in your pursuit of a boyfriend or vice versa.

"In nature, you learned to run for cover during a lightning storm. When a dog gave chase, you picked up a stick to protect yourself.

"You learned life lessons either by your parents advising you or you learned the hard way by direct experience.

"As you grew into your twenties, relationships grew more complicated, you worked a job with acerbic bosses and cantankerous fellow employees. You discovered many different aspects of how people operate in the world.

"Along the way, you picked up new understandings and created game plans on how to deal with your circumstances.

"All the while, you became a better you. But sometimes, you wondered about your choices or predicaments.

"I'm reminded of the ancient king who held court each day. He beckoned the local sage for words of wisdom. Each day for a year, the sage brought the king an overly ripe piece of fruit along with a witty statement. When the sage left, the king tossed the fruit into a hole in a pillar where it fell to the basement, untouched.

"One day, after the sage gave the king the overly ripe fruit, he turned to exit, but noticed the king tossing the fruit into the pillar hole."

"What are you doing?" asked the sage. "Did you not know I gifted you with a gem in the middle of each fruit?"

"The king made an excuse before the sage exited the throne room. Quickly, the king ordered a knave to recapture the fruit."

The king cut it open to reveal a valuable gem. He said, "I never knew such beauty could be found inside an aged piece of fruit."

"The king ordered his staff to recover the gems from all the fruits in the basement. The gems of knowledge enlightened him, which allowed him greater understanding. He became a better king for all the people of his realm.

"The great writer Thomas Moore said that every person faces the deadly turpitudes of living: obsessions, addictions, depression, loss of meaning, judging others, violence, anger, hate and prejudice.

"It's your challenge to connect with the divine in you. You might call it the "spiritual" within you. Choose to identify with your higher self. That quest creates a transformation that leads to your better well-being and better choices.

"When bad things happen to you, decode the experience to see the gem. As you discover the synchronicity of the lesson, take advantage of it. Synchronicity coupled with purpose equals "coincidence."

"Once you step into the "flow" of life, those synchronicities multiply because your energies coordinate with the natural vibrations of the universe.

"Engage these talents: walk in the light, walk tall, walk with a song, walk strong, walk wise, walk with hope, walk with joy, walk with purpose and walk with passion. People notice your demeanor. You attract them to their own higher self.

"Take advantage of a bitter experience, betrayal of a friend, unfair treatment by another or any of the overly ripe experiences of life. You will find a "gem" in the rotten fruit that will enhance your life beyond all ordinary understanding."

That night, after his story about discovering the "gems" of life, I sat there with an appreciation that everyone brings 'skin' to the game of life. Whether it's a campfire with strangers or spending time with your family, this thing called 'living' allows special moments, special times and special people you meet on your bicycle travels.

And to those of you, I am going to meet this summer while I pedal across America, I'm excited to greet you. I'm excited to share it with you. I want to hear your story. Together, let's make this a better world of understanding and acceptance. To that, I say, keep pedaling. It's a hell of a ride.

(Sandi eating lunch on the Lewis & Clark Trail.)

Chapter 34—Gnarly, mystical energy that flies out of your body, onto the pedals, and into the wild blue yonder

One thing equates to your quest: adventure may not always be comfortable, but it's still an adventure.

As we traveled down Big Sur on the West Coast of California, we awoke to birds squawking in the trees and the sound of waves crashing on the beach. Seagulls bickered with one another while pelicans glided over the crest of waves. We stretched, cooked breakfast, pulled up the tent, and packed the gear.

For the entire morning, Sandi and I cranked up 1,000-foot cliffs only to descend back down to 300 feet. The blue Pacific Ocean waters sparkled like trillions of diamonds. Aspirin-white waves crashed onto sandy beaches. Every kind of bird flew in every kind of formation. The road resembled a thin snake with no end as it slithered around every contour of the terrain.

At one moment, we traveled through dense woods and just as suddenly, upward along a barren rock cliff. Out in the water, rock islands featured hundreds of birds such as cormorants, pelicans and seagulls. Otters slapped their flippers as they floated on their backs. Seals played in the surf.

The stunning scenery around us made the pedaling incidental. It felt like when those kids rode with E.T. across the full moon. A feeling swept over us like we were riding through a dream. We pedaled an elegant serpent meandering on the wings of the Pacific Ocean.

Some call it "satori" while others feel an almost drug-like "high" racing through their systems. The Greek philosopher Aristotle spoke about it in his Nicomachean Ethics book. He attempted to define happiness.

Essentially, he said that human happiness is not so much an outcome or end-state, but a realization of one's true nature. Or, fulfilling one's potential and living with a sense of daily joy. That certainly describes bicycle touring or even day rides on your steel fun machine.

In one sense, in this highly complex world, many of us yearn for simple lives, peaceful lives and tranquil lives. A bicycle tour brings out the very essence of "satori" in that you engage several very basic needs in life: sleep, eat, pedal, purpose, explore and live creatively. We define "satori" as the perfect moment. It may last seconds, minutes or a lifetime. Another term, "eudemonia" hits when you combine your bliss with your path. Once into eudemonia, you effervesce with joy. Past that, the world breaks other peoples' hearts, but for this moment in your life, you enjoy the pure daily joy of living.

The Big Sur creates gnarly, mystical energy that flies out of your body, onto the pedals and into the wild blue yonder. You stop to gasp at the beauty at every ocean point vista overlook. Of all the wonder of the West Coast of California, the Big Sur captures your youth to leave memories for your lifetime.

(Stopping for a rest along Big Sur, California.)

Chapter 35—A Sense of Glee, Joy, Celebration

> ***"Movement equates to the lifeblood of bicycling. You move through space and you move through time. You move into the morning until you pedal into the evening. You transfer energy from your body to the pedals to the rotation of the wheels. At each point, the sun lights your path while life gallops along its own journey. You realize a wondrous connection to the natural world as you roll through it at 12 miles per hour. You might call it the perfect speed of life. Bicycling might be deemed one of the spiritual miracles of the universe."***
>
> ***—FHW***

The night before, we slept in the pines along the road on the Lewis & Clark Trail in Montana. We left the main highway on a dirt road that looked very little traveled. Gorgeous scenery everywhere we looked! The night sky featured millions of stars, a full moon, and meteors slashing across the ink-black of space. It was almost like they put an exclamation point at the end of a beautiful day of riding. We cooked dinner over our one-burner stove.

For some reason, the food tastes like a Waldorf-Astoria high-class seven-course dinner every night while pedaling all day. And the trimmings, well, you just can't beat the sound of a Great Horned Owl hooting in the distance, or crickets chirping, or a squirrel chattering in a nearby tree. Before sunset, we watched two hummingbirds working a flower patch near our camp.

And the sky, well, those thunderheads lit up with the setting of the sun. Purple-pink dominated the heavens while we sat on our 'boulder' chairs watching the Natural World entertain us.

In the morning, we awoke to a sunny sky, dew drops on the grass, and a few spider webs that had been weaved during the night, one of them on the corner of the seat tube and top tube of Sandi's bike. We felt bad that we had to dismantle it.

After breakfast, we were packing up when a rancher stopped by in his pick-up truck. He rolled down his window, "I don't want to alarm you folks, but there's a big grizzly walking down this road in this direction about a mile away."

"Thank you," I said. "Sandi, let's gracefully get these bikes packed and get the hell out of here..."

Have you ever heard of "flashing packing"? Well, we quickly, with a sense of urgency, flash-packed our bikes within minutes. We jumped on them and pedaled out to the road with a keen sense of really being alive. I mean, I've been face-to-face with grizzly bears on my journeys through Alaska. Lucky to be alive after having starred one down outside my tent on the Russian River one morning when I woke up. It wasn't my day to die. He looked at me only five feet away, and then, walked down to the river. I nearly peed my pants. That's another story I will tell in Chapter 58.

On the road, eastbound, we calmed down rather quickly as we pedaled along beautiful meadows filled with flowers. One patch of White Mountain daisies covered five full acres. It stunned us as it rolled with the terrain and glistened in the morning sun. We heard the bees humming from one flower to another.

"Sandi," I said. "Let's get a picture of you in the wildflowers."

"I'm game," she said. "You want me to take my clothes off to make them authentic?"

"Dear," I said. "Just make it a PG picture showing that you're enjoying yourself."

"Well, since we just escaped certain death if that grizzly had come upon our campsite, yes, I'm thankful to be alive. Tell me why I married you again?"

"Remember, I said I loved adventure when we first met," I said. "You said you liked adventure, too. So, here you are...let's get a picture of you on this adventure."

Sandi walked into the field. She gave a dozen poses from different stances. (Two I can't show on social media!) The picture I love best is the one she reclined in the flowers and stuck her feet up. She outstretched her arms as if accepting the beauty, joy, energy, spiritual blessings and warmth of Mother Earth.

Ralph Waldo Emerson, a dear friend of Thoreau said, "The Earth laughs in Flowers."

"Flowers" by Albert Lainghton

They are autographs of angels, penned
In Nature's green-leaved book, in blended tints,
Borrowed from rainbows and the sunset skies,
And written everywhere–on plain and hill,
In lonely dells, mid crowded haunts of men.
On the broad prairies, where no eye save God's
May read their silent, sacred mysteries. Thank God for flowers!
They gladden human hearts, Seraphic breathings part their fragrant lips,
With whisperings of Heaven.

Following the Lewis & Clark Trail, Montana, on tour through the endless energy of flowers lining the roads of our lives.

(Sandi relaxing in a field of wildflowers.)

Chapter 36—Two Irishmen Across America: Wearing One Pair of Underwear

> ***"With friends, you laugh with abandon, you talk with freedom of expression, you smile with a sense of joy, and you face the world with courage. A best friend is one of the miracles of the universe."***
>
> ***—FHW***

You meet all sorts of people on a bicycle tour. Some quiet, some talkative, some open, some closed and some able to make you laugh until your jaw cracks. On my ride up the Continental Divide, in Riverview, Colorado, I met two Irishmen riding coast-to-coast across America—Gerry Mulroy and Dave Turner from Drogheda, Ireland. Both are over 50 and both are filled with Irish humor.

That first night, at the Mangy Moose Café, they drained a few pints while they struck every funny bone in my body. From that night for the next 10 days, when they cut west at Madison Junction, Yellowstone National Park, I laughed often and hard. Their humor caused me to wake up in the middle of the night, laughing.

At one point, we mounted our bikes and pedaled along the Firehole River. We saw elk and bison grazing in the rich watershed. Later in the day, we reached Firehole Falls with its bubbling pools, steaming vents and beautiful designs coloring the runoff. Nature's artwork captivated us like few other sights on the planet at those pools.

At one point, a road crew stopped us for 15 minutes. The guy held up a stop sign. A motorcyclist waited right beside us.

Two SUVs rolled up with their windows rolled down, with the wives in the passenger front seats. At that moment, Gerry told his story about how Dave and he had been wearing the same single pair of underwear across the entire United States—to save on washing. The motorcyclist took note, the Stop Sign-holder listened hard and the two ladies in the SUVs leaned their ears into the tale.

"Yes, I brought one pair of underwear when we started on the beach in Virginia eight weeks ago, but Dave forgot his pair in the motel," said Gerry. "Each night, after a shower, I switched the outside in, and next night the inside out. I did that every day for a week. Then, I threw them over to Dave and he did the same. Wear them all day and then, turn them inside out and outside in. After two weeks, we followed the usual routine. Then, so as to save that one pair, we turned them front to back and back to front. "

Gerry, a master storyteller sucked everyone into his 'one pair of underwear' saga with pertinent gesticulations and facial contortions. By that time, the ladies in the SUVs couldn't stop laughing. The motorcyclist checked his underwear, and I could not contain myself. The Stop-Sign holder roared with laughter.

"After a month," said Gerry. "We would throw the one pair of underwear up against the motel room shower tile. If it stuck like Velcro, we would wash that one pair of underwear. If not, I would take the next shift by wearing that underwear for that week. That way, we discovered we could cross the entire the North American Continent wearing only one pair of underwear."

I asked Dave, "What did one of you wear when you weren't wearing the one pair of underwear?"

"Commando!" Dave said.

The ladies in the SUVs could hardly contain themselves—they laughed so hard. I nearly lost control of my bike from my belly laughter. The motorcyclist said, "I need a drink." The Stop Sign holder said, "I've got to find a new job."

I leaned over to the ladies in the SUVs, "After a week of this humor, I need special counseling." They roared with more laughter. Finally, the Stop Sign-holder let us pass and we pedaled forward. As usual, Gerry carried a smirk on his face.

"In the sweetness of friendship, let there be laughter and the sharing of pleasures. For in the dew of little things, the heart finds its morning, and life is refreshed." K. Gibran

(Dave, Frosty, Gerry riding through the Grand Tetons.)

Chapter 37—Ever Change the Oil in Your Knees?

"How does it feel to be on the front end of a bicycle journey that promises hardship, true grit, the unknown, and it's bound to test your body, heart, mind and spirit? Long distance bicycle touring challenges you in other ways: patience in dealing with fellow riders who haul their own emotional baggage. Everybody travels with a delicate bag of tricks in their personal backpack. You face constant emotions. You may cry thinking about the loss of a loved one while pedaling. That event may burn deeply into your mind—and the only way to release it—to cry. And then, there's the joy of the moment!

That's the magic of long-distance bicycle adventures. You renew your mind, you tear down and build up your body, you choose your path to the end of the ride. You face crotch rot, sore butt, cramping legs, sweaty body and a voracious appetite. With the magic of bicycling, you become the adventure."

—FHW

Heat punctuates the air in South Georgia every summer. Humidity sticks to the skin like a plastic sandwich wrap. For riding, the combination is torture. All I could think about while sweating my way down the road was the next convenience store where I could buy a half gallon of ice-cold orange juice.

How much did I sweat on Route 82 headed into Waycross? It was so hot and humid like pedaling inside a steam sauna. Sweat dripped from my scalp, before running down the back of my spine where it soaked into my shirt. From my forehead, it ran down into my glasses where it pooled on the rims. Some of it escaped down my nose where it dripped onto the top tube, then splattered onto my legs. Sweat hung from my chin and ear lobes until I shook it off. It ran down my arms, glistening through the hairs until it soaked my riding gloves. Rest stops made it worse when it dried and left salt cakes on my body and clothes.

Nonetheless, I was having a good time. A passing car's bumper sticker said it all: "A bad day of bicycling is better than a good day of work." It was true, I didn't mind the sweat because I was exploring the South. I'm not saying that it was scads of fun, nor was I in comfort, but at that moment in Georgia, that's the way it was—hot and miserable. I accepted it because complaining would be useless. It is times like that, especially on a bike, I just live; I accept the moment. That's the special intrigue of bicycle touring. Sure, I love riding on the flats on an autumn day. It's easy pedaling, and the air is cool. I'm comfortable and dry. It sure beats busting my butt going up on a 6,000-foot climb on a hot day. But here's the catch. The flats have their own beauty, but it doesn't compare to the mountains. Given the choice, I'd take the mountains even with the price of the climb.

That's the point—I accept the flats when they are happening, yet love the mountains when it's time for climbing. I couldn't change any of it at one moment anyway. I take it a day at a time.

No doubt about it that muggy day in South Georgia. I couldn't wait for a convenience store. I was ready to buy their entire stock of orange juice. I was dehydrated and I couldn't drink fast enough to replenish my fluids. Ahead on the left, I spotted a dilapidated paint-chipped building kitty-corner to the pavement. Gray moss hung down the sides of the faded white paint and red dust lined the windowsills. Coke and Pepsi coolers with their colored logos stood like military sentries on both sides of a broken screen door. Two faded red Texaco gas pumps with broken glass over the meters stood out in the sun. A bent tin roof provided shade for two long benches alongside the building. I looked like a dripping fountain as I rode up near the gas pumps and laid my bike against a pole. Two old men stared at me, but said nothing. Off to the side, a thin, gray-haired black man in tattered clothes sat gumming his ice cream.

Seconds later the door slammed behind me, kicking up a dozen flies on the screen mesh. Inside, a dirty wood floor led past a huge lady sitting behind the counter, knitting a sweater. She wore a basketful of curlers in her hair, with three extra chins tumbling down from below her lips. I headed for the cooler.

"How ya'll today?" she asked.

"Just fine ma'am," I replied. "Sure, am thirsty. Does it get any hotter than this?"

"You better believe it, son," she said. "Last week, it was 96 with the humidity over 90."

"How can you stand it?" I asked.

"The weather is like the flies," she replied. "You can't do nothin' about 'em, so you just get used to 'em."

"I guess you're right," I said. "Do you have any half-gallons of OJ? I only see quarts."

"What ya'll see is what ya'll get."

"You got any cookies?"

"Yes sir, near the bread on the second aisle over."

I paid for two quarts of orange juice and a bag of chocolate chips. Seconds later, the screen door slammed behind me, kicking up the flies again. An old geezer had pulled up to the pumps and was filling his pickup with gas. He complained about the heat. The two old men continued staring at me in silence. I wondered if they were alive.

After swigging the first quart, I inhaled a handful of cookies. A mongrel dog got up from behind the Pepsi cooler, walked over, and sniffed me. He looked at my bag of cookies with pleading eyes. "Okay buddy, here's one for you, but that's all you get unless you want to pedal my bicycle down the road." I flipped him a cookie. He walked back to his hardwood bed and began crunching on his prize. I grabbed the orange juice and belted down half the jug. The cold liquid slid down my throat and filled my stomach. After chewing on the second handful of cookies, I noticed my chain was dry. I tossed the bag of cookies onto the pack along with the second jug of orange juice. After unzipping my tool pouch, I grabbed the spray can and spun the crank backwards. The chain rolled through the pulleys, threaded its way around the freewheel, and back toward the middle chain ring. Most of the lengths were dry.

"You gotta check this chain more often," I muttered to myself. "This chain's dry as a bone."

I sprayed both pulley axles and drenched the freewheel. I cranked the pedals backwards slowly, spraying the chain as it came off the lower pulley. No matter how careful I was, oil sprayed onto the rim. As I squatted there, sweat dripping down from my brow and chin, the black man shuffled toward me. I was nearly done when he stood over me.

"Ever change the oil in yer' knees?" he mumbled.

"What?" I asked, looking up at him.

"You ever change the oil in yer' knees?" he repeated more clearly.

At first, I didn't know how to answer, but then I thought about it saying, "Only when they squeak, sir."

He laughed through his gums. The last of his ice cream cone vanished into his mouth.

"How far have you ridden that bicycle anyways?"

"From the Golden Gate Bridge in San Francisco," I said.

"Naw! You ain't gonna tell ole Charlie a lie now are ya'?" he said. "The devil gonna take you if you don't tell the truth now ya' hear?"

"It's true, I rode this bicycle starting from the Golden Gate Bridge. I've been on the road for three months. It's no big deal. Lots of people have ridden across America on a bicycle."

"Well, I'll be hanged," he said. "I never dreamed a man could ride across this whole country."

"Some people have ridden a bicycle around the world."

We got to talking, ole Charlie and me. This 91-year-old man, wearing tattered clothes, was the son of a slave who was freed by Lincoln back in 1865. This toothless man, with clouded black eyes, yet a clear mind, possessed more historical knowledge than a history book. His father was brought over to America in chains on a slave ship to pick cotton in the Carolinas. When things heated up over the abolitionist movement, his father was sold to a tobacco grower in Waycross. After the Civil War, things didn't change much for his father, except he got married and fathered five children. Charlie was the youngest. He never went to school and to this day couldn't read or write. He had worked on farms all his life and had outlived his wife and four kids, save one.

He felt that Franklin Roosevelt was the greatest president, but he wished that Jesse Jackson would one day live in the White House. If Jesse couldn't make it, then Bill Cosby would make a good second choice, to keep some humor in politics.

This intriguing old man captivated me for an hour. He was an enthusiastic, walking, talking history book. He hadn't been out of the county in his 91 years, but he had listened to radios, then television, and stored everything he had learned in a lucid memory. As he talked, a pattern of his life and his attitude illuminated every historical perspective. What held my attention was his span of reference. He was born in 1889 before electricity, cars and paved roads. In his time, he had seen the entire modern world develop with unbelievable speed.

"What was the greatest moment of your life?" I asked.

"There was such a great many moments Charlie had seen, but maybe when Mr. Neil Armstrong walked on the moon, that has to be the greatest moment of Charlie's life," he said. "All his life, Charlie has been lookin' up at that ole man in the moon, but when Mr. Armstrong walked on it, well, that was the greatest moment."

"How about the worst?"

"Lotta' worsts young fella'," he said. "These many years later, Charlie can't figure out why human beings have to keep hurtin' each other."

"What's the most important thing in life?" I asked.

"After good health, it's got to be love. You get to love someone. And someone gets to love you."

Later, Charlie departed with his 70-year-old son. I watched as they sped away down the dusty dirt road leading into the Georgia backcountry.

The next day, I reached the Atlantic Ocean. My coast-to-coast adventure ended, but Charlie and dozens of other people convinced me that nothing ends until you die. Without question, living is an attitude manifested by spirit.

Bicycle touring is the spiritual vehicle for adventure that I call traveling at “human speed.” It beats the measured pace of walking yet surpasses in quality experiences the alacrity of 60 miles per hour. You can smell the flowers along the way. The day is yours and the road leads you anywhere in the world. Along the way, some of the people you meet, share the simplest, basic truths in life. Have I ever changed the oil in my knees?

Only when they squeak.

(Lady selling fruits and vegetables from her pickup truck in South Georgia.)

Chapter 38—Wonder of Bicycle Travel: Magic Moments

> ***"What does a man (woman) need—really need? A few pounds of food each day, heat and shelter, six feet to lie down in - and some form of working activity that will yield a sense of accomplishment. That's all in the material sense, and we know it. But we are brainwashed by our economic system until we end up in a tomb beneath a pyramid of time—payments, mortgages, preposterous gadgetry, playthings that divert our attention for the sheer idiocy of the charade.***
>
> ***The years thunder by, the dreams of youth grow dim where they lie caked in dust on the shelves of patience. Before we know it, the tomb is sealed. Where, then, lies the answer? In choice. Which shall it be: bankruptcy of purse or bankruptcy of life?"***
>
> ***—Sterling Hayden, Wanderer***

When the eclipse of the sun occurred in 2017, we stood on the edge of the precipice of Niagara Falls. With the crystal clear green water raging over the edge, it tumbled downward into white mist. The sun caught that vapor to create a double rainbow across the chasm. Above, a one-quarter eclipse of the sun energized the sky while hundreds of sightseers cheered with delight while looking at that natural phenomenon through their gray-colored protective glasses.

"We're watching a natural trifecta of Nature's epic moments," said Don. "I don't know how it can get any better than this."

"You got that right," said Gerry. "This ice cream cone sums it up for me... life is good on my bicycle."

It could happen in the morning when you pedal down the highway to see dewdrops sparkling off the leaves of a cherry tree. You stop to pull cherries off the tree along the Lewis and Clark Trail in Oregon. Their succulent sugars bathe your mouth with magical energy and cause your taste buds to turn summersaults on your tongue.

How about that moment when you saw a DQ along Route 66 in New Mexico? You could not stop yourself from buying an ice cream cone that slid down your throat with all the joy of a culinary waterslide that you loved when you were a kid. It splashed your entire being with happiness.

Do you remember that night by the fire with new cycling friends camping in Morro Bay, California on Route 101, with Arctic Terns, Canada geese and another 50 species of migratory birds squawking in the water? How about those flames licking the night air while you watched your dinner bubble up on the coals—ready to be devoured by your hungry body? The magic of a day well lived day on your bicycle!

Remember that ride across Kansas when the sun hung low in the sky to create your own shadow that stretched 30 yards across the highway into the next field? Your shadow followed you, delighted you and at the end, when the sun burned into the western sky, you found yourself missing its magic—when your shadow suddenly vanished—poof! Yet, the memory delighted you!

How about that moment this summer, pedaling with your friend on East River Road along the Yellowstone River, Montana headed south toward Yellowstone National Park? The western sky burned scorching orange colors into the thunderheads in the heavens at the end of the day. You felt a slight mist of rain falling lightly on your shoulders. As you raised your eyes to the east, a double rainbow touched down where the sun blazed on a 100-acre meadow of summer green. Talk about magical moments!

"Don, look to the East," I yelled.

"Holy catfish," my friend said. "My God! It doesn't get any better than this!"

Can any greater joy come from life than living inside the 'moment' of an adventure? It may be a fleeting 'high', a stranger that changes your life, an animal that delights you or frightens you, a struggle where you triumphed, or even failed, yet you braved the challenge. Those moments present you with uncommon experiences that give your life eternal expectations. That's adventure!

(Rainbow over the mountains north side of Yellowstone National Park.)

SECTION II: TOURING SOUTH AMERICA

Chapter 39—Corridor of the Giants

"Raw adventure takes guts, gumption and true grit. On this rugged ride over the Andes, we marshalled every bit of courage we could gather on one of the roughest roads in South America. Rain, snow, winds, lightning, gravel, raging rivers and altitude tested us. At the same time, our courage brought us to the doorstep of humanity's quest to explore this amazing planet. We succeeded."

—FHW

No matter how long you live in your own town, the time comes when you want to explore outside the city limits. Maybe something "excites" you out there beyond the horizon. At first, it may seem frightening. I cried the first time I flew to a foreign land. Each time, however, it got easier. My interest was piqued because I grew confident that riding in exotic lands offered me special glimpses into cultures different than my own. South America exceeded my expectations.

Not only that, there is something enthralling about sitting on your saddle on your bike at the top of South America and pointing it southward. You're on the front end of a grand adventure. Thousands of miles separate you from Tierra del Fuego a short hop from Antarctica. Along the way, you're in for some amazing life experiences.

"You know, this is what we came for," the mud-covered bicyclists said. "This is the toughest riding of my life. What's even better is that I think it's going to get worse."

He talked about a little-known dirt track cutting through the Andes from La Paz, Bolivia to Arica, Chile. It's called the El Camino Highway. It's rough, tricky, sometimes treacherous, and always challenging. Nearly 300 miles long, it starts out at 12,000 feet, rises to 15,500, and plummets to sea level. This dirt road crosses astounding Andean landscapes on its way to the Pacific Ocean. It's not for the faint of heart, nor for those who need a sag wagon. This bicycle expedition provides raw adventure. Few roads in South America equal this ride for pure serendipity.

Back home, friends and acquaintances bombarded us with reports of danger "down there." We would be gunned down by drug cartels, or thieves would leave us marooned in the desert stripped of our clothes but save our underwear. I admit it, with all the press reports, I felt concerned. Pedaling through Third World countries might be courting danger. I didn't show it to anyone, but I too felt nervous. Washington DC offers a special hotline to inform international travelers about the current risks in every region of the world. After talking with them about our intended route through South America, they advised us not to travel south out of Bogota, Columbia to Quito, Ecuador. Too much guerrilla warfare going on. No problem, we'll fly over that area. We hated the idea of stopping bullets with our tender bodies.

For the most part, however, people in countries around the world, live quiet, routine lives. Except for a few hot spots, folks go about their daily living without much excitement.

My riding partners, Doug, Bryan and I knew the route from La Paz, Bolivia to Arica, Chile was mostly unpaved. It featured altitude changes, severe weather patterns, and no medical facilities. Food and water contamination became a valid concern. A breakdown could end the ride for any one of us. We beefed up our bikes with 40-spoke rims and bought the best racks available. We packed rain and cold weather gear along with spare chains and derailleurs into our panniers. We could not find out about food supplies, so we carried six days of provisions. That amounted to 90 to 100 pounds of gear on each bike.

La Paz, Bolivia, population one million, is a large metropolitan city located in a valley that resembles a huge football stadium sunk into a gigantic hole. The city is 1,000 feet below the altiplano. (The altiplano is a treeless, high-altitude plain of land in Bolivia that averages 12,000 feet.) A four-lane expressway winds along the edge until it drops to the metropolis at the bottom. Two cultures exist. Third World misery inhabits the rim above the city, while order and relatively clean conditions prevail below. Dramatic snowcapped 21,000-foot peaks surround La Paz. On a clear day, beautiful panoramas startle a first-time visitor.

We spent four days in La Paz. The toilets didn't work and we faced contaminated water. Buildings were in disrepair—not much different from any metropolitan city in the USA. Cars were run until they dropped dead in their tracks. Even then, they were resurrected like a cat with nine lives, with wire and tape, and pushed back onto the road until they died again—beyond any hope of a tenth life.

We pedaled out of the city. On a sunny summer day, cold winds greeted us. The Bolivians live their lives in a crisp, thin-air environment. Evenings turn chilly with the setting sun. Native costumes reflect the need for warm clothing. We rode past women dressed in heavy wool dresses with multiple layers of sweaters topped off with black fedora hats. Out in the middle of nowhere, shepherds sat near flocks of sheep or llamas. Although they never initiated a greeting, they replied to ours. Their small children stared at us. One young boy began crying when we stopped to rest near him. His mother grabbed him into her arms for security. He had probably never seen touring mountain bikes, or people our size. Doug stands 6'4".

Bolivian men dressed in heavy wool pants and shirts. They wore ragged jackets but rarely a hat. Their jet-black hair, smooth dark skin and dark eyes fit the quietness of their demeanor. All the ones we passed plowed fields or harvested crops within stone fenced fields. Cows pulled one furrow plows and wagons featured wooden axles and wheels.

We enjoyed the smooth blacktop, but it changed 24 miles out of town. Before turning off the main highway at Viacha, we stopped at a small gas station and grocery shop to fill our tires, water bottles and packs with food. Our six days' worth of provisions included rice, lentils, bread rolls, pasta, vegetables, oatmeal, and cans of tuna. By the time we were ready to leave, a small group had gathered around the bikes. We never liked it, but they crowded in close and handled everything on the cycles. In order to keep an eye on the gear, we stacked the bicycles in tandem and left one person standing guard.

Heavily loaded, we pedaled to the edge of town, and headed west. The fat tires on our mountain bikes dropped onto the dirt. From one way of riding to another. New rules and different dangers. The gravel required a whole new riding technique.

Where we hit the gravel, flat land made pedaling easy. That changed when the serpentine road wound upward toward distant peaks shrouded in the clouds. Ruts and large puddles riddled the roadbed. At times, we picked our way through a minefield of holes. We forded two small streams the first hour. Tricky riding! Bryan got stuck in the mud at one river crossing. Doug crashed into some soft sand and stood up looking like a freshly plowed-up mouse.

"That happened so quick I couldn't put my foot out," he said, a bit dazed.

"Good thing I wasn't too close behind you," Bryan added. "I almost ran over you."

"Let's do another hour of riding and call it a day," I said. "What do you say we pitch our tents by a stream?"

"Sounds good to me," Doug said.

We found a knoll near a river, but out of the constant wind that blew softly throughout the day. I set my tent facing the sunset. The clouds were back-lit as I watched the drama from between the nylon flaps. There is something peaceful about the end of the day, when the last bird calls out its song and the sky fades into twilight. After eating dinner, I took a sponge bath and slid into my sleeping bag. It's a fact that bicyclists rarely suffer from insomnia. Not so at 12,000 feet. We felt the effects of high altitude sickness called 'soroche' by the Bolivians. No matter what time we went to bed or how tired we were, we woke up out of a dead sleep at three every morning, until we became acclimated.

We filtered our water from the stream the next day before cranking up the winding road. Erosion-scarred hills drained down to the road. Dark tundra grass covered the earth along a river valley that we followed. No reference points of humanity existed.

Later in the afternoon, after completing a climb, we faced a wide valley with a thunderstorm advancing from the south. In the distance, white summits peeked out of storm clouds, then vanished into a gray mist. Darkness swallowed the valley with rain sweeping across the sky. Jagged lightning bolts slashed the air below us. I stopped to wait for my friends.

"That lightning scares the daylights out of me," Bryan said, riding up.

"It doesn't thrill me too much either," I said. "What do you think Doug?"

"It's passing to the east, so we should be all right if we wait a half hour."

"Let's eat while we're waiting," Bryan said.

We munched on sandwiches and watched the storm move away from us with rain falling on the tundra for miles. Soon, it looked safe enough to ride through a gap in the clouds. We coasted into the valley. Three miles later, we pedaled down a muddy, twisting road that led to a wide river. Riding became impossible in the muck, so we got off to walk the bikes. In seconds, clay squeezed up into our fenders and brakes, freezing the wheels. By the time we reached the river, we were dragging our bikes. We spent an hour washing the soggy clay out of our tires, chains and rims.

With each day's ride, the land grew harsher. The road was pitched and rutted. We forded a dozen streams, sometimes getting stuck in the middle. At times, the sand washed over our rims.

We worried about our food supply because we were getting low after four days. We reached a village where a military unit was housed in a walled compound. It was a passport check. They were enthralled that anybody would ride bicycles on a road as grueling as the Camino.

A colonel came out to shake our hands along with a captain who was amazed at the gear on our bikes. Fifteen minutes later, they let us go. The town looked abandoned, with no one in the muddy streets, so we didn't have much hope for finding food. A few blocks later, we looked through the dark doors of a mud house to discover carrots, onions, and potatoes. What a find! The shopkeeper had fresh bread and cans of peaches. We cleaned him out.

On the outskirts of town, we rode up to a transportation fiasco. Two large trucks were stuck nose first and five feet deep into the mud of a 150-foot-wide river. Dozens of men shoveled dirt, but the trucks sank deeper. To get an idea of how poor they are, we realized that this was the only supply route from Bolivia to the seaport. Yet, they couldn't afford one bridge over a river that was 150 feet wide, and over two feet deep. We portaged our bikes across.

Miles later, we climbed up a canyon. It took four hours and some gut-busting leg work. We crossed five more streams. At the top, cathedral-shaped boulders offered a dramatic skyline relief, but nothing compared to the huge summit called Mount Sajama west of us. It loomed 21,500 feet into the sky. Deep canyons along the road dropped a thousand feet below us. For two hours, we pedaled as the peak rose higher in front of us. We dodged hundreds of mud puddles, gully washouts, and a few dozen mini-lakes in the road. Onward the Camino stretched, ever reaching out in front of us like a ribbon in the wind, appearing and vanishing with the rolling contour of the land.

Near sunset, a black sky moved across the mountains. Lightning cracked the clouds into flashing sections and thunder rolled down from the alpine heights. It swirled over us and roared into the valley off the eastern face of Mount Sajama. Doug and Bryan ducked into a culvert beside the road. The lightning came closer. We were unprotected.

"We better camp right here," I said, riding up. "Besides, we're gonna be miserable in the rain. I can't see riding for another hour. Let's call it quits."

"What about being exposed on this flat ground to the lightning?" Bryan asked.

"Once it moves out of the mountains, we don't have that much chance of being struck," I answered. "Although it can strike anywhere it wants. But we're close to the ground, so we should be all right."

"Great!" Doug lamented. "Let's get the tents up before the rain hits."

We laid the bikes down in the dirt and pulled our packs off. We pitched the tents as rain swept toward us. Electricity charged the air. We pulled the gear into our tents just as sleet, then hail pounded us. The wind tore at our tents. An hour later, with the last rays of the sun lighting the summits, the storm rolled across the valley.

We awoke to a cold, overcast morning. A gray shroud entombed the mountains. All around us, tundra wilderness.

Climbing into the higher elevations, we followed the meandering road as it slipped between two huge peaks. Behind us, Mount Sajama dominated the sky. Ahead, a row of five 19,000-footers made their own bid for the most awesome award. One cone-shaped volcanic peak, Mount Payachatas at 20,000 feet, jutted into a brilliant blue sky. We pedaled through a corridor of giants. Each one stood four miles high.

At one river fording, we decided to take baths in the glacial runoff, which was relatively warm. When I say 'relatively,' that means above freezing. After four days of being scuzzy and disgusting, no matter how cold it was, we took baths. There's nothing quite like bathing in an icy river. It's like filling your bathtub with ice cubes and jumping into it for ten minutes. It lets you know you're alive because every cell in your body is screaming, "COLD PAIN!" It hurts so much that you question why you do things like this to yourself.

We followed the Camino into a wide valley. Llamas grazed in small herds. Traveling on my bike carried me back thousands of years to a place where time didn't exist in clocks or schedules. It was either morning, afternoon, or night. No calendars marked the progression of the year to the few mountain people who lived in thatched-roofed mud huts scattered along the valley. Only the weather expressed the time of year. A sense of peace flowed out of the timelessness.

Late in the day, we again stripped the bikes to portage them across another river too deep for our axles. At the Bolivian border, we dismounted and walked into the office for our passport stamp. We met a very casual border guard. I used to worry about these guys, with all the stories about border officials, but so far, we hadn't had any problems. We walked out and headed over to a small cafe. We ordered rice, tomatoes, potatoes and onions. Half an hour later, the cook filled our orders. The cafe was a shack with a wood-burning stove in the rear and a few tables out front. The pope's picture graces the walls of restaurants all over South America, and just as often, a nude girl's photo appears with him. This time, three nudes surrounded the pope.

We made our final assault over the pass at 15,500 feet to the border of Chile. Bigger rocks bedeviled us as we continued climbing up the mountain. We suffered constant jolting and lurching through the rocky minefield. Sometimes we couldn't react fast enough and would take a tumble. Spokes were another worry. Constant pounding could break them or warp a rim. This road was tough on bikes and riders alike.

After two more hours of solid climbing, we reached a plateau. Everywhere, broken rock. No vegetation grew or any animals except a black condor soaring overhead. Laboring up the incline, we felt the effects of a 15,500-foot-high altitude when we had to stand on the pedals. We gasped for air when our bodies needed extra oxygen, but it wasn't there—not in abundance.

On our left and right, Mount Payachatas, Mount Quisiquisini and Mount Guayatre punctuated the sky. Each stood over 19,000 feet. Even at our altitude, those mountains dominated the corridor of giants that we had been riding through. By the time we reached the pass, broken rock lay everywhere upon the land. Grapefruit-sized rocks made riding difficult. Ahead, Lake Chungará filled a valley at the foot of Mount Payachatas, which we had now circled to its far side. At the crest, we coasted downhill toward the border station. We bounced and bucked all the way.

We stopped at the border where we had to register the bikes and get our visas stamped. Because of 'bureaucratic' paper shuffling, we were forced to stay five hours at the border for a maximum of 15-minute work. But the one thing you don't do with civil servants is getting them upset. They can hold you up for days, so you just keep smiling through your anger. Around 6:00 p.m., we were stamped, sealed and delivered. By now, it was freezing. As we thanked the guards, cursing under our breaths, we walked the bikes out into what was becoming a blizzard. They smiled and wished us luck. After holding us for five hours, they didn't seem to think we should mind that they had cost us lots of wasted time, and now we were in frigid misery.

Nonetheless, we started out with snow swirling around us. We were told a cabin was two miles down the road. As we pedaled our bikes into the storm, I stopped to take a picture of Bryan and Doug vanishing into the snow. After taking the first shot of them, I noticed some interesting ducks near the lakeshore. They were black, with non-webbed feet, white or yellow beaks and two raised eye sockets.

As I looked around, a half dozen different kinds of birds floated in the water near the shore. They included black and white seagulls, diving ducks, gray ducks with long curved necks and some geese—all living on a lake at 15,000 feet. The icy water alone would dissuade the heartiest foul, but add a few blizzards in the summer, and it is a wonder they would live there. By the time I finished shooting, heavy snow limited my visibility to 30 yards. I was cold, shivering and getting wetter as I rode. My gloves were soaked. I kept pedaling along, figuring two miles could mean anything from one to ten. If that cabin didn't come into view soon, I was going to pitch my tent and jump into my sleeping bag to save myself from freezing to death.

The road got worse, which meant I was taking jolts in rapid succession. Keeping my bicycle vertical was a major consideration. I continued riding through the gray mist and snowflakes, hoping for a glimpse of the cabin. It's an amazing feeling being so high in the sky that I was not only in the snowstorm, I was in the clouds that created the storm. On my right, the lake was barely visible. Quick glances showed me many of the black ducks still lining the shore, tucking their heads back into their feathers to keep warm.

With one glance towards the water, I couldn't believe my eyes. "What in the hell is that bird doing at this altitude?" I said to myself. "No, it can't be. I must be losing it." I thought I saw a pink flamingo standing near the shore. No way! Not at 15,000 feet! I must be suffering from hypothermia. Upon a second glance, I saw not one, but three pink flamingos. These were tropical birds. Why would they be living at this altitude and in such inhospitable conditions? No matter how cold I was, I had to get a shot. I uncovered my camera and snapped two pictures. All the while, I cursed the border officials. Back on the bike, I told myself one more mile before tent time. I would catch up with Bryan and Doug in the morning.

A short time later, I spied the cabin marking the boundary of Parks Louca National. Bryan stood at the door. By then, a mantle of white covered the ground. I shivered numb from the cold. I cooked some hot soup and retired.

We jumped out of our sleeping bags at sunrise. The sun melted the snow at the lower elevations. Outside the cabin, Mount Payachatas pierced the sky across the lake. Its regal white robe reflected off the still waters of Chungará. On the shoreline, the black ducks turned out to be Tagua Gigante. Morning shadows moved across Mount Payachatas as the sun rose higher. Along the green moss-covered shoreline, four pink flamingos danced in the water. They danced to stir up the water for their food. We watched the ritual. As we squatted for pictures Bryan said, "You know, as mad as I was yesterday at those border guards, I have to thank them for what we're seeing this morning. This is incredible. When I saw those flamingos through the snow yesterday, I thought I was suffering from altitude sickness."

"Yeah, me too," I said. "I thought I was seeing things but here they are."

An hour later, I rode several miles behind Bryan and Doug. I was still sick in my guts from some kind of bacteria I picked up in Peru when we hiked to Machu Picchu. I had suffered the “Inca Two Step” for weeks.

As I struggled along, I looked up into the sky to see black dots around 18,000 feet. I pedaled along at 15,500 by myself.

Seconds later, to my amazement, two twelve-foot wing-spanned condors were gliding 30 feet off my handlebars and looking over at me. I was so flabbergasted; I could hardly speak. They were just curious as they looked over at me.

"My God," I exclaimed. "You guys are enormous...like a couple of B-52 bombers."

They didn't make a sound. I wondered if they thought I was a piece of meat or just invading their air space. My first thought was to get my camera out and take a picture, but to my horror, I had shot the last picture at the border.

Looking back at the two birds, I knew I had made a huge mistake in not reloading the camera. Maybe 30 seconds later, they tipped their wings northward and caught an updraft.

They soared into the wild blue yonder. Minutes later, they were two black specks in the sky. But for me, they will remain 30 feet off my handlebars for the rest of my life. They are the reason I named my touring expedition touring bike, "Condor." He has taken me to great heights and has helped me fly with the condors in the mountains of South America.

Several hours later, with clouds closing around the higher elevations of Mount Payachatas, I caught up to Doug and Bryan on a rest break. They were astounded by my story and wished they would have been with me.

The gravel road wound around the backside of the mountain allowing closer views of its glaciers. Once past the volcano, the road climbed again onto a rocky plateau. We reached a high point in the highway, then down it fell into dark green tundra grasses. We rode through alpine terrain. The road carried us through valleys along braided streams. Ducks lived in some of the tundra ponds while Vicunas, a wild skinny version of the llamas, grazed on distant hills. Kangaroo rat creatures hopped across the road. Down we rumbled, bouncing along the rocks and ruts in the Camino. The canyon we traveled into grew wider as the road followed mountain flanks and descended into a large open area where we could see for miles to the west. Distinct changes in the vegetation became apparent at the lower elevation. The road hugged the steep sides of the mountains like a slithering serpent. We rarely pedaled as the road dropped.

From our lofty perches in the high mountains, we plunged downward along hairpin turns. Soon, the peaks became higher, and more pronounced as we dropped lower. No traffic, save an occasional rodent scurrying across the road. Trees grew along the route, then cactus. An hour later and several thousand feet down, we made our way onto a flat plain that opened into a rock-strewn sand-dune valley. Before us, no vegetation, no birds, no animals, not even a fly—utter desolation—a moonscape of tan, brown and red canyons. We picked our way along the dirt until we rode onto the asphalt.

For 54 miles, we sailed along the snaking highway that led through desert dunes. Nothing lived out there.

The wheels spun fast and free. Smiles spread wide across our faces. At 30 miles, a second canyon joined ours, giving us a muddy river to follow. We rode along a world of white dunes and blue sky.

We pedaled our bikes into the driest region in the world, the Atacama Desert of Chile. A few hours later, we reached the outskirts of Arica with the Pacific crashing against sandy beaches. In one day, we had gone from blizzards, glaciers, pink flamingos and condors to the utter desolation of a desert, by dropping from 15,500 feet to sea level.

Few raw adventures remain on this crowded planet—the Motto Grasso Jungle of Brazil, Antarctica, the Australian Outback, perhaps the deepest reaches of Africa, and the Camino International Highway of Bolivia and Chile. It proved a rough, merciless road that carried us back through time, up into pure mountain majesty, and allowed us a glimpse into nature's showcase. That adventure had to be earned with each crank of the pedals and the pitching of our tents at every desolate campsite. But the campsites were the ultimate experience when we set our front flaps looking into the face of a howling storm over Mount Sajama or woke up to a mantle of white—covering Mount Payachatas—garnished with pink flamingos.

We ventured into South America for this kind of adventure. It was the meanest. It was the worst. It was the toughest. Ah, and it was the best.

(Camping in the raw wilderness.)

Chapter 40—Barks, Growls and Fangs

"A dog is man's best friend; but only when he's yours."

—John Brown, cyclist

They raise the hackles on the back of my neck when I hear them coming. Often called man's best friend, they can be a bicyclist's worst enemy. Dogs!

They take their guard duties seriously 24 hours a day. Dogs come in a variety of colors, sizes, temperaments, and enthusiasm. They love a good chase. From their property line to a point down the road, dogs consider bicyclists fair game. Most of the time, they lie around the yard sleeping. But as soon as a rider goes by, all hell breaks loose.

The first thing you hear is their bark. A quick glance shows you their location, at which point, you make a decision to stand on the pedals to outrun them or stop and defend yourself by getting behind your bike. It's an adrenaline rush. If they're big, you fear for your body. When you're far enough ahead of big dogs, you dare them to chase you, because you want to see them run in vain. In the end, you know they are doing their job, and you never take it personally.

However, I have been known to yell unkind words about their family tree.

The one time I was afraid for my life happened on a dirt road outside a village in Peru. I was headed up La Raya Pass toward Bolivia. Along the road, about 50 meters from the route, a farmhouse stood out against a mountain backdrop. Green grasses lined a winding driveway from the house to where I was on the wagon-wheel-rutted road. Through the nameless village I had ridden, several dogs had attacked me, but they were too small to do any damage. I yelled at them, which kept them at bay.

When I passed that farmhouse, three BIG dogs lay on the ground near the front door. I was looking at the house when one of the dog's heads jerked upward. He had caught my scent and barked. His two buddies jumped to their feet like a couple of Al Capone's bodyguards. I kept pedaling, knowing that my best bet was to get out of their territory.

The race was on. I hammered the pedals, trying to get as much distance away from them as possible. Up that driveway, they raced, with their fangs showing as they barked in tandem, much like "Butch" in the “American Flyer” bicycle movie starring a young Kevin Costner. At that point, I was in trouble. I had no more than 100 yards on them at the beginning. They closed fast. By the time they reached me, I had passed the line of their territory. But they didn't stop. I kept pedaling as they came up alongside me. In the frenzy of the chase, they started charging in at me, trying to get at my legs. I pulled my pump from its bracket and started waving it. The pump extended to its full length which made it look like a long stick.

"Here's a Zefal sandwich for you sons-of-bitches!" I yelled. (Later, upon thinking about it, they WERE sons of bitches, so it was a compliment.)

The dogs did something at that moment that I had never seen before. One broke off to the opposite side of me, and the other placed himself in front of me. I felt like a moose cornered by a wolf-pack. Those dogs weren't fooling. I must have looked like their evening meal.

Waving my pump and yelling like a wild man, I stopped and picked up a rock. I hurled it at the lead dog. The rock winged past his shoulder. He retreated. I whirled just in time to see the side dog flying through the air at my body. I lunged sideways, avoiding the snap of his teeth. Still waving my pump at both dogs, I picked up two more rocks and began throwing and yelling at them. One rock nearly hit the leaping dog and the other grazed the third one. They backed off as I grabbed a handful of rocks and began throwing and cursing at them. Not caring to get hit by the rocks, they ran to a safe distance away, still barking.

I hoisted my bike to an upright position. Shaking from fright, I threw my foot over the top tube. Glaring at the dogs with rocks in my hand, I slipped into the toe-clips. I tossed one more rock at them to let them know I meant business.

Seconds later, I settled into a slow even cadence, cranking upward along the winding road. I have to admit it, dogs make a bicycle adventure exciting at times. But given a choice, I'd rather be attacked by a pack of chickens!

(Sliding down a snow field.)

Chapter 41—A Desert Thief

"Only a baseball player should be allowed to steal and get away with it."

—Ty Cobb

"They'll steal you blind," my friends said before I launched myself on a world tour.

"Not if I'm smarter than the average bear," I said confidently. "No one is going to get a dime off me."

Famous last words.

Anyone who has traveled through developing world countries has a litany of stories about how their friends were "ripped—off" by cunning thieves. Nearly every traveler has suffered some form of theft. What they never mention: thievery runs wild everywhere in the world. Every week in the USA, enough goods are stolen to fill one hundred box cars of the Union Pacific Railroad.

But I'm smarter than the average traveler. I make it a policy NEVER to leave sight of my bike or gear, not for a second. I never put myself in situations where I could be cornered. When traveling in a strange land, I keep a sixth sense of potential danger. My antennas are out at all times and caution is my password.

Many veteran travelers have told me their stories of deft thieves everywhere in the world stealing them blind.

One fellow traveler, an Aussie named Murray whom I met in the Galapagos Islands off the coast of Ecuador, had been backpacking around the world for two years. He figured he had heard every trick in the book from other travelers. They tell them at the dollar-a-night hostels in cities around the world.

Some of the tales show how creative thieves can be. The reasoning behind travelers being fair "marks," especially with their cameras dangling from their necks, stems from the perception that travelers are rich. By the fact they are traveling, makes them wealthy in the thieves' eyes and makes them fair game.

Murray walked along the street one night toward the Grand Casino Hotel in Quito, Ecuador. It was one of those hotels on the "Gringo" trail that cost $90 a night and featured cheap food. Anyone can find these places by carrying a travel book about the country they are visiting. The hotel was a run-down place with graffiti on the walls and toilets that didn't have seats. Patrons "hover" during their morning constitutional. Even more disgusting is the practice of throwing used toilet paper into a corner box. If you're twentieth into the community bathroom on any particular morning, it's not a pleasant way to start the day. However, you get used to it.

On his way to the Grand Casino, Murray was crossing a bridge when two guys walked up to him, one in front and one behind. Before he knew it, streams of warm oil cascaded down his face and over his shoulders. When he turned to see what was going on behind him, the guy who had approached from the front cut the strap on Murray's camera and ripped it off his neck. Both men sprinted away, leaving Murray with oil dripping onto his pack and clothes, minus a camera. He couldn't chase them with his 40-pound pack, and he couldn't leave it, because the other thief would come back and steal that, too. That's why Murray now covers his pack with a heavy gauge sack and never leaves his camera in view. By the time he told his story, five other people spoke about their experiences. Everybody laughed about the episodes, but not the ones who had suffered the loss of their gear.

Upon crossing the border from Ecuador to Peru—Doug, Bryan and I walked our bikes through the crowd. We watched carefully, as we strategically placed our bikes in a triangle so we could keep an eye on each other’s cycles. But that wasn't enough. We were nearly out of the crowd when a nice-looking guy walked alongside my bike opposite me. He started talking to me in perfect English about what a wonderful day it was and welcomed me to his country. I was talking away with him when Doug who was in the back of me said, "Frosty, watch his left hand." In a flash, I glanced down his arm where he had unzipped my travel kit pouch.

"You bastard!" I yelled, as I shot my arm out in a karate chop and belted him across the neck.

He faded into the crowd in seconds.

"Did you see that guy try to steal my gear?" I yelled, my heart pumping a mile a minute.

Doug's steady voice came back, "Just keep cool and keep watching each other's packs. We're not out of this yet."

It was true, we needed to keep calm, because we were most vulnerable if we panicked. We kept watching until we moved away from the crowd.

A month later, we had crossed the Andes out of Bolivia and were riding through the Atacama Desert of Chile. This 1,000 mile long desert that stretches along the Pacific coast is the driest in the world. The only human encroachment is the Pan-America Highway that snakes through this moonscape of desolation. Roadhouses dot the route at intervals between Arica and Santiago.

We were physically broken the day before by a headwind that blasted up from the south. We had cranked into an angry invisible wall. That night we camped on a dune. We were exhausted as we pushed the bikes off the highway through the deep sand. We camped alone with the universe and a zillion stars. None of us had much to say as we cooked our dinner, ate quietly and passed out on our air mattresses.

In the morning, I ate oatmeal with my last banana. After slicing it up, I slipped my Swiss Army knife into the left-hand pouch netting of my handlebar bag. I put it there because it was handy for peeling fruit. I cut the skin off fruits in foreign countries to ensure myself against contamination. A half-hour later, we broke camp and headed south.

Pedaling for the next five hours was like riding in our own instant replay movie. Golden-hued sand dunes slid by our view as if cloned from the same one a dozen miles back. It was a monotonous repetition mile after mile and my butt was killing me. In the afternoon, we reached a roadhouse.

The building looked like a square box with a front porch. A long bench stretched out in front of both sides of the front door. A tin roof provided shade for travelers. On both sides of the door, large glassless windows opened to the road. Inside, tables and chairs awaited patrons. A half dozen men stood around outside, drinking beer and talking. Since no one was sitting on the bench to the left of the door, we stacked our bikes in tandem under the window. My bike was on the outside. I grabbed my day pack, which carried my cameras and other valuable gear, and walked inside. We decided to sit at separate tables so we could write in our journals.

"Can you see the bikes?" Doug asked, when he sat down at his table.

"Yeah, I can see them, no sweat," I said. "I'll keep an eye on them."

Sitting inside, I could see out the window to the bikes. They were within spitting distance from me. Even when I wasn't looking, I could see them from the corner of my eye. A few men walked over to look at them. I kept a sharp eye out. Soon, they walked away. I went back to my writing. Minutes later, an old guy came over to the bikes. At first, he stood next to mine, with his hands in his pockets. He bent down looking closely at my water bottles. His body was sideways to me, so I couldn't see his left hand. As long as I could see his every move, I didn't think about it. Minutes later, he walked away. I kept writing.

An hour later, Doug, Bryan and I loaded up on gallons of water and headed south into the desert. We camped that night on a nearly identical campsite that we had camped, on the night before.

The next morning, I didn't have any bananas, but apples would make a nice condiment for my cereal. I reached for my knife in my handlebar bag, which I brought into the tent each night along with my gear. The knife was gone along with my dental floss. I looked through my day pack, handlebar bag and my jacket. No knife.

"Any of you guys borrow my knife?" I asked out the front flap of my tent.

"Haven't touched it," came the replies.

"It's gotta' be here," I grumbled. "It didn't sprout legs and walk off on its own."

"Maybe one of those desert rats stole it yesterday," Doug ventured.

"No way," I said. "I had my eyes glued to the bikes the whole time we were stopped at that roadhouse."

Sitting in my tent, my mind was in a quandary as to where I might have put the knife, but I knew it was in the side pouch of my handlebar bag, because that is where I always put it. But then I started tracing events back at the roadhouse, and as incredible as it seemed to me, I instantly knew how and when it was stolen.

"You're right Doug," I said. "One of those guys stole my knife right in front of my eyes."

"How? You had your eyes on the bikes the whole time," Bryan said.

"I sure did, but I didn't have them on my handlebar bag," I said.

"What do you mean?" Doug asked.

"Well, when they were looking at the bikes up close, I was all eyes," I said. "But later, an old guy came over and spent a few minutes bending down looking at my water bottles. Then he stood up sideways to me. That's when my knife was stolen. I'll bet he was using his left hand to wave his friend back and forth until his buddy could reach a hand up from the front of the bike and grab the knife. That's the one thing I couldn't see on my bike because it was farther-most out from the window, so the edge of the window cut off my view.

"Now you have a story to tell at the next hostel," Doug said. "But don't worry, you have the last laugh."

"Great comfort you are," I said. "So, what's the last laugh?"

"That's easy," Doug said. "When you're long gone from this desert retreat, he will be here for the rest of his life."

What's it like living in the Atacama Desert? It's clean and clear. It's hot and dry. Its rocks and sand, waves and rippled by the wind over an eternity of time. It's a quiet place, but it is not a fun place. That guy is still there, and I hope he is enjoying my knife. The desert thief.

(Riding into the high country.)

Chapter 42—Sometimes you have to go without a mirror in order to see yourself

> ***"When all the blandishments of life are gone, the coward sneaks to death, the brave live on."***
>
> ***—George Sewell***

When bicycle adventure stretches into weeks, months, or even years—profound changes occur. New perspectives arise that seldom emerge in daily routine existence. In South America, we rode so far from civilization for weeks at a time that we never looked into the mirror. It almost got to a point of living like an animal, except we did brush and floss our teeth. However, in the process, we moved into a nomadic form of life. A person does a lot of thinking while on a long-distance tour. Endless thoughts rumbled through my mind while riding in the Atacama Desert of Chile, the driest desert in the world.

On such a long tour in the desert, basic living dominated. I woke up to the sun at dawn. Hunger pulled at my stomach and a hearty breakfast filled me with energy. Later, after having washed the pot, I take a bath with my shower bag or none at all. I stretched my muscles. With that done, I stuffed the panniers and broke camp. Each piece of equipment had a special place on my bike's frame. Everything was simple, straightforward, black and white.

What time is it? The present. What day is it? Today. Where am I? On the planet Earth. What's in the news? Good question. Stress? What's that? Anything new in my life? Every mile. Positive expectations? Moment to moment.

If I'm with a pedal partner, our conversations run the length and breadth of the globe. We talk about life—the meaning or non-meaning of it—along with the futility, frustration and turmoil in the world. At the other end of the scale, we talk about people and places. We are grateful for our fortunate circumstances. What's up ahead is a favorite topic because it holds expectations. If it is mountains, we know clear streams will be our constant companions on climbs and descents. Something about moving water makes our pedaling up a mountain grade seem effortless. Along the route, we know lakes await us, with abundant wildlife.

One important aspect of traveling with a partner is the emotional bonding that takes place. I know what love feels like when I've toured with someone. I've fallen in love with my best friends on our shared adventures. My female friends have shared wonderful campfires under a starlit sky, swam in turquoise pools, watched desert sunrises and climbed over ledges to see the world from behind a waterfall.

When I'm alone, I talk to myself. Those solitary times make me appreciate moments of fellowship. My whole day is brightened when someone stops to talk along the highway or at a campsite. I'm as interested in their journey as they are in mine. Travelers enjoy a different mindset—their spirits exude optimism through discovery. Sharing it creates a mutual high.

The one thing I notice as weeks turn into months is that I'm less concerned about things that don't affect me. Every day flows naturally into new people, sights, and perspectives. A deep peacefulness pervades my demeanor. I used to wonder what happened to bring on that peacefulness, and one day I figured it out. Do you know that most people look into the mirror every day of their lives? When they do, they become critical of themselves. They aren't pretty enough or handsome enough. They focus on minor flaws. They might not like their nose shape, eye color or lips. They compare themselves to someone else. It's an endless cycle of self-denigration. Youth slips away each day, and their minds argue against it. That mirror reflects their personal insecurities. It focuses them on themselves instead of the quality of their lives. You can't SEE depth of character or caliber of personality in a mirror. It's the one aspect of a human being that presents itself through daily interaction with others.

Perhaps looking in a mirror determines self-esteem, whether high or low. That's unfortunate, because we are what we are. No two are the same; everyone is unique. When I was a kid, my brother Rex possessed golden book good looks. Girls fell over themselves when he walked by. I never quite measured up, no matter how many times I combed my hair. I compared myself to my brother, and later, to those handsome faces on the magazine covers. No way could I be that handsome and no way could women look as beautiful as the stars on the silver screen. Yet, I had been measuring myself against others, and ignoring my own qualities. One day, a friend of mine, Mike Mason, told me he was tired of me berating myself. He told me that I had one of the greatest assets he had ever seen in a person.

"What is it?" I asked. "Will it make me money?"

"Don't you get it?" he answered. "You have the greatest gift I've ever seen."

"What good is it doing me? Why can't I see it?" I asked again.

"It's your enthusiasm," he said. "You can't create it or buy it. You have it in spades, and it's going to be with you all your life. It's your gift to others, the joy of being alive."

"I have never complained since. Thanks, Mike."

Ever wonder why so many of those handsome and beautiful movie stars have such tragic personal lives? They marry among themselves on physical attraction. Their spiritual, emotional and personal selves get lost in the hype. Do they share common interests? Do they have similar backgrounds? Did they take time to become friends who liked each other? What happens, is one day, they both have to get down to daily living together. If either one lacks a balanced self-concept, or they don't have common interests, the relationship is doomed. No matter how good-looking someone is, it's their character that expresses itself to the world each day.

On a spring tour, my friend Jack complained that he wasn't as good-looking as 'those other guys.' He lamented about not being tall enough. He bemoaned his skinny build. Yet, in reality, Jack was good-looking. He possessed average height, but I never considered height a measure of his humanity. I told him that I was tired of his maligning himself, and asked him to say positive things or nothing at all. I asked Jack if he would like to give up his full head of hair for another man's six feet of height, but sparse hair. If he were taller, better looking, or perfectly built, would he date more women? Would our friendship become better? I told him it wouldn't matter to me if he were the ugliest person on earth. Some of the most physically beautiful people in the world are the ugliest, saddest, and most loathsome.

Character reaches beyond good looks. It reaches deeper levels of BEING that have nothing to do with the physical world. Character is not a comparison or judgment. It's an acceptance of one's self and feelings for his or her friends. A short time later, Jack came up to me with a big smile on his face.

"What's up?" I asked.

"You know that talk we had a few months ago about accepting myself?"

"Sure."

"You know something, I've been taking stock of my life," he said. "I've got a good job, a great girlfriend, a nice house, sports and good friends. What you said has finally gotten through to my brain. I like myself."

"Great," I said. "You know, you have to take inventory once in a while to realize how good your life is."

"Thanks," he said.

"Thank you, Mike," I answered, thinking back to my old friend who had helped me.

In the end, I'm convinced that friends walk into one another's lives to help each other out. They offer support during rough times and enhance the joy of the good times. They make a day on the snow, or water, or dinner or movies a time of celebration.

What if someone you know lies or plays unfairly? What if their dishonesty angers you, whether it be a public figure or someone you know? They obviously look into a mirror too much but can't see themselves. In the end, dishonest people sink to a level with others like themselves, or no one at all. Their prison lacks human interaction based on respect. I never feel angry at dishonest people, because I know they pay the ultimate price—no self-esteem and loss of quality friends. I can't think of a worse fate.

On a bicycle adventure, I rarely look into a mirror to see myself. Soon, I forget about what I looked like. I'm just me. Doug is himself. Pam bubbles with her usual excitement. Bryan talks his head off. Sandi laughs all the time. John tells his jokes. Gary smiles. Gerry sings songs. Dave contemplates the world. My friends and I go along without worrying about our clothes, how we look, what we do for a living, or what the Joneses have. We simply accept ourselves and each other with no conditions. The moment is the only thing that is important. Participating at that moment means we're not looking at reflections of ourselves, rather, we are living. In that participation, comes unconditional self-acceptance.

Samuel Johnson said: "The fountain of content must spring up in the mind, and they who hath so little knowledge of human nature as to seek happiness by changing anything but their own disposition, will waste their lives in fruitless efforts and multiply the grief they propose to remove."

Sometimes you have to go without a mirror in order to see yourself.

(Gerry and Dave riding into deep canyons.)

Chapter 43—Even My Teeth Can Taste It

"Three years ago, I was 16 days into a bicycle tour up the east coast. At this time, I'm in Maine. On this date, three years ago I was on the C & O rail trail just outside of Washington DC. Tonight, in Maine, there is a chill in the air, the foliage is past peak, it could snow at any time. I'm saying, what the heck was I thinking 3 years ago. I survived that trip. I actually wish I was on it again. I have a big part of me screaming to just do it. I may be challenged, but I know that I would not be disappointed. As uncomfortable as it may be, I have learned, and I will preach, we are capable of so much more than we think. However, we may never know until we put ourselves right in the thick of it."

—Chris Baker Bailey

We headed east out of Port of Natales, on the coast of Chile at the southern end of Patagonia's. In the bay, a dozen black-necked geese watched us ride past them. At the edge of town, we dropped our bicycles off the pavement and onto a dirt road. Ahead, our route wound through rolling hills toward distant mountains. Some were snow-covered with glaciers plainly visible. Scrub trees grew intermittently across the terrain. Rocky, treeless mesas stretched before us. Being close to the bottom of the world in South America, roads lacked route numbers. Whereas most towns have many roads leading away from them, this was the only road coming into or going out of Natales. So, few signs of humanity existed, it felt like we had pedaled to the ends of the earth. After starting six months previously at the top of South America in Caracas, we welcomed the lack of people.

Twelve miles later, a three-mile turnoff brought us to a cave where ground sloths, over six feet tall, once lived. These bear-like creatures inhabited the cave that resembled an underground amphitheater. A second attraction called the "Devil's Chair" stood near the cave. No one was in the parking lot, and we hadn't seen anyone all day. Tourism was limited to international travelers who had the means to visit this remote region.

Further along the route, we followed a difficult gravel road. It turned from a hard surface to soft, then heavy rock and back again. Baseball-sized stones challenged our forward movement. We kept strict attention to riding. Otherwise, the road would drop us in a second. With the danger came beauty as glaciers peeked out of the clouds with each change of the winds in those high places.

In the afternoon, we reached a government control station where we turned off toward Torres del Paine, meaning "towers of the pine." The stone-covered road snaked along a high plain with mountains, mesas and buttes stretching out in front of us. We cranked over rocky terrain for another ten miles before turning toward the park. Peaks stood black against the late afternoon horizon. We rode toward them. No trees grew on the rocky landscape.

On the south side of the road, I stopped to take a picture of a vicuna. To my surprise, it walked up to me. The wild animal was a version of a llama and a distant cousin of a camel, so I didn't feel any threat from it. When I finished snapping a picture, it walked right up to me, with a curious look on its face. I was almost afraid, but what could it do to me? Before I knew it, the vicuna's face was two feet from mine. He looked right into my eyes when suddenly, he sucked in a lung-full of air and spit in my face. I wilted from his breath which smelled like rotting fish. I backed off, cursing at him. He had sprayed saliva all over me, and it too, had the smell. I jumped on my bike and tried to catch Doug and Bryan.

Two miles later, they had stopped by a large lake, to watch a half dozen ostrich-like Rea birds run from them. I saw one of them as I came up. It felt like we were entering a prehistoric zone of wild creatures. It was time to camp and I needed a bath.

"Did you guys see one of those vicunas along the road?" I asked when I pulled up.

"Yeah, we saw two."

"I took a picture of one, but he walked up to me and spit in my face," I said.

"You smell rank, like rotten fish," Bryan said.

"That settles it," I said. "Let's camp here. I'm getting a bath."

"Yeah, for our sake as well as yours," Doug said. "Why did he spit in your face? Did you call him a dirty name?"

"Funny, funny," I muttered.

As we walked the bikes across the rocky ground, a minibus loaded with tourists drove out of the park. I walked no more than twenty yards off the road when the driver honked. Looking around, I saw several dozen curious faces and lots of cameras clicking at us. It had happened so many times before, I didn't think about it. But the look on their faces was telling—like they would trade places in an instant, because what they saw intrigued them.

After waving to them, we made our way to the lake. We pitched our tents and took baths. Thankfully, the vicuna's stench washed off with copious amounts of soap. Walking up to the tents, I felt hungry.

"You know, I'm hungry," Bryan said.

"Cook up some of that famous spaghetti of yours," Doug said.

"Never mind my cooking," Bryan said. "I'm thinking about my Mom... hey Mom, what are you doing right now? Making lasagna? Send some down, mom! I'd love to eat a plateful of lasagna with cheese melting down the sides... I'll bet you're making some chocolate chips this afternoon, too. GOD, I could eat some chocolate chip cookies dipped in milk. And, oh, what else, um, a loaf of fresh bread. I've been eating apples all day. I'm starving."

"Mom, if we could only have Scotty beam you down, you could cook us up a wonderful dinner," Doug said.

"I'm gonna make spaghetti, but it's not gonna cook fast enough," Bryan said.

"Yeah, well, your spaghetti is not what you'd call Chef Boyardee," I said.

"It's not too bad," Bryan said, defensively.

"That's the trouble, it IS pretty bad," Doug said.

"What I'd really like," Bryan said, "are brownies for dessert, with tons of walnuts and semi-sweet chocolate, a triple batch, yeah, that's what I'm gonna make when I get home."

"Or apple pie right now would be great, too," I said.

"Peach pie, or blackberry pie," Bryan added.

"Or pumpkin pie with ice cream on top," Doug said. "Make that—HOT pumpkin pie right out of the oven, with vanilla ice cream dumped over the top."

"I can't believe how hungry I am," Bryan said.

"For post-dessert, you have those humongous, juicy strawberries dipped in melted white chocolate," Doug said, running his tongue around his lips at the same time.

By now, we were standing together with our minds running wild about food. The more we thought about it, the more we dreamed up our favorite dishes.

"Melted white chocolate," Bryan whispered, then gasped, his mouth salivating. "Why am I so hungry? I've been eating lousy apples. They just don't cut it when you're riding 60 miles over gravel. I need something more substantial... like a dozen chocolate eclairs."

"Yeah, something nutritious like that," I said. "You know I have the perfect bicycle food if we could get to a grocery store in the States. I'd buy a gallon of vanilla ice cream, two pounds of bananas and three jars of fudge topping. First, I'd microwave the fudge into a perfect stream of smooth tongue-caressing liquid. Then I'd cut the half-gallon into three pieces. Then I'd slice the bananas over the ice cream. Next, I'd pour a full jar over each mouth-watering mound of ice cream. Then, I'd wait a minute for the chocolate to ever so delicately melt and mix with the ice cream until the whole dish transcended into a new food group called 'The Ultimate Bicycling Food.'"

"I'm gonna pass out," Bryan yelled, his tongue slurping around his mouth. "Is it possible to suffer death by chocolate overdose?"

"I've got it," Doug said. "We'll throw a dream food party when we get back, with blueberry muffins, with banana nut bread right out of the oven and butter dripping down the sides."

"Yeah, and what about breakfast guys?" Bryan leaped in with his tongue now thinking for his brain. "Couldn't you go for a stack of 15 banana pancakes—where you toss them on the griddle and they bubble up, then you slice bananas over the top, then turn them over and smell the banana cooked into the pancake. Then you slap them on your plate and melt butter over the top, and next, you pour maple syrup on them, and as it drenches the stack, you grab your fork, and then you DIVE-IN with it. You take a big chunk and shove it into your mouth, and that's when your taste buds do hand-springs."

"Oh yes," Doug said, his eyes growing larger with anticipation. "Even my teeth can taste it."

"Yes, and then after that," I said. "I'll make some walnut chocolate chip cookies. As soon as they come out of the oven, I'll dunk one into a glass of cold milk and watch it sizzle, and then pop it into my mouth, lightly brushing my lips before it melts down over my tongue and then the hot chocolate drips down between my teeth and finishes up running down my throat. Then I will follow it up with a ten more cookies and a quart of milk."

"Yes, Yes, Yes!" Doug agreed, almost delirious with thoughts of food running wild in his brain.

"Oh Mom, where are you when I need you?" Bryan whimpered, clasping his hands in prayer.

"Wait a minute guys," I said. "If we were back home right now, we could have that food, but we couldn't have this adventure."

"Yeah, I guess you're right," Doug said. "We're on a dream adventure and our friends back home wish they could be here, but we're standing here wishing we could be home at the dinner table."

"Yeah, so let's cook up dinner and enjoy ourselves," I said, walking back to my tent. "We're in the middle of paradise."

"Ah, I guess you're right," Bryan muttered, walking away. "But I'd sure love just one hot chocolate chip cookie dunked in milk..."

(Cooling our feet off in an icy stream.)

Chapter 44—Danger Rides a Wild Wind

> ***"Heaven is a one way ticket, and a Hearse doesn't have a travel rack for luggage. Besides, I'm not ready to go."***
>
> ***—Bryan Delay***

You may think dramatic events occur while bicycle touring. It's true, remarkable happenings do occur at times depending on a country or the terrain. Around every bend in the road, potential exists for something delightful to occur. I use the word "delightful" because it wouldn't be fair to say dramatic—although, some things happen that can be described as sensational. Once in a while, the word "danger" comes up. For the most part, however, bicycle touring is peaceful.

Nonetheless, all of us experience a few dangerous times in our lives or we witness something extraordinary. Many people like the adrenaline rushes of violence. Sports fanatics love professional football where people hurt one another. Others go to auto races with the expectation of seeing a crash. I think long distance touring riders see less perpetrated events and more spontaneous natural occurrences that excite the mind in spiritual ways. It's true I harbor high expectations each day, but I let them unfold naturally. Touring proves pleasant most of the time. However, there are times when it's not so pleasurable.

Doug, Bryan and I were on the tail end of our ride around South America. Palm trees and sunshine greeted us as we pushed through the thriving city of Santos on the coast of Brazil. People were interested in our journey and asked us what we thought of their country. It was beautiful except the ocean for miles up and down the coast was filthy brown because billions of gallons of raw sewage were piped into the ocean daily. Signs along the beaches warned bathers that the ocean was contaminated, but people still went swimming. We made comments about it, but Doug brought us to the sobering realization that New York City until recently pumped 200,000,000 gallons of raw sewage daily into the Hudson River, and still does it many times a year when the treatment tanks exceed their capacity. The coast of New Jersey and all the gunk that washes up there is no different than the coast of Brazil.

Nonetheless, we had a great time riding along the beaches. It's hot and humid in Brazil. It rained every day and the sun came out to boil us after we were soaked. It was still early morning when we headed out of town and many Brazilians waved to us when they passed in their cars.

We pedaled in the breakdown lane of a four-lane divided highway. The highway department had placed speed bumps on the road, about two hundred yards apart, extending across the breakdown lane. We slowed our bicycles to get over them. Those bumps would destroy a car's undercarriage if rolled over at high speed. We watched the traffic speeding by us, then brake to go over the bump, then gun the engines again, only to brake a few seconds later.

We had passed over the first bump and were nearing the second one. Doug was 10 yards ahead of us and Bryan was one bike link ahead of me. A strong side wind blew across the highway. Paper flew across the road and got hung up in the weeds beside the pavement. Cars slowed down for the speed bumps. We breathed lots of diesel smoke from passing trucks.

Without warning, a sickening screech erupted out of the din of traffic behind us. Except this was a Brink's armored truck and it was sliding sideways past my left shoulder. Two cars were stopped at the speed bump, and traffic had boxed the truck in from the left. The driver may have been daydreaming, because he was in a full panic stop as he headed toward the right shoulder of the road sideways—straight for Bryan. I pulled hard on my brakes, nearly somersaulting myself over the bars. Bryan didn't react to the screeching tires, nor did he see the truck careening toward him. In an instant, the armored vehicle slammed into one of the cars that were barely clearing the speed bump and bounced in front of Bryan.

As it did, I saw Doug look back with the fear of death on his face as he stomped on the pedals to speed up and away from the truck that was about to flip and roll over him. Instantly, he vanished behind a wall of gray steel that was rising like a stage curtain in front of me. As quickly as I saw the underside of the truck's body, it rocked back upright. Bryan, now braking for all he was worth, slammed headfirst into the truck's side panel. He bounced back and up from the truck like someone had set him up for a kill shot in volleyball. His legs and arms flailed wildly as he flew out over the shoulder and down the embankment. When he sailed into the air, my heart took a shot of fear that squeezed the breath out of me. I leaped off my bike running for Bryan as he tumbled off the road.

"Oh my God!" I screamed. "Oh my God!"

By some kind of miracle, Bryan who is an ex-hockey player, rolled with the fall, and finished the tumble on his feet. I was running toward him when he yelled, "I'm all right, I'm all right!"

I raced over to check him. He had a small cut over his left eye, and was dazed, but other than that, he seemed okay. His helmet had saved him from having his block knocked off. Doug raced back from around the truck. He was fine. A lot of people asked us if we were all right. Other than a broken brake handle and bent handlebar, the bike was operable. We got back on the bikes and rode away.

After something as dramatic and frightening as nearly losing my life, and that of my friends, my mind buzzed with frenzied thoughts for the next hour. What if that truck had lost control without braking and simply run Bryan and me down from behind without a sound? What if we were farther off to the left and had been pinched between the cars that the truck had hit? What if it had rolled over on Doug and killed him? What if I had died or been injured?

Friends have asked me that question before. "Don't you worry about being killed on the road."

I always answer with an emphatic, "No."

What they don't realize is that anyone can get killed or injured at any time or anywhere. It makes no difference whether you're at home or 10,000 miles away in another country. Being alive has been and always will be a dangerous prospect. In the caveman days, you might have died from other animal attacks or starvation. Today, you may be run over by a car, or drop out of the sky in a plane.

The only way you may guarantee that you never suffer in harm's way is to stay in your house for the rest of your life. What for? Anyone who is afraid of dying is afraid of living. Anyone who fears taking a bicycle trip around the world is unrealistic about their own safety driving through the traffic of their own city. Death and danger lurk everywhere in life. No one is exempt, and tomorrow is not guaranteed to anyone.

After an hour, I settled down again. Doug and Bryan pedaled ahead of me. Their cadence put a nice rhythm back into the day. I watched Bryan's chain roll up around the freewheel in a smooth flowing motion. We were back in the saddle, riding the road, like nothing had happened. I was grateful for being alive. Sure, I could stay home and be out of harm's way, but that's not what living is all about.

An old friend of mine, Dan McCormack, once told me that great sailing ships look noble and majestic while tied to their moorings in the harbor, but that is not where they belong. They were built for cutting through the blue waters of the seven seas, for billowing clouds, and for crimson sunsets in exotic lands.

The men and women who sail them know the dangers and the rewards of the journey. The same is true for long distance touring riders.

There will always be danger riding the wild wind, but it's not the fear of it that counts, it's the adventure that opens any individual to the highest potential of his or her life.

(Waterfalls cascading white magic.)

SECTION III: TOURING AUSTRALIA

Chapter 45—Dead from the Neck Up!

"It's lonely without a friend to share the road."

—Doug Armstrong

Australia captivates everyone's imagination. Exotic creatures that defy description, hop, jump, fly and crawl around the Land of Oz, its nickname. Desert dominates nine-tenths of Australia. It's an ancient continent with most of its mountains flattened by millions of years of erosion. Along its coasts, breathtaking beauty abounds in a variety of temperate zones from rain forests to 7,000-foot Mountains in the Snowy River Range of Victoria. Legends have it that British convicts populate Oz. Nothing could be further from the truth. Aussies are some of the kindest people on the face of the earth. They possess a dry sense of humor that keeps life in perspective. "No worries me mate," is their answer to problems that are trivial and not worth an anxiety attack. Riding a bicycle in Oz provides an experience of friendliness.

A mate invited me to a party in Sydney on a Saturday afternoon a week prior to my departure on my trans-Australia crossing. A group of Aussies were singing, joking and getting pissed (drunk). They sang about the hard times in Oz, and a collection of other ribald lyrics about wine, women and the Outback. At one of the high points of the party, they sang Yankee songs in my honor. Their best one was, "I'm an old cowhand, from the Rio Grande." After singing a few stanzas, a chap named Richard asked me what a Yank might be doing in Australia.

"I'm going to ride my push-bike across your country," I answered.

"You're gonna do what?" Richard asked again.

"Ride my push-bike to Perth."

"Do you know how far that is?"

"Oh yeah," I said. "Over 3,000 kilometers."

"Did you know that you're going across the Nullarbor Plains, mate?"

"Yes, I saw it on the map,"

"Do you know what Nullarbor means in Aborigine?" he asked.

"No, what?"

"It means 'treeless,'" he said after swigging on Foster's beer. "There ain't a tree for 2,500 kilometers, and it is 38 degrees (app. 115 Fahrenheit) at this time of year. It's nothin' but a bloody desert. You'll cook like an egg in a fryin' pan."

"It'll be a great adventure," I said.

"You know what mate?" he said. "I reckon you're dead from the neck up!"

Richard was right about the Nullarbor. The highway shot straight toward the horizon, bisecting the land into two equal halves of nothing but desert. When I hit Ceduna, *"The Gateway to the Nullarbor Plains,"* three signs warned travelers of animals to watch out for—wombats, camels and kangaroos. They might have added the Emu, an ostrich-like bird that inhabits the Outback. When drivers hit one with their cars, a large repair job results.

Nothing could have prepared me for that ride. I suffered under a merciless sun. The heat sucked the moisture out of my pores faster than I could pour it back into my body. I carried five gallons of water in plastic jugs. A thousand times I asked myself, "What was I doing out there?", "Why hadn't I listened to Richard?" I cooked daily in the saddle and broiled at night in my tent. To top that off, Australian bush flies attacked me every time I stopped. Those demonic monsters respected no one, and they seemed to be searching for water themselves in that desolate land. As soon as I stopped, they attacked my eyes, mouth, nostrils and ears. I prayed for head winds. I prayed for tailwinds. I got no winds. At night, flies circled my tent in an expectant swarm, trying to find a break in the netting. I lay there in my underpants, sweating in the evening heat, cursing them and waiting for sleep to take me away from their noisy torment. The one good thing I remember was staring up at an uncommonly clear night sky with millions of twinkling stars complimented by the Southern Cross.

Each morning, I woke up before sunrise, ate breakfast and pedaled into the quickly rising heat of the day. It never dropped below 95°F at night and the mercury popped 115°F. by the afternoon. It was like breathing air from a portable hairdryer.

The Outback defies description. Its vast landscape of red clay, and white sand reaches the horizon in every direction. Scrub bushes grow close to the ground, but they too give way to the burning 160° heat at ground level at midday. In many areas, nothing grows.

The only companion that I could count on was the sun—always shining and blistering hot. Because of it, and the endless immensity of the land, the Outback swallowed my confidence. There were no reference points, no humanity for hundreds of miles. Traffic on the trans-Australia highway—is virtually nonexistent. A true sense of solitude crept into my mind. Roadhouses were 120 miles apart, but they were nothing more than wooden buildings with gas pumps outside. When I reached one, my spirits rose because I knew that cold pop awaited me in their generator-powered coolers. I stalked into the house, swatting bush flies and headed straight for the cooler. A liter of icy orange pop vanished into my mouth within seconds. I grabbed another before walking up to the cashier to pay the bill. A half-hour later, the roadhouse rippled in the heat waves of my rearview mirror and quickly vanished, as if it had never been there. I was back to drinking tepid water and watching miles of nothing slip past.

This routine repeated itself for weeks, until one day in the middle of the continent, I approached a turnoff where the highway touches the ocean. It's called, "The Great Australian Bight."

The naturally formed bay known as the Great Australian Bight came into existence when Australia and Antarctica separated around 50 million years ago. The coastline of the Bight is dominated by the Nullarbor Plains, an exposed limestone bedrock that was, in fact, a former seabed millions of years ago.

Before reaching it, however, I cruised along, minding my own business when up ahead, I saw something move across the road. The closer I came, the bigger it grew. Finally, I focused on it. A Camel! It was a big, shaggy camel—out in the middle of nowhere. He walked up to me, sniffed my pack, and then trotted north into the Outback. Later, I found out that more than 35,000 wild camels roamed the desert in Oz. They were brought in from the Middle East for transport trains from Adelaide to Alice Springs and on to Darwin, right up the middle of Australia. When mechanized transport arrived, the camels we turned loose in the desert.

Late in the day, I turned off the road for a short ride to the Great Australian Bight on the coast. Rugged cliffs, 200 feet above the ocean, offered spectacular views. It was the only relief I had enjoyed from the bush flies for several weeks. After eating a snack, I pedaled back toward the main road.

At the juncture of the highway, a large emu stood in my way. He wore a coat of black feathers, stood five feet tall and weighed around 90 pounds. The bird walked right up to me, expecting a handout. He had panhandled other tourists who had stopped at this scenic turnout. I tossed him a piece of my apple.

After taking a few pictures, I decided to be on my way. The bird began running alongside me. My bike had eighteen gears, so I started cranking it up the freewheel. With every increase in speed from me, the emu ran faster. With nothing else to do, I decided to see how fast the bird could run. I clicked into high gear and held a good 24 miles per hour for a hundred yards. It didn't faze the emu. He thumped along with me, not even breathing hard. I, however, was gasping and sweating like a horse. Enough of this! I slowed down to my usual 12 miles per hour. The emu again matched my pace. What the devil?! If he didn't mind running alongside, I didn't mind his company. I talked to him—asking him about his family and kids.

"How's your mother-in-law?" I asked. "Get along with her pretty well? How does she deal with this heat? Do any of your kids play cricket?"

After no answer, I continued, "Do you know of any ice-cold swimming pools around here buddy? Have any friends who sell ice cream sandwiches? Man, could I curl my tongue around a fudge bar right about now."

The emu never looked over during the whole conversation but kept a perfect stride with me.

This new partnership continued for 30 miles. I really enjoyed George's (his new name) company. But it was time to call it a day, so I turned off the highway and pitched my tent a hundred meters off the road. George walked into the bush with me and stood while I cooked dinner. I threw him another piece of apple. He also gulped water that I offered from my water bottle. An hour later, with the sun set, George's black silhouette pressed against the sky as he seemingly stood guard outside my tent.

"You don't have to stay here all night George. Go find your friends. I'm out of apples."

George didn't budge. I finished dinner and went to bed with him standing outside my tent. Around three o'clock, I woke up.

A glance outside my tent revealed George standing guard. I felt safe.

The next morning, I woke up with my new friend standing in the same spot.

"G'day George," I said. "This is going to be a test of your character to run 150 kilometers, today mate."

George snaked his beak down to my tent flap.

"Okay, you want some food," I said. "Just wait till I finish eating, okay?!"

"Crazy bird," I said, talking to myself. "This is outrageous. I'm out in the middle of nowhere, 12,000 miles from home—and here you stand guard over my tent all night—in this one tiny spot on the face of the earth, and all you want is a piece of apple. It's a cheap price to pay for your friendship George."

"Squaaaaaak...."

"I couldn't agree with you more," I answered. "But you gotta' work on your vowels, my friend."

I packed my gear and walked out to the road with George following. I fed him a piece of bread. He again took up his effortless stride alongside my bike. It was like having my own dog as my best friend and traveling companion. After an hour, I stopped for a drink and squirted water into George's face. He pranced around in a circle like a banshee, crowing a weird sound. He loved the water.

"You're one crazy bird," I said. "Here, have another shot."

I squirted a steady stream into his face. He opened his beak and caught the water like a funnel. It drained down his throat. When half my bottle was gone, I stopped. He flapped his wings and danced around some more, squawking happily. He loved the attention. We were buddies.

Minutes later, I pedaled west, with a blazing sun rising high into the sky. Sweat dripped off my nose and chin onto the top tube. I looked for George, but he wasn't with me. I looked back.

He was gone. "I'll be darned," I said. "I enjoyed George's company."

I pulled around in a big circle on the highway, but no George was in sight. The Outback stretched to the four horizons.

Some kind of joy faded from my spirit when George quit our partnership. Loneliness crept in again, but I told myself that it was better to have enjoyed him than never to have met him at all. He proved one lesson to me that day—all great journeys through life are better, when shared by two.

I looked around one more time, but the Outback rippled in the heat waves. Better get on with it. I had half a continent to go.

Alone.

(Sunset after a long day in the saddle.)

Chapter 46—Dancing in the Water

"Bicycle touring is sheer ecstasy."

—Pamela Hardaway

Riding north of Perth, Australia grinds along in sweaty work. Temperatures quickly rise every morning to 110°F top. It's a lonely road with minimum traffic. All a bicycle rider can do is sing songs and count white lines that slip by too slowly. Port Hedland remains a distant dot on the map, too far away to imagine for weeks. The highway winds along the Indian Ocean coastline, but a rider never sees the water.

Of the few attractions in the guidebook, I wanted to see the Pinnacles of Cervantes. I turned west off the highway but faced a 26-kilometer sandy road that wound along the coast. A dense growth of thicket grew beside the primitive trail. It took me the rest of the day to push, pull and pedal my bike to the Pinnacles. My vitriolic mouth surprised me. Nothing is more anger provoking than when I can't get my bike rolling. I surged with anger especially when I dumped it in the soft sand. I knew I would have to get out the same way I came in, which put me in a nasty mood.

Although Australia is a large continent, its population numbers only 26,000,000. The West Coast is scarcely populated. North of Perth, its no-man's land. I spent half the day getting to the attraction with no one passing me. Loneliness swept over my spirit.

Even with my best efforts, darkness fell upon me before I reached my destination. It couldn't be more than a kilometer, so I decided to awaken before sunrise and shoot some pictures.

The best photographic shooting is before eight in the morning, and after five when shadows enhance images.

Before falling asleep, I heard kangaroos foraging in the bush. In seconds, I fell asleep, too exhausted to even give myself a sponge bath.

Birds start chirping before dawn everywhere in the world. A flock of gulls provided my alarm clock in the morning. They fought over something on the beach a hundred meters away. A rush of wings flew over my tent.

In minutes, I packed and got moving. A large, thicket-covered sand dune lay ahead of me. The road angled toward it and cut a switchback from right to left and up over the top. A golden sunrise sprayed light over the top of the dune. I cursed the thick sand as I stood on the pedals for the increasing grade. At the point where the road began climbing, I heard a crash in the brush. Above me, a 150-pound Gray Kangaroo bounded out of thicket and along the ridge. I had startled it. Another crashing sound... a second roo, a female, bounded after the first. The kangaroos were catching lots of air as they escaped. Right on their tails was a baby roo, hopping like a pogo stick...boing, boing, boing, boing trying to catch up. In a split second, they were in full flight, their dark silhouettes bounding along the ridge with their tails trailing behind, like the mice in Disney's "Fantasia." I grabbed my camera, but the scene vanished in seconds. The kangaroo family disappeared over the ridge.

At the top of the dune, the sun blazed purple or gold over the horizon like the crown on the head of the Statue of Liberty. Below me an entire city of nature's skyscrapers—the Pinnacles of Cervantes. Nature had carved sandstone into five-meter-high towers that dotted the land. Various shapes, both bulbous and skinny stood silently in the sand. Long shadows swept across the red or orange grounds. As I stood there, two large heads, 40 yards away, broke the stillness and looked back at me, their ears perked for any sounds. Out of the thicket, a tiny head popped up—the baby roo.

On the ridge, I walked among the pinnacles for an hour. Wind and rain had carved them into this silent city, where few pedestrians tread, save a few kangaroos and gulls.

The ride back to the main highway took me the better part of the day. Amazingly enough, I didn't curse or get upset. Everything I saw that morning was worth the struggle of the previous day and the return. I pedaled up the road.

I'll admit it, being on a bicycle adventure by myself proved lonely business. I rode along with no one to talk with. I camped night after solitary night with the gut ache of loneliness. I talked to myself. My journal was filled with lonely items, even self-doubt. Why was I out there in the middle of West Australia? What was the point?

My friends were going to work and coming home to their families. They lived normal lives. They look at me with wonder thinking I've got it made being able to travel around the world. They don't understand that tradeoffs are required in any choice. If they want lots of free time, they have fewer financial abilities. With a heavy work schedule or family, they must give up free time.

We have choices in how we live our lives. Once a choice is made, I think each person must pursue it vigorously, and if they become unhappy, it's time to change life directions. The key is the courage to act. In the action comes an opening opportunity. At my lowest emotional points, even when I'm hanging on by my fingernails, I expect the positive—maybe not at that point, but in time I'll get there. To think any other way, results in depression, and the certain destruction of myself. The one thing I've learned along the world's highways—is there are no guarantees. No one can coast downhill all the time. No perfection for humanity exists in this world. No security from pain or death. Anything good or bad can strike at any hour. It's what I make of a situation that counts. That's what happened on this ride, when I was feeling so low that when I looked up, all I could see was the bottom. Loneliness does that to me. It sucks the energy out of my mind. It hurts. My body feels weak, unable or unwilling to go forward. But I push it toward tomorrow. I will climb out of this valley of loneliness. I know I will.

Late in the afternoon, I was thinking of pulling off the road at the next turnoff to take a swim in the ocean. I felt sweaty and hot. It was getting time to pitch camp, too. Where was that road? The one thing about being so far away from civilization is that there are no reference points. In the USA, you can't get away from Wendy's, MacDonald's, Pizza Hut and Kentucky Fried Chicken outlets. In Australia's Outback, it's so vast that I lost confidence that other humanity even existed.

A road with "Shark's Bay" on the sign-post came into view. I turned toward the ocean. In the parking lot off the beach were a couple of cars. I could tell West Australia cars by their license plates. It was the year after they had won America's Cup from the USA. They had printed on their plates: "West Australia—Home of Australia's Cup." Any time I stopped to talk, they could tell I was a Yank and gave me a hard time about losing America's Cup. It was a national mania for them to win it. It galvanized Australia's collective pride.

When I stopped, a man stood by his car with a curious look on his face.

"G'day mate," he said. "How ya goin' on that push-bike?"

"Pretty good," I said. "But I'm ready for a bath. It's been a couple of days so don't get too close to me."

"No worries," he said. "Here, take a bit of sardines and go feed my friends."

"What friends?" I asked.

"In the water," he said.

Beyond the waves, in waist-deep shallows, two men and a woman stood among four large gray dorsal fins that ripped through the water. Whatever they were, they were big fish. I looked back at the man.

"Have a go at it mate," he said. "They're friendly."

Two minutes later, I stood in the middle of four 300-pound dolphins swimming around me on Monkey Mia Beach. They popped out of the water in front of me and squawked into my face. One of them swam between my legs. I hung onto one of his dorsal fins for a wild ride in the surf. When I dropped off, the dolphin swam right under me, nearly flipping me out of the water like a beach ball. I swam right in the middle of some of the smartest, friendliest creatures on the face of the earth. Their rubbery skin slid by my legs and under my hands. These frolicsome mammals sent a shiver through my body. They displayed incredible energy and playfulness. There I was, right in the middle of them, having the time of my life.

In my journal that night, I wrote about dolphins dancing in the water. They splashed me. I tugged on their fins, and they pulled me around the water. They looked me in the eye, and I looked back, one sentient being to another. In an instant, they were gone.

The experience reminded me of my fading youth when I used to watch fireflies at night. I sat in the darkness and suddenly—there was a firefly—cavorting about, flashing its taillight, on and off—hiding in long grasses—appearing—vanishing—appearing again. Then gone. For good. I stood up, with the exuberance of a child that was making room—oh so gradually and a little painfully—for the depth and wisdom of the man. I stood between two worlds belonging to neither, partaking of both, knowing the moment, so fragile, so fleeting, is all there is.

(Two spoked wheels wrapped in rubber; locked onto a steel frame, makes for one of the most unique adventure machines on this planet.)

SECTION IV: TOURING ASIA

Chapter 47—Face to Face with a Cobra

> ***"Ever bike? Now that's something that makes life worth living! ... Oh, to just grip your handlebars and lay down to it, and go ripping and tearing through streets and road, over railroad tracks and bridges, threading crowds, avoiding collisions, at twenty miles or more an hour, and wondering all the time when you're going to smash up. Well, now, that's something! And then go home again after three hours of it...and then to think that tomorrow I can do it all over again!"***
>
> ***—Jack London***

Mount Everest rises 29,035 feet into the sky over Nepal. Its Nepalese name Chomolungma, means "Earth Mother." For my brother Howard and me, this culture provided a dramatic change from anything we had ever experienced. Riding through the streets on my bicycle in Kathmandu, Bachtapu and Patan proved distressing to my sense of balance. These cities thrive with human misery beyond most westerners' comprehension.

Even for those who have enough to eat, the squalid conditions of great numbers of people left me gasping for understanding. Children with deformed bones and bodies looked up with pathetic eyes and uplifted hands for a few rupees from passersby. Trash and garbage lay everywhere in a profusion of chaos. Venders featured freshly killed chicken and water buffalo meat presented to the public on wooden tables in the street, accompanied by a cloud of flies. In a short time, I had to swallow my sense of trying to understand this strange land and accept it. Otherwise, I would have been emotionally torn to pieces.

One of the good things in Kathmandu was the cheap price of lodging. Howard and I stayed at the Star Hotel. We stayed a week, exploring the nooks and crannies of the city. Bright colors were everywhere. Women's costumes brightened the market bazaar with reds, oranges, greens, and yellows. Temples featured Buddha's eyes glaring at every person walking by. Vendors offered an array of fruits and vegetables we had never seen. Merchants displayed metal works, cloth and beads along the streets. Boys on tricycle taxis stared at us when we passed. The poverty overwhelmed us, but Lance pointed out that it wasn't any different than in inner-city New York. He was right. Nearly every society houses poignant forms of human misery.

We decided to ride to Pokhara about 180 miles away. That city was the beginning of many major trekking routes into the Himalayan Mountains of Nepal. The climb out of Kathmandu proved a killer. Combine altitude with steep grades, and our lungs gasped for oxygen. Our legs suffered, too.

The second day into the ride, we stopped along a river to watch a funeral (on the other side of the water) of a young Sherpa boy who had died from a fall. His family had placed him on top of a pile of sticks. They bound him in linen, except for his face, which was covered later. People walked by his body to pay their respects. His parents gave his belongings to relatives. They sang a song of celebration. No one seemed to be sad during the ceremony. Finally, they covered the boy's face before throwing more sticks on top of his body and lit a fire. It quickly consumed the corpse. After it was thoroughly burned, several men used poles to throw the remains into the river.

"I reckon that's the most sensible way to finish a bloke's time on this earth," Howard said. "Dust to dust. That's the way it's supposed to be anyway. That's the way I'm going."

"That makes two of us," I said. "I can't see taking up a lot of room after I'm gone anyway."

What we had seen provided one of the most natural ways to dispose of the dead. The longer I stayed in Asia, the more I understood their customs. They may be considered Third

World but live in sublime connection with nature. Their lives are basic to the earth, in balance with it. I felt a new kind of peacefulness in Nepal, a sense of present-moment living—in harmony with life.

Two days later, we rolled into Pokhara. Around us, stunning mountain scenery with snow-covered peaks jutted into a clear blue sky. The sun's intensity bore down on us and we were hungry as we moved into the city center.

"Let's get a good hot meal," Howard suggested as we rolled through the dirt streets.

"There's a place that looks as good as any," I said, motioning off to our left.

"Let's do it," Howard added.

We stacked the bikes in tandem against the glass windows of the restaurant. Stacking made theft more difficult. We could never allow our bikes to be not watched for a second. Gear vanished when unattended.

Howard secured a table before I walked into the cafe. Wooden tables and chairs made up the only furniture on a dirt floor. I threw my camera down on the seat next to me. A bearded fellow came over to take our order. We asked for Dahl Bot, rice, bean, and leaf green food plate. It was the standard staple for most people in Nepal. They allowed extra helpings which was the custom. It cost less than 50 cents a meal. Add some unleavened bread, and we were happy riders.

When our waiter walked away, a thin, white turban-covered man dressed in linen Serapis walked through the door carrying a stick over his shoulder. At the end of it hung a medium-sized wicker basket secured with rope. The Indian man sat down ten feet away from us. He placed the basket in front of his folded legs. At first, we didn't pay much attention, but something caught Howard's eye.

"Bloody hell," he blurted out, pointing down at the man.

"Look at that thing flare up," I gasped. "Is this a joke? Look how big it is! Hey Howard, that damn thing's coming our way."

Before us, slithering ever closer, a 6-foot long, fully flared cobra held our complete, undivided and total attention. It kept moving closer, flicking its tongue. We sat there, a captive audience of two, looking into the snake's eyes, transfixed by the motion, solidly riveted to our bench.

"What's the deal here?" I spoke ever so clearly. "This guy would be arrested back home."

"We're not home," came Howard's sobering reply.

The snake transfixed us. It crawled across the dirt floor of the restaurant toward us. What were we supposed to do? Nothing in my life ever prepared me for being in this scene. I was taken by surprise, unable to react. This stuff happens with Indiana Jones in the Temple of Doom, but not to a couple of small-town bicycle riders. Right? Wrong!

Seconds later, because we hadn't responded, the man let the snake crawl to within 24 inches of our legs, which brought us an immediate response. We leaped up, sticking the bench in front of us to fend off the cobra.

"What's the next move?" I asked, totally confused.

"No moves at all unless you wanna' die," Howard said.

"What IS this guy's problem?"

As if to help us understand, the man thrust his free hand into the air with a few pieces of rupees.

"Money, ah yes, the bottom line, he wants money," Howard said.

"Here, give 'em whatever he wants!" I said.

At that point, I would give him my last dime just to save our lives. The man extorted us with terror. We slapped a pocketful of coins onto the chair and shoved it toward him. He grabbed the money, then gripped the snake by the back of the head and shoved it into the basket. Seconds later, he tied the knot, stood up, and walked out to the street, vanishing quickly into the crowd. It happened so fast, my cocked camera lay on the table, leaving me with the only pictures—in my mind.

Chapter 48—Billions on Bicycles

"I can see the Wall of China from here."

—Astronaut Buzz Aldrin

Millions of people around the globe ride bicycles. But I have never been so affected by bicycle riders than when I rode through the streets of Beijing, China. That country houses 1.4 billion people. Their main transportation vehicle? The bicycle.

With 21 million people in the Capitol City of Beijing, more than half of them bicycle to work each day. They use their bicycles so much for work they don't think of them as recreation. The city lies on an arid plain in the northeast just below the Great Wall of China. North of the capitol, barren mountains conceals the tombs of the Ming dynasty. The countryside is rough and rocky.

Inside Beijing, it's a world of black, one-speed bicycles with bells on the handlebars. Each bike is the same, with a small lock on the seat that stays to dead bolt the spokes. A rear rack holds any amount of goods including chairs, tables, washed clothes, chickens in bags, hay, vegetables and children.

People use busses to go to work, which is packed every day. Shunning the busses, more than 10 million people ride their bicycles to work each day. I reached the city in autumn. With millions of bicycles, sidewalks and paths won't do the job. In Beijing, triple-lane, paved bike paths serve as the main arteries throughout the city. Where the traffic slackens, multiple-lane roads suffice.

On my first morning riding around the city, I was stunned at the number of people pedaling slowly, at the same speed to their destinations. No one was in a hurry or passed others. No one shifted gears and everyone dressed the same. At every stoplight, bicyclists backed up by the hundreds. When the light changed, a large dark amoeba-like mass of people oozed into the intersection, some turning left or right, most going forward.

I couldn't understand why they weren't in a hurry until a lady stopped me in the street near Tiananmen Square.

"Are you an American?" she asked in accented English.

"Yes, ma'am."

"Are you having a good time in China?"

"Yes, ma'am," I replied. "But I'm pretty curious about your bicycles. How come everyone is going the same speed? It looks like they're going to a funeral."

"Young man," she said winking at me. "This is a socialist society. No one is allowed to get ahead of their neighbor, so why try to go faster?"

That statement struck me as I rode toward the mountains that week to see the Great Wall. On the way, I visited the Ming dynasty tombs. Much like the Great Pyramids in Egypt, monarchs possessed grandiose needs to build elaborate monuments for themselves. The tombs proved no more than huge gray stoned basements about fifty feet underground, which took decades to build. The one I visited had two secondary chambers for the ruler's wives. When he was buried, his two wives were killed, so they could be put into the tomb with him. Unfortunately, the arches were too small to allow the passage of the wives' caskets. In order for the wives to be near their husbands, the funeral procession carried the extra caskets into the main burial room. Seventeen trunks of jewels were left in the grave.

It seemed vain, but I've seen how the high and mighty around the world have created extraordinary monuments to their self-perceived greatness. If anyone upstairs is looking, I'm sure The Great Spirit must be laughing at our childish antics. The human race is truly a magical mystery tour.

Approaching the Great Wall, I had to climb more than a thousand feet. The wall loomed across the mountainous skyline in front of me. A rush of feelings swept through my mind.

When I was a kid, I saw a picture of the Great Wall in my 10th-grade history book. I told my teacher, Mrs. Rainwater, that someday I would walk on it.

"You will never talk about the Great Wall because China is closed to all foreigners," she said.

"Maybe for now," I said. "But my dad said that everything in the world constantly changes. I'll get my chance one day."

On that cold November afternoon, I cranked hard on the pedals, closer and closer to my boyhood dream. When I reached the wall, a hoard of Chinese gathered around me, trying to sell T-shirts, flags, and other trinkets. After buying a shirt, I parked my bike alongside one of the stairs leading to the top of the wall.

Climbing up those steps was like being at the end of a twenty-year dream. I don't know what it was that drew me to that wall as a kid, but there I was, as a man, walking into my dream. I didn't shout, nor was I excited. I walked up to the top of that wall with a deep feeling of gratitude.

Around me, treeless brown mountains stretched to the north as far as I could see. The wall stretched more than 8,850 kilometers (5,400 miles) across the top of China. It took hundreds of years to build—sacrificing millions of lives. The wall stood more than 30 feet high and 20 feet thick. It featured towers at high points on the tops of mountains where it peaked and ran east and west for as far as I could see.

Several hours later, I headed back to Beijing. Sometimes, when I see such wonders of the world, I think I've experienced the greatest moment of my life. But down the road, something else pops up. It may not be as spectacular in comparison, but in its own way, it holds something special. Each country I visit offers different cultural flavors.

I've seen good things and bad things and people to match. Sometimes, I'm in such beautiful places that I want to stay forever—to be forever happy. But life won't allow that kind of happiness. No matter how beautiful or how much fun some experience is, I can't hold onto it. I have to move into the next day, or a new day will dawn on me no matter what. I carry wonderful memories, but each experience prepares me for the next moment.

I looked back at the Great Wall as I coasted down the steep grade. One more glance. It was gone. My dream became a dream again.

SECTION V: TOURING NEW ZEALAND

Chapter 49—One of the Rarest phenomenon's on Earth

"Cycling in the middle of the rainy season in that region was not at all easy and perhaps wise, but what can I say, the mountains are still the mountains. That's how I am. I spent the next six days under water, a furious downpour or drizzle, between often ruined and flooded paths. My motivation now lies flooded in the soles of my shoes. Some friends have asked me how I manage to ride in such a seemingly hostile environment.

"I think there are two ways of experiencing this continent. Either by passing over it, watching the wheel speeding on the asphalt from one country to another or by letting it absorb you without resistance. And I don't want to miss anything; I want to assimilate all I can of this land that is so different from my own. The encounters are ten, a hundred, or a thousand, spread over the whole day and even into the night. All days."

—Filippo Graglia, a Taubabou on the Horizon

Even the dogs don't bark at bicyclists in New Zealand!

If ever you imagined a paradise for touring bicycle riders, New Zealand is it. The South Island with its 12,000-foot glacier-covered summits possesses extraordinary mountain vistas. But it doesn't end there. Animal life abounds along the rocky seacoast, including countless shore birds. On the domestic front, sheep. More than 21,000,000 of them outnumber the human population seven to one. Four million-year-old Moeraki Boulders "hatch" out of the sand along the coast. Kiwi birds hide in the darkness while penguins and sea lions frolic in the surf.

Doug and I spent three days in Christchurch. It features a lovely Victorian City where characters like the Wizard and the Bird Man catch everyone's attention. The former is a self-proclaimed theologian who walks into the city center daily and preaches a sermon on almost any subject that catches his fancy. His "sermons" cause wild reactions among tourists. Milder-mannered, the Bird Man is a walking perch for hundreds of seagulls that inhabit the city. His avian friends trust him and fight for the honor of perching on his cap.

At one of the museums, we enjoyed riding a Penny Farthing. In fact, an American named Thomas Stevens was the first man to ride a bicycle around the world from 1884 to 1886. He pedaled a High Wheeler, its other name.

But paradise sometimes exacts a price. We rode south out of Christchurch with a brisk tailwind. Being blown down the road is like a free ride. It's like when you jump on a horizontal elevator at an airport. You enjoy an invisible "assist" that speeds you up with little effort. You get to laugh and sing and sit in the saddle with little effort. A hundred miles south, we headed west on Route 79 toward Mount Cook National Park, into the heart of the highest mountains in New Zealand. We pedaled with side winds blowing us across the highway, but that wasn't too bad.

We made our way through a valley until we reached Route 8 in Farlie. A wide open plain covered with brown grasses brought us to a vista overlooking the turquoise waters of Lake Tekapo. We cut across its lower end and coasted for the next few hours on a tailwind that was whipping along at over 50 miles per hour. It was so much fun...that is until we hit Route 80 at Lake Pukaki, headed directly into a 50-mile-an-hour zephyr. This hit us like the granddaddy of headwinds. Sixty-miles per-hour gusts thundered down from the canyons in front of us.

Twenty-four miles separated us from the camping area in the park. It might as well have been a 10,000 feet climb with 16 percent grades. We stopped for a drink at the intersection.

"You sure we want to do this?" Doug asked.

"No kidding, man," I said. "This is an inland hurricane. We're gonna be blown off the road. I don't know how we're gonna make it."

"We'll be in Granny gear the whole time," Doug said. "Let's get it done."

From there, our five-hour ordeal began. With the mountains in front and to our left and the white caps on the lake, we cranked into a savage wind. An invisible force ripped at our bodies. Normally, we hammer out 24 miles in two hours. Not in that wind. We cranked along, heads down, hands gripping the bars and fighting for balance. Blasts of wind howled in our ears. For the first hour, a narrow canyon directed a cyclone at us. The road was straight for three miles but looked like it was forever. We were in the Granny gear the whole time, even on slight downhill grades. After six miles, we reached the storm-whipped waters of Lake Pukaki.

The wind intensified as it exploded off the flat surface of the water. We had been riding together, but one blast sent me crashing into Doug. After that, we kept a short distance between our bikes. On we cranked into this brutal gale-force wind. Up ahead, swirling clouds played wildly in the mountains at the end of the lake. We saw the birthplace of this raging tempest. It thundered and howled at us. It ripped violent patterns onto the surface of the lake. That wind continued doing everything in its power to keep us from our destination. Hour after gut-busting hour, we fought our way into this tempest of sound and fury.

Near sunset, we dragged our weary bodies into the camp area of the park. Doug decided to take a rest. I pitched my tent, tossed the panniers inside and grabbed my camera. The sun settled over the peaks. Shadows moved up the west face of the mountains to my left. Glaciers hung to craggy peaks above me. I wanted to catch the sun making its final lighting assault on the glaciers for this day. I ran along a huge glacial moraine with my pack bouncing on my shoulders.

At the end of the camping area, it turned to bush and moss-covered rocks. I followed a primitive trail that meandered upward along a ridge line. It climbed steeply offering me a glimpse of five large glaciers. Further up the hill, a gray glacial river came into view below me. In front, an enormous canyon stretched into the distance, the result of a receding glacier whose "toe" was barely perceptible under the south face of 12,500 feet Mount Cook. The clouds broke momentarily giving me a full-blown view of its south face. Brilliant mountain energy! Along the canyon, back toward me, on sheer vertical cliffs thousands of feet high, four glaciers clung to their rocky perches.

Nearer my location, about a mile on the right, a large gravel avalanche shoot, now still, cut its way through dark green vegetation. In front of me, where I stopped to sit on a rock, I had a grandstand view of the merging of two glacial canyons. The one closest to me had 300 feet high banks that resembled a canal trough. In that zone, ice overlapped gray rocks, which protruded like broken glass shards on a ghetto sidewalk. Along the rock fields, sinkholes made indentations, and 500-ton boulders lay around like broken eggshells. On the left side of the canyon, nine glaciers in various formations poured like cake batter out of the mountains. Beneath each glacier and mingling around the base of the ice floes, dozens of waterfalls cascaded down the jagged rock.

Above this grand mountain scheme, white and gray twisting clouds folded into changing formations like ghosts in a Disney movie. Even more dramatic was the thrashing and thundering wind. It rushed through the canyon to my right with the deafening roar of cannon fire. Each volley blasted the ridge where I sat. The blasts bellowed over the water of the glacier lakes below me, ripped up the ridge, and roared by me at 60 miles per hour. I was nearly blown over the ridge at one point and dropped to my stomach to save myself. The grasses were being blown so hard; they looked like water running over a dam.

As I watched this drama, wonder crept into my soul. I let out a yell. At times like this, when the wind blows, the ice cracks and rumbles, rivers roar, and the mass of nature's moving parts unite to create a natural movie with a screen that stretches across the sky—it's at these times I know my life equates to delicate perfection. Living is right and good. I have no doubts that I live at the top of my game as I sit here in a howling windstorm with my spirit soaring and my eyes full of blue, gray, aqua, white, ice, water and mountains rising to collide with the sky.

Upon returning to camp, Doug and I were invited into a Kiwi couple's van for dinner. We talked for two hours before the wind died. We walked out at 11:00 o'clock just as a full moon broke over the summit east of Mount Wakefield. A slight drizzle fell west of us across the Saffron Glacier, which we could see from our location. What we witnessed; I've never seen before nor since. Its existence requires the most exceptional of circumstances to occur. That night, we saw one of the rarest wonders of the world.

"Would you look at that?" Doug said.

"Holy catfish," I said. "What do you call something like that?"

"I don't know," Doug answered. "It's not a rainbow, so it's got to be a...moonbow, yeah, that's it, a moonbow."

Across the sky to the west, created by the blazing light of a full moon, and a clear sky to the east—a fully arced rainbow swung from the ground, up over a mountain, into the night sky, back down into the white glacier field, and touched down again on the rocky ground in the distance. The brightest colors were green and yellow, but red and purple glistened in the drizzle, too. Within the arc, a white mist curtain brightened the darkness.

"That is a once-in-a-lifetime happening," Doug said.

"You know, this makes everything we suffered today worth it," I said. "This is so amazing that I can't even believe it!"

My friend and I stood there watching the moonbow. In silence, we heard other things. Perhaps the heartbeat of the universe.

Chapter 50—Rain, Rain, Rain and Then, Some More Rain

"What a thing it is to sit absolutely alone,
in the forest, at night, cherished by this wonderful,
unintelligible, perfectly innocent speech,
the most comforting speech in the world,
the talk that rain makes by itself all over bridges,
and the talk of the watercourses everywhere in the hollows.
Nobody started it, nobody is going to stop it.
It will talk as long as it wants, this rain."

—Thomas Merton

Pedaling through the rolling hills south of Auckland, New Zealand, I headed toward Rotorua's volcanic area. Sheep grazed in pastures along the road. When one of them saw me, it sprinted away, causing a panic-stricken stampede by the rest of the flock. Many times, when I rode along with sheep on both sides of the highway, they bolted in opposite directions and I felt like Moses parting a white sea of woolly water.

In a village north of Rotorua, I bought two days' supply of food. Cranking out of town, I noticed another bicyclist ahead carrying a large pack on his back, but nothing on his racks. I caught up to him to say hello. He greeted me with "Ohio-go-ziee-mus," which means "good morning" in Japanese. As we pedaled in tandem, he spoke a small amount of English.

"Where are you riding from?" I asked.

"The lake region north of Auckland."

"That pack looks pretty heavy," I said. "Isn't it killing your crotch?"

"No problem," he said.

He hailed from Kyoto, Japan. Itsuhicko, a gardener, was taking his first trip away from home. Additionally, it was his first bicycle tour. He had ridden more than 600 kilometers on his way to Wellington. I couldn't comprehend how he could ride that far with a heavy pack on his shoulders. The pressure pain on his crotch must have been killing him. Five pounds will cause severe pain for a rider in a matter of a few hours. Anything more would be debilitating. Riding alongside Itsuhicko, I noticed he was wearing a pair of soft slippers, no socks, no toe clips, no padded gloves, no handlebar pads, no helmet, no padded cycle shorts, and no sunglasses, with no water bottles, no mirrors, and a cheap vinyl seat atop a 10-speed non-touring bicycle. He couldn't possibly be enjoying the ride! His feet would have to be killing him, along with his hands, butt, and shoulders.

We rolled along together until Itsuhicko signaled for a water break by a roadside park. We leaned the bikes against a picnic table. He un-shouldered the leather pack and slung it onto the table. I stepped over to pick it up. My worst horrors were verified. This fellow rider, 5'5", 130 pounds, was carrying a 35-pound pack. That amount of weight hung on his tender shoulders and pinpointed on a few square inches of his butt bones. He endured agonizing pain. Pressure pain is the worst kind of hurt. I was astounded at his ability to withstand the misery.

"Itsuhicko," I said. "You must be crazy to carry this much weight on your body. Aren't you in pain?"

"Itsuhicko not crazy," he said, smiling. "No problem."

"Here," I said, hoisting the pack onto my rear rack. "I'm going to save your butt for the next couple of days."

"No, no, Itsuhicko carry pack," he said, grabbing it away from me.

"No, damn it," I said. "I'm going to carry this for you before you have to get a bionic rectal replacement. Now let me have it."

"No, I carry pack," he said. "It my pack. I carry pack."

He grabbed the pack out of my hands and began pulling it apart to get to a few things he wanted. He pulled out a large metal alarm clock.

"What do you need an alarm clock for when you're on vacation?" I asked. "Who cares what time it is! Get rid of that thing. Burn it."

"Itsuhicko no burn clock," he said. "Must tell time."

“Dude, on a bicycle tour, we don’t worry about time,” I said. “We don’t care what time of the day it is, or the day of the work or the month of the year. The only thing that matters is that it’s time to ride.”

“Frosty, crazy,” Itsuhicko said.

Next, he pulled out a pair of leather shoes, three pairs of pants, a coffee pot, two belts, two glass plates, a half-gallon water bottle, a large portable radio, a bag of apples, rain gear, a heavy tool kit, sleeping bag, air mattress, camera, tripod, and tape-recorder. With the amount of gear in his pack, he could have held a rummage sale and made a fortune. I stood there frowning.

"You know something, you are truly crazy with a capital C," I told him, laughing. "You're gonna kill yourself with that kind of weight mashing your butt."

"Butt okay," he said. "No problem."

He wasn't going to budge on the pack, so I gave up trying. The kind of pain he was experiencing would cripple me in 20 miles on the first day of riding. He had been traveling for two weeks. When we returned to the road, I couldn't help wondering how much our culture controls us. Our thinking is determined by how our parents raised us and what region of the world we grew up in. How we act or react is governed by the country of our birth. Here I was, riding down the road with a Japanese gardener, who was suffering incredible pain every second of his ride, yet he couldn't allow me to carry his pack to relieve the pain.

Later in the afternoon, the sky turned gray, then dark. Everything quieted as a storm front moved overhead. We pedaled along until we found a field for pitching tents. It was flat, but we found two raised mounds to give us a three-inch rise off the ground. That should be enough, and it didn't look like a bad storm. We finished setting the tents up when the rain began pattering against the nylon. Each of us tossed our gear inside and dove in with it.

Darkness prevailed when the rain pelted my tent in earnest. But I sat high and dry on my air mattress. I prepared a bowl of hot rice and veggie dinner. I could hear Itsuhicko's cook stove working, but he wasn't saying anything.

"Everything okay over there," I yelled out through the downpour.

"No problem," he replied. "Much rain, though."

"Yeah, it's raining cats and dogs," I said.

"Where cats and dogs?" he asked.

"Uh...oh, forget it, I couldn't explain it if I wanted to," I said, knowing that he would never understand that saying.

Rain. It's beautiful, but in a tent, it's wet. I stacked my gear along the sides to guard against any seepage that might make its way into my tent. I threw my daypack down for a pillow and rolled out my sleeping bag. My air mattress was soft as I laid back to sleep. In the pitch black of the night, I heard raindrops slapping the tent. A few sheep bleated from an adjacent field. That continued for a few seconds because I fell fast asleep.

"What's this?" I thought as I woke up in the night.

Water had seeped into the back of the tent and soaked the end of my sleeping bag. I pulled my feet up to avoid the wetness of the bag. The rain fell in buckets. I dozed off.

Sometime later, I woke up feeling water invade my sleeping bag, wetting my left elbow. I turned over, but it soaked my right elbow. I lay there awake, feeling a bit cramped. Water soaked through a section of my knees. I tucked myself more into a ball to avoid the wetness. Dry. That's better. I was now safe once more, but I felt uncomfortable curled up like that. I tried to change my position, but water struck not only my knees and elbows, it seeped across my air mattress into the region around my rump. This sucked and I sat up fully awake. Water attacked my every move. I couldn't figure out how it was draining into the tent so quickly. By the minute, my condition deteriorated. That's it, I've had it. I clicked on the flashlight. Oh my God! An inch of water pooled into every section of my tent. It wasn't just seeping in either. I shined the light against the sidewall. The water level in my tent matched the water level outside the nylon. That meant I might be a submarine captain.

I sat in the darkness, my knees up to my chin and arms wrapped around my legs. Water soaked my butt. The sleeping bag: totally hopeless. The rain continued. I shivered. Sitting there, I wondered why I had allowed this to happen again. That's right, it's happened before. Each time it does, I promise myself that every campsite from that point onward must be picked as if a monsoon might rage that night. I promise myself to put the tent on high ground, waterproof the seams, and dig trenches to drain the water. But as the memory of the last drenching fades from my mind, I get careless. I forget to seal the seams and pitch the tent in dry riverbeds, or in a depression. What do you know? Then it happens again, and I chastise myself. I tell myself what a complete nincompoop I am—that I must have a 5-watt light bulb for brains—that when the brains were passed out, I was not only at the end of the line, I was in the wrong line. What does it take to get it through my thick skull so that I could prevent such misery? I make a new pact with myself: this will never happen to me again as long as I live on this earth.

Half an hour later, I heard the first birds chirping, signaling a new day. The rain slowed to a drizzle, then stopped. The first light cast a sullen glow across my tent. In minutes, I surveyed the damage from the rain. Everything except my camera was soaked. I unzipped the flaps. Outside my door, a fully arced rainbow stretched across the sky and touched down on both ends. Right behind it, the sun had cracked the horizon. I looked around. Itsuhicko and I were two islands in a small lake. At one end of what was once a field, two seagulls floated in the water.

"Itsuhicko," I yelled out. "Are you alive?"

What came out of his mouth, I couldn't repeat in Japanese, or for that matter, I don't think it would translate too well in English, either. After his tirade about the rain, and the flood, he stuck his head out of his tent. I looked over at him, and we both started laughing.

"You crazy!" he snorted. "I no follow crazy American no more."

Outside the tent, I sloshed around in two inches of water. My feet squashed around in the grass beneath the miniature lake. Packing the gear proved a struggle. It weighed twice more as normal. I loaded my bike and Itsuhicko stuffed his soaked pack with his wet gear. From the way he hoisted that pack onto his shoulders, it must have been 50 pounds. There was no way he could endure that kind of pressure pain, but I didn't say anything.

While walking out the pasture gate, we looked back at where we had camped. We couldn't tell because even our mounds were underwater. Overhead, the sky threatened more rain as clouds moved across our path.

"You crazy American," Itsuhicko said.

"It wasn't my brightest idea for a campsite," I answered. "Just don't tell your friends back home about this. We Americans need all the help we can get."

Less than a mile down the road, I could see the pain on my friend's face. Each stroke on the pedals was killing him. His butt suffered severe agony at that point. He looked at me.

"Big problem," he said, stopping. "You help?"

"No problem my friend," I said.

He un-shouldered the pack and loaded it onto my rack. Even my mountain bike shuddered under the weight. I strapped the pack down.

Minutes down the road, Itsuhicko said, "My butt thank you."

Then it began to rain...

SECTION VI: TOURING GREECE

Chapter 51—Songs and Gifts of Food

"There is more to life than increasing its speed."

—Gandhi

Socrates made his reputation in Athens, Greece. The weather in this ancient country is sunny and dry. But it is a desolate land and barren mountains make agriculture difficult. The Greeks, however, gave the world great literature and architecture. The Acropolis stands over the city in mute testimony of a glorious past. I had wanted to see the Parthenon with its seven sisters. After spending a week in Athens, Sandi and I had toured the statues, ruins and trinket stores. Our favorite stops were the Greek pastry shops and we danced ourselves crazy at a Delphi wine festival. The only trouble is, Greek men, dance together and they wanted me to dance with them. I was more than surprised when I had my butt pinched.

On the way toward Patras on the coast, we worked off the pastries, pounding the pedals through the mountains. We passed donkeys carrying carts of sticks and oxen pulled heavy loads while men with whips trailed behind. Goats and sheep grazed on sparse patches in the low areas.

Near Patras, we enjoyed a fruit vendor who offered apricots, figs and plums. I wasn't feeling too well because of a bacterium that I somehow had digested in Athens. We pulled into a small park in a residential area outside the coastal town. In minutes, three dozen kids gathered their parents and ten dogs. We leaned our bikes up against a tree and started pitching the tent.

"Sandi, I gotta' lie down or I'm going to throw up," I said.

"That's okay, I'll set the tent up," she said.

I lay down on my back, facing toward the darkening blue sky. I closed my eyes. In moments, I felt the presence of others and opened my eyes to 15 little faces staring down in a circle around me. Giggling and laughing, they started chirping questions at me. It was Greek to me, so I sat up with my arms folded around my knees, and they sat down, imitating me. My audience grew to more than 20 kids. I couldn't understand their questions, but with sign language, we started a conversation. They pointed to themselves and gave a name. I repeated each kid's name. Then they wanted to know Sandi's and mine.

She, too had joined the circle after putting the gear into the tent. After our names, they wanted to know our country, where we started, and where we were going. Then they wanted us to sing a song. I sang an Elvis Presley song, "You ain't nothin' but a hound dog." They went wild. They wanted another song, so we sang "Moon River." They loved it. Now our audience grew to more than 40 kids and parents, none of whom could understand English. Yet we communicated beautifully. We asked them to sing a song. The whole group looked at us when a parent began singing, and they joined in what must have been a national ballad. Their voices melted softly into the warm evening breeze. All those faces looking at us, singing their hearts out...just melted our hearts. What a moment in time, shared with people 10,000 miles away from our home, singing their spirits out to us on a warm night on the shore of the Adriatic Sea.

Afterward, when the crowd dispersed, kids walked up with gifts of food. When we finally zipped up the tent for the last time that night, we had four loaves of bread, six tomatoes, two bags of fruit, chocolate, fresh figs, grapes, and two hot dishes of food that were similar to quiche—absolutely delicious.

When I lay down in my sleeping bag, I nearly jumped out of my skin. Something sharp cut into my arm. I thought an asp had bitten me, which would have been the death of me. Luckily, it was a kitten that had been slipped into our tent while we were singing, and it found my bag was the best place to curl up. I gently put it outside the tent.

Sleep settled over us, but a few hours later, a chorus of barking dogs startled us. From one side of the street, three dogs launched their attack. After their vocal cords gave out, a second group across the way barked themselves into a frenzy. Then some smaller dogs yipped and screamed their two cents worth. This barking marathon continued until dawn. A few minutes of silence settled over us when a rooster announced the coming sunrise. This must have been the signal for the dogs to go to sleep. When I got out of the tent, they were oblivious to the world.

We were invited to a morning breakfast on the front porch of a family that we had met the night before. Once again, families from around the neighborhood gathered to greet us. We couldn't speak a word of Greek, nor could they understand a word of English. An hour later, we headed out to the road, kids running alongside us. We waved to their parents and spoke the only word we knew in Greek. "Ehfkhahreesto" (thank you) they smiled and repeated the same to us.

In all my travels, I couldn't begin to repay the kindness I've received from people around the world. Kindness is an international language.

Chapter 52—The Oracle of Delphi

"The Oracle said that I was the wisest of all Greeks. It is because I, of all Greeks, know nothing."

—Socrates

You probably watched the movie, "Achilles" where Brad Pitt played the legendary Greek warrior who traveled across the Mediterranean Sea to assault Sparta. He fought against the Spartans but could not conquer the high walls of the Spartan fortress. Thus, his legions departed but left a wooden horse outside the gates. The Spartans took the massive horse inside the fortress gates. Inside the horse, Achilles, along with his band of warriors, jumped out of the bowels of the Trojan horse and opened the gates to the Greek fighters. They ransacked Sparta.

In the end, Achilles lost his life to an arrow that hit his heel, and poisoned him to death because, as legend has it, when his mother dipped him into the river, she held him by his heel, thus not protecting that single point in his body from attack. That's why you hear of their "Achilles Heel" when someone suffers injury or loss.

When you ride your bicycle through Greece, its beauty overwhelms you as the Mediterranean Sea sparkles off to your side. Islands shimmer in the deep blue waters. Fig trees grow in orchards. Rock-strewn mountains cover the dry landscape. At the same time, Greeks throw their trash everywhere into gullies, streams, under bridges, and just about anywhere except a landfill or trash can. It's pretty sickening. Humans toss their trash in every country in the world.

But the one extraordinary aspect of traveling through Greece remains the incredible amount of ancient history you pass through. Conquering armies invaded Greece dozens of times. The Greeks suffered greatly.

And through it all, Greek engineers built the Parthenon in Athens, which must be one of the "Seven Wonders of the World" in its grandeur. To stride upon it is to walk in the footsteps of emperors, wise men, madmen, and holy men.

After seeing all we could see in Athens, we pedaled the bikes toward the Oracle of Delphi. In Greek mythology, it means, "The navel of the Earth."

Gary and I climbed through some rugged terrain with jagged mountains piercing the sky above us. We also cranked up 2,100 feet of altitude as we arrived from the east. We passed what was formerly a training field for athletes who played in the games. They trained with weights, javelins, rings, leather balls, and other athletic equipment.

"Man, this is like walking into the past," Gary said. "This is beyond incredible how those Greeks built such huge buildings without cranes or engines to lift those ten-ton carved rocks into place."

"Yeah, when you look at this kind of architecture, it's almost beyond my imagination how they could build such extravagance," I said.

"I'm going to climb to the top of the kiva," Gary said. "I want to get a shot of you speaking to the crowd."

"Go for it," I said.

Gary spent five minutes hiking to the top of the 5,000-seat arena. When he got to the top, he yelled down, "Are you ready to give your speech."

"Yeah," I said. "Four score and seven years ago..."

Gary took the shot. I gave my little speech like many other thespians from 3,000 years ago. When I thought about it, kings, queens and conquering armies all passed through the Oracle. The picture is so good that I have it on my office wall these many years later.

Everything that remains of the Oracle stems from enormous rock structures of buildings, the Oracle itself that stands near an ancient spring, and a massive kiva that seats around 5,000 people.

Above that, we walked across something like a football field with rock stands on both sides. It's apparent that people as far back as 1,400 BC like to be entertained.

Dating back to 1400 BC, the Oracle of Delphi created the most important shrine in all of Greece; in theory, all Greeks respected its independence. Built around a sacred spring, Delphi was considered to be the omphalos—the center (literally navel) of the world.

People came from all over Greece and beyond to have their questions about the future answered by Pythia, the priestess of Apollo. And her answers, usually cryptic, could determine the course of everything from when a farmer planted his seedlings, to when an empire declared war.

After tramping all over the grounds, we visited the museum at the base of the Oracle. It's phenomenal with crude statues carved out of rock from 1,000 years ago, but then, we could see a progression of how the sculptors refined their work right into the Bronze Age.

As the Greeks grew in their knowledge and understanding of the world, their art also became more refined. Aristotle, Plato, and Socrates along with mathematicians, began to figure out the laws of Nature. That's why Greece is known as the "Cradle of Civilization."

Aristotle said, "It is the mark of an educated mind to be able to entertain a thought without accepting it."

Because the Oracle enchanted us so much, we camped out and returned the next day. It's quite a "heady" experience to tramp around ancient ruins from 3,000 years ago. It's almost like you could hear the cheers as the athletes played the games while the spectators roared with approval. Not much has changed in the 21st century with sports arenas housing 100,000 cheerings and/or booing fans.

"Man, I gotta tell you," Gary said. "Between the Parthenon and this Oracle, I'm pretty much blown away by the ancient Greeks. Their extraordinary architecture, their sculptors, their myths...all of it just mesmerizing to me. This is one of the high points of our journey. Hard to believe we started in Norway in the land of the Vikings and ended up here in the Cradle of Civilizations."

"Yeah, there's something about bicycle travel that brings greater perspective," I said. "I can't put my finger on it, but I feel it in my bones. Maybe the physical and mental effort to get to these places brings a greater appreciation. It's not easy and it's not fast, but man, it's truly unique."

"You got that right," Gary said. "I think it's time to get moving to Corfu. More ruins, more artwork, more history. It doesn't get any better than this."

We filled our water bottles, talked to a few tourists, and then, like millions of other visitors to the Oracle, we rolled away with only memories and pictures of our visit to The Oracle of Delphi.

(Frosty making a speech to the ghosts of the past at the Oracle of Delphi.)

SECTION VII: TOURING THE LAST FRONTIER OF ALASKA

Chapter 53—Hyderized

"We can never have enough of nature.
The sight of must refresh us,
inexhaustible vigor, vast and titanic features,
the seacoast with its wrecks,
the wilderness with its living and decaying trees,
the thunder-clouds,
and the rain which lasts for weeks,
and produces freshets.
We need to witness our own limits transgressed,
and some life pasturing freely
where we never wander."

—Thoreau

British Columbia. Its mountains span the horizon in every direction. Pine trees march across the landscape, scaling lofty peaks, stopping only at the tree line. Rivers rage from beneath gargantuan glaciers. Trout and salmon swim through crystalline waters and leap over waterfalls that splash through old-growth forests. The vast wilderness swallows your imagination.

Sandi and I had cranked our way west from Prince George's toward Prince Rupert on the coast of British Columbia, the rainiest city in the world. At Kitwanga, the Cassiar Highway, Route 37, led us north toward Stewart. A big sign on the highway read, "NORTH TO ALASKA." Within a few miles, the pavement dropped off onto gravel. Our loaded mountain bikes kept our full attention as we navigated the rough road. Many times, the gravel turned to sand, which left us pushing through the soft spots. We had to stop often—take off our shoes and shake out the sand. Each day, we found ourselves deeper into the wilderness. At one point, we stopped on a ridge overlooking a valley. The ground fell away from our wheels, stretching into tree-covered ripples that reached up to glacier-covered mountains. On the far side of the valley, waterfalls tumbled over cliffs and splashed into frothing white water that flowed into emerald lakes.

"Look at the distance to that glacier," Sandi said. "It must be over five miles and it still looks big."

"Yeah, but look over your left shoulder about thirty yards away, in the trees," I whispered.

"A bald eagle," Sandi said.

On a branch of a dead tree, a glistening black feathered eagle with a snow-white head sat preening itself. When the bird noticed us, it flew over the valley.

"What a beautiful bird," Sandi gasped.

"Yeah, and we're gonna see more as we go along."

We crossed the Cranberry River by midday. Hard gravel made riding easier as we rode one day to reach Meziadin Lake Junction. Two gas pumps stood out of a concrete slab in the middle of a muddy parking area. Puddles, tire ruts, and holes dotted the lot. We stopped for lunch in a rickety mobile home. Some of the most weathered-looking men we had ever seen sat around red and white checkered vinyl-covered tables, smoking and drinking coffee.

We ordered sourdough pancakes, which were offered even in the afternoon. The cook was so impressed with our bicycling up the Cassiar that he gave us all we could eat. My hunger told me I could eat a dozen, but when the cook came out with the first stack, his pancakes rivaled a medium-sized pizza. We slapped on butter and drenched them in maple syrup. It dripped over the sides of the steaming cakes. By the time I finished my plate, I knew three more would stuff me. Sandi looked full with the first stack. The men finally realized that we were riding bicycles. They craned their necks, looking out the window at the bikes leaning against the railing.

One grizzled man pulled on his dusty beard. He wore leather from head to toe. He puffed a pipe between sips of coffee. I could tell he wanted to talk with us. I looked him in the eye, which gave him an opening to talk.

"Where you two headed?" he asked.

"Up the Cassiar," Sandi said.

"You gonna head over to Hyder?" he asked.

"That's forty miles out of our way," I replied.

"I don't think you wanna miss that interesting side trip," the old man said. “It’s called Glacier Highway.”

"Why is that?"

"Coz you’ll ride past giant glaciers hanging off the valley peaks," he said. "Be sure to visit Hyder. It'll be the best experience you'll have on the Cassiar."

"You game Sandi?" I asked.

"Yeah, why not? We have the time, and that's what we came for."

"Heck yes, we're gonna check it out," I told the man.

"You'll be glad you did."

"Thank you, sir."

We loaded up on water and more food. Lake Meziadin made a perfect camp setting that night with mountains rimming it and trees growing down to the water's edge. We took sponge baths after our feet rebelled against further advancement into the glacier-fed lake. A campfire kept the mosquitoes at bay. That night, the temperature headed into the low 30's. We dove into our sleeping bags and zipped them up around our faces. I kept my wool socks on for extra warmth.

In the morning, we broke camp for an early start. I wasn't quite sure what our mentor had in store for us, but he didn't want to spoil it by giving us further information. His mysterious approach piqued my interest enough that I wanted to see what was out there. Sandi checked the map only to see the road led to the coast and ended in the town of Hyder, Alaska, the southerly city reached mostly by road in Alaska. It looked like it was located deep in a fiord.

As we pedaled, the lake swept south of us and west toward a snow-covered mountain range. We rode through canyons with steep rock walls rising on both sides of the highway. Well past the lake, we threaded our way through tightening canyon walls that led up to pine-covered slopes. The terrain rose to dark tundra grasses that led to rock and snow. After a hard pull on a steep, loose gravely incline, where our back tires slipped out from under us, we crested the hill, lathered up with sweat.

"Look at that," Sandi exclaimed.

"That's incredible," I said.

"That old guy did us a big favor," she said.

"No kidding."

Above us, three glaciers hung from their mountain perches. The tip of one glacier melted over a cliff. A waterfall dropped 1000 feet to the canyon floor. The white spray from the windswept water burst into a rainbow that waved back and forth as if someone cooled themselves with a Japanese hand fan. Melting water from the largest glacier tumbled into white froth down to the road. Small icebergs floated like corks in a lake formed by the melting ice. As we stood astride our bikes, a one hundred and fifty-foot high block of aqua-blue ice separated from the main body of the glacier.

"Sandi, look at that thing break away!"

"Get that shot."

As I pulled my camera, a crunching, ripping sound echoed across the water. The large chunk toppled into the lake and a wall of ice splashed into a semi-circle. A wave rolled across the surface until it crashed against the beach below us.

"Look, it is popping back up," I said.

"It looks as big as a battleship," Sandi added.

"There goes another one."

A white column of ice two hundred feet high split from the main glacier. The ensuing wave washed into a silt-laden river that frothed over a rocky bottom. A steam cloud lifted off the water and settled into the low spots along the road.

"This is something like I've never seen before," I told Sandi.

"Yeah, let's go see more of it."

We coasted down the incline toward the glacial lake. The jagged toe of the glacier resembled a Great White shark's mouth full of teeth—impressive but foreboding at the same time. Dozens of waterfalls fell from snowfields a mile above the road. Farther along the route, we spotted a large glacier bottlenecked between two steep cliff walls. It resembled a moose's face painted aqua or white.

"You see that glacier up there," I said, pointing.

"Yeah, it's pretty big."

"How far do you think it is from here?"

"Maybe a mile."

"Let's go climb it."

"Great idea."

"I like you, you know that?"

"Only because I cook for you."

"HEY," I said. "I wash dishes, don't I?"

"You can carry the water and food, too."

"Of course, dear..."

We loaded two quarts of water and food into my daypack. In minutes, we dropped down from the road into a field that grew steeper as the slope neared the mountain's base. Gophers scurried along the ground and jumped into their holes when we surprised them. We may have been the first human beings they had ever seen. With each step, the incline grew sharper. Halfway up, we reached a gray-silted river that cut us off. We had to keep our shoes on to ford it because sharp rocks lay everywhere in the streambed. The frigid current rose midway on our thighs, so we held hands to help each other. One slip and we could be swept downstream. I tested the bottom with every step. Once across, we crawled over a steep rock pile left by the melting ice.

"You feel the wind?" Sandi said.

"It seems to be swirling and it's getting colder. I can feel the moisture in the air," I said.

We climbed another hundred yards to the base of the glacier. Water drops pelted us, and a chilling wind slapped our faces. We zipped up our jackets and pulled our hoods over our heads. From under the glacier, a swift, icy stream eight feet wide boiled over the rocks as it cascaded down the slope in a bubbling froth.

"Yiee, this is great," Sandi yelled.

"Can you believe how cold it got?" I asked. "I'll bet it dropped twenty degrees. This wind is whipping around because of the temperature changes."

"Yeah, it's incredible," Sandi said. "It looked peaceful from the road. Now, we're in the middle of a miniature storm. Look at this blue color on the ice. It even feels cold. Can you smell what I smell?"

"Yeah, I can almost taste a fresh coolness within the ice," I answered. "It smells so fresh. It feels like having my lungs cooled off with peppermint."

"Look at the layers in this chunk of ice," Sandi said. "It's full of rocks and sand. It looks like the rings on a tree—only they're flattened out like a birthday cake."

"Yeah," I said. "Look back at our bikes. They look like specks on the road. This is a great view of the canyon."

"Let's get off this glacier," Sandi said. "My feet are freezing and I'm getting soaked from these raindrops."

"Okay," I said, digging into my pocket. "I want to leave a penny to show we were the first to climb up here."

"Sounds good, but who would ever find it?"

"Who cares? We know it's up here. That's all that matters."

I placed a penny in the crack of a large boulder. Sandi took my hand as we headed down the rock piles and crossed the stream. Along the way, Sandi stuck a pink fireweed flower into her hair. She looked like a princess making her way down from the throne room of the mountain gods. We started running like the “Sound of Music” as we neared the bikes. We scrambled up the road embankment toward the bikes.

"Did you feel different up there under the glacier," she asked.

"Yes, I felt cold, wet, and alive."

"That's it, me too, like every cell in my body wanted to jump out of my skin."

For the rest of the day, we cranked down a narrow dirt road. Dozens of glaciers hung from their perches as much as a mile above our heads. Waterfalls dropped out of the clouds that hung along the mountain flanks. We reached Stewart before dusk. At the western edge of town, a vast ocean bay opened up before us, with cliffs dropping vertically into the sea. Waves crashed against the rocks. A mile over our heads, glaciers clung to the summits.

We rode through town toward the American side to a tiny fishing village named Hyder. A sign going into town read, "The Friendliest Ghost Town. Population 87." Hyder featured the main street covered in dirt and lined with broken-down houses. It was like walking onto a movie set. We stopped at a place called “The Alaska Inn.”

"Let's have dinner," I said.

"This looks like the only place in town," Sandi added.

We walked into a bar with stuffed animals adorning the walls. Hats, horseshoes, traps, bumper stickers, and life preservers hung from the rafters. Several tables were filled with couples. Two bearded men at the bar were talking but watched as we walked to a booth. When we sat down, Sandi noticed dollar bills covering the walls. A person's name was written on each one. A waitress walked over to us.

"Where did this money come from?" Sandi asked.

"Everybody asks that question," she answered. "We're so far from civilization; we don't get many visitors. For some reason, people think it's an honor to be here. They leave a little memory of themselves."

"How much do you figure is on the wall?" I asked.

"We've got over $25,000.00 tacked up," she replied. "Now, what would you like for dinner?"

"I'll take this bill-covered wall to go," I said.

"You can only have the evening salmon special," she said, not appreciating my stab at humor.

"We'll take two specials," Sandi said.

"Two specials coming up," she said.

"Have we seen the sights today, or have we seen the sights TODAY?!!" I said.

"Yeah, that hike was one of the best things I've ever done. That storm at the edge of the glacier was amazing."

"Hey, you folks over there," one of the men at the bar called out to us in a drunken voice.

"Who? Us?" I replied.

"Of course, you two, that's who, come over to the bar," he said. "I've got a surprise for you."

"I think that guy is a bit drunk, so maybe we should humor him," I told Sandi.

"What if he..."

"Hey, you folks come over to the bar and get Hyderized," the man said. "You've got to be Hyderized before you can officially be welcomed into this town."

"What's he talking about?" Sandi asked.

"I don't know..."

"Come on, you two," the other man said, motioning.

"They're coming over to our table," Sandi said.

"Are you steppin' up to the bar to get Hyderized or ain't ya?" the first fellow hissed through his missing front teeth.

"We're not drinkers," I said.

"That don't make no difference," he crowed. "This is special. Now come up and meet my fren' Jed."

The guy grabbed me by the arm and pulled me along with him. I could have resisted, but I didn't want to create a scene. Besides, there wasn't much he could do to me physically. Sandi followed us to the bar.

"This is my fren' Josh Clayburn and I'm Jed Decker," he hissed through his teeth again. "We saw you were new in town and wearin' those funny shorts, so we wanted you to get the official greetin' of Hyder."

"That's right," Josh said. "Jed and I have decided to help you two with the keys to the city, err, I mean keys to the..."

"Keys to the village Josh, ain't you got no mind, man?" Josh admonished his friend. "Now, are you two ready?"

"What do we have to do?" Sandi asked.

"Now you're talkin'" Jed grinned with a mouth full of gold teeth. "You see these two glasses of clear liquid?"

"Can't-miss 'em," I said.

"All you have to do is knock it back in one gulp, and you will be officially Hyderized for the rest of your natural-born lives. It's truly an honor," Josh said.

"What's in the glass?" I said, picking it up and sniffing the contents.

"NO, NO, NO! You can't smell it," Jed said.

"So what is it?" I asked, realizing that it was liquor.

"Um, it's...GLACIER WATER, that's what it is, just a little glacier water, won't hurt ya' none," Josh said. "Now just take the glasses and throw them to the back of your throats in one gulp."

"I don't know about this being glacier water," I said, holding the glass.

"Me either," Sandi said, grabbing hers.

"You gotta drink it to be Hyderized," Josh urged.

At that moment, I looked at the bartender and two other patrons who had come into the bar. They nodded in agreement. It wasn't more than a swallow, so it wasn't going to kill us.

"Here goes nothing Sandi," I said, throwing the drink back into my mouth.

"Me, too," she said, raising her glass to her lips.

"Argh," I yelled as the drink burned my throat.

"This is awful," Sandi gasped. "Water please, bartender, water, get me a glass of water."

Everyone in the bar laughed at our reaction to the glacier water. As I drank a glass of water to rinse the booze down, tears filled my eyes. The bartender thought it was cute when he put a match on my glass and watched it light up in a blue flame. Sandi and I had swallowed some 151-proof rum.

"I feel like I've just been kicked in the throat by a mule," I told Sandi.

"I feel like my brain got run over by a train," she added.

"Are we Hyderized now?" I asked Jed.

"Yup, you and your lady are officially welcomed to Hyder, Alaska."

Back at the table, we drank two more glasses of water to rinse the taste out of our mouths. Everyone seemed to enjoy the show. Our waitress arrived with our salmon dinners.

"Is there such a thing as hyderization?" I asked her.

"Oh yeah, it's a visitor's official celebration for being here. Since you two drank your glacier water, I'll get your cards to prove it," she said. "But just remember, don't drink more than one glass, or that stuff will knock you for a loop."

"I feel like I stuck a blowtorch into my stomach, so why would anyone drink a second glass of that firewater?" I asked.

"I guess folks don't have much to do around here," she answered, walking away.

"I don't understand that one," Sandi said. "You could climb mountains, fish, sail, backpack, camp, and more in a place like this."

"It's probably easier to drink," I said.

"I don't understand why," Sandi said. "That stuff is poison."

"What the heck. We're Hyderized. Did you see the sign above the street when we drove in?"

"Yeah, the one about this being the friendliest ghost town?"

"Maybe this is the perfect place for Jed and Josh. They're a couple of characters."

"Yeah. Let's eat; I'm starved."

"Boy, this salmon tastes good. How's yours?"

"Good, real good."

(The Bear Glacier on Glacier Highway, BC)

Chapter 54—Earthquake Under a River

> ***"Traveling is a brutality. It forces you to trust strangers and to lose sight of all that familiar comforts of home and friends. You are constantly off balance. Nothing is yours except the essential things. air, sleep, dreams, the sea, the sky. All things tending towards the eternal or what we imagine of it."***
>
> ***—Cesare Pavese***

"My butt is killing me," Sandi said as we neared Dease Lake Junction on Route 37 in British Columbia.

"Mine too," I said. "But look around us. There's nothing but wilderness."

"Yeah, it's beautiful."

A few hours later, we reached the junction. The sun burst through the clouds, casting an orange glow on the leaves. We stopped at a log cabin gas station/grocery store.

"Howdy," I said to the man behind the counter.

"How do their partners," he replied, stroking his beard.

"We're looking for a campsite and the best fishing in this neck of the woods."

"Well now, there's a pretty fair spot about a half mile north of here. You'll be on the banks of the lake in a peaceful cove. There's a good supply of wood and a grassy spot you can pitch a tent."

"How about the fishing?" I asked.

"Well sir, just about any place you can throw a line in the water," he answered. "But if you wanna catch 'em by the buckets, go back south about a mile and look for a river about fifty yards off the road. There's a path that leads through the brush to a sandbar near the bank. Just toss your lines in there and you'll catch a fish with every cast."

"Every cast?" Sandi exclaimed.

"That's right, but there's one small problem," he said.

"When is catching fish a problem?" I asked.

"You might catch something you're not lookin' for."

"Like what?"

"Bears...mean ones, ornery ones, and bad ones," he answered, grinning. "All they have to do is decide between you and the fish once you get down there on their table."

"What's so funny about that?" Sandi asked.

"It's not funny young lady," the old man said. "Last week, a big brown smashed through the front door without knockin' and made a mess of my dry goods. Bears ain't much for solvin' things peaceful-like. But don't let me worry you none folks."

"Ah, heck no, we're not worried," I said. "All we have to do is decide between bears and fish...ah, it's just a matter of who gets to eat who...ah, but we've got bear spray enough to stop a grizzly."

"You're a lot of comfort," Sandi said, rolling her eyes.

"Kiddin' aside, don't worry about it," he added. "They'll leave you alone. Just make a lot of noise goin' down to the river. Keep your campsite clear of food, and you'll be fine."

"Wonderful," Sandi said.

We pulled our bikes off the side of the building and headed for the campsite on Dease Lake. We enjoyed a smooth gravel road because it hadn't rained for a week. A steep path led down to the lake. We stacked the bikes near the shore. Glass-clear water revealed hundreds of rocks scattered over the lake bottom. Trees circled the shoreline.

"This is beautiful," Sandi said.

"Let's pitch the tent and catch some fish before it gets darker," I said.

"We better be sure to keep the food in a tree away from camp," Sandi advised.

"You don't have to tell me twice," I said. "That guy might have thought he was funny, but he scared me."

We pitched camp, gathered firewood and rigged the fishing poles. A short ride took us back to the river the old man told us about. Sandi followed me through the thick brush toward the sandbar. We talked loudly and whistled to alert any bears in the area. I carried my canister of bear spray, at the ready. At the water's edge, a swift current raced along the fifty-yard-wide river. Large boulders lay in the shallow streambed.

"See any bears?" Sandi asked.

"Naw, we're cool."

On Sandi's first cast over the swirling waters, a grayling trout struck the lure.

"I GOT ONE!" she yelled. "Yahooo, this is great! Look at her fight, look at her jump, wow, this is fun."

"It's a good sized rascal, too, and it's still fighting...here, grab the line...that's it, now pull it in, yeah, got it," I said. "It must weigh two pounds."

"Here, you try it," Sandi said, pulling the lure out of the fish's mouth.

I cast out across the water.

"GOT ONE!" I said, on the first cast. "Look at that son-of-a-gun walk on water with his tail... look at him fight. That guy wasn't kiddin', a fish with every cast."

"A fishing paradise. These fish are so far into the wilds, they've never seen an artificial lure. If the fishing is this good from now on, we'll have so much fun," Sandi said. "Here, let me grab yours, yeah, that's it, bring it a little closer, there, got it. What a beauty."

"Just keep your eyes peeled for bears," I warned. "They might think we're stealing their dinner."

We caught trout for the next half-hour, one with every cast. We tossed them back. They weighed nearly three pounds and measured 17 to 20 inches. Near dark, we headed back to our campsite and ate dinner.

That night, a storm moved across the mountains west of us. Lightning splintered the sky. Thunder rolled across the lake, awakening us.

"Look at this," Sandi said, nudging me.

"What is it?"

"Look at the sky."

"Yeow, what a shot of lightning," I said. "We're in for a bad storm."

"It looks pretty nasty," Sandi said. "Did you stake the tent down real good?"

"We'll be fine."

Overhead, black clouds swirled in the sky, blotting out the moon. Lightning cracked the air and thunderclaps vibrated the wind that pounded across the lake. Soon, water drops splashed into the lake. We heard it coming at us as torrents fell from the sky. Within minutes, a blast of wind lashed into our tent, nearly tearing the stakes out of the ground. A lightning bolt across the lake spread into three fingers and burst into the trees. A tree exploded into pieces.

"Did you see that?" I gasped.

"My God!" Sandi said. "If that bolt hit us, we'd be fried."

"We should be safe with these tall trees around our camp," I said. "It'll strike a tree first and follow it down into the ground."

"Or split the top of the tree off, which will land on our heads."

"What do you have to think up things like that for?"

"Could it be I'm scared?" Sandi frowned.

The wind howled across the lake. Sheets of water poured out of the sky and pelted our tent. Drops trickled down the inside of the nylon. Water soaked the toe end of our bags. I woke up feeling cold water on my heels.

"Are you dry?" I asked Sandi who nudged me.

"Sure, like a fish."

"We can't do anything until morning, so let's make the best out of a bad situation. I should have sealed the seams better. That's why the water is leaking in on us."

The storm tore at our tent for five hours. It poured out of the sky in buckets. The lightning passed, leaving a constant thudding of raindrops pounding our tent until daybreak. We were soaked, with water covering the floor of the tent, and soaking our bags. We put on our jackets to keep warm. The dawn broke with sunshine flickering through the trees. A hawk sounded a greeting to the morning as the sun burned off the mist. Water drops fell from the leaves and pattered onto the tent. Sparrows chirped in the branches.

"Say good morning to the sun," Sandi said, looking out of the tent.

"That's the best news I've heard in six hours."

"Let's get this gear on a clothesline to dry it out."

"Sounds good," I said. "Let's get breakfast and go fishing on that river while our gear dries."

"You go," Sandi said. "I want to write in my journal."

"Okay."

I grabbed my bike, along with my fishing gear, and walked up the steep road to the main highway. Rain-filled puddles dotted the road. I plowed through them, back to the sight where we had caught the fish yesterday. As I neared the trail leading to the river, I felt the ground shaking faintly.

"Feels like earthquake tremors," I muttered to myself, as I stashed my bike alongside the road and walked into the bush.

The closer I came to the river, the more the ground rumbled. When I reached the river, it had risen over two feet. The ground shook under me. I started to get frightened before I saw what was causing the earthquake tremors. Out in the river, surfacing like dolphins breaching, large gray boulders, some three feet in diameter, bounced downstream, being carried along by a raging current. The added volume from the rain had changed the river's once peaceful current into a giant watery earth-mover. Each time the boulders hit on an uneven spot, they shook the earth. Their total sum effect shook the ground violently near the water. Once I realized what was going on, I laid down on my back and got the wildest vibrating body massage of my life.

Chapter 55—The Worst Experience of My Bicycle Life

> *"There are no guarantees in life;*
> *Not today, not tomorrow,*
> *Not ever."*
>
> *—Duncan E. Littlefair*

Rex and I had pushed our bikes through the Wrangell Mountain range to the coastal town of Valdez, Alaska. We had ridden alongside the oil pipeline that stretched from Prudhoe Bay more than 800 miles south to the ocean. The large silver cylinder crossed rivers on swinging bridges, burrowed underground in places, and climbed hills at other times. It delivers 1.5 million barrels of oil per day, and it takes a week to reach the loading docks.

Along the road to Valdez, glaciers tumbled down to the highway. We pedaled through snowfields. Camping was a test of our resolve in the early summer. Temperatures dropped in the shadows of the 18,000-foot peaks. Near the coast, the road plunged downward along a raging white water river canyon. We stopped our bikes above the village.

In front of us, distant waterfalls from steep cliffs surrounded the port village of Valdez. Tankers, the length of three football fields, floated in the water. One-room houses lined the shore and white columns of smoke curled upward from their tin chimneys. Seagulls flew in circles and bobbed in the water near the oil storage tanks lining the docks.

We coasted downward until we reached a cafe. Inside, every animal that walked, crawled or flew in the state of Alaska held a place on the walls, or someone's head. Bearded men in plaid shirts and dirty jeans shoveled food into their mouths. We ate dinner and asked about the ferry schedule that would take us past the Columbia Glacier and into Whittier, Alaska. We found two large dock crates for our campsite that night.

At 5:00 a.m., a ship's whistle woke us. We purchased tickets and rolled our bikes onto the ferry, along with dozens of passenger cars. When the cargo was loaded, the ship cast off. Our vessel plowed through the narrow inlet on its way to deeper water. Looking back, we saw a light mist clinging to the mountains above Valdez. Two hours out to sea, we saw our first icebergs. A blue sky stretched across the horizon and was broken only by stunning snowcapped mountains. We stood on the side of the ship.

"Look over there," Rex said, pointing.

"A bunch of seals enjoying a free ride on those icebergs," I said.

"There's more over there on that big slab."

"They're everywhere."

"LOOK! Over there! Those seals are jumpin' out of the water."

"It's a whale," I said. "I think it's a killer whale. Look at it cut through the water."

"Where? Oh yeah, I see it, wow, what a monster!"

Over the loudspeaker, the captain spoke, "Good morning ladies and gentlemen. If you look off the port side, you'll see hundreds of seals sunning themselves. Many have caught the scent of that killer whale, about one hundred yards off the port bow. He's stalking his prey near that cone-shaped iceberg. Get your cameras ready for some pictures. This whale is one of the most dangerous species in these Arctic waters. It will attack any animal."

"Look at him slice through the water...oh my God, he's got a seal," Rex yelled.

What happened next took my breath away. The whale leaped onto the ice and grabbed a baby seal. As the whale slipped back off the floe, he flipped the seal into the air. When it came down, he cut it in half with one powerful bite. The water turned bloody. A dozen seagulls circled, ready for any remaining food. Seconds later, the whale dove, leaving the screeching seagulls with a few morsels of food to fight over. Minutes later, we saw the killer whale far behind us, looking for more prey.

"Your attention please," the captain spoke again. "We will be steaming near the Columbia Glacier soon. It's one of the largest ice floes in the world reaching 41 miles into the mountains. The ice is over 5,000 feet thick in places and three miles wide at its terminus. This glacier travels down the mountain about six feet a day. If we're lucky, we'll see large chunks of ice separate from the body and splash into the water. Keep your cameras ready for action."

Our ferry steamed toward the glacier. At first, we watched a wall of ice rise out of the water. Our ferry swept a wide turn as we sailed closer. At 100 yards away from the glacier, we heard a 300-foot wall of ice separate from the main body.

"It's breaking loose," Rex said.

"No kidding," I said, raising my camera.

An avalanche of ice, about 50 yards wide, 200 feet high and 100 yards long slid into the water. When it hit the bay, a splash sent waves over the ocean. We churned past the glacier on our way to the open sea.

Late in the afternoon, we reached Whittier, Alaska. The ship docked at a railroad station on the coast. A train departed in the morning that carried visitors through the mountains. Not caring to spend our money on a hotel, Rex and I opted for a campsite on a hillside a half mile out of town. It was a great night under the stars with a sheet of the Northern Lights blazing across the sky. We were about to douse our campfire when two men in their mid-twenties got out of a pickup truck and walked up the hill.

"Howdy. How you doin' tonight?" Rex greeted them, offering a handshake.

"Pretty good...so how come you folks are up here anyway?" asked the taller man.

"We're camping out waiting for the train to take us through the mountains in the morning," I said. "You're welcome to share our campfire. Grab a log and have a seat."

"Thanks, appreciate that," the second stranger said.

"So where you headed?" Rex asked.

"We can't find jobs, so we're leavin' the state," the tall one replied.

"What kind of work do you do?" I asked.

"I'm an oil driller..."

As he was explaining his job, his buddy said he had to take a whiz and walked away from the campfire. Before I knew it, the other guy grabbed Rex in a chokehold. I was so surprised, I stood up yelling.

"Get your hands off..." my words died on my tongue as an arm clamped around my throat.

I was stunned and staggered for a second. I had better break this guy's hold or Rex and I would be dead meat. I stepped to the side, grabbed my left fist with my right hand, and drove my elbow into the stomach of my attacker.

"Uhm," he grunted, releasing his grip at the same time.

For the first time since I was in Army combat training, I was in a rage. My system loaded up on adrenaline. My heart pounded against my chest, and blood raced through my arteries. Everything became clear and distinct. I sprinted over to Rex and kicked his attacker in the ribs. He staggered backward and fell down. Rex sucked in a deep breath. In a flash, I picked up a burning log and swung it across the knees of my attacker who had recovered and was charging me from behind.

I whacked him. He yelled in pain.

As the other attacker charged, Rex side-stepped him and kicked him in the midsection. The man doubled over, groaning.

"Get a rope!" I yelled.

"I've got plenty," Rex yelled back, his fury exploding.

I ran over to the guy I had belted in the knees. He was lying in the fetal position, holding his knee.

"Put your hands behind you," I ordered him.

He rolled over crying in pain. Rex tied him up. We walked over and tied up his buddy. They couldn't move by the time we finished.

"I'm gonna drive their truck into town and talk to the police," I told Rex. “Here, take this bear spray and spray them until they choke half to death if you need to.”

"You okay?" Rex asked.

"Geez! That was scary wasn't it?" I said.

"No kidding," he answered.

We collapsed—afraid, happy to be alive, thankful that we prevailed and realizing that we could have been one of those stories in the newspapers had we not been stronger, smarter, or luckier than our two adversaries.

Chapter 56—Nature's Applause

"To survive, our minds must taste redwood and agate, octopi, bat and in the bat's mouth--insect. It's hard to think like a planet. We've got to try."

—James Bertolino

"Time's wasting," Sandi said, scrambling out of the tent. "Let's get to the river."

"Calm down," I said, following her. "Those fish aren't going anywhere."

"You have any spinners?"

"Sure do!"

Sandi and I had ridden down Route 1 from Anchorage, Alaska, into the Kenai Peninsula. We had camped at the intersection of the Kenai and Russian Rivers. The Kenai was a deep, wide, turquoise river. The Russian, shallow and narrow, snaked through deep woods below us. Every campsite had fresh salmon being smoked or iced. Our neighbor had given us a fresh salmon steak cooked to perfection last night.

We scooted our way down a steep bank to the banks of the Russian. A dozen fishermen cast their lines over the water.

"FISH ON!" a man yelled across the water.

"Look at that guy," I said.

The angler's rod bent down into the water like a palm tree in a hurricane. A Silver salmon took the line upstream. The man ran along the stream bank following the fish. Other fishermen ducked or back out of the way. It took him ten minutes to land the salmon.

"That's my idea of fishing," Sandi said, throwing his line over the water.

Below us, in the clear, dark depths, 20 and 30-pound Silver and King salmon raced upstream. Sandi hooked one on her second cast.

"Whoa, it HIT!" she yelled.

Sandi yanked on her rod. A salmon shot past us, headed upriver. The fish leaped out of the water, dancing on its tail across the surface.

"Help me," Sandi said. "I can't hold it."

I tried to help her, but the fish raced upstream, ripping yards of line off the reel. Sandi ran alongside the bank to keep it on the line. I ran with her.

"He better get tired soon, or I'll lose him," Sandi yelled.

"You keep winding him in, and I'll get ready to grab him," I said, not knowing what a task that might be.

The fish stopped when I caught up to Sandi. Again, it shot upstream. The line sliced through the water.

"Keep it tight," I said.

"He's gotta be getting tired," Sandi said, breathing hard.

"It's a race as to which of you goes down for the count first," I said.

The salmon swam upstream leaping out of the water several times. Doug held him on the line. It was tiring enough so I could wade into the water near the big fish.

"Got it," I said.

"What a catch!" Sandi said. "He's at least 20 pounds."

"Maybe more."

"What a fight! My arms feel like rubber."

I caught the next one, but let it go. We had enough salmon to feed us for several days. I thought we could get one of the other fishermen to smoke ours for us, so we could eat it on the road. As we sat by the bank, another fisherman came up to us.

"You guys might like to hike upriver to a spot where the salmon leap over high falls."

"What about the bears?" I asked.

"Just make a lot of noise."

We put our gear into the tents and put on our pants and tennis shoes. The fishing crowd thinned out as we hiked our way over the trail. It led over fallen tree trunks, rocks, and through heavy brush. I whistled regularly, not wanting to meet a bear face to face. We walked along the banks where thousands of fish swam upriver like silver darts. In bends of the river or behind logs, large schools of salmon rested a dozen across and five layers deep. When a fish swam forward, another took its place. The water was black with salmon.

We climbed over fallen trees, and high ledges and fought our way through deep woods. We forded the stream several times, soaking our shoes.

"I sure hope this is worth it," Sandi said.

"No kidding," I added.

"Now I know why those bears are such good fishermen," Sandi said.

"Heck yeah, they can't miss with those fish piled up so close in the stream. Must be a million of them."

"That's for sure," Sandi said. "Do you hear that noise?"

"Yeah, it sounds like a standing ovation," I joked. "It's got to be the falls. Maybe nature is cheering us on."

We rounded a bend in the river several minutes later. Before our eyes, we walked up on one of those jaw-dropping sights seen on National Geographic specials. White water plunged down from a fifty-foot-high ledge and frothed over three smaller levels of rocks. Near the bottom, behind a large rock, hundreds of fish gathered for their turn at the rapids. Every few seconds, a salmon drilled through the water, powered by its tail—the fish shot into the air wiggling wildly. Upon hitting the water, it shot back into the air and vanished into the white froth like a torpedo.

Many fish flopped back onto the rocks when they didn't make it up the rapids.

"Look at that fish over there on the rock with a bite out of its side," I said.

"Yeah, it looks like a grizzly bit a chunk out of it before it got away."

We sat down to watch for a while. Salmon jumped through the rapids in a never-ending pattern of wiggling bodies flying through the air. I leaned my head back and closed my eyes. White noise filled my ears. No, it wasn't noise. It was applause. That's what that water was doing—applauding. Nature was putting on a show for us and adding applause.

Sitting there, eyes closed, I imagined the sights before me with the fish leaping. Just to make sure I was right, I opened one eye. Sure enough, they were still leaping.

Nature sure is an odd entity.

It was beautiful, yet sad seeing those fish struggling up the river. They fought hard to get to their birthplaces to start a new generation, then died. I guess there are two sides to everything. Nature creates such beauty in a storm but that same weather can destroy everything in its path. Sunshine is nice, but in a desert, it kills plants and animals. The tops of the mountains look beautiful against a blue sky, but the minus 30-degree temperatures up there would freeze me to death.

An hour later, we decided to get back to camp. I stepped toward the stream.

"This pisses me off," I said, reaching for two soda pop cans.

"What's that?" Sandi asked.

"You know everywhere we go, some slob has already been there throwing trash in the most beautiful places. How can someone hike up to a place like this and dump their six-pack and litter is beyond me. I just can't figure it out."

"Yeah, and no matter how much we pick it up, more people throw it down."

I picked up the bottles and trash and stuffed them into my pack. I wish it were as easy to separate the chemicals and other poisons we throw into our rivers, lakes, and oceans around the world.

When people do what they do to this planet, I wonder if they have ever taken the time to listen to the applause.

Chapter 57—Scuzzy, Yukky, Grubby, and Stinky

> ***"Close living for many days rubs away your veneer—your body aromas remind you, that you too are an animal."***
>
> ***—Rex Wooldridge***

Alaska is big and its sky is vast. Towering mountains breach the blue expanse with their snow-covered summits. Clear air stretches from one horizon to the other. On the land, wildlife forage for food. In the sky, golden eagles soar on crisp thermals, always watchful for a meal. Bald eagles cruise the skies looking for carrion along the Yukon River. While riding a bicycle through this last frontier of America, the immensity of the land swallowed my imagination. At times, glaciers from some of the peaks, crash down alongside the roads. There is nothing quite like Alaska. It's a land standing in the shadow of North America's tallest mountain (20,310 feet) Denali, "The Great One."

Rex and I had reached Wonder Lake campground via bus, 85 miles into the interior of Denali National Park. We camped 29 miles from the base of Denali. As we stood there in the morning, thunderheads drew away from the great white face as if impelled by invisible forces. Morning shadows stretching over the features of Denali created a new dimension from what we had seen the evening before.

We had stayed up most of the night watching Denali and the midnight sun producing a spectacular light show. During the late hours, pink-gray clouds streaked across the mountain in wisps until temperature changes drew thin vapors away from the peak, revealing a stunning view of the mountain. The orange-pink-yellow rays of the setting sun kept us in constant suspense until 2:00 a.m. when ebbing light seemed to draw the cloud cover once again over Denali.

At 4:15 a.m., we jumped out of our tents when a British fellow yelled excitedly, "The Mountain's out! It fills the sky!"

We walked over to a tundra pond where Denali reflected in the glass-still morning waters. The mountain's white brilliance startled us. It grew larger as the sun rose into the Arctic sky. The shadows across its face grew shorter with each passing minute. The silent drama unfolded while a dozen people clicked pictures.

Luck held us in her arms! Denali rises so high into the sky it affects weather conditions for 100 miles in every direction. Clouds cover it more than 60 percent of the time. But this morning, they drew back with the rising sun, giving everyone in the park a fabulous view.

"Let's get packed," Rex said. "That bus will be coming in another hour."

"What's the hurry?" I asked.

"Well, we've been here three days, and we've seen the best view of the mountain. Besides I'm getting low on food," Rex said. "Not only that, a guy I talked to last night said he had traveled across the Denali Highway and said it was fantastic. Tons of wildlife along the way."

"Guess you're right," I said. "We've seen the best of this mountain for the past couple of days."

Wildlife strutted before us on our way out of the park. Everyone must take a bus that bumps and jolts over an 85-mile-long dirt road, ending at Wonder Lake campground. Dahl sheep walked along craggy cliffs. Caribou ran down the road in front of the bus while moose browsed in ponds. A golden eagle swooped through the valleys. A mama grizzly stood on a hill near the road. Her cub ran around like a child possessed, obviously wanting to play tag. She whacked it on the noggin, sending the cub sprawling. It jumped back up, shook itself off, and then leaped into a tundra pond. Back at the park entrance, we picked up our bikes at the ranger station where we had cabled them to a tree.

"We're looking at three days on that road," Rex said. "It's only 140 miles from Cantwell to Paxson, but it is gravel. Could get rough if it rains."

"We better load up on food."

"Okay," I said. "We can make it as far as the junction tonight. It looks about forty miles away from here on the map. I need to get a bath too. I feel like I've been dragged through camel dung and left to dry for three days. I can't stand myself."

"I can't stand you either, and I'm as smelly as you are. One whiff of my pits just about knocks me out."

We loaded our bikes with food and water. Nice to be on the road again after a week of hiking around the park. Alaska is wild except for a few cities that give the illusion of civilization. Less than 550,000 Alaskans live in the state that comprises 1/5 of the USA's landmass. Most of those people live in Anchorage, Fairbanks and Juneau. That leaves the land to the wild creatures.

The road to Cantwell wound through dense forests and hilly terrain. My legs weren't used to pedaling. Within the hour, they settled down to a steady cadence. We reached the junction in the evening, but in the "Land of the Midnight Sun," we had plenty of light. Our bike tires dropped off the pavement onto the gravel. The gravel road wound through some pines and vanished over a ridge.

"First stream we come to is bath time," Rex said. "I'm going to bed tonight smelling like a rose."

"Sounds good to me."

We climbed through the trees until we reached a rolling plain with mostly dark tundra grasses covering the landscape. Mount Deborah stood in the distance. Because of the cool temperatures, we didn't sweat much. We were dirty from not bathing for a week.

It feels miserable when you ride for a few days without washing. The dried sweat combines with dirt to make your whole body feel scuzzy, yukky, grubby and stinky. You feel despicable. Long-distance bicycle riders know the feeling because it happens often. With a rise in the terrain, you sweat again, which starts steaming through your parka. New odors tweak your nose and since you hadn't smelled them before, you wonder about yourself. Close living for many days rubs away your veneer—your body aromas remind you that you too are an animal.

I start dreaming of a hot bath where I can soak away that scuzziness swirling around my nostrils. That's the way I was feeling after cranking up that rise. Except I knew we weren't going to find a hot bath out there. No matter what, I was jumping into a stream. I knew that rivers in Alaska originated from glaciers, but that didn't impact upon my mind at the moment.

"There's a river up ahead," Rex yelled.

"Great! Let's pitch camp."

As soon as we stopped, the mosquitoes made their assault on our bodies. I pitched my tent and jumped in to change.

"These skitters are ready to eat us for dinner," I told Rex, as I walked toward the river, with an air brigade swarming around my head.

I kicked off my shower sandals and dipped my foot into the river.

"Rex, come over here quick!" I yelled. "I need your help. These mosquitoes are eating me alive. This water isn't just cold man, it is liquid ice. Hurry up, swat these devils."

"Just dive into the water," Rex said.

"Are you crazy? It's freezing."

"If you don't take a bath, you won't be able to live with yourself, so quit pussy-footing around—get wet."

I walked into the water up to my crotch. My skin instantly responded by erupting into goosebumps right up to my neck. Rex swatted the mosquitoes but a few bit me. My body told me NOT to sink below the surface, but my mind told me I wanted to be clean. A battle raged within me until I heard Rex said, "Go ahead, and get it over with."

With one last hesitation, I dropped below the surface like a brick. The frigid water attacked my skin like dry ice. Every cell in my body told me what a fool I was for pulling this crazy stunt. I clutched my soap as I shot out of the water like a dolphin trying to fly.

"AHEEEEEE," I yelled. "I'm gonna die."

"You'll die clean," Rex added, laughing.

I lathered up in double time, trying to reach every part of my body, to get clean. My hair took a bit longer, but soon, I was soaped up. Again, I plunged downward into the current. I rubbed my hands over my body to get the soap off my skin. The sledgehammer cold water nearly knocked me out. Pure agony engulfed me, but in seconds I burst out of the water.

Rex stood near me, swatting the insects while I toweled down and struggled into my tights. He took his bath moments later. I laughed with glee knowing what kind of misery he was experiencing.

The sun sank low in the sky when we sat down at a campfire. In the distance, a wolf howled at a rising half-moon. After writing in our journals, we slipped into the tents for a night's sleep.

In the morning, I woke up with a start. I heard some kind of animal outside my tent. I smelled it, something with a bad case of halitosis.

"Rex, you hear what I hear?" I whispered.

"Yeah, I can see it."

"What is it?"

"A grizzly."

"Oh shit," my voice died down.

I crawled out of my sleeping bag feeling a strange kind of fear welling up inside me. I felt like that once before when I was with a friend and he drove us into a near head-on accident. The pit of my stomach turned to acid and I was paralyzed with terror because I thought I was going to die. Outside my tent at that moment, was another kind of death—something that I had admired from the distance the day before, but now, a wild creature looking for food. It could be gentle, and it could be savage. At that moment it could let us live or eat us, and we would not have much to say about it. Weighing in at over 900 pounds, it was interesting to note that grizzlies make a living with their claws and teeth. I could see its brown fur right outside my tent flaps. I froze in place, not knowing what to do. I said nothing. Rex must have been thinking the same thing. Make no sounds and pray the beast left us in peace.

Seconds passed. I clutched my legs in pure fright. Rex and I could live or die depending on the grizzly's appetite. Minutes passed as the big fellow grunted around our tents. I sat in a state of mental paralysis. My heart thundered against my ribs and I could hear it in my head. My hands shook and I felt blood racing through my arteries with increasing amounts of adrenaline being dumped into them by the second. I wanted to escape, but my mind knew that a grizzly can outrun a horse for a short distance, so I sat there.

They say your life passes before your eyes when you're about to die, but that wasn't true with me. I couldn't think of anything. Yet I heard everything the bear did, DISTINCTLY. It dug around my tent, snorting, and grunting. It sniffed the nylon and left a long trail of saliva across my roof. Five minutes passed as the bear worked its way around the end of my tent. Its shadow loomed across the nylon. That's when I heard a ripping of the fabric at the back of my tent. I looked over my shoulder to see four long, black claws poking through the tan nylon of my fragile dwelling. Every cell in my body said, "RUN!" But my mind said, "Stay." An instant later, the claws withdrew. The grizzly worked his way around to the front. His odor filled my lungs with fear. Soon, he dug for something ten feet away from the tent. I saw him through the crack in my flaps. Then something caught his attention in the brush, and he ambled toward it. His dirty butt vanished into the bushes.

"Frosty," Rex whispered. "Are we going to live?"

"It's a toss-up," I answered. "We better keep calm, so we don't attract his attention."

"I've been scared to stone the last ten minutes anyway, so don't worry about me moving."

"I've never been so scared in my life."

"I'm still scared."

We waited for what seemed like an eternity before seeing the grizzly appear on a ridge a hundred yards away from us. He was headed away from us without looking back.

"Let's get the hell out of here," Rex said as he crammed his sleeping bag into the stuff sack.

We broke camp in record time. While looking back over our shoulders, we cranked with exceptional power. It must have been the adrenaline stored up while we were in the tents waiting for the grizzly to maul us. He had decided to find his food elsewhere. We headed in the opposite direction.

"You know how close we came to going to that single track in the sky?" Rex said as we rode away. "I can't begin to tell you how scared I was. I couldn't function. So many things went through my mind. I remembered every article I ever read about campers being dragged out of their sleeping bags and mauled. I just couldn't believe it was happening to me, but it was, and it scared me out of my wits."

"You took the words right out of my mouth," I said. "It could happen any night we camp in the wilds, because this land is their land."

"Yeah, that's what I notice a lot up here," Rex said. "No telephone poles or buildings anywhere in the wilds. It may be one of the last places we can ride and see it the way it's supposed to be."

For the next hour, I was deep in thought. We could have been killed. I felt sick inside. I pondered the stories I had read in newspapers about people dying in the wilderness. Some froze to death because they marched into the wilderness unprepared. Others died by not wearing a life vests in an overcrowded boat. A few died in avalanches because they ventured into the backcountry. Many mountain climbers fall to their deaths. Outside the wilderness, more die because they don't take the time to buckle their seat belts. Sometimes, big airliners fall out of the sky. There are so many ways of dying, but those deaths don't affect us because we are so far removed. It's like it won't happen to me. Friends ask me if I'm afraid to die on one of my world adventures. Sure, it's true I could die on the road if some driver ran over me. I could die on a plane, too.

I don't think about death because it is a waste of time. It's negative energy. I do everything in my power to ensure I don't put myself in danger—I wear a helmet, fly two orange flags on the side and top of my bicycle, don't go into countries where I'll get shot, and check my food and water for cleanliness. But after I've covered the bases as well as possible, I figure life is for living. I don't sit around worrying about it. Nobody is guaranteed anything.

We followed the soft/hard dirt road over hills and through shallow valleys. Our hands took a beating. We gripped the bars to keep them upright. After crossing a glacial plain, we climbed 1,000 feet to a ridge. At the back of us, thousands of tundra ponds dotted the valley. In the middle, a braided river swept along, continually weaving into and out of itself.

Near the edge of a cliff, we laid the bikes down to take pictures. The vast pond-covered plain below us stretched north toward the glacier-covered mountains. As we stood there, the sun forced its way through pocket holes in the clouds. Large steam columns seemed to prop up the sky like the poles of circus tents. From that point along the Denali Highway, we had bicycled into the center of the world's highest vertical mountain range. Denali soared 20,310 feet high to our west, Mount Hayes stood 13,382 feet to the north, and Mount Sanford rose 16,237 feet to the southeast and the lesser mountains of the Talkeeta Range 9,000 feet to the south.

"Can you believe this sight?!" Rex said. "We're in the middle of some pretty high peaks. Look in the valley. There must be thousands of ponds along the river, and they look like tiny mirrors."

"It runs right up to that glacier at the foot of the mountains...hey look, a herd of caribou off to the left, see 'em?"

"Yeah, sure do," Rex said. "This sight is worth our brush with death."

We jumped back on the bikes heading east. The road was bumpy. Late in the afternoon, we camped on a high ridge looking north toward glacier-covered peaks.

The next day, the road and weather were in our favor. We made good time to Paxson where we crossed over the Delta River. The water was glass clear, but something was happening in the shallows of the riverbed.

"You see that water?" Rex said. "It's blood red!"

"Yeah, and the blood is running upriver against the current."

"Look closer," Rex gasped. "Those are fish... oh I know what they are."

"What?"

"I read it in an outdoor magazine. Those are Sockeye salmon going upstream to spawn. They turn bright red when they hit the fresh water after being in the ocean for a few years."

Before us, thousands of 10 to 15-pound fire-engine red salmon raced against the crystal clear current. Some rested four to five deep behind large rocks in the river. The white sandy bottom rendered a perfect backdrop for this color show. It was like when I cut my finger as a kid and stuck it under the faucet. My blood turned the water red. That's what these fish were doing on their way upstream, which created an extraordinary visual experience. Their endless numbers colored the water red.

I stood there in amazement at nature's creative hand. I was glad the blood-red color was in the river and that I was seeing it with my own body in one piece.

Wherever that grizzly is today, I am thankful he spared us. I will never forget the sight of those claws cutting through my tent and the smell of his being in my nostrils.

SECTION VIII: TOURING ANTARCTICA

Chapter 58—A Moment Frozen in Time

"Good God! This is an awful place."

—Robert Falcon Scott
(upon reaching the South Pole)

(Note: the author lived and worked in Antarctica at McMurdo Station, a base where Robert Falcon Scott originated his epic journeys to reach the South Pole in the early 1900s.)

In the morning, a whiteout howled across McMurdo Station, Antarctica with 100-mile-per-hour winds and minus 80-degree temperatures. I had been confined to my barracks for two days as a 'Condition One' storm worked its way over the icepack before me.

By late evening, the weather turned placid but a biting minus-60-degree temperature kept most people inside. I, however, bundled into my cold weather gear—insulated boots, heavy mittens, five Thermax layers, fleece, three hats, face protection, along with ski goggles—and headed out the door to ride my bicycle over the ice runway.

Yes, there were bicycles at the scientific station for me to ride. There was a report of some emperor penguins on the ice. I HAD to see them no matter what the cold. I jumped on the bike looking like an overstuffed bear with all my cold-weather gear on. My breath vaporized as I rode toward the ice-covered ocean. My lungs burned with each inhalation of polar cold. About a mile around the cove, the setting sun glinted off the roof of Robert Falcon Scott's Discovery Hut. He had died 80 years ago on his last attempt to reach the South Pole. The Hut had stood on the point of McMurdo Sound since 1902. It gave mute testimony to the courage those men displayed in their polar adventures. This was a cold, miserable place.

I rode along a path that led toward the ice pack in the sound. It's hard to describe pack-ice, but it is jumbled-broken ice chards being heaved and smashed into multiple shapes-triangles, domes, squares, tubulars, and wedges—like an Erector Set gone crazy. However, near the shore, it was reasonably smooth with a thin veneer of snow from the blizzard.

Above me, a gold/purple sky glowed brazenly in its final glory into the crevasses of the Royal Society Range across the sound. For once, a rare quiet softened the bitter edge of the crystal-white desert before me. One of the glaciers, more than ten miles across at its terminus radiated liquid gold from the setting sun. Stepping through some shallow snow drifts, I sank knee-deep, until I pulled through and gained the edge of the ice. Even with polar weather gear protecting my body, the numbing cold crept through the air, as if it were trying to find a way into my being.

The bike frame creaked at the cold and the tires made a popping sound on the snow I pedaled over. The big boots I was wearing made it hard to keep on the pedals. But I persevered and kept moving forward. Across the ice, I looked through the sunlight and saw four black figures approaching. I shaded my eyes with my gloved hand. They drew closer, their bodies back-lit by the sun on the horizon. It was a family of Emperor penguins. I dismounted from my bike. From our survival classes, I learned to sit down so as not to frighten them. By appearing smaller than them, they might find me interesting.

Slowly, I lowered myself into the snow, cross-legged, like an Indian chief. Minute by minute, they waddled closer—straight toward me. Three big birds, about 80 pounds each kept moving dead-on in my direction. The smallest followed behind them.

Another minute passed and they were within 30 feet of me. The lead Emperor carried himself like a king. His silky black head color swept down the back of his body and through his tail. A bright crayon yellow/orange streaked along his beak like a Nike logo. Under his cheek, soft aspirin-white feathers poured downward, glistening in lanolin. His wings were black on the outside and mixed with black/white on the front. He stood at least 40 inches tall, and his enormous three-toed feet were a gray reptilian roughness with blunted talons sticking out. He rolled his head, looking at me in a cockeyed fashion as if I was the strangest creature he'd ever seen.

I don't know what made me do it, but I slipped my right hand out of the glove and moved it toward him—slowly. The rest of the penguins closed in. The big guy stuck his beak across the palm of my hand and twisted his head, as if to scratch himself against my skin. I felt glossy feathers against my hand. He uttered a muffled coo. The rest of the penguins cooed. Their mucus membranes slid like liquid soap over their eyes every few seconds. I stared back, wanting to say something to them, but realized I could not speak their language. However, at that moment, we shared a consciousness of living.

My frozen breath vapors hung in the air briefly before descending as crystals toward the ground. I battled to keep from bursting with excitement. Within seconds, one of the other penguins pecked my new friend on the rump. He drew back. With that, he turned and waddled away. Following the elders, the little one gave one last look at me, as if he too wanted to scratch my hand, but was afraid, and turned with his friends. As they retreated, their wings were out, away from their bodies like children trying to catch the wind in their arms. The baby Emperor was last to go.

My hand turned numb, so I stuck it back into the glove. As I sat there, I remembered once when a hummingbird landed on my finger—and I remembered the sheer delicacy Nature shared within that warm spring day in the mountains. Here, in this frozen wasteland beyond the borders of my imagination where man does not belong, Nature touched me again today with its pulsing heart and living warmth. I only hope my species learns as much respect for our fellow travelers as they show toward us.

I stood up, tightened my hood and looked for the penguins. They were gone. Only the pack ice rumbled toward the horizon. I turned to my bike. It's hard to believe that two rubber tires laced together with spokes and rims—and attached to a metal frame could carry me from the Amazon Jungle, to Death Valley and on to where the bolt goes into the bottom of the globe. That simple machine laying in the frozen snow had taken me to far-flung places on this planet and it had allowed me magical moments beyond description. That moment with the penguins probably was the best it had ever done by me. I remounted it and turned toward the barracks.

The ride back didn't seem so cold.

SECTION IX: BICYCLE TOURING

Chapter 59—Pedaling into the Future

> ***"Whatever befalls the earth befalls the sons of the earth. Man did not weave the web of life; he is merely a strand in it. Whatever he does to the web, he does to himself."***
>
> *—Chief Seattle*

Life thrives along a country road. It whistles, chirps, snorts, bleats, and munches. Birds fly patterns much like a clothesline, from tree branch to fence post. Cows stare at me in slow motion like spectators at a tennis match. Sheep bolt at the slightest noise as if the sky is falling and run away, not knowing why or where they're going. Horses prance up to the fence lines, curious as to what I'm doing that's different than most humans that pass by in their cars. Dogs don't care—they love chasing me and nipping at my legs.

What's different to my fellow creatures—is that I've been exploring the world astride my bicycle for many years. Millions of pedal strokes have etched memories into my thighs. My legs remember the 16,000-foot passes in the Andes. They remember the cold, wet winds that tore at my body during summer snowstorms. These same legs suffered through endless miles of parched earth in the Atacama Desert of Chile, the driest in the world. Not to be outdone, the Australian Outback with 115-20 Fahrenheit temperatures tore moisture out of my legs and suffocated my lungs. The tundra swallowed me with its vastness on the Arctic Circle. On that colossal, thriving continent of Asia, people stared in wonderment at my journey.

The years pass much like campsites I've left in regions around this wondrous green globe. The kindness shown me in my travels by people throughout the world cannot be repaid in a thousand lifetimes. But the one point that always comes home is that people care. They wonder, too. "Why are you riding that bicycle?" they ask. Few understand my reasons because they can only know the "why" of something by participating. That takes effort, which many people in the modern world would rather avoid.

Riding a bicycle into an adventure is much like walking. The philosopher Duncan Littlefair said that when you walk, you fall forward but catch yourself with your other foot. You fall forward into the unknown, into the emerging moment. That's what bicycling allows, a constantly emerging opening opportunity into the future. It's not dramatic—it's poetic and manifests itself in deep spiritual appreciation. In time, while riding a bicycle, the big things mean little, while the basics of life become all important—eating, sleeping, quenching thirst, shelter, companionship, warmth, and protection from the environment.

When I was a kid, riding my bicycle along the beach, my friends and I raced to inspect a piece of pollution up ahead. It might be a Japanese glass fishing ball or a bottle with a note in it. That's changed now. On the beaches around the world, I've seen colorful flower-like displays of plastics, glass, and Styrofoam. But these bouquets will not attract honeybees or hummingbirds. On the pristine waters of Lake Titicaca, the highest navigable lake in the world, in Peru, plastic debris floats alongside ancient reed boats. On once mighty cliffs overlooking the Mediterranean Sea and along sandy beaches, automobile carcasses lay upon the land like misshapen rocks, somehow not lending beauty with their presence.

Black oil spots, replete with dead birds, speckle the beaches along Australia's western coast. Dolphins wash up with the tide, having died with the latest onslaught of toxicity created by humans. I've pedaled into the Himalayas of Nepal, where so many trees have been cut down that once mighty mountains break in half and slide sideways down erosion shoots the size of battle ships. Riding through large cities, I've choked on the fetid air that blackens my lung sand burns my eyes.

In the rain forests of Brazil, we might as well begin calling them "fire forests" because so much smoke vomits into the air from the 60,000 square miles that are burned annually. My lungs suffocated on the smoke as I rode through their once vibrant beauty. In Alaska, I watched Bald Eagles, our nation's historical symbol, die by the dozens as they dove into the black muck of an oil spill created, not by one drunken captain but by an entire American public intoxicated with driving theirV-8 powered cars singularly off to work each day. Maybe the deaths of those eagles signal a harbinger of our own future. For certainly, we are falling forward into it, but with our eyes closed, almost afraid to put our other foot out to save ourselves.

Yet we can. We must. We are in a global village where every action by any neighbor bares great impact upon all of us. At this moment, we are in a crisis. It's interesting to note that the word "crisis" in Chinese characters means the same thing as the word "opportunity." Literally translated, "crisis" means “opportunity riding the dangerous wind." Because we created these problems facing humanity today, we can solve them. And like every person who has shown me kindness in my travels, human beings all over the earth want to help.

We Americans consider ourselves ethical, but we continue selling chemicals to countries around the world. We want to save the rainforests, yet we sell South

Americans chain saws and tractors to cut their forests. We buy their beef to make more profit off our hamburgers. We enact Clean Air, Clean Water, and anti-pollution laws to raise our speed limits, buy larger-sized eight-cylinder cars, and create more chemicals that make DDT a minor player on the toxic stage.

At some point, each of us must take a stand. Like riding a bicycle, we must get back to basics. We have to understand that if we're going to get to the top of that next mountain, we must put our whole body, mind, heart and soul into it. Like a bicycle rider, we cannot depend on someone else helping us to the top. Each of us must pedal our own bike. Each of us must make choices that will stop the Greenhouse Effect, acid rain, ozone depletion, rainforest destruction, and chemicalization of our natural world. Whether we are a president of a large corporation or a janitor, we each have an important interdependence toward one another and this planet. We must take personal action toward the common good of our home, this small green biosphere, out in the black void of space.

I continue pedaling forward into the future. A big mountain awaits me, and it's going to be a tough, nearly impossible climb. We're all faced with a nearly impossible world ecological situation. Yet with each day, I have an opening opportunity to make a difference. Each of us possesses that same opportunity in our own spheres. The more of us that join in the common goal of saving our planet home, the more successful we will be.

Life thrives along a country road. The sun shines overhead while the meadowlarks sharpen their voices for a morning songfest, and chickadees do loop-d-loops above the tall spring grasses. Sheep munch fresh green shoots as I pedal past, and horses prance along the fences wishing they could be as free as me. Chickens search the ground for an unlucky worm. In the sky, a red-tailed hawk soars on the rising thermals. A covey of white-winged butterflies dances above fields of clover. It's another lovely day for pedaling my bicycle through the natural world.

Let's give future generations a chance to enjoy this wonderful, too.

EPILOGUE

REFLECTIONS IN THE PAVEMENT

> ***"The general conclusion is that wealth and power have never been long permanent in any place...and that they travel over the face of the earth, something like a caravan of merchants. On their - arrival everything is found green and fresh; while they remain, all is bustle and abundance, and, when gone, all is left trampled and down, barren and bare."***
>
> ***—William Playfair***

Riding down the highway allows my mind wandering time. I think about life, about what I have seen, about my joys and sorrows. Some thoughts drift pleasantly through sunny meadows in my mind, and others lie heavy in the darkest recesses. Happiness. I've had my share. Problems. They come with living. Hurt. Can't get away from it sometimes. Disappointments. A part of life. Love. It flutters above my handlebars, never quite understood or totally realized. Friendship. I am blessed. Health. I preserve it. Freedom. Humanity's greatest need. Travel. Bicycling provides one of its ultimate expressions.

WHY I GO

Whenever I go on my journeys or even plan them, the people I talk with exclaim how lucky I am and that they would like to go. Many want to travel, but for various reasons, they can't or won't, and have justifications for not going.

Is the excuse the reason, or is it the answer?

They would love to go. Instead, I DO go. I go with others like me or by myself. My fellow adventurers are the Walter Payton, Michael Jordan', Chris Everts, Serena Williams, Peyton Manning, Tom Brady, and Valerie Krueger of traveling. Our efforts are not applauded on the broad scale of stardom, yet we are a handful of individuals who walk the Great Wall of China, bicycle across a continent, explore the Galapagos Islands and climb to the top of Everest. We don't get paid for our exploits, but the rewards supersede financial gain. For those of us who crank the pedals, bicycle adventuring gives perspectives into our inner souls.

THE MEANING OF LIFE

My favorite bird is the Blue Footed Booby bird. As I walked through its nesting area on the cliffs of the Galapagos Islands, each pair stood at their nest protecting their young. Upon coming in for a landing, both their feet came in nearly vertical, then slapped down with near crashes when they landed too fast. Over the water, their pinpoint accuracy dumbfounded me. Like a guided dart out of the sky, they dropped toward their prey beneath the ocean's surface. These birds dance as a mating ritual. They play well in my mind. Nature plays well in my heart and I thank the booby bird for giving me a free show. The boobies, doing what they do best, offered me a window into the meaning of life.

For each step up the ladder of material acquisition, you must be prepared to sacrifice either time, emotional stability, or daily lowering of personal happiness levels. The bigger the buck you chase, and the harder you work for it, the more you lose your balance in the scheme of life. That balance is happiness.

When you maintain a balance and are able to back off, slow down or retreat to a peaceful part of your mind in your pursuit of material goods—it is the key to spiritual depth. I think it is possible, but you must understand yourself and your limits. How do you figure that limit? As soon as you become more unhappy than happy—it's time to back off and take inventory. If it's money you want, and if you can handle the unhappiness with the goal, then you can use the goal to offset the unhappiness. The key is to make a goal achievable and within a reasonable amount of time. Because if you go too far into the world of working for wealth, you get so wrapped up in the material goods, you lose touch with yourself and your balance.

I think a Blue Footed Booby bird flies only at its altitude and speed and dives to its level. When the wind is too strong or the fish too big, the bird backs off. Even though a booby isn't too intelligent, it is an intuitively smart creature—and happy.

A PLACE WHERE TIME DOES NOT EXIST

On the Galapagos Islands, seals line miles of beaches like teeth on a comb. Birds nest on the rocks in such numbers, they create a mantle of snow on the rocks from their excrement. Black Iguanas blend with volcanic rocks. Dolphins leap in the blue liquid ocean waters. Penguins "fly" underwater chasing schools of fish. The islands are a well-stocked zoo without cages.

On Island Espanola, we walked among seals snoozing on the rocks. Hundreds of black Frigate birds, with eight-foot wings, soared above us. Sleek Blue Footed Booby birds sailed high above the waves before doing 90-degree turns straight toward the water, dropping like darts from 100 feet up. Pelicans glided above incoming waves before plunking down to catch a fish. Penguins waddled out of the surf.

The amazing thing about everything around us was the harmony of the animals. Lizards perched next to curve-beaked birds that paid no mind as they pecked for food in the soil.

Iguanas slept near seals that snoozed near dozens of crabs. We walked through 50 acres of Blue Footed booby nests. Climbing over the rocks, we watched Waved albatross jump off cliffs in order to take off.

I took a few steps over a busy ridge when I came face to face with a daddy and mommy booby and their chick. Soft downy fluff covered the baby. Its eyes, beak and feet were black. Brown and white feathers covered the parents. Each had turquoise blue feet. When I got close, the male hooted like the sound of a whistle without the ball, and the female squawked at me.

Even though they seemed stupefied on the ground, once these sky pilots lifted into the air, their sleek bodies with three-foot-long wings allowed them swift and certain movement along the cliffs and glide over the surf. These birds were meant for flight—graceful and effortless.

Nothing can compare to seeing and hearing these animals in their own front yards. When I came in contact with them, eye to eye, that was the heart of the interaction, animal to animal, creature to creature. As I walked through this huge wildlife sanctuary, the mist rolled over the cliffs. The eternal movement of water and life pervaded my senses. We live and we die. Everything is the same except the players. They live their span, then vanish. It was in this place that I realized that time does not exist.

IT HURTS TO LEAVE

Leaving always hurts. It pains me in a place in my mind that I cannot describe. A few weeks before leaving on a bicycle adventure, I suffer tense pains in my stomach every time I think of the coming journey, of the change. I'm leaving a comfortable routine of work, play, and friends.

At the airport for my South America adventure, my friend Paul chattered as I walked toward the plane. Tears yes, I always cry, as if I'm afraid. Off I walked into that tunnel, and with a last glance toward him, I was swallowed into the belly of the plane bound for the unknown. Moving through the seats, I was aware of my tears drying as I looked at the strange faces.

How can I explain my need to reach out, to explore and experience? Is routine life too mundane or less meaningful? Why would someone with a comfortable home and job with a great sports routine and friends travel to a new continent and risk disease or even death?

My only answer—I need to explore this world in the time allotted to me. I suspect this 70 or more-year span is a one-time journey. When it's over, I will never, ever walk upon this planet again. Others may think they are coming back in another human body or other forms, but I am not taking any chances. With that in mind, I want to absorb everything possible in my time here. When I ride my bicycle, the road in front of my house connects to the farthest reaches of the globe. It goes everywhere to the end of my life.

I'D TRAVEL HUMBLE EVEN IF I WAS RICH

Why would anyone check into a dollar-a-night hotel in a developing country? The toilets don't flush, and the showers run cold. Everything is broken down. Is it worth saving money to endure poor conditions? Absolutely! I like traveling with those who crawl around the earth, my fellow riders, and backpackers. They travel with nothing more than the bare necessities and a handbook of the country they're exploring. They live an unscheduled life, which opens them to spontaneous situations.

Even if I were rich, I wouldn't go on a guided tour, or check into fancy hotels. That kind of lifestyle is alien to me. Sure, it's fun having money, but I'd rather be with those who talk more about living than what they own. I avoid people who display their egos in their clothes or the status they've attained. Traveling modestly makes the adventure more interesting.

I'd travel poor even if I were rich.

LOOKING TO THE SIDE

Riding through a developing country tears at my guts. While riding, I look to the side of the highway where children stare from broken windows in cardboard shacks and incredible filth. Children, by the millions, live in housing that most USA citizens wouldn't let their dogs inhabit. It's hard on my emotions.

There is no escape for these people from the iron bars of their poverty. Their condition is filthy and futile. I don't know how to express my exasperation. We, humans, spend a million dollars a minute worldwide, 24 hours a day, every day, for military preparation to kill each other when billions of us are dying from lack of food, sanitation, clean water, and education. It is beyond my understanding of reason, of compassion on the part of the leaders of the world. What is even sadder is the fact that it has always been and it will always be. My sadness overwhelms me.

At any moment, I can hop on a plane and fly away in comfort. Nothing is fair or good or right about this eternal condition. My only way to deal with it is to maintain a cool, rational mind to protect my sensitive, emotional side, because there is nothing I can do to change what I see. I crank harder on the pedals, moving away from it, but it's there and I remember.

ULTIMATE CAMPSITE ONE

In the Andes, roads cut over 15,500-foot passes. At the top of one pass, we found ourselves caught in a dark cloud mist. The road dove steeply following a treacherous valley floor. A river crashed alongside and vanished into still deeper recesses of the canyon. Doug and Bryan rolled downward ahead of me. We plunged deeper into the mist. Soon, green shrubs and trees appeared like apparitions in the silence.

Further along, momentary breaks in the mist allowed us incredible views down a steep gorge where the terrain dropped to sharp V's and faded into the mist. After 45 minutes of freewheeling, we followed a bend at the end of the valley and began to climb. Thirty minutes later, shrouded in gray wisps, we coasted downward into an eerie fog. At that late hour, darkness mingled with the cloud mist. Bryan stood at the roadside. "Let's camp here," he said. "This is the ultimate campsite."

Below us, just off the road, a flat piece of ground hung above a cliff that dropped off into nothingness. Momentarily, a break in the cloud showed the cliff plummeting 3,000 feet straight down, but the soupy gray mist blocked our view. We set up the tents before cooking dinner.

The next morning, blue skies broke over the valley revealing our perch, which equaled a condor's nest. A stunning sunrise created vapor columns streaming across the valley. Sunlit snow-covered peaks in the back of us glowed in white/blue/green. We dangled our legs over a cliff while eating breakfast. From our front doors, we looked across 100 miles of the mountain range.

Beats waking up in the city any day.

HEAD WINDS SUCK!

What is the one thing that puts the kibosh on my cycling day? Is it rain? Is it snow? Is it a gravel road? Is it a torrid heat wave? Is it a 12,000-foot pass with a 12 percent grade? No! None of those!

Then what makes me say bad words and foam at the mouth? What causes my lips to form utterances so fowl my mother would wash my mouth out with soap and send me to my room?

You guessed it—headwinds. I dislike them. No, I HATE headwinds. They are the bane of my existence, the pain in my butt, the devil's torture, a living nightmare.

Headwinds depress me, pick on me, and laugh at me. They are the scourges sent upon me by my enemies to make me suffer. My legs complain, my hands hurt, and my shoulders ache. Sand gets into my teeth. Tumbleweeds blow into my spokes. My feet hurt. If I had three wishes from the good witch of the east, I would have her banish them from the earth and make a law against them.

If I haven't made myself clear, it comes down to this: HEADWINDS REALLY PISS ME OFF!

I CRY INSIDE

In the village of Santa Rosa, Ecuador, whores cost $1.20 a trick and a new pair of shower sandals goes for $1.50. That's how cheap life is in the developing world. Beggars in the marketplace are pitiful. I cry inside as I drop money into their tin. It will mean nothing to them nor will it do anything to help. While walking through the city, I came upon a man with his arms cut off below the elbows, who had no teeth and only one eye with a broken pair of glasses on the one eye. He stood with a sign and a cup held out. He was sickening, pathetic, sad and filthy—the epitome of misery.

At an outdoor market, an old lady with a blackened face and blind with oily, dirty clothes marched around to stalls, tapping her heavy wooden cane to beg. Several times, she begged at empty stalls, talking to the air—with no luck—she turned 90 degrees and walked five more steps to the next stall, where vendors remained silent or shooed her away so she would not disturb customers. Ungodly pathetic. It reminded me of the time I saw an eight-year-old blind boy at a pagoda in Kathmandu, Nepal. A man dropped his keys into the child's hand. When the boy tried to figure out what kind of money it was, the man laughed and took the keys away. Humans can be heartless and cruel to one another.

After seeing so much human misery, I know I can't do a single shred of anything to change it. Still, it sickens me to see it, and I see a lot of it around the world. How do people get picked for such horrid life paths and conditions in their lives? When it comes down to it, it's the luck of the draw—like a good fortune for some and bad fortune for others.

In the end, I understand why the great writers Poe, Twain, Gibran, Hemingway, and others became embittered. It's a terrible life for many.

When I think of my own tragedies, I admit it, losing my dad when I was 17 devastated me. Vietnam terrified me because death was merely a draft notice away, and my college roommate died in the steaming jungles of Cambodia. I lived in fear of dying daily and hung on to hoping the war would end before my draft deferment ran out. My divorce rocked me for five years, the pain lingered for ten. One of my best friends betrayed me. Many of my friends have suffered from nasty breakups. In too many cases, most people, as Thoreau said, "Live lives of quiet desperation." I cry inside, as much for them, as for myself.

IT'S EVERYWHERE GETTING WORSE

Although I don't need to see road signs or mileage markers, I can always tell when a town or village is near in any country of the world. The trash and garbage intensify.

What is it about human beings? We are dismantling this planet's ecological systems. In the process, we are destroying millions of other animals and plants. While riding my bicycle, I see junk along the roads, dead fish in the rivers, NO fish in the rivers because of so much toxic input, plastic bags lining the riverbanks and flying like flags from tree branches for dozens of miles, trees being slaughtered by the millions, and air that poisons my lungs. I see the construction of homes and the use of plastics that are destroying habitats. We humans are making a mess of our earth. Our numbers are growing to 240,000 new human beings per day, a net gain of more than 83 million more per year. We cut 500,000 trees down per hour without replacement. We are causing the extinction of more than one million animals on this planet in this century. What are we doing about it? Not much, and no matter what we do, no one wants to deal with the real cause—human overpopulation. Somehow, we refuse to deal with responsible human reproduction. It keeps getting worse and worse and worse.

What's going to stop us? Nature! At some point in time, nature is going to check us, in a cruel fashion, in great numbers and even greater suffering. In the end, Earth will balance us out. It's a sure bet we won't do anything significant fast enough to alter the coming disasters. It's just too bad that we're taking so many plants and animals down with us.

THAT'S THE WAY IT IS

We rolled into town, almost praying for a shower and hot dinner. The first hotel made our day with four beds, a cold shower and clean sheets.

We decided to eat first. There's a different appreciation in a developing country. Walking into a restaurant is a compromising experience. The floor may be wood, concrete or dirt. Cobwebs may hang from the rafters, and flies crawl over everything. With no doors to stop them, dogs and pigs wander back and forth begging for food. Silverware and plates are rinsed in oily water, then pronounced clean enough for the next customer. Seating consists of benches or hard-backed chairs shoved up under broken tables or boards. His floors are littered with trash. Chickens search around the tables for tidbits.

Whatever we ordered, we asked for no meat because it was fly infested. Most foods were greasy, but as long as it was cooked well, we were safe from food poisoning. We never drank the water because it was drawn from polluted streams. We tried to be as careful as possible and hoped our gamma globulin shots would protect us from possible hepatitis contraction.

When bicycling through much of the world, we must compromise, because that's the way it is.

THE TOUGHEST RIDING OF MY LIFE

Riding a gravel road over La Raya Pass in the Andes headed toward Bolivia, I had an absolutely miserable day. I was wet, - freezing and shaking at nightfall. The 80-kilometer ride was one of the worst of my life. I pounded down a corrugated gravel road all day. My arms and butt hurt. My rectum bled when I - defecated. I was tired from no sleep brought on by altitude sickness at 13,000 feet. The road pounded my guts. At 3:30 PM, a rain/hailstorm hammered us, and we huddled by a rock. Doug, Brian, and I started freezing from being wet. Later, we cranked our way over the pass. With freezing fingers, I pitched my tent and dove into my sleeping bag. It wasn't until two hours later that I warmed up again.

The next day marked the fourth straight day of physical torture on our bikes. At dawn, I unzipped my tent to look at a 113-kilometer ride into Puno. It was a study of dogged determination. My body ached in every cell. I was suffering from the Inca Two Step, which left me weak and sick. I hadn't slept more than four hours per night because of the altitude, and my air mattress leaked. My lower back hurt, my left wrist was jammed from horsing the handlebars, and my shoulders were killing me with muscle tension.

For the entire ride, the endless misery of the gravel demanded my attention. Sometimes it was worse than usual, when the rutted rippling caused my bike to bounce every second front and back end. The bouncing jolted my butt and spine as it slammed my hands into mush. I couldn't go fast, I couldn't go slowly. It was like self-imposed torture. At times, it was so bad that we tried to ride the footpath along the railroad track, but that too became a problem with it being too narrow and unpredictable. A treadmill of misery. To add to the excitement, dogs from nearby farms attacked us, snapping at our heels.

By the time we reached a town on the other side of the pass, I was sick, exhausted, weary and hurting. Up ahead, pavement. Upon reaching it, I got off my bike, knelt down on all fours and kissed the road. Nothing like being thankful for the ending of the toughest ride of my life.

KEEPING CLEAN WITH ICE WATER

What's it like jumping into an icy stream or lake? First, you have to be dirty enough so you can't stand yourself. When sweat and grime build to a crescendo of odor, no matter how cold, you will jump into the icy water.

There is a method to the madness, however. First, sandals, soap and towels are close at hand. The first two steps into the water let your bottom half know what kind of pain your top half will suffer. Pain? Sort of. I guess it's more of a shock discomfort. Complete sensory shock. You wade into the lake, splash a little on your legs and arms, take a deep breath, and dive. You do feel pain in your head if the water flows from a snow field. It freezes the blood. It hurts so much, you have to surface immediately. You use biodegradable soap to lather up. Once covered, you slip back under the surface and rub yourself clean. Seconds later, a dry towel and clean clothes make the world feel nicer. You feel like a million bucks after an evening bath.

It's worth freezing your butt off for.

THE SEVENTH CONTINENT

In Ushuaia, Tierra del Fuego, South America, I stood on the beach of the most southerly city in the world. It's located in a fiord at the bottom tip of the continent. A Greenpeace ship steamed into the harbor with a large sign that read, "World Park Antarctica."

As the human race invades that icy seventh continent, I can't help but accept that we shall destroy it, too. We've already started toxic waste dumps, dumped oil in the coastal waters, and burned hazardous wastes, and built airport runways through penguin rookeries. It seems such a simple reality to me that we leave that continent alone. Instead, many nations are lining up to plunder it.

Will we ever learn?

CLIMBING AND COASTING

Along the coast of Brazil, 14 to 16 percent grades tested my resolve as a bicyclist. My Granny gear of 24 to 34 wasn't low enough for the steepness combined with the humidity and heat. During a midday climb, I soaked my clothes completely in the first five minutes. Sweat dripped through my mustache. Water beads fell from my nose, my chin, and my ears. My jersey dripped from the sleeves. With a heavy gasp, I stopped Condor to catch my breath. Judging from the lay of the pavement, it was the steepest grade of the trip.

Back on the seat again, I slipped into the toe clips and cranked. My breath fell short and quickly as I needed tons of oxygen to get up that mountain grade. One hundred meters later, I stopped for a stalled truck on the road. Its engine failed to carry the lumber cargo up the grade. I pedaled past them. Soon, I caught up to Doug sitting by the roadside.

"What's up?" I asked.

"Just a case of overheating," he answered. "I got 'that' feeling and decided to rest in the shade and pour water over my head."

Another ten minutes later, sweat poured off our bodies like raindrops. We overheated again. We got off and walked. It was too steep, so hot, and so humid that we gasped for breath. We pedaled, then climbed, then pedaled for the next hour. Every curve seemed to move toward another climb.

"It never ends," I yelled to Doug.

Another 45 minutes into the climb, a miracle dropped out of the side of the mountain in the form of a waterfall pouring from the rocks. Doug and I dropped our bikes and headed for the fountain. We jumped in with our helmets, gloves, glasses, and clothes on. Nothing can describe the euphoric sensation of pleasure I felt. Cold water drained down my neck and shoulders. It ran into my glasses creating distortions on the lenses. I moved under the flow to get it on my back. It was pure joy and utterly wonderful.

We took turns dipping our heads into the water until we had cooled down. Around us, jungle spread across the landscape. Humidity showed itself in the steam columns rising up to the clouds. It's uncomfortably hot and muggy in the Brazilian rainforest.

After much celebration under the fountain, we jumped back onto the bikes and continued our climb. Fifteen minutes later, we reached the top, drenched with sweat.

Moments later, I rolled over the downside. My bike gathered speed. Coasting. Love it! My gravity-motor kicked into high-speed gear. Something absolutely thrilling overcomes my body when I'm on a downhill ride. My mind leaps with excitement and my spirit soars. What was so hard on the one side of the mountain was wonderful on the other. It's the Yin/Yang of life. One is infinitely more pleasurable than the other, but both are necessary for each to exist. Besides, the steeper the climb, the more incredible the scenery.

As I increased my speed, the wind tugged at my body and dried my sweat. I followed the snaking road down toward the sea. Off one curve, beautiful white sands and breakers stretched to the horizon. Down I plunged through jungle growth, flowers, birds and insects. What had taken hours to climb, took only twenty minutes to descend. At the end of the incline, the road leveled, and my legs instinctively began pedaling again.

Climbing and coasting—are both a part of the incredible adventure of bicycling.

SECTION X: HOW TO BECOME A LONG DISTANCE TOURING RIDER

Chapter 60—What it's like being a Long Distance Bicycle Rider

What is it like being a long-distance touring rider? Is it exciting? Does it make traveling special? Why do I ride? What makes me do it? How is it traveling on a bicycle? I am asked these questions often while I'm on tour and I try to explain it to folks, but they don't have the background to understand. Still, I try to explain my feelings.

On an emotional level, it's a sensory involvement with natural forces surrounding me. It's a tasting of the wind, a feeling of the coolness, and the warmth—swirling clouds above me and grasses bending in soft breezes. Touring puts me in intimate contact with sunrises and sunsets.

Along seacoasts, I watch waves charge their white fury against sandy beaches. Touring, in its elegant silence, allows me to see an eagle swoop out of the blue and with its talons extended, grab a mouse and lift it into the sky headed toward its nest. Touring allows me to see a kangaroo hop across the road in Australia or ride into the teeth of an approaching storm.

There are quiet and wild moments depending on nature. When I am a long-distance touring rider, I get caught up in the forces that whirl and swirl around me, and I feel at peace with them. The normal everyday occurrences of life, which seem extraordinary to many people, are normal to me. Why? Because I place myself in a wilderness 'orbit' that is natural, in synchronization with the animal world—far away from the maddening din of humanity's cities.

One of the things I enjoy as I ride along, is the ease with which I move through the Natural World, both plant and animal. My journey carries me through deserts, mountains, forests and plains. As I ride along, three aspects of living become important with every turn of the pedals. Whether I ride through a country or across a continent, I meet people and see the sights. For me, the most important thing is my connectedness, a combination of what I feel is important in keeping my life in relationship with the natural world, and therefore, myself—and that is—keeping my body, mind, and spirit, in balance, like on a wheel, somewhat like a freewheel. Even though I'm changing gears, whether it's the three front derailleur chainrings or the seven on the back end, I'm keeping a good combination of changes and adaptations to the earth around me.

I think bicycling is a lot like that. I ride into each day having no idea what's going to happen. I ride with a positive attitude, and invariably, good things happen. It's rare that I ever ride into a negative situation—because life is generally positive. Some people may complain that it's raining out today, so that's a negative. I don't see it that way. Rain makes flowers bloom. A mountain rises ahead. I have to drop into granny gear. My legs ache, and my hands hurt—yet that's a positive because it's part of the process of moving into the unknown, experiencing it, and finding out what it's about. It's a lot like anyone's life as they grow toward their own fulfillment. Each day, I feel as I ride my bike into the unknown, the pedals move around in a constant rhythm of adaptation to the different kinds of terrain, and so do I, with my body, mind and spirit.

Starting with the body, a long-distance touring rider is concerned about the health of his or her body. That concern translates into taking care of it. I exercise all the muscles, not just the ones for riding a bike because it's important to keep everything balanced.

My nutritional approach is vegetarian with an emphasis on raw natural foods—vegetables, fruits, nuts, grains. I compliment them with whole breads and pastas. I avoid meat and dairy products. This nutritional stance gives my body maximum clean-burning fuel to push the pedals throughout the day. It makes me capable of responding to any physical needs whether it be hot, dry deserts such as the Atacama of Chile, the Outback of Australia, or a 15,500-foot pass in the Bolivian Andes. I can move through them with confidence because my body maintains a balance.

The five bodily senses play an important part of the day in a bicycle tour. I feel everything around me. I taste, touch, hear, smell and feel nature. I taste the rain on my tongue and touch the bark of a tree. I hear an owl hooting and smell a skunk. My senses soar because I am involved with the swirling forces of nature. I sweat in the desert and get chilled in the mountains. I am wild on my bicycle with the wind blowing past me.

Touring fills my mind with expectations. Something new lies around the bend in the road ahead. It can be confusing or frustrating. Most of the time, however, it's a positive experience. If you pinned me down, I would go with the word—serene. Nature creates inexplicable beauty. I love seeing it for the first time and my mind swallows it in big gulps.

Unfortunately, with the passing years, my mind has been forced to accept the incredible destruction wrought by humanity on this globe. Human beings destroy our natural heritage at an astounding rate. I am hopeful for a change of consciousness, but it's not probable that it will occur in time to alter our present global course of self-destruction.

Ultimately, my spiritual being moves through the natural world. I pedal, change gears, drink water, see an eagle, watch a storm, and sleep beneath the stars. These activities affect something deep down in my spirit. It's the balance in my life. It's something I can't really know, yet it seems to grow as I get older. It's a feeling inside me about life, which leaves me at peace with myself. When I keep my spiritual life balanced, my spirit connects with the natural scheme of nature. By keeping in balance I accept life on its terms and deal with it. If I win or lose, or I'm sick or healthy or whatever, I move forward in a spiritual way, with a positive feeling toward life.

Bicycling is that beautiful vehicle that I can push forward at what that wise old bird Chian in “Jonathan Livingston Seagull” called "The perfect speed, and the perfect speed is being there." I'm definitely THERE on a bicycle—body, mind and spirit.

Chapter 61—How to Live the Dream

You see them in the outdoor magazines—climbing mountains, canoeing down the Amazon River, walking around the world, bicycling from Alaska to the bottom of South America, rowing a boat to Antarctica, and sailing across the Pacific, and Scuba diving on the Great Barrier Reef. Men and women around this planet live some wild adventures that seem crazy at first, but as you see or read their stories, it dawns on you that they are living their dreams.

Why would Valerie and Verlen Krueger from Lansing, Michigan, paddle their two canoes from the top of North America through the middle of the continent, and then paddle across the Caribbean and enter the Amazon Basin of South America and paddle thousands of miles through the interior to end up at Ushuaia, Tierra Del Fuego, at the bottom of South America—taking three years and risking death along the way? I don't know, but they did it.

One woman, Ann Kanabe, bicycled from Prudhoe Bay, Alaska on the Arctic Ocean, more than 15,000 miles through Canada, the United States, Mexico, and Central America. The length of South America to the bottom in Tierra Del Fuego. She decided to do it. The human spirit knows no boundaries.

I think each human being has some kind of journey to make. Deep within each of us, a longing to explore and extend our limits bubbles from birth. Like the child who wants out of his or her crib to explore the front room, that same child in time wants to see what's in the front yard. Later on, that person wants to explore what's down the block and beyond the city limits. What's out there? For each individual, it's what he or she hasn't experienced. Therefore, it holds mystery. People read or watch TV about life in other lands, but that's not good enough for everyone. Any people want to see it for themselves. There is something about smelling, hearing, tasting, touching and feeling a new place for the first time. It adds to one's spirit and life force.

Some people pick books, movies and television for their journeys. Some travel around their country in a car. Some fly planes, while others prefer backpacking. Others choose to remain within their city's boundaries. Travel is a personal endeavor.

I chose bicycle adventuring. Why? Because bicycling possesses rhythm. Look at nature—it is round. Our planet is round. Raindrops are round. Animals' and insects' eyes are round. Everything in life is cyclical. The bicycle's wheels are round. They roll in a steady rhythm throughout the day. I don't know if the human body evolved to fit a bicycle or not, but look at how the two work together. No other machine humans have created returns so much efficiency from the amount of energy output. Bicycling involves my body, mind and spirit during the journey. Not only that—it's fun. Remember when you were a kid on your bicycle? You had fun on it, didn't you? It doesn't change—in fact, it increases because as an adult, you're aware of the fun you're having.

No other traveling mode gives me such fulfillment and contentment at the end of a long day. I meet more people on my bicycle than on any other mode of travel. The greatest advantage of bicycling is that I cover great distances cheaply and in an environmentally responsible manner.

Those are some of the reasons why. But people ask me other questions. How do you get so much time off? How do you make the money? Doesn't it cost a fortune to travel?

How do I live my dreams? It's not easy because I am not wealthy, nor do I have a financial benefactor. I've had to work my butt off, plain and simple.

The key to taking a long bicycle adventure or any adventure is to focus on it. Make a date for the day when you will take off.

If it takes two years to save money, decide it's worth your efforts. I've met many people on the road, both men and women, alone or in tandem, who worked two jobs for a year or two or three. They worked over 80 hours per week including weekends, with only one goal, and that was to make a pile of money so they could explore the world for one or two years.

That means they didn't buy clothes, gadgets, new cars, and other fancy goods. Some lowered their living standards to a single-room efficiency. Some took menial jobs they disliked, but they never lost sight of their goal. I've worked 90 hours a week sometimes to earn money for a bicycle adventure. It mattered little to me what the work was, as long as it got me to my goal. I've bartended, cleaned toilets, driven trucks, painted houses, swept industrial floors, moved furniture, lifeguarded, washed dishes, waited tables, and worked in a hospital cleaning bedpans. The point is, we have 24 hours a day, seven days a week. It's what we choose to do with that time that helps us succeed with our goals.

For example, if I start working 80 hours per week, two jobs, maybe three, I will have no free time, but the money will be there for me at the end of 12, 18 or 24 months. Whereas another person may work 40 hours per week for the same period, and he or she will have plenty of free time. But when it's over, they will have scant savings. I, however, will be sitting on a bankroll. Time passed for both of us, and it's over now. The difference is, I have plane tickets for China, Russia, Australia, Africa, South America and Europe. That's how you can live your dream of travel.

You can also become a steward, dance instructor, lifeguard, and housekeeping person on an ocean liner. You can become a stewardess on an airplane. You can become a dive master. You can also become a bicycle guide for a Tour Company. It's an endless avenue for living your dream of world travel.

Set your goal. Begin somewhere. Explore boldly. Establish your initiative. Lock on to your vision. You can't 'want' to do something because the universe can't work with a 'want'. I 'want' to do something won't cut it. It can and will work with 'intention'. I 'am' riding across America on my bike. Once you 'intend', the universe will pull you into your vision or dream.

One more important point—it's inexpensive to travel by bicycle and tent. Your only costs are food, and in developing countries, that's a few dollars a day. You can't live in an apartment as cheaply as you can bicycle around a continent for a year.

Limitations stop many of us. If you decide to get married but want to travel, you may have to defer children for the time you need. Although, I have met bicycling couples with their two kids strapped into a 'bugger' for year-long rides. If you're locked into a job but want to quit because you're unhappy, you have to make a plan, so you can work toward it, even if it takes several years. Maybe you have a good job and you and your wife want to travel, but you don't want to quit. Many times, you can take a leave of absence without pay. You may want to wait for retirement. I've met couples on the road in their seventies, busting overpasses with the gusto of much younger bicyclists. Sometimes, you're boxed in, with few choices. In that case, it's better to take care of your responsibilities before making travel decisions.

Women who want to bicycle travel have distinct concerns. You may want to have a male friend along. Going alone might be pushing your luck in certain countries. But if you had two or three of you, you would be relatively safe in many countries. In such places as Australia or New Zealand, you would be reasonably safe. Use your own discretion and common sense.

The adage, "do it while you're young," is the best bet. When you're young, you have time to burn, and few cares to worry about. More importantly, bicycling around the world offers you tremendous life experiences in appreciating different people and cultures. Your return from these adventures will enhance your personal values, and give you greater compassion and a strong sense of global humanity. This earth of ours is a lovely piece of real estate winging around the universe.

See as much of it as you can in your lifespan.

Chapter 62—Everything you need to know for long-distance bicycle adventure

> ***"Riding a bicycle flat out brings joy throughout a person's mind, body and spirit. Pedaling scintillates every cell in one's body toward some kind of nirvana, state of grace and/or total bliss. It might be deemed something like the ancients equate to enlightenment. Whatever you call it, the feelings ring from the rafters of your mind. Everyone enjoys that smile on your face and in your spirit when they meet you on tour on your bicycle."***
>
> ***—FHW***

GETTING STARTED

Please note that bicycle touring puts you out on the highway where there are cars and trucks flying past you at 60 miles per hour. Many drivers are texting, calling on their cell phones, swatting at flies on their dashboards, and/or turning around to yell at their kids to settle down. While this book gives you suggestions for the journey, the publisher cannot, and I cannot take any responsibility for your choices to ride a bicycle on the roads of the world. You travel at your own risk.

THE RIGHT BIKE

Everyone carries a bias about something dear to his or her heart. When it comes to bicycle touring, I've tried various approaches to equipment. Many of my lessons have been learned the hard way.

Experience proves a stern taskmaster. I've stood in rainstorms with a breakdown, wondering why I hadn't listened to a friend who had been through it. Maybe I didn't listen because I thought I knew it all. Wrong! Even with miles and years behind my wheel, new ideas pop up daily. I'm willing to learn from other riders, because each one has a different style that incorporates something better into his or her bicycle touring operation.

Ben Franklin said it best: "Penny wise, pound foolish."

That wisdom holds true to this day. It applies to the bike you buy, and your gear.

More than once, I've been asked for advice on what kind of bike to ride. Am I biased? You bet. My inclination for bikes and equipment comes from a long trail of mistakes. You may obtain a host of experts' opinions, and they are valid relative to each person's needs, and aspirations in touring.

Light touring machine or heavy mountain bike?

Hands down—buy a mountain touring bike. It's the best thing to happen to bicycle touring either nationally or internationally. Cost? If your touring plans mean two weeks per year in the USA, buy a bike in the $600.00 range. For international tours of six months duration, spend $1,500.00 or more and save money in the long run. For those who want the best, a custom-built mountain touring bike will cost $2,500.00 to $4,500.00. It's a lot of money and it's a lot of bicycles. The bike you see in the pictures of this book is a custom-made Franklin Frame that I bought for $2,500.00. That was 31 years ago. The touring geometry is outstanding. It fits me like a glove and rides like a dream.

Some people will tell you that a mountain bike is too heavy. Balderdash! We're talking five pounds more at the most. That goes for both men and women. You won't feel the weight. They say it handles harder. No way. Your body adapts to any load. That bike will become as comfortable as your favorite easy chair.

Why a mountain bike? First of all, comfort levels increase because of the fat tires. Buy ridged 1.75 tires for a smooth ride. A mountain bike offers a better, softer ride. You don't get front-end shimmy from being overloaded in the panniers or handlebar bag. Another big plus is the rarity of flat tires on a mountain bike. I've gone five months without a flat. No conventional touring bicycle can boast that. Those 1.25-inch tires get cut or worn out much too often. I love the security of knowing my tires are sturdy, especially on a long downhill, high-speed coast. Additionally, you can load a mountain bike up with tons of weight and not worry about spokes breaking (26-inch versus 27-inch rims), or wheels warping out of true. Best tire: Schwalbe Marathon Plus Tour.

Customize that mountain bike for touring. Replace the straight bars with wide drop bars or butterfly bars. That will give you three hand-holding positions. Buy an Aero bar that will give you a place to rest your forearms and take you over the front of the bike for hours of comfortable riding. That means your shifting levers must be relocated on the down tube, or bar end shifters are available. Yes, there are new shifting levers on the horizontal section of drop bars and/or butterfly bars. Purchase what you like best. Install a 40-spoke rear wheel, if available, for added endurance, especially for international touring.

Buy the heaviest gauge and highest quality spokes for that back wheel, and make certain the person who builds your wheel knows what he or she is doing. Check around and get several opinions. By investigating, you will discover the best bike person in your town. Be aware of fast talkers who seem to know it all. Ask them how much and where they have toured. Do they know how to fit a bike into your body? Make sure they do it. Learn how to do it yourself. It's important to get a perfect fit. Your enjoyment depends on it.

Two items in the drive train stand out as very important to me. I install a front Granny gear 24-tooth chainring with a 34-tooth low-end freewheel gear (cassette). No sense in killing yourself on climbs. Best rear derailleur? I won't go anywhere without a Deore XT. That derailleur outlasts anything on the market.

For those who love 'light touring', yes, by all means, buy a light touring bike. For women who want a lighter ride, yes, buy that bike that works for you. In the end, do your due diligence and buy the right bike for you.

You will develop your own style given a few miles, but it's nice to feel confident in your bicycle when you start out with a quality machine that fits your needs.

E-bikes: many great choices to give you and your spouse an extra lift while riding. Make sure you buy one with a kickstand and solid rear rack. My best advice: Hai-Bike with four speed-assist selections, excellent rack, 75 miles on one charge and solid German technology. My wife bought one and loves it. She completed the Lewis & Clark Trail on hers. Also, she rode the West Coast with it. Very dependable. Check with Consumer Reports on E-bikes to make sure you buy a dependable ride.

PREPARING FOR INTERNATIONAL BICYCLE TOURING

Going on a bicycle tour to some exotic country? Developing country? Whether you're going for three weeks or six months, you have dozens of things to take care of before boarding the airplane. Preparing for an international tour is like battling a four-alarm fire. When you think one blaze is under control, another one needs immediate attention.

Begin preparing NOW—three to six months in advance. If you work forty or fifty hours a week, solid preparation will keep you from going crazy a week before departure. In my own world tours, I've found each continent needs specialized consideration. For example, in America, you can expect a bicycle shop in the next town if you need a spare part. In Africa, forget it. Whether you crank your bicycle across the Arctic Circle in Norway, push through the Andes Mountains in Peru, or sweat your way across the Nullarbor Plains of Australia—the success of your journey depends on what you do before you leave.

The key to that success is the COMPLETION of your "To Do" and "To Buy" lists months before you leave. When you make your target date seven days to a month in advance of departure, you can relax at the bon voyage party without having an ulcer. Additionally, your health during the ride may depend on your advance preparation.

To make things easier on you, major and minor areas of concern will be covered. You may refer to "What to take and how to pack it," in this chapter. As you begin to acquaint yourself with the enormity of international touring preparation, get out a pen and a paper, and start a list.

BICYCLE AND EQUIPMENT

Two to three-week guided tours usually enjoy a sag wagon and mechanics to repair and maintain your bicycle. With those tours, your bike, whether you rent or bring your own, is not as critical a factor in the success of your tour. However, buy a bike and gear that will serve you well, so you may ride in confidence. Before going on tour, a basic tune-up is a must. If you buy a new bike, be sure to ride it 300 miles and have the wheels trued. Be certain to have the bike fitted to your body.

For persons riding into developing world countries, a mountain bike (converted for touring by adding drop bars or butterfly bars, 40-spoke hole hubs, extra quart water bottles, anatomical touring seat, aero bar, lower gearing, and fenders added) is highly recommended. It not only offers a superior ride on gravel roads; the tires last longer with far fewer flats. Make sure the quality of the bike and components matches the length of your ride. Insist on sealed bearings, but if you can't buy them, make sure your hubs have been overhauled. Carry tools that work with every part of your bike. Take a course in bicycle repair.

Highly recommended: In the past several years, those 'Aero' or 'Scott' bars have become vogue in racing circles because they lower the body resistance and create a bullet-like profile that is more streamlined. The big discovery for touring riders is a whole new form of comfort. By resting your arms on the bar, you rest your whole upper body and your butt. It allows for many more comfortable miles by taking the pressure off the triceps and shoulders. I highly recommend adding them to your comfort gear while on tour.

TENT, SLEEPING BAG, AIR MATTRESS AND COOKING GEAR

If you're on a guided tour, these items may not be important because lodging and food will be provided.

For those on individual tours, this equipment is extremely important. A quality, self-standing tent in the \$250.00 to \$350.00 range is a good bet. Be sure to seal the seams, carry extra seam sealer, and carry a waterproof ground mat.

A three-season sleeping bag at three pounds (down or fiberfill) good to 10 to 20 degrees Fahrenheit will keep you warm in most conditions. If you get caught at a high altitude, you may wear your tights, mittens, sweater and cap to bed for extra warmth. The BEST air mattress is a 3/4 length self-inflating Thermo-Rest by Cascade Designs. I buy my gear at REI.com, LLBean.com, EMS.com, and NorthFace.com, because they give outstanding guarantees on their equipment.

Cooking gear includes a large pot, a secondary pan, utensils, cups and a stove. Buy a stove that will burn many kinds of fuel for international destinations. An MSR International is one of the most popular and costs around $89.00. Talk with an REI employee for your specific needs and he or she will fill them. For the USA, a Coleman Primus with propane bottles works great.

DAY PACK OR SMALL BACKPACK

On top of your back rack, you may want to carry a 3,000 to 4,000 cubic-inch capacity pack with three external pockets. It can be your utility pack for easy access to your camera, film, valuables and food. Carry your most often used gear in it. When stopping at a restaurant or whenever leaving the bike unattended for a few moments, you can release the bungee cords and sling the pack over your shoulders.

RAINPROOFING YOUR GEAR

No doubt about it, you're at the mercy of the elements on a bicycle tour. Your equipment must be kept dry. Wrap everything in plastic bags. Keep your rain suit easily available. Make certain your film, digital cards and camera gear are securely rainproofed. Do the same for your sleeping bag and tent.

INTERNATIONAL TOURS

When riding in a foreign country, you're subject to different conditions. You may be vulnerable to infectious diseases, tainted food and water. You need extra precautions with eating, drinking, and medicine. Boil, drop or filter your water, and eat only cooked foods. I use an MSR or First Need water filter. They are inexpensive and effective. Always peel fruits and vegetables. Wash your hands and keep your eating utensils clean. Drink only water you have filtered.

In a developing world country, you can expect a case of food poisoning at some point in your tour. Once you feel it coming on, induce yourself to vomit, and keep vomiting until your stomach is empty. Drink plenty of water to rinse out your system. This procedure will save you from prolonged suffering. If not food poisoning, you may pick up a new bacterium that doesn't agree with your intestines. In that case, you must tolerate the alien bugs until your system settles down to normal again.

Because you will not be able to bathe every day, carry anti-fungal ointment. Take a washcloth and wipe yourself down nightly with water. This will help prevent fungal growth on your skin. For poison ivy or skin rashes, carry a Micatin cream. You can buy an MSR shower bag in order to take a three-minute shower every night.

Your passport is vulnerable to theft. Always keep it on your person or at arm's length.

IMMUNIZATION AND INOCULATIONS

Don't you love this category? It's a real pain in the rump, but necessary. Tell the nurse which countries you will be visiting and get your inoculations card completed with each shot or series. Take no chances with yellow fever, tetanus, typhoid, diphtheria or cholera. Insist on a Gamma Globulin shot for the best, but not perfect, prevention available for hepatitis.

Tell them how long you intend to tour, so they can adjust the dosage accordingly. Seek out all information you need in this area, and act upon it. Call or write the Center for Disease Control, U.S. Department of Health and Human Services. The number is in your local phone book under U.S. Government. Or, look up online! For shots, call your local hospital immunization department. If you demand answers, you will receive them. In this area, preparation and prevention are keys to your health.

Upon returning to the USA from a Developing world country, have a blood, urine and feces check to make sure you haven't picked up any liver flukes or other parasites. If tests are positive, begin treatment immediately.

In countries where malaria is present, you must start taking pills two weeks before leaving. With two or more people on the tour, take them on the same day, so everyone can remind each other during the ride. Follow instructions as your doctor tells you.

PASSPORT

This one can be a real hassle. Pick up the application at the post office. Fill it out and provide all documentation exactly as required. One mistake, and they will write you a letter with the needed items for the completion of your passport. In the meantime, your application is scattered between their office and your house.

Make certain you send them RECENT (within six months) official passport pictures and sign them on the back. Use those same pictures for visa applications. When applying for visas to different countries, use a travel agency's courier services. If you have any problems in processing, call your congressional representative. For peace of mind, make a list of the locations of American embassies in the countries you plan to visit.

Keep a dozen extra pictures for an international driver's license, hostel card and other needs that will pop up on an extended tour. Color or black-and-white pictures are acceptable.

For extra precaution, take a photostat copy of your passport, driver's license and birth certificate. Put them in a separate compartment.

CAMERA EQUIPMENT

When the adventure ends, the pictures you snapped will be your most prized possessions. That is, if you didn't soak the camera in a rainstorm, or forget a spare light meter battery.

Camera gear needs special attention, whether you carry an expensive digital mirrorless, cell phone or a sure shot automatic. Keep your camera in a waterproof bag and insist that airport security people hand-inspect it. Always ride with your camera in a plastic bag and out of the sun. Carry a small tripod.

CUSTOMS

Before leaving the states, have customs officers document U.S. ownership of your bike, camera equipment, expensive jewelry and any other gear you consider worth claiming as previously purchased property. Otherwise, you could be liable for import taxes upon your return. Even more important, you could be charged more than $100.00 for an import tax in a developing world country!

NUTS AND BOLTS INFORMATION

Carry theft insurance for all your valuables overseas. Check with your insurance agent to make certain your bike and gear are covered.

Schedule a dental checkup and have everything in order before leaving. If you have a problem in a developing world country, you may suffer prolonged pain.

Money matters are very important. Purchase American Express traveler's checks because that company has the most offices throughout the world. Carry debit credit cards (Visa and MasterCard) that are honored internationally. Send your company $500.00 to $5,000.00 of debit credit, so you will have that to draw on if you're not back in time to pay a bill. You may need it in a pinch.

Make certain their expiration date is after your return. ALWAYS keep them in your money belt. I keep my passport and valuables on my person 24 hours a day and within arm's reach when taking a shower. When sleeping in a hostel, stuff your valuables into the bottom of your sleeping bag. Camera gear can go into the closed end of your pillowcase on your hostel sheet. NEVER assume your gear is safe from theft. It will be gone in seconds if left unattended.

For additional financial preparation, you can order foreign currency from your own bank. If you arrive in a country during a festival or other holiday, you will have at least $50.00 worth of their money for your immediate expenses. Carry a credit/debit card that you can plug into any ATM machine in most countries and retrieve needed money.

If there is any question as to safety, write the embassy of the country you want to visit. I avoided Columbia completely on my tour through South America. Hostile guerrilla action broke out on the routes I had to take to get to Ecuador. My body is allergic to bullets and jail, so I never take any chances.

For complete information from USA sources, call the Citizen's Adviser Center in Washington, D.C. at the phone number (202) 647-5225; if a problem exists in a country, call (202) 647-6173; if a situation merits further investigation, call the Security Department, 24-hour command center at (202) 647-2412. Consider their suggestions seriously in your travel decisions.

Carry a booklet with addresses and phone numbers of embassies in a foreign country. Check-in with the USA embassy staff and out when you leave a country.

DRUGS: Anyone who carries or consumes drugs in a foreign country is absolutely out of his or her mind. Jails in developing world countries are loaded with Americans who thought they wouldn't get caught. I can't stress this enough: STAY AWAY FROM DRUGS OR ANYTHING THAT LOOKS, FEELS, OR SOUNDS SUSPICIOUS. If someone traveling with you carries drugs, insist he or she gets rid of the contraband. If they refuse, separate yourself from them. You may be considered an accomplice. Police in developing world countries lock you up and throw away the key.

Purchase your plane tickets two or three months in advance for possible discount prices, and assurance that you have a plane seat. Shop for an airline that charges the least for a bicycle as extra baggage. Some airlines charge $150.00 for your bicycle ONE WAY.

Break your bike down and pack it into a sturdy box. Be sure to secure the front forks by placing a block of wood in the axle and taping it in place. Unscrew the rear derailleur from the dropout. Tape it to the chain inside some paper or a rag. That will save it from being bent or have a shop do it for you. Be advised that you must know how to reconstruct your bike at the destination, so learn how to break it down and put it back together.

Learn a few valuable phrases in the language of the country(s) you may visit. Learn to say, "Hello, goodbye, good morning, good night, where is the toilet? How much? Yes, no, Mr., Mrs., please and thank you."

Carry a phrase book to help you along. People will warm up when you make an effort to speak their language.

If you won't get back before April 15th, you need to fill out a Federal Income tax extension form. By proving you were out of the country, you have an automatic 90-day extension (you can show a copy of your airline ticket). However, you must have enough paid into the IRS in order not to suffer penalties.

If someone is taking care of your house, or you are renting it out, you need to fill out a Power of Attorney form giving someone you trust the legal right to handle your personal affairs, such as eviction of destructive renters or those who bounce rent checks. Leave that person with extra funds to pay for emergency or unexpected bills.

Fill out a will and register it in probate court. Notify your benefactor. It costs less than $10.00 to register.

Make sure your insurance payments are in order. Car, house, bike and any other insured items must have up-to-date premiums paid.

Carry a travel handbook that gives you the ins and outs of each country and major cities. Carry a Youth Hostel book with locations and phone numbers.

Today, with smartphones, you enjoy 24/7 connections to the world. However, you may need mail at some point.

Leave a travel itinerary with loved ones of post office addresses in major cities. Tell them to address the envelope with your name, c/o Poste Restante, Central Post Office, City and Country. Poste Restante is the international word for general delivery. You can pick up your mail at a post office by showing your passport. Tell your friends to write to each address three weeks in advance of the tentative dates you have written down on your itinerary. If you're not sure where you will be and don't want to write all your friends each time with a possible new address, you can have your friends write to one address in the states at your best friend's or parent's house and have your mail forwarded from there. It's easier that way. I can tell you that letters are like Christmas gifts and mean so much when you are a long way from home.

Another nice communication mode is ‘Hotmail’ or ‘Gmail’ on the computer. You can pick up email virtually around the world today. You dial up your personal code and you can write and read letters to and from your friends. Check with any carrier to get hooked up.

Create a FB account where you can write stories and exhibit pictures from your travels. You’ll be amazed at the audience that follows you.

Carry the international dialing phone number of your local bicycle shop. If you suffer a major breakdown, they can express mail you a replacement. By keeping stocked with parts from the pack list, you should be covered.

When traveling through multiple countries, you must have a plane ticket home, and enough money to show you are financially responsible while touring that country. Otherwise, authorities may not let you enter their country.

Check with your travel agent to see if you need a visa for a particular country, or whether they give an automatic 30-day visa. Once you arrive in a country that has granted you an automatic visa, but you didn't obtain one for the next country you will visit—you can apply at the embassy in the Capitol of the country you are now touring. Remember to take extra pictures.

Always be cordial and smile. Be as neat and clean as you can and act respectfully toward authorities.

For anyone going on a long-distance tour, buy a special padded seat cover with the latest silicone cushioning. It will save your rear end. For double insurance, seats now offer this material, and you can add the cover for ultimate comfort. I ride a Serfas Full Suspension Hybrid touring seat. It is around $45.00.

PHYSICAL CONDITIONING

Your physical preparation is one of the most important keys to enjoyment while on tour. Ride your bike every day for a month before departure. If you're headed into the mountains, find some steep grades where you live, and ride them with your loaded panniers. If none exist, ride a high-resistance stationary bike at the local health club.

If you fail to prepare your legs, a slight strain or ligament pull will finish you abruptly on a bicycle adventure because it will get worse with every added mile. Make sure you avoid that: get into pedaling shape as well as butt shape.

BIKE SECURITY

Your bike security at night or while visiting a monument is important. Either check into a safe hotel where you can keep the bike in your room (I cable it to a pipe or anything secure), or have someone in your party stay with the cycles and gear. Lock the bikes to something solid and keep equipment in your tent at night.

ATTITUDE

Patience: In developing world countries, during any situation, remain calm, patient and respectful. Learn to accept their ways, even though they may be frustrating and different from your own.

One last point on international bicycle touring—you are pedaling into strange lands, meeting new people and experiencing different cultures. You will have the time of your life. Leave excess baggage like prejudice, discrimination and discourtesy at home. Stretch your emotional, mental and spiritual wings to learn about the world. Ride as a personal ambassador from your country. The impressions you make on people will remain with them forever. Share a smile, kind words and good things will come your way.

Enjoy a grand bicycle adventure in good health and high spirits.

WHAT TO TAKE AND HOW TO PACK IT

One of the most frustrating feelings on a bicycle tour is when you dig into your pack for something and can't find it. Even worse is realizing you didn't bring it. It can be as small as a pair of tweezers or as important as a spoke wrench. The best way to prevent such a calamity is to keep a pack list that you can check off before leaving for your adventure.

Special precautions must be taken in five areas each time you load your gear into your panniers. When you need an item, you want it easily available. That goes double for your first aid kit.

International tours require extra attention to detail, and at least three months of advance preparation.

EQUIPMENT ORGANIZATION

Organizing your equipment is the best way to have it ready for your use. If it's small, light and you use it often, the best storage place is a zipper pouch on the rear panniers or your daypack. Depending on how you stand your bike, items used often need to be on the free side of the bike. For efficiency, group common items like a toothbrush and soap in the same nylon 'ditty' bags. These drawstring pouches are handy. You can use clear plastic bags to separate clothes into organized compartments. You can do the same for tire repair tools.

When your gear is packed, especially on your first trip, it takes a few days of rearranging everything to place it where you like. Once that's accomplished, draw a schematic of where everything is placed. Use it for quick reference when packing for future rides.

WEIGHT DISTRIBUTION

The first rule in bicycling touring is: If you don't need or use it, leave it. Why? Simple—weight adds up quickly. Every excess pound you pack will cost you in bike stability and miles covered daily. When riding with four panniers, you need to pack the heaviest equipment—like stove, fry pan, and cable lock—into the lowest sections of your rear panniers. That will keep your "lean" weight closer to the ground. Lean weight means the amount of weight you have on the bike and where it is located. If you pack heavy items higher up in the panniers, the bike will be top heavy.

When loading your bicycle, you need to balance weight from side to side. More weight should be in the rear panniers than in the front. If you experience a shimmy in your handlebars, it means you have too much in your handlebar bag. Keep less than four pounds in it. If a shimmy persists, lighten your front panniers and check the side-to-side balance. Traditional touring bikes with light frames and skinny tires have a shimmy problem more than touring mountain bikes. That's why I recommend a mountain bike for touring.

CAMERA EQUIPMENT CARE

Keep your camera equipment in plastic bags at all times. While on tour, dust swirls around you from cars and the wind. Also, you must be concerned about rain. Large zip lock freezer bags work well, and you can see through them and reuse them. Keep camera gear in the daypack cushioned over your sleeping bag and air mattress rolls.

DAYPACK AND INTERNAL FRAME BACKPACK

A small daypack will keep many of your valuables safe and ready for use. They are as handy as any book pack that you used back in school. It'll carry your camera and valuable gear that you want with you at a moment's notice.

A 2,000 to 3,000 cubic-inch internal frame pack with three side compartments is an excellent addition to your versatility while on tour. You can store your air mattress and gear, along with extra digital cards, valuables and food. Make it the easy-access pack to your most often-used gear. If you happen to find yourself in a backpacking situation, you're ready to go.

RAINPROOFING YOUR GEAR

No doubt about it, you're at the mercy of the elements on a bicycle tour. Your equipment must be kept dry. Wrap everything each morning in plastic bags. Keep your rain suit available. Make certain your camera gear is rain proofed. Do the same for your sleeping bag and tent.

NIGHT LIGHT IN YOUR TENT

Miner's lamps cost $20.00 and will give you ample light for writing in the tent or cooking dinner outside.

CYCLING SHOES, GLOVES, GLASSES, SHORTS AND HELMET

Buy the best, most comfortable cycling shoes you can afford. Do not ride with tennis shoes. You need the plastic or steel shank on the bottom of the shoes to give you protection from the pedals. Without that shank, you will be in a lot of pain and cause your legs to waste a lot of energy to compensate.

Buy a good pair of cycling gloves to protect you from pounding your hands to death. The first week of a cycling trip, keep shaking your hands at regular intervals so you won't crush the ulnar nerve in the palm of the hand. If you have 'aero' bars, you will be able to give your hands a rest. That bar will take the pressure off your ulnar nerve. I highly recommend it.

With the ozone vanishing, you need to buy 100% UV glasses to stop damage to your eyes. I wear the very best eye protection. I buy the sunglasses with leather side blocks to protect you from the wind and they have a cord to keep them around your neck.

Buy two pairs of cycling shorts, either regular touring shorts or Lycra. Make sure you buy the suede-padded shorts instead of leather because sued is easier to wash and wear. If you are riding in extremely sunny weather, you might want to wear thin Thermax protection in the form of a shirt that covers your arms and neck. If it's blistering sunshine, wear thin tights to protect your legs from hours of radiation from the sun. A tan looks nice, but the damage to your skin accumulates into wrinkles, and potential skin cancers. Your body does not need all that sun. Protect your face daily with maximum sunblock.

Always wear a helmet. One person on average per day dies in the USA while riding a bicycle each year. Over 50,000 persons visit hospitals with broken bones and cuts bad enough to need medical attention after bike crashes each year. The most serious accidents are head injuries because people weren't wearing helmets. For touring, be certain to have a visor on your helmet for sun protection. They can stitch you up, and they can set your broken bones—but they can't pour your brains back into your head the right way. Wear a helmet. If the helmet doesn't have a visor, you can buy one at a motorcycle shop and drill new holes and fit it on yourself.

INTERNATIONAL TOURING

Any time you ride into a foreign country; you're subject to different conditions. You may be vulnerable to infectious diseases, tainted food and water. You need extra precautions with eating, drinking and medicine. Boil, use drops or filter your water, and eat only cooked foods. Always peel fruits and vegetables. You might consider becoming a temporary vegetarian once you see how dairy products and meats are left out in the sun with flies crawling everywhere.

Because you will not be able to bathe every day, carry an antifungal ointment. Take a washcloth and wipe yourself down nightly with water from your bottles. This will help prevent fungal growth on your skin. For poison ivy or other skin rashes, carry Micatin cream.

Your passport is vulnerable to theft. ALWAYS keep it and money on your person, in a pouch around your neck or in your pack. Your daypack should always go with you on a break, or have a trusted friend watch the gear while you go to the restroom.

During a tour in foreign countries, preventive maintenance is very important. Check your spokes often and take plenty of spare nuts and bolts. Two spare tubes and one extra tire are a minimum. Carry enough patch gear for 20 punctures. You will need a freewheel puller wrench, chain breaker and rear derailleur. In developing world countries, strongly consider a mountain bike converted for touring, i.e., put drop bars on it, 'aero' bars, and ride with 1.75 tires with a 40 spoke 26-inch rim. For heavily mountainous countries, try a 24 front 'Granny' gear chain ring to a 34 teeth rear freewheel or cassette climbing gear.

THE BIG ITEMS

Your tent, sleeping bag, daypack and air mattress are the bulky pieces that must balance over the rear axle. Strap your tent forward under the seat and your sleeping bag behind it. The air mattress will fit over the tent. The second set of crossed bungee cords will secure your daypack. Check for hanging straps or bungee cords—EVERY TIME you finish packing your bicycle. Otherwise, you will wrap them around the freewheel or spokes. The results can tear up your wheel alignment and worse.

FUEL BOTTLE AND GEAR PLACEMENT

You will find your own style for placing equipment. However, the fuel bottle is a potentially troublesome item. Some riders place it in their lower water bottle clip on the down tube. You can wrap it in plastic and set it upright in the rear pouch of your panniers. In either case, be certain to secure the opening from leakage. This pack list may be customized to suit you. This is a very large pack list that covers everything from A to Z. Use or discard items as you need them for yourself.

PACKING LIST

TOP OF FRONT PANNIER RACK

1. Sleeping Bag and Silk Cocoon in Waterproof Stuff Sack
2. Handlebar Bag
    a. Front of Bike White Light (3 AAA)
    b. Rear of Bike LED Red Warning Light (2 AAA)
    c. Chamois Cream
    d. Tire Pressure Gauge
    e. Riding Carb Fuel
    f. Eyeglass Cleaning Liquid & Cloth
    g. Sunglass Case W/Reg. Glasses
    h. SPF 100 Sun Block
    i. SPF 50 Chap Stick
    j. Hand Sanitizer
    k. Swiss Army Knife
    l. Mobile Phone
    m. Camera, extra digital cards
    n. Travel Wallet

LEFT FRONT PANNIERS

1. Instant Oatmeal
2. Hot Drink Mixes (tea, coffee, hot chocolate)
3. Peanut Butter
4. Bread or Tortillas
5. Three One-Gallon Freezer Bags
6. Three One-Quart Freezer Bags
7. Three One-Pint Freezer Bags
8. Riding Carb Fuel (Dried Fruit, Apples, Bananas, Oranges)
9. Stuff Sack with Energy Bars
10. Sports Drink Mix

RIGHT FRONT PANNIER

1. Spice Shaker
2. Vegetable Broth Cubes
3. Dinner Staples (Pasta, Lentils, Couscous, Quinoa, Etc.)
4. Dehydrated Evening Meals
5. Salad Fixings
6. Extra Riding Carb Fuel (Dried Fruit, Apples, Bananas, Oranges)

RIGHT REAR PANNIER

1. Outside Pocket
    a. First Aid Kit
    a. Folding Water Container
2. 0.6L Fuel Bottle in Freezer Bag
3. 325mL Fuel Bottle W/Pump
4. MSR 2.0 L Pot w/Strainer Lid
    a. Brunton Cook Stove
    b. Dish Towel
    c. Matches
    d. Pot Gripper
    e. Fork
    f. Liquid Soap

    g. Scouring Pad
5. Snow Peak Individual Cook Set, MSR cook set, you decide for your needs
    a. 0.8 L Cooking Pot
    b. Lid
    c. 10 oz. Cup
6. Gallon Freezer Bag
    a. Plate
    b. Long Handled Spoon
    c. Long Handled Knife
    d. Stove Wind Shield
7. Repair Kit
    a. Assorted Bandages
    b. 3 Tire Irons
    c. Open End Wrenches, 7-10 Mm
    d. Allen Wrenches, All Sizes to Fit Bike
    e. Leatherman Squirt Pliers
    f. 6" Adjustable Wrench
    g. Chain Tool
    h. Three Grease Rags
    i. Nuts, Bolts (Assorted)
    j. Chain Links
    k. One Tire Patch Kit (6-8 Patches)
    l. Brake Cable
    m. Gear Cable
    n. Brake Blocks
    o. 4 – 6" Plastic Tie Straps
    p. Short Length Elect. Tape
    q. 26 X 1.5 – 1.75 Presta Valve Tube
    r. Tent Seam Sealer

LEFT REAR PANNIER

1. Outside Pocket
    a. Clothes Drying Net Bag
    b. Insect Repellent
    c. Cable and Combination Lock
    d. Chain Lube, Grease Rag & Small Tube of Grease Remover Hand Cleaner in Plastic Bag

2. Street Clothes Stuff Sack
    a. 1 – PR. Lt. Wt. Long Pants w/zippered Legs
    b. 1 – Lt. Wt. Long Sleeve Shirt w/roll up sleeves
    c. 1 – Pr. Lt. Wt. Underwear
    d. 1 – T Shirt
    e. 1 - SwimSuit
3. Bike Wear Stuff Sack
    a. 1 – Pr. Biking Socks
    b. 1 - Thermax Long Sleeve Jersey
    c. 1 - Thin Sun Protection Long Sleeve Jersey
    d. 1 – Pr. Riding Shorts
    e. 1 – Pr. Biking Tights
4. Cold Weather Stuff Sack
    a. 1 - Under Armor Top
    b. 1 - Under Armor Bottom
    c. 1- Stocking Cap
5. Shower Sandals in Net Bag
6. Toiletry Kit
    a. 30 Days Flaxseed
    b. 30 Days Aspirin
    c. 30 Days Glucosamine W/MSM
    d. 30 Days One-A-Day Vitamin
    e. Sewing Kit
    f. Gore-Tex Repair Kit
    g. Disposable razors
    h. Toothpaste
    i. Toothbrush
    j. Dental Floss
    k. Comb
    l. Travel Wallet Contents List
7. Small Net Bag
    a. Microfiber Towel
    b. Deodorant Bar Soap in plastic bag

TOP OF REAR PANNIER RACK

1. Duffle Bag, preferably oblong and squared off
    a. **Rain Protection Plastic Bag W/Closure Device**
    b. Tent in Stuff Sack
    c. Poles in Stuff Sack

- d. Ground Cloth & Rain Fly in Stuff Sack
- e. 14 Tent Stakes in Bag (1 Extra)
- f. Air Mattress in Stuff Sack
- g. Lightweight Camping Chair
- h. Plastic Bag for Bicycle Seat Rain Cover
- i. 30' Of Nylon Cord
- j. Mini Clothes Pins

2. Red & Black Daypack

- a. **Rain Jacket** Rain Cover Plastic Bag W/Velcro Strap Closure
- b. Rain Jacket
- c. Rain Gear Stuff Sack
  - i. Rain Pants
  - ii. Rain Booties
  - iii. Helmet Cover
  - iv. Gloves
- **d. Gallon Plastic Freezer Bag**
  - i. Gear Location Schematic
  - ii. Maps
  - iii. Bike Specs.
- **e. Zippered Pocket**
  - **i. Night LED Head Light (3 AAA)**
  - ii. Ear Plugs
  - iii. SPF 50 Chap Stick
  - iv. Nighttime Eye Cover
  - v. Spare Batteries
    - 1. 3 - AAA
    - **2. Camera**
- f. **One Roll Camper Toilet Paper in Plastic Bag**
- **g. Small Net Bag**
  - **i. Phone Charger**
  - **ii. Camera Battery Charger**
- h. Quart Freezer Bag
  - i. Postcard Stamps
  - ii. Journal
  - iii. Address List
- i. Two Pens
- j. Two carabineers on Outside of pack
- k. Water purification tablets
- l. Cell phone
- m. Lap top computer

REMOVABLE BIKE ACCESSORIES

1. Frame Mounted Air Pump
2. 3 Water Bottles
3. Handlebar Mount Warning Bell
4. Rear View Mirror
5. Two 14" Bungee Cords
6. Four 20" Bungee Cords
7. One 11" Bungee Cord
8. One Short 27" Safety Flag
9. One Long 6' Safety Flag
10. Two Parking Brake 11" Velcro Straps
11. Bike Computer(1 Cr 2032 + 1 12v)
12. 3 Spokes with Nipples Mounted on Left Chain Stay
13. Two Extra Halo Sweat Bands on Aero Bars

WEARING TO RIDE

1. Helmet
2. Halo sweat band
3. Sunglasses
4. Short sleeve bike jersey
5. Bike shorts
6. Bike socks
7. Bike shoes
8. Bike gloves
9. Riding food in jersey pockets
10. Hydration pack

NEEDED (make yourself a 'need to buy' list)

1. Long handled peanut butter spreading knife 8" REI camp knife
2. Adjustable nylon webbing straps instead of bungee cords
3. Better Velcro straps to attach grey handlebar bag to sleeping bag and front pannier rack
4. Ink marker for tire tube to mark leak

On departure day pack added

1. Lip Balm
2. Bike Repair Book
3. Camera Instructions
4. Destination Tour Book
5. Blanket & Pillow
6. Toiletry Kit
7. Sunglass Case W/Sunglasses
8. Eye Cover for Sleeping
9. Riding Clothes
10. Riding Shoes
11. Bike Computer
12. Radio w/earphone

On Departure Day Pack (again, use as backup)

1. One Roll Toilet Paper
2. Trowel
3. Packable Broad Brim Hat

Travel Clothing

1. Long Pants
2. Long Sleeve Shirt
3. North Face Shoes
4. Normal Socks
5. Poly Underwear
6. Prescription Glasses

Ship Back – UPS (You may want to ship gear back to lighten load, example)

1. North Face Shoes
2. Normal Socks
3. 2 Duffel Bags
4. Blanket and Pillow
5. Eye Cover for Sleeping
6. Radio w/earphone
7. Tool Kit stuff

8. Straight Blade Screwdriver
9. Side Cutters

MAIL BACK ON LEAVING DESTINATION CITY OR COUNTRY

1. Tour Book
2. Bike Repair Book
3. Camera Instruction

First Aid Kit

- 6 -10 4x4" Pads for Cleaning Wounds and Soaking Blood
- 4 - 6 4x4" Non-Stick Pads for Covering Wound
- 1 – 2" Ace Stretch Wrap
- 1 Triangular Arm Sling
- 4-8 Large Safety Pins
- 4-6 Bandage Strips With 2 To 3 Inch Square Pads
- Tape, 1 Inch Wide, Surgical Tape (3-6 Yards or Meters).
- 6-10 Packets Or 1 Small 2-3 Oz. Bottle of Wound Sanitizer/Cleaner Betadine, Hibiclens, Peroxide, Baby Wipes or Soap and Water
- 1 Small Tube Triple Antibiotic Salve for Dressing Cuts and Abrasions
- 1 Small Tube, Hydrocortisone, 1% Or 2.5%, Topical Usage Only. Reduces Inflammation, Rashes, Saddle Sores and Allergic Reactions.

- 10-20 Tablets/Capsules Tylenol, *Acetaminophen*: For Muscle and Body Pain, Joint Pain, Headaches, Fever, Allergies, Cough, Cold, And Flu
- 10-20 Tablets/Capsules Motrin Or Advil, *Ibuprofen*: Anti-Inflammatory, Pain Killer
- 5-10 Tablets/Capsules Benadryl, *Diphenhydramine Hydrochloride*: General Anesthetic, Antihistamine, Anti Swelling, Sleeping Pill, Sedative, Anti Bleeding - Called: Nuprin, Medipren, Brufen, Anti-Vomiting/Nausea, Motion Sickness
- 3-4 Band Aids ½" Wide (1.5 Cm & 2.5 Cm Wide),Keep Some in Tool Kit, In Small Plastic Bag
- 3-4 Band Aids 1" Wide (1.5 Cm & 2.5 Cm Wide),Keep Some in Tool Kit, In Small Plastic Bag
- Moleskin- Prevent Blister
- Molefoam – Protect Blister
- Solarcaine -Sunburn Relief
- Imodium Ad- Anti-Diarrheal
- Visine - Eye Irritation
- Eucerine - Moisturizing Lotion
- Rolaids - Anti-Acid
- Lotromin Af - Anti Fungal
- Calamine - Sting / Itch Relief

Safety and extras for national and international travel

1. Take a six-foot, fiberglass orange/lime green flagpole, lock to back rack.
2. Take a three-foot, fiberglass orange/lime green traffic side flagpole, bungee into traffic side.
3. Two extra tires, two extra tubes, 20 patches.
4. One extra chain.
5. Extra rear derailleur.
6. Extra freewheel or rear cassette.
7. Passport, shot records, international driver's license, Scuba Diving Card, extra passport-sized pictures, hostel card, silk sheet for the sleeping bag, bird book, Frisbee (optional), Hacky sack, snake bite kit, 30 feet of nylon cord, spare toe clip, extra nuts, washers and bolts, toe clip strap, swimmer's goggles, malaria pills, small binoculars, metric conversion card, bear repellant spray.
8. When traveling on a train, boat, or plane, make sure you buy a NEW fuel bottle and mark it a 'water' bottle with duct tape. If the TSA people try to confiscate it, they will, put some water in it and drink it to show them. Otherwise, they will take it away from you, and you will be without a fuel bottle when you reach South America or Africa or some other place.
9. Spare brake cable, spare gearing cable, spare brake pads, spare pulley, photocopies of passport, driver's license, sewing kit, MSR stove cleaner and repair kit,

birth certificate copy, water purification tablets, suture and thread, folding gallon container, spare spokes front and back, spare reading glasses, chain oil, chain breaker, freewheel cog remover, spare ball bearings, bottom bracket puller, pocket vice, crank remover, crazy glue, valve stem remover, swimsuit, cable and combination lock.

INTERNATIONAL TOURING RECOMMENDATIONS

When riding outside the grocery-store-and-fast-food borders of the United States, you open yourself up to new culinary challenges and dangers. In America, you can count on clean water. The U.S. Department of Agriculture inspects meats. Most people speak English. You enjoy smooth roads and easy living.

You're sick of it, right? Too many motorhome mentalities! Cable TV hookups in campsites! Every town in America looks like every other town. First, you see the Golden Arches, followed by Wendy's, Subway, Arby's and Pizza Hut. Everyone walking out of a fast-food restaurant looks like they need special coaching from Jenny Craig and the TV program: Biggest Losers! Ye gads! Whatever happened to regional flavor, small-town diners, personal dress and style? Does anyone remember what an old-time hardware store smells like? Do they know the wooden floors creak? Not a chance!

Sounds like you're ready to see how the other 95 percent lives. Hold onto your handlebars and pull up your Lycra shorts because you're in for one heck of a surprise. You face amazing sights and experiences in the developing world.

Always be aware of your potential circumstances on tour in developing countries. Be smart! Be prudent! Be prepared! Your life may depend on your thoughtful and measured actions. You cannot hope someone will rescue you like they do in the movies.

Anytime you ride into a foreign country, you're subject to conditions you won't find at home. You may be vulnerable to infectious diseases, tainted food and contaminated water. You need extra precautions with eating, drinking and medicine.

Riding Outside the United States

While on tour in any one of more than 190 countries, give or take a revolution every five years, you will notice many differences. The freedoms you take for granted at home may be turned upside down in other countries. The way people dress on the altiplano, treeless land above 12,000 feet in Bolivia, is different from the natives in Bali. People in the Middle East bow to Allah five times a day and the women are covered except for their eyes. Australia's kangaroos may enthrall you with their 40-foot leaps. Europe's architecture and history will seduce you. The cultures, languages, animals and people you visit will change dramatically from country to country. Your patience and understanding will be challenged often in foreign lands.

Please enjoy that people around the world offer smiles and friendships. They laugh, cry and struggle through different parts of their lives, just like you do. You travel through the 'village' of humanity.

Along the way, you need to adapt. That 'adaptation' is key to your success. When it comes to eating, you face challenges and fabulous experiences.

First, you face a 90 percent certainty of suffering from food poisoning or bacterial disruption of your stomach and colon. Whether it's giardia cysts, worms, dysentery, hepatitis or food poisoning—you're headed for the bathroom. The key: accept its inevitability, treat it, endure it and get on with your tour. Take along medicine for diarrhea and pills to kill parasites. Obtain those medications in your doctor's office.

Water on International Tours

The primary concern on international tours: water! The rule remains simple:

- Always filter your water.
- Use purification tablets to ensure safety.

Make certain when you're filtering water to avoid mixing droplets of unfiltered water with filtered water. Just one unfiltered or untreated droplet can cause you sickness. That's why a purification tablet gives you a second line of defense in making your water safe.

No matter how much time it takes to filter water, do it painstakingly. It can mean the difference between miles of smiles and days of lying on your back with giardia making your colon feel like it's an arena for a bumper-car rally.

Diseases

Several diseases await you while on tour in developing countries. Be prudent and you will save yourself from most of them. Take every preventative shot in the book to protect yourself. Your physician can provide immunizations for you.

Hepatitis causes one heck of a lot of misery in developing countries. To combat it, take gamma-globulin shots that last up to six months. So far, so good! Make sure you take the shot several weeks before the trip and avoid taking a gamma-globulin shot with any live virus vaccines. Your doctor will know about that.

If you contract hepatitis, you will feel like someone used your body as a practice target for a bow and arrow. You will be weak, your eyes will turn yellow, and your urine will darken.

You can contract hepatitis from food or water. If you come down with it, see a doctor as quickly as possible.

The Inca Two-Step, or Montezuma's Revenge, or Buddha's Belly give you an idea of a 'bowel affliction' called diarrhea in the United States. You will spend entire days on the toilet and your face in the lavatory! If you discover blood in your feces, along with cramps in your stomach, it could be dysentery. You may need to take tetracycline. See a doctor.

Upon returning from any international tour, have your feces, blood and urine checked for bugs.

Food Transport Over Long Distances

One of your biggest challenges will be transporting food and water across long stretches of desert or uninhabited mountains. Be sure to look at a map and find out how far it is to the next food and water. We have carried as much as six days of food with us when we rode from La Paz, Bolivia to Arica, Chile. Our bikes looked more like pack mules than touring machines.

Our supplies included 10 days' worth of oatmeal, dried beans and rice, dried bread and rolls, tuna, dried fruit, potatoes, carrots and onions, and other sturdy, non-perishable foods. With rice and beans, and oatmeal—you can enjoy protein and carbs to power you anywhere.

In desert situations, like the Atacama Desert of Chile, or the Sahara in Africa, you're looking at hundreds of miles of sand. You won't see a fly or mosquito. You will need to bring four gallons of water with you to ensure making it to the next roadhouse. That's especially important on the Nullarbor Plains (treeless) in the Outback of Australia, where temperatures exceed 120 degrees Fahrenheit and higher. The sun sucks water out of your skin like a wet-vacuum. I've toured 100 miles in Death Valley at 116°F, and 190° at ground level. I have downed five gallons in one day, and never hit the bathroom!

Preventative maintenance and health on tour

Because you will not be able to bathe every day, carry antifungal ointment, or take a 1.5-gallon' shower bag' with you offered at most camping stores. You can rinse down, soap up, and rinse off within three minutes. Just hang the bag on a tree and, voila, you're clean for sleeping. Great invention! Still carry the anti-fungal ointment! Also, carry cortisone cream for poison ivy.

During a tour anywhere, preventative maintenance: is very important! Check your spokes and screws daily to make sure they are tight. Gear ratio: 24 to a 34-rear granny! No need to bust your guts when you can spin with ease!

There's a reason you're traveling along an adventure highway. As John Muir wrote, "Camp out among the grass and gentians of glacier meadows, in craggy garden nooks full of Nature's darlings. Climb the mountains and get their good tidings. Nature's peace will flow into you as sunshine flows into trees. The winds will blow their freshness into you, and the storms their energy, while cares will drop off like autumn leaves."

Be smart. Stay prepared. Enjoy the peace and silence. It's all good!

Baker's Dozen Suggestions

You will develop dozens of personal habits while touring. Your gear will be placed where you want it, and you will evolve an almost ritualistic style of doing things.

Of course, the most important thing you can do is buy a good bike and have a touring veteran fit it to your body. Have the bike fitted at four junctures:

- Fit the right-sized bike for your height.
- Fit your seat to pedal height. With your shoe heel at the 6:00 o'clock position, while sitting in the seat, have someone hold you straight, you need to have a 10 percent bend in the knee. This will give you maximum pedal, muscle and power coordination.
- Fit your knee to your pedal axle. You should be able to drop a plumb line straight from the back of your patella to the axle of the pedal. The pedal will be located at the 9' o'clock position on the left side of the bike. Adjust your seat to make sure you're exactly in line with your patella and the axle for a perfect fit and comfort.
- Fit the length from your seat to your handlebars. A general rule of thumb is to place your elbow at the tip of the seat and your longest middle finger will touch the handlebars for a perfect riding angle and fit. Go to a professional bike shop to get it done for you if you are unsure.

Buy a bike from a good bicycle store where you will enjoy good service after the sale. If you buy mail orders, be sure you know what you're doing or have a friend who knows what he or she is doing to help you select the best bike.

Here are that Baker's dozen ideas:

- No matter how much you ride, someday you will take a fall. Since you don't know how bad the fall will be, you must anticipate the worst and wear a helmet. About 2.5 Americans die daily from falling off bicycles. That's 900 a year. Most of them cracked their heads like an egg yolk and didn't live. About 50,000 suffer broken bones, cuts and other injuries. Wear your helmet so you don't become a statistic. Buy an ANSI-approved helmet and strap it on every time you get on your bicycle!
- Buy the best sunglasses you can afford to protect your eyes. Protect yourself from deadly radiation from the constant sun burning down on your face and body by covering your body with long sleeve jerseys and tights.
- Buy an excellent pair of shoes designed specifically for bicycle riding with a steel or plastic shank along the footbed to give your even pressure and comfort. Without a good shoe, your food will feel more pressure and pain than you can imagine. Check performancebike.com; bikenashbar.com; REI.com.
- Learn how to maintain and repair your bicycle. Take a bicycle repair class with hands-on instruction. You need to be able to take apart your head tube, hubs, bottom bracket and freewheel or cassette assembly. If you're on a world tour, you need to be able to true your wheels and possibly rebuild a rim! You must know how to repair a tube or save a tire with 'duct tape' to the side walls to get more mileage when you're in a remote village in South America. Take the tools you need and know how to use them.
- Your nutrition on a bike trip is important. Stay as close to high carbohydrates and simple proteins as possible for maximum efficiency. You will gain more stamina, power and endurance from pasta, grains, fruits, cereals, vegetables and bread. You may want to take multiple

vitamins on an extended tour for 'added' nutrition. Your body suffers considerable depletion of resources while pedaling for days on end.

- Also, in order to defend against skin cancer, cover your body with long sleeve jersey and tights and a hood down from your helmet to protect your ears and neck. Use 50-block sunscreen and lip balm.
- Drink liquids constantly. Water provides the best drink on tour.
- While touring in high mountains, allow your body to acclimate itself to the altitude. If not, you could suffer from altitude sickness. If you push too hard, or too fast, you could suffer from pulmonary edema. If you feel weak, or short of breath and start coughing, drop below 10,000 feet and stay there for a few days until you feel well enough to climb again. Cerebral edema is a more serious sickness because it affects your brain. You will suffer a pounding headache and possible double vision. If you do not take action, death could result. Descend to below 10,000 feet and get medical attention.
- When taking airlines and trains to major destinations, you will have to box your bike for transport. Visit a bicycle shop and pick out a box that fits your bike, or ask them to save you one, or check out their dumpster for extra boxes. Learn how to break your bike down and put it back together so you won't depend on a bike shop.
- You will attract lots of attention while touring and many people will invite you into their homes. I have never encountered a problem, but you need to be cautious, especially if you are a woman. You might accept lodging only if you meet a family or couple. I would shy away from single men asking you over to stay the night. Also, many men enjoy a faster cadence and move ahead of their women partners. This is important: if you're on tour with your wife or a female companion, ride behind her so you stay together. If you pedal too far ahead, she will feel alone and vulnerable. She will be highly agitated given enough time, and your relationship will suffer—along with your tour. Trust me on this one, guys!

- Dogs can be the bane of your bicycling tour. They will frighten the daylights out of you and worse, bite you. You could be sent to the hospital for stitches or rabies shots. If a dog or dogs attack, they usually bark first, so you know they are coming. It's worth your efforts to deal with their attacks quickly. Always be alert for dogs by keeping an eye on a house or any areas you think of house dogs. If you can outrun dogs by pedaling past their territory, go for it. You can carry a dog repellant spray, or better yet, pull your traffic side three-foot-long fiberglass safety pole out from under your bungee cords and show it to them by waving it back and forth. That 'whip' will calm them down quickly and they will leave you alone. If pressed, carry a few stones in your handlebar bag and throw them at the dogs. Carry an air horn or Mace to ward them off. Aim at their faces. As a last resort, dismount your bike and walk behind it as you move out of their territory.
- Always be prepared for survival situations by carrying ample water, food and shelter. Carry minimum amounts of food that will keep you fed for up to seven days in remote regions. Make sure you can stay warm in a summer blizzard at a high altitude. Bring those waterproof glove protectors and rain booties to keep your hands and feet dry and warm.
- Leave the road and find camp 1.5 to 2.0 hours before dusk. If you happen to get caught in the dark, attach a front LED headlight and a rear blinking LED red light. You can carry a blinking strobe light to let traffic know your presence.

Breaking down and packing your bike for travel

Secure the right-sized box for your bike. You can buy a plastic box at bike shops if you plan to have a safe place at your destination to store it. If not, a cardboard box will work fine.

Break down your bike by taking off the handlebars, front wheel, pedals and seat and pulling off the rear derailleur. Take the rear derailleur off the dropout, tape it to the chain and encase it in cloth with tape. Do not forget this procedure or you may suffer a bent dropout hanger and possibly a broken rear derailleur. Lock the front forks with a plastic axle and secure them with tape. That will stabilize the forks from breakage.

Secure all nuts and bolts and pack the bike with paper so it won't move inside the box. Place the front rack under the forks. The front-wheel will fit beside the frame opposite the chain drive side. Tape the pedals to the frame so as not to lose them along with the bike seat and shaft. Slip a piece of cardboard between the wheel and your bike so it won't suffer scratches. Everything you can do to keep the bike locked solidly still in the box is important. Toss in your six-foot fiberglass safety flag and three-foot fiberglass traffic-side safety flag along with empty water bottles. Tape it up with plastic tape. Tape all four corners, and all seams for extra strength on international journeys where they throw your gear around without regard to damage to your precious bike.

Best safety gear on the planet for cyclists

Let's cover the most important safety device on your bike: be sure to hose-clamp that six-foot-long fiberglass pole with orange/lime green and white safety flag to your rear rack. A second three-foot fiberglass safety pole with an orange/lime green flag will fit under your bungee cords that secure your rear pack to the rack—about 18 inches into traffic. In town, you can shove it closer to the bike, so you won't be such a 'wide' profile trying to maneuver around cars in heavy traffic.

The total effect is two oranges, flapping flags that can be seen a half-mile away. They get the attention of approaching drivers both front and rear. When you garner their attention, you are less likely to suffer consequences. You must remember that you are sharing the road with at least 2,000 pounds of steel traveling at 65 miles per hour. Just one yawn or sneeze, a glance back at the kids, or a daydream could have a car running up the back of your panniers. Those flags are your lifeline to safety. Engage them as if your life depended on them. Buy at a bike shop, K-Mart, Walmart or Target.

Finally, remember you are pedaling down the adventure highway. You're an ambassador for your state or country. What you do affects others. Things you say or do last a lifetime to those you encounter. Make your tour a positive experience for all you meet. You will be rewarded with magical moments that last a lifetime in your heart and mind.

Chapter 63—Camping techniques, Bear and mountain lion safety, Safe Water, Personal Hygiene, Cooking, Cleaning, Human Waste, Leave No Trace, Wilderness Survival

> ***"To many Americans, the wilderness is little more than a retreat from the tensions of civilization. To others, it is a testing place—a vanishing frontier where humans can rediscover basic values. And to a few, the wilderness is nothing less than an almost holy source of self-renewal. But for every man, woman, and child, the ultimate lesson that nature teaches is simply this: man's fate is inextricably linked to that of the world at large, and to all of the other creatures that live upon it."***
>
> ***—Unknown***

Every time you step into the wilderness, it provides you with uncommon splendor and beauty. What can you do to preserve it? Answer: "Leave No Trace!"

By following the established protocol in this chapter whether you ride a bicycle, backpack, climb mountains, fish, raft, canoe, hike, sail, or do any other wilderness activity—take only photographs and leave only footprints.

For sure, my dad always told me, "Son, when you go camping, always leave the place nicer than you found it."

To this day, I have picked up a half-million pieces of trash in my life, if not more. I volunteer to pick up rivers, roadways, campgrounds, mountain paths, and any place I see trash. Yes, it's frustrating that many careless outdoor people toss their cans, bottles, and glass containers without a blink. I also advocate for a 10-cent deposit/return law like Michigan's to stop the incredible littering of the landscape. It drives me crazy that billions of humans take no responsibility for their landscape around the planet.

Nonetheless, all of us enjoy a stake in our world's well-being and our own as we live this great life adventure. I hope you become one of the people that care and care deeply. This Chapter will show you how to preserve the wilderness.

Whether you hike, backpack, canoe, climb, bicycle or any other mode of adventuring—these techniques will guide you.

WILDERNESS CAMPING

CAMPING AND COOKING IN ESTABLISHED CAMPGROUNDS:

Making Camp
Cooking and Food Storage
Camping and Cooking in a Primitive Area
Make Camp in Primitive Areas
Building Campfires Safely in the Wilderness
Fire in Your Tent
Candle Lantern
Sanitation and Human Waste in the Wilderness
Cleaning and Hygiene
Bear and Lion Country
Rules for Camping in Bear and Lion Country
If a Bear or Mountain Lion Should Confront You

When adventuring shelter and food take on a whole new significance, especially internationally. If you venture into developing world countries, being ill-prepared may cause you great discomfort. In the USA, it's not hard to find a camping park, motel, or bed and breakfast. You have many to choose from in every state and most of Canada.

In the developing world outside cities, lodging is next to impossible to find. That's why you must carry your own tent, sleeping bag and air mattress. For cooking meals, you need a stove, cookware, fuel, water, and food supplies. When you're prepared with the basics, bicycle adventuring internationally will offer miles of smiles. Nothing beats a good night's sleep on a full stomach.

The most important gear a cyclist can carry is a top-quality tent. It must be big enough, light enough and waterproof. Quick "pitch time" is a nice extra. With so many tents on the market, how do you choose? You may have a friend who knows tents because he or she camps often. They have learned by experience. Have them go to the local camping outfitter with you to discuss the relative differences between tents. Buy good gear. Do you want to go cheap? Be my guest, but you will pay a terrible price in misery.

If you're on your own, a few tips may help in your purchase. For camping, your tent should be self-standing and six pounds or less. It should have a waterproof floor and sidewalls. Rip-stop nylon is your best bet for durability, or if you can afford it, buy a Gore-Tex fabric tent. Make sure the tent has a loop to hang clothes and candle lanterns from the ceiling. Make certain the tent is taut enough, so it won't flap in the wind. Get shock-corded poles for easier setup.

Make certain the rainfly covers the outside edges of the tent. Is your tent long enough? Can you sit up in it? Will you have room for two people and your gear? Is it warm enough for three seasons? A light color will be cooler in the summer and stand up under ultraviolet damaging rays better. Zippers should be YKK plastic. Make certain your tent features "No see 'em" netting. Check for good ventilation low in the tent you buy. Some manufacturers stand solidly behind their tents with excellent guarantees. Compare for a top choice. Purchase seam sealer and apply it to the rain fly and corners of the tent, wherever the fabric has been sewn.

Once on the road, a few good habits will keep your tent in top condition for years of use. Purchase a nylon-backed plastic tarp for a ground cloth. Cut it to fit 2" inside the outside boundary of your tent. This will help stop sharp objects from cutting your floor and it will keep out moisture. You need to cut it 2" less all around the tent so it won't catch rainwater and pool it in the under you in the middle of the night.

Set up your tent every night as if it was going to rain. Find a high spot in the land and check for rocks and sticks before laying down the tarp. Never leave your tent out in the sun for extended lengths of time. Ultraviolet rays will damage the fabric. When taking down a tent, fold the poles and put them in a safe place immediately after you pull them out of their sleeves. This will prevent them from being stepped on. Count stakes each time you put your tent into the stuff sack. After a rain, either dry out the tent in the morning or at the earliest moment. For storage, make certain your tent is bone dry before putting it away for the winter.

After your tent, purchase a warm, comfortable sleeping bag. You have two choices: goose down or fiber fill. Having used both many times, it's this bicycle camper's opinion that for three seasons of bicycling, a three-pound, 20-degree Fahrenheit, and fiber-fill mummy bag is your best bet. It dries easier and stands up to usage for many years longer. Downshifts and leaves cold spots after a time and the loft breaks down. However, you may have a friend who swears by down for its compact ability and lighter weight. It becomes a personal decision.

No matter what your choice is, buy a quality mummy bag from a reputable company. Make certain it's long enough and features a contoured hood enclosure with a drawstring so all that is not covered when it's cold is your mouth. Make certain your bag is designed so the baffle flap drapes DOWN over the zipper from the inside. Gravity will keep that baffle covering the entire length of the zipper and stop any cold air from entering your bag. Expect to pay more for a down bag.

Keep it in a waterproof bag and stuff sack when riding. If you forget, you will be sliding your bare body into a cold, wet bag one nightstand wonder why you didn't pay attention to these suggestions. Don't laugh, I have slept in wet, cold bags before.

No matter how good your tent and sleeping bags are, misery stalks the bicyclist that fails to sleep on an air mattress. The best self-inflating air mattress on the market for cycling is a 3/4 length, 1" thick Thermo-Rest mattress by Cascade Designs. Buy a stuff sack to go with it. It's the best investment for comfort in the world.

While camping, you need cookware. A copper-bottomed stainless-steel set with two pots, and plastic cups is light and handy. Keep a scrubber and soap in the pot. A plastic fork and spoon are light. If you're traveling in a first-world country, go with a propane gas stove, and carry two extras. For overseas touring, go with an MSR International stove that burns any kind of fuel. Your Swiss Army knife is a vital part of your cooking utensils, along with a carrot or potato peeler. Add a small plastic cutting board. Always wash cookware after dinner, especially in the wild. You don't want a grizzly sniffing your toes in the middle of the night.

Depending on how loaded you are, and the length of your adventure, a sleeping bag, tent and mattress will be set on your back rack. You may have a front rack with a platform perfect for a sleeping bag. You need a bigger bike to fit this style of packing. Be sure to carry plastic bags to waterproof your sleeping bag. It wouldn't hurt to do the same for your tent and mattress.

The one thing you cannot count on during an adventure is a campground. Well before you begin looking about 1½ hours before dark, have water bottles filled and an extra full gallon. If the water quality is questionable, purify by tablets, drops, or filtration. Purchase your food in advance. Such things as toilet paper, matches and stove fuel should be secured.

If you find a campground with showers and you're willing to pay the price, go for it. Try to keep away from dogs and loud music.

Often, you are nowhere near an organized campground, or in the case of the developing world, no such thing exists. You're on your own. That's a plus, because it offers you a chance to experience nature, animals and solitude.

The best way to find a campsite is to look for a dirt road that leads into the bush, trees, rocks, or out of sight of the road. If you can find a place near a river, lake or stream, so much the better (Please bathe with biodegradable soap). When you find a suitable spot, away from traffic, pitch your tent, EVERY TIME, as if it were going to rain. Exceptions are the Sahara Desert. I have broken my own rules a few times and it cost me dearly with a ruined camera and miserable nights floating around in my tent or trying to dodge the wet spots creeping up on my body as the bag absorbed more water. Pitch your tent on high ground. Check for rocks, twigs and roots before laying down the ground tarp. Set the front door away from the wind and possible rain. This will give you a windbreak for cooking too. Make certain all stakes are secured and the rain fly is taut. Be sure to keep the ground cloth under the tent. Once the tent is secured, take the gear off your bike and put it into your tent. Cable locks your bike to a tree including both wheels. A combination lock will allow everyone in your party to use the same lock without using a key.

CAMPING AND COOKING IN ESTABLISHED CAMPGROUNDS

When camping in an established campground, many obstacles are overcome immediately. You enjoy a picnic table, water, washing facilities and a seating area at your command. Nonetheless, you need to buy food and load up on water two to three hours before sunset in case you don't reach an established campground. Always check your map for locations.

Making Camp

After finding a spot in a campground—one to two hours before dark—you can:

- Pitch your tent on high ground.
- Roll out the sleeping mattress and sleeping bag.
- Place all your gear in the tent. Always put your gear in the same places, so you know where to find specific items, even in the dark. Always place your flashlight or miner's lamp exactly in the same place so you can grab it when you need it.
- Make sure your 'miner's lamp' is on your head and ready to work as darkness falls. These LED headlamps can be purchased at camping outlets. You may look like a coal miner walking around in the dark, but you will find it very useful.
- Remember NOT to place any food in your tent, especially in bear country. Rule: cook and eat 100 yards from your tent, and then, hang food 100 yards from your tent. That means you may have to eat first, then, cook

and eat food, and then, hang food in trees 100 yards from the final campsite. Don't believe me? Think you can get away with it? So did I! But when you wake up during the night with a grizzly or black bear pummeling you inside your tent or looking at you when you open the flaps—don't say I didn't warn you! In bear country, always carry bear spray with you from REI.com and other camping stores. It could save your life. I guarantee that you will be scared enough to wet your pants, but you could live!

- If you are not in bear country, you 'can' leave food in your tent as long as you remain in the tent. If you leave, or you have food odor in your tent, little critters will eat their way through the nylon and ruin your tent.
- Lock your bike to a tree or to your helmet inside your tent (if there are no trees or something to cable the bike). To do this, run the cable through the bike frame, then into your tent and lock it to your helmet strap. When you zip up the tent, the cable acts like an umbilical cord between it and your bike. If someone tries to make off with your bike, they won't get far before you notice half your tent being pulled away.
- Always light the match before turning on your gas burner. Never turn the gas on first, unless you want to make it like a Saturn rocket and blast yourself to the moon.
- Set up your food and fixings, cutting board, utensils, pans, water bottles and spices.

- Prepare your meal.
- Enjoy!
- Wash, clean and dry all your pots and utensils. Replace and secure.
- Secure food in a tree or bear box, or if you're looking for an exciting night of terror, leave it in your tent!

Cooking and Food Storage

Before cooking your meal, make good use of the stove burner for heating water for tea or hot chocolate. If you're cooking by a campfire, let the wood burn down so you get an even heat from the coals. You'll also have to tackle the problem of balancing pots on the coals.

Once you have prepared the food for cooking by chopping and cutting, place the food into the cooking pot. As your dinner progresses, keep an eye on the food to keep it from burning.

After dinner, wash everything with soap and rinse with water. Leave no food out for the animals. Keep extra food in a locked food box—a wooden or metal box used in some campgrounds where animals are a concern. If there are no food boxes, and you're in a bear or mountain lion country, do not store food in your tent. Hang your food in a tree 300 feet from your camp.

Leave none of your gear out in the rain. Either store it in the tent or under the tent vestibule.

Camping and Cooking in a Primitive Area

Camping in primitive (wilderness) areas presents several challenges that must be considered. You must be more responsive to your environment, i.e., disposal of human waste, water contamination and generated food and paper waste. You are more susceptible to bears, raccoons, squirrels and wild pigs charging into your camp looking for food. If it's a big old grizzly, he might be looking for you because he carries the latest copy of the Gourmet Bear in Search of a Bicyclist. Take precautions when camping in the wild.

Again, make certain you have loaded up on extra water two to three hours before dusk. Or carry a filter that can purify water if there are ample places to fetch it—such as in the mountains or in lake regions.

Next, look for a campsite well off the road and hidden away from the sight of others. Not only is it a good idea to 'vanish' into the wilderness for personal safety, but you will also sleep better without hearing traffic all night. Remember your earplugs and use them!

Most dirt roads or trails on public land will lead to a 'stealth' camping spot. Try to get behind trees, brush, hills or a mountain. You want to be concealed, along with your fire or candlelight.

Be certain to keep your tent 25 feet away from fire. Ashes will burn through the nylon in seconds. Place your tent on high ground, so that if it rains, you won't wake up feeling like you're being swept over Niagara Falls. Special note: eight out of ten persons reading this advice will choose to learn this lesson the hard way! Trust me, you will wake up in the middle of the night wishing you sported gills!

Make Camp in Primitive Areas

- Secure food and 1.5 gallons of water two or three hours before dusk.
- Look for an abandoned road or trail and 'vanish' into the landscape.
- Pitch your tent on high ground. The sight should be safe from lightning and potential washout from a rainstorm.
- Roll out your air mattress and sleeping bag.
- Place all your gear in exact same place every night.

- Place your miner's lamp near your headrest. Once your tent and gear are secured inside, either lock your bike to a tree or run the cable from the bike to your helmet inside your tent.
- If you have a campfire, make sure it is 25 feet away from your tent. If that is not possible, use your stove for cooking.
- Spread your tablecloth on the ground outside your tent. Tablecloth can be a yard square of plastic.
- Secure your candle lantern where you can use it.
- Organize all your cooking gear and food in front of you.
- If you are using a stove, make sure it's stable. You don't need a scalding injury while away from medical help.
- If you drink coffee, hot chocolate or tea, boil your water first.
- Prepare food. Cook food. Eat like a ravenous wild maniac!
- Wash dishes and clean up all traces of food.
- Always leave the bottom zipper of your tent open if you leave camp to take a bath or for any other reason. Whether you have food in the tent or not, curious squirrels or chipmunks may bite their way through the nylon to see what's inside.

Building Campfires Safely in the Wilderness

If you enjoy ashes in your soup and burning embers in your potatoes, make yourself happy—cook on an open fire! It's SO romantic and mountain-Manish! It's primordial! Humans have enjoyed campfires before the wheel they invented the wheel. It beats watching television, unless you think watching the latest episode of "American Idol" gives meaning to life!

You need to remember a few points about making a fire to keep it safe and under control:

- Always check for, and obey, no-burn rules. Use common sense when camping in a dry area.
- Build a protective rock ring around the fire. You can wet the ground around the fire ring if you have ample water.
- Keep the fire away from tents and other fabrics. Watch out for your Lycra or Gore-Tex. One flying ember will burn a hole in it.
- Keep your eyes on the fire at all times.
- Build the fire away from overhanging tree branches or dry brush. If you build under some low-hanging branches, you might turn the tree into a bonfire. Explain that to the local fire department chief after you've taken her away from her husband and two kids at suppertime. On second thought, maybe she would mind a little adventure away from hubby and the kids...! Finally, avoid building a fire against a large rock or cliff because it will leave unsightly smoke scars.
- Keep a water supply handy in case you need to douse the flames.
- Let the fire burn down before you place your pots in the embers. You want a slow, even heat on your food.
- If it's windy, eat pork and beans out of a can, or a sandwich, or energy bars. Avoid the chance of a runaway fire.
- Before hitting the sack, be certain to put the fire COMPLETELY OUT by smothering it with water or dirt.

If you fail to put it out completely, you could cost people their lives and homes. Put that fire out COMPLETELY!

- When finished with the fireplace, spread the rocks out and return the fire area to its natural appearance. Spread the ashes and place leaves and brush over the fire pit. Really give nature a chance by keeping the wild beautiful. "Leave no trace!"

Fire in Your Tent

On those rainy or windy days, your first inclination might be to cook in your tent. Don't!

Okay, I know you're starving to death, and you hunger for a Big Mac, or Chipotle's Special or a Giant pizza. Again, don't cook in your tent!

There are so many little things that can and will go wrong when you have an open flame burning in your tent. I'm as careful as a person can be, but once, I nearly turned my tent into a bonfire! Avoid learning this lesson the hard way.

Candle Lantern

The only flame, and I haven't done it in a long time because of miner's lamps with LEDs, is a glass and aluminum-encased candle lantern. Even then, I never leave it in the tent unattended. Make sure it's either hanging from the roof on a string or resting on a flat surface such as a notepad or book.

A fire inside your tent is nothing to fool with, and that's not a lesson you want to learn the hard way!

Sanitation and Human Waste in the Wilderness

It's very important to follow a few rules when camping in primitive wilderness situations:

When washing dishes, heat the water and use bio-degradable soap. If you're washing in a lake or stream, make sure you discard the soapy water onto the soil at least 15 feet away from the lake or stream water so it drains into the soil. Rinse your cooking gear thoroughly.

Pack out what you pack in! I pick up the trash of careless campers. I honor Mother Nature by leaving a place cleaner than I found it. In the immortal words of the great philosopher Goethe, "Do not think that you can do so little, that you do nothing at all." Avoid burning anything, especially plastic, but do take it in a bag to a proper trash can up in the next town or wherever it's proper and responsible.

Since no toilets are available in primitive campsites, please follow strict wilderness rules:

- Find a spot 20 to 30 yards away from your campsite and away from a water source.
- Dig a hole four to six inches deep. Do your business. Cover your waste with soil. If that is not possible, cover with a rock or leaves. Carry your TP in a 1-gallon zip lock plastic bag and another 1-gallon zip lock bag inside it. Roll your 'soiled' TP into a ball with new TP and place it in the second zip lock bag. No, you don't have to touch the soiled TP. Again, "Leave No Trace!"
- You may burn your used toilet paper in the campfire. If dry conditions exist or combustibles are present, just carry the used TP in the zip lock bag and toss used TP at the next proper disposal.
- In Chile, my friend Doug nearly burned an entire wheat field because the flame he used to burn his toilet paper ignited to the dry stalks. The next thing I knew, Doug waddled toward me with his shorts around his knees, screaming, "I just crapped in the wrong place!" We

grabbed six water bottles and ran back to the fire, squirting it with our tiny water guns. A passing motorist and an old lady stopped to help us. You can imagine her shock and confusion when she saw Doug with his shorts at his ankles and me screaming and squirting at the flames. She didn't know whether to help us or faint. Moral of this episode: be careful where you strike a match to your toilet paper—and pull up your pants before you light it!

- Also, clean your hands with 'hand sanitization' or soap and water, or at least rinse your hands.

Cleaning and Hygiene

While on tour or on any adventure, you're living at a basic level. You're closer to being an animal than you've ever been. Bugs will try to invade your tent and mosquitoes will buzz around your head. Spiders will spin webs across your tent at night and they will be eating their 'catch' when you step out the next day. "You'll go to sleep under the moonlight and wake up with the sun. The morning alarm clock might be the laughing call of an Australian kookaburra bird. It's natural, but it's dirty out there on a bike, or backpacking, or mountain climbing or any extended outdoor activity.

That's why you must maintain good sanitation and hygiene practices.

Wash your hands before preparing food. Be certain to use bio-degradable soap in the wilderness. If you don't have any, use any soap or hand cleaner, but make sure you use it. Avoid throwing soapy water into a stream or lake. Throw it onto the land where it can drain into the soil.

After any use of pots and pans, make certain to wash and rinse them. Use your camp towel to wipe them or let them dry in the sun. Please honor Mother Nature and she will bless you with wonders around the next bend in the road or turn of the river.

Bear and Lion Country

> **"Bears are made of the same dust as we, and breathe the same winds and drink of the same waters. A bear's days are warmed by the same sun, his dwellings are over-domed by the same blue sky, and his life turns and ebbs with the heart pulsing like ours. He was poured from the same fountain. And whether he at last goes to our stingy Heave or not, he has terrestrial immortality. His life, not long, not short, knows no beginning, no ending. To him life unstinted, unplanned, is above accidents of time, and his years, markless and boundless, equal eternity,"**
>
> **—John Muir, hiking in Yosemite Valley, California, 1888**

Camping in Grizzly, Black Bear, and Mountain Lion Country

The grizzly is North America's symbol of wilderness. His domain reaches from Yellowstone to Alaska. To catch a glimpse of these great animals fills your eyes with wonder. His wildness defines the wilderness. He remains "king" in his domain.

Nothing will scare the daylights out of you faster than coming face-to-face with a bear. Few animals will kill you faster than a grizzly if she feels threatened. If she comes in the night, you will feel terror like never before because you have the added uncertainty of darkness. The sound of her grunting will drive your heart into a pumping frenzy, and your blood will race around your body like a Formula One race car at the Indy 500.

I shivered in my sleeping bag while a grizzly dragged his muzzle across the side of my tent one morning in Alaska. His saliva left a mark on the nylon for a few weeks, and a mark for a lifetime on my mind. I'll never forget the three-and-a-half-inch claws that tore through the back of my tent... that day. I lucked out!

Bears prove capricious, unpredictable and dangerous. They search for food 24/7. Anything that looks edible to them makes for fair game. They eat berries, salmon, moose, deer, mice and humans without discrimination.

That's why this section deals with camping with a grizzly bear, black bear and mountain lion country.

If you travel, hike and camp in remote regions of North America, or other areas of the world, sooner or later, you will camp in bear country. It's not something to be feared, but it is something you must respect. You are in his dining room.

The key to your safety and survival in Mr. Grizzly's domain: is respect! You must honor the rules of the wilderness. You must follow those rules each and every time you camp, hike, or otherwise make your way into his territory. You may not get a second chance.

Imagine looking into a grizzly's eyes, backed by his 800 pounds of teeth and claws, and pleading, "Gee, Mr. Bear, could you give me a break this time...I'm really sorry I left my chocolate chip cookies inside my tent...can we make a deal, like, I'll give you my first-born child...please, pretty please...."

Never assume a bear won't walk into your life.

At the same time, you cannot camp in fear. During my many journeys to Alaska, I enjoyed extraordinary moments watching rogue grizzlies fishing for salmon and mother grizzlies playing with their cubs. Great wonder and amazing moments!

I also had the living hell scared out of me because of my own carelessness.

By using common sense and following the rules, you can minimize the chances and danger of a bear confrontation. But your safety cannot be guaranteed. You could do everything right, and still, run into a bear—especially if he's trying to find food for his evening dinner!

However, since I've alarmed you, let me put this in proper perspective! Former Governor Sarah Palin lives in Alaska. She alleges she has outrun a few grizzly bears. Therefore, if you're camping with Sarah, the only thing you have to do is run faster than her!

If you follow nature's rules, your chances of a bear confrontation are less than a lightning strike. Therefore, go ahead and enjoy yourself. And if you do encounter a bear, you will return home with great bear stories that will keep your friends glued to your every word.

Remember: food and food odors attract bears, which makes them overcome their fear of humans. Be smart and keep food odor off your body and tent, and away from your camping site.

Rules for Camping in Bear Country

Camp in an area least likely to be visited by bears. Stay away from animal trails, large droppings, diggings, berry bushes, beehives, and watering holes. Don't swim in streams where salmon run. If you do, you may end up running for your own life.

Make absolutely certain your tent has no food odor in or on it. If you have spilled jam or peanut butter, grizzlies, especially like Skippy's Crunch Style, on your tent fabric, wash it clean.

Cook 300 feet away from your tent. Wash your gear thoroughly. Do not sleep in the same clothes that you wore while eating and cooking dinner.

Make sure you avoid keeping perfume, deodorant or toothpaste in your tent. Keep anything that has an odor in your food bag and hang it away from your camp.

Hang your food in a strong 1.5-millimeter-thick plastic bag at least 300 feet from your tent. That means your camp, cooking and food hanging areas are in a triangle, 300 feet apart. If a bear does amble into your sector, he will go after your food bag, and more than likely, he won't bother you.

Bear-proof canisters that can carry several days of food supplies cost about $100.00 and can be purchased at most camping outlets mentioned in this book. REI.com

After you have hung your food, take out a wet cloth and wipe your face and hands to ensure you have no food odor on them.

Finally, brush and floss your teeth. You wouldn't want a tiny piece of food between your molars to be the reason you inadvertently invited Mr. Grizz to feast upon your tenderloin body at night. Can you imagine the coroner's report in Whitehorse, Yukon, "Gourmet camper was mauled last night because he left one little piece of fried chicken between his teeth... he could have starred in the movie "Dumb and Dumber."

Also, remember to employ the same sanitation rules you learned in the primitive camping section.

Hanging food: Attach one end of a parachute cord to a rock or carabineer and throw it over a tree limb. Use the other end of the cord to tie your food bag. Pull the bag into the air at least 12 feet above the ground, at least five feet from the tree trunk and at least five feet from the limb where the cord is hanging. Secure the parachute cord by tying it to a limb at the base of the tree or some other tree.

A second method for hanging food: Loop two bags over a limb so they balance each other and let them dangle with no tie-off cord. Some bears have figured out to follow the tie-off cord and release it by batting or pawing it—mostly in Yellowstone where so many careless campers visit. This second method should discourage a bear's efforts. Again, keep it 12 feet off the ground, at least five feet away from a tree trunk.

A third method: throw a line over the branches of two trees about ten feet apart. Throw the same parachute cord over the line and hang your food bag between the trees on the line. Do what works best for you.

Grizzlies do not intentionally prey on humans. As long as they are not drawn to any food odor, you should enjoy a good night's sleep.

If a Bear or Mountain Lion Should Confront You

Okay, you've followed the rules, but you wake up to the sounds of a bear outside your tent or something else that's breathing and prowling through the night mist. Your nostrils fill with the stench of something that's got a really bad case of body odor.

You don't carry a gun, but you do have your Swiss Army knife! Yeah, great! The bear would snatch it out of your hands and use it for a toothpick afterward! If you did carry a gun, it would only piss him off! But you kept your bear repellant spray right next to your sleeping bag, so you pull it out. Yes, the bear spray will stop a grizzly better than a gun.

At that moment, you wish you could sprint like an NFL halfback or fly like an eagle!

What to do: Stay calm. Remember that bears and mountain lions don't like humans. It could be a deer, moose or elk. Unless you're in bear country in early spring, when a bear is just out of his den and hungry, he may only be curious and sniffing around.

I have been told that a good strategy is to play dead inside your sleeping bag if you're attacked by a grizzly. If you're with another person, you may opt to run in different directions. At least one of you would live! Keep that bear spray in your hand!

No hard and fast rules exist that guarantee anything in this situation.

During the day, be alert. If you come in contact with a grizzly, try to move out of his area. Never run! Make a lot of noise by blowing a whistle if you're hiking. If a bear sees you and charges, turn sideways and do not look at him directly, but do point your bear spray at his face. He may still attack you, but then again, if you are not threatening, he may not. If he continues charging to within 20 feet, spray a stream of bear spray at his nose, and follow the stream with your own eyes until you hit him right on the nose and continue the stream. It will stop him. Make sure your friend carries a second can of spray to continue the point-blank spraying if needed. Some folks carry wasp & hornet spray for backup.

If you don't have bear spray, shame on you, but if the attack continues, drop to the ground and assume the cannonball position with your hands over your head to protect your head and stomach.

If you run, he will chase you down. At this juncture, you may want to...cry, pray, scream or faint. It may not do any good, but it may make you feel better. If your prayer isn't working, make a quick conversion to another religion and pray faster. If you die, you died while on a great adventure, which makes it a bit heroic. It's better to die this way than suffering a heart attack while eating chocolate bon-bons on a Barker Lounger in front of an NFL game with the remote glued to your hand.

Black bears: when confronting black bears, you have a much better chance of survival. Stand your ground. Do not drop to the ground or play dead. Don't look into his eyes; stay on your feet and keep that bear spray pointed right at his nose. Don't look scared, even if you're wetting your pants with fear. Maintain your composure until the black bear leaves your area. Practice using bear spray or hornet spray.

Mountain lion: if confronted with a mountain lion or puma, stand your ground and make yourself appear larger if possible, by spreading out your hands and/or hopping up on a log or rock. Move away slowly and keep the 'bear' spray aimed at the lion. If you have a child with you, pick him or her up and hold the child close to you. With a cat, you can fight back, and it may run away. It also may run if you throw rocks at it. Do not run yourself. Again, it's between you and lady luck.

Adventure is not always comfortable, but it is still an adventure. I am a firm believer that neither bliss nor adventure is ever obtained by staying home in your rocking chair.

As a final note, be confident that you will make your way through bear country safely when you follow the rules of Mother Nature. When you respect Mother Nature, she will respect you right back.

I can see you sitting around the table with your friends after your adventure in Alaska:

In your journal, "Yeah, I woke up one morning on the Kenai River when I heard a blood-curdling growl...I thought the sun was shining through my mosquito netting, but it was the pearly whites of a 900-pound grizzly...well sir, I didn't have much time to think, so I pulled out my Bowie Knife—kinda' like Daniel Boone—and stared back into that grizzly's eyes. That's when I gave him a toothy growl of my own. It scared him so badly, he scrambled up a tree, where we used him for an umbrella to keep the 24-hour sun from burning down on us while we ate fresh salmon steaks on the campfire and talked to Alaska Governor Sarah Palin in the next campsite."

Jack London would have been proud!

Tent Camping

Release the valve on the air mattress first so it is ready when you get everything inside. A key to camping success is having everything where you want it, when you need it. That means replacing the same gear in the same pouch every single time you use it. ALWAYS zip up a pouch immediately after taking out or putting something into it. Make it a habit.

Before cooking dinner, you might want to take a bath first, before the sun goes down and the air cools. Soap, towel and shower shoes are all you need. If it's a swiftly moving stream, be careful with your bottle of biodegradable soap.

A special note on campfires. Gather your wood before dark. Pick up kindling and larger branches. Stick with dead wood. Be sure the fire pit is a safe distance from your tent (20 feet). Sparks carry on the breeze and will melt nylon in seconds. Make certain the flames won't catch adjoining grass or overhanging branches on fire. A circular rock firewall is a good safety factor. Place paper and kindling at the bottom. Light the fire, get it going and keep adding larger and larger wood until you have a good flame. If you cook on an open fire, keep your pot in a heavy plastic bag to keep the black soot from smudging your gear. If your campsite is in a dry zone where fire hazards are high, use common sense when building a fire, and decide not to build one, if it's a high wind area. ALWAYS put the fire totally out with water at night and in the morning. Clean the pit and spread the rocks around. Replace twigs and leaves over the pit before you leave.

When you're ready for sleep, use one of your panniers for a pillow and a sweater to make a cushion. Or, purchase an air pillow at a camping store. Be certain to check for mosquitoes by shining your flashlight around the tent. If you see any, extinguish them. Now you're ready for sleep. Or are you? If you are in the deep wilderness where bears or other large meat-eating animals live, leave no food in your tent. Put it in a plastic bag and hang it in a tree, 300 feet from your tent. Be certain to brush your teeth and wash your face and hands so no food odor is on your person. If you have fruit in your tent, and if it's touching the floor, ants will cut the nylon in a few hours. Don't give them the chance. Any time you leave camp for a hike, do not leave food in the tent, and leave it open so chipmunks can get in. If they can't, they will chew holes through your tent.

In the morning, you may need to take your daily constitutional. That's fine. Just remember the rules of camping. Bury your feces if possible. As for your toilet paper, burn it, bury it or wrap it up and carry it out to throw away or burn at an appropriate time. You may carry a one-gallon plastic zip bag for the TP, and a second one to carry soiled TP out of the camp to be tossed in a waste can. You can burn your TP and use prudent judgment in high-fire areas of dry grass. It's that simple. In fact, leave the campsite cleaner than you found it. Burn or carry out the trash and put it in a proper disposal. No matter how trashed a place is, you don't have to become a part of the problem, you can be a part of the solution.

When breaking camp, pack your gear and clean out the tent. Pull your stakes and count them before dropping them into the bag. Do not let them lay on the ground where they can get stepped on. Pull the tent poles and immediately break them down and place them in nylon sleeves. Fold the tent along with ground cloth and place it in the stuff sack. You might try changing your folding pattern periodically, so you don't cause premature deterioration on waterproofing and fabric. Strap your gear on the bike. Walk the bike out of the area, and go back to look over everything to see that you have all your gear, including the food bag that hung from the tree. Don't be surprised if you walk up on a bear scratching his head trying to figure out how to get to your food bag.

When you're satisfied that you have everything secured, it's time to pedal. If the campsite was beautiful, you may have taken a few photographs for memories of your home in the woods.

When you follow a solid routine for camping each night, you wake up refreshed and relaxed. Camping goes hand in hand with great wilderness adventures.

> ***"While bicycle adventure-touring turns from days into weeks and weeks into months, you turn a corner in your mind, your heart and your spirit. You tap into a wellspring of eternal emotional bliss. You push two pedals that give your body renewed energy with every stroke. You see things differently while gaining whole new perspectives. You transform from one person into a whole new individual every day. Ironically, no psychologist can figure it out. But you know! The energy of the universe charges through every cell in your body to create pure enchantment."***
>
> *—FHW*

THE END.

ABOUT THE AUTHOR

Frosty Wooldridge, Golden, Colorado, lives each day with gratitude, boundless enthusiasm and a sense of purpose for everything he undertakes. He graduated from Michigan State University with a post-graduate degree from Grand Valley State University in Allendale, Michigan. He loves mountain climbing, scuba diving, swing dancing, skiing, tennis, racquetball and bicycle touring. He has rafted, canoed, backpacked, sailed, windsurfed, snowboarded and more all over the planet. He writes and speaks on overpopulation and environmental challenges facing humanity. He has taught at the elementary, high school and college levels. He has bicycled 150,000 miles on six continents and 15 times across the United States. His feature articles have appeared in national and international magazines for 30 years. He has interviewed on NBC, CBS, ABC, CNN, FOX and 100 radio shows. His website contains more information for anyone aspiring toward a spectacular life:
www.HowtoLiveaLifeofAdventure.com

Friendship appreciation: Few get through this life without friends. Thank you Doug Armstrong for your steadfast friendship while exploring the world. To you, Bryan Delay, thank you for a great ride through South America. To Bryan Hallack for friendship and world exploration. Wow, Don Lindahl for your humor on so many adventures. Thank you, Gerry Mulroy, for your music, humor and friendship. And to you, David Turner, what a ride my friend. Don Collins and Sally Espstein, thank you for your friendship and inspiration. Bob and Marie Johannes, thank you. Thank you, Cynthia Schoen. Thank you, Jim Ament. Thank you for a great ride, David Christie on the Continental Divide. Also, Denis LeMay and our 1999 Continental Divide ride. Thank you, Zeb and Deanne Bell, for years of friendship. Thank you to the entire Paul and Kathleen Corrigan family for making all my world travels possible. And, to you Tim Costello, endless thanks along this life path. Thank you, Fred Elbel, for your friendship. Thank you Luciann Graziano. Thank you for your wise counsel Ken Hampshire. Love riding with you

Frank Cauthorn. Thank you for your lifelong friendship Herb and Carma Johnson. What great rides we've shared Robert Montgomery. Thank you, David and Deb Martin for our rides and friendship. Best to Gary Hall. Love you Tali and Dave Montessi. Thank you, Gary Millennor, for your friendship. Love you both, Gary and Marty North. Best to Lindy and Robert Padfield. Thank you, Jeff Rense, for years of great talks. Best and love to Gregg Roberti, Laurie, Lauryn and Adam. Thank you, John and Sharon Stchur. Thank you, Ed, and Hildy Steinberg. Best to Marylou Tanton. Love you Archie Visser. Very best to my brother Rex with love. Thank you, Tim and Barbara Davis. Thank you, Chuck Wilder.

Facebook adventure pages:

How to Live a Life of Adventure: The Art of Exploring the World

Bicycle Touring Unique Moments

Bicycling Poets

Frosty Wooldridge

Other books by the author:

Handbook for Touring Bicyclists—Bicycling touring grows in popularity each year. Men and women around the world take to the highways and the "open air" is their kitchen. On the pages of this book, you'll discover how to buy, carry, prepare and store food while on tour. Discover the ins and outs with a "Baker's Dozen" of touring tips that are essential for successful bicycle adventuring. Whether you're going on a weekend ride, a weeklong tour or two years around the world, this handbook will help you learn the artistry of bicycling and cooking.

Strike Three! Take Your Base—The Brookfield Reader, Sterling, VA. To order this hardcover book, send $19.95 to Frosty Wooldridge by contacting him through his website. This poignant story is important reading for every teen who has ever experienced the loss

of a parent from either death or divorce. This is the story of two brothers losing their father and growing through their sense of pain and loss. It is the story of baseball, a game that was shared by both the boys and their father, and how baseball is much like life.

An Extreme Encounter: Antarctica—This book transports readers into the bowels of million-year-old glaciers and katabatic winds, to the tops of smoking volcanoes, scuba diving under the ice, intriguing people, death, outlaw activities and rare moments where the author meets penguins, whales, seals and Skua birds. Hang on to your seat belts. You're in for a wild ride where the bolt goes to the bottom of the world.

Bicycling Around the World: Tire Tracks for your Imagination—This book mesmerizes readers with animal stories that bring a smile to your face. It chills you with a once-in-a-lifetime ride in Antarctica where you'll meet a family of Emperor penguins. Along the way, you'll find out that you have to go without a mirror, sometimes, in order to see yourself. The greatest aspect of this book comes from—expectation. Not since Miles from Nowhere has a writer captured the Zen and Art of Bicycle Adventure as well as Wooldridge. Not only that, you may enjoy a final section: "Everything you need to know about long-distance touring." He shows you "How to live the dream." You will possess the right bike, equipment, money and tools to ride into your own long-distance touring adventures. If you like bicycling, you'll go wild reading this book. If you don't like bicycling, you'll still go wild reading this book.

Motorcycle Adventure to Alaska: Into the Wind—"Seldom does a book capture the fantasy and reality of an epic journey the magnitude of this book. Trevor and Dan resemble another duo rich in America's history of youthful explorers who get into all kinds of trouble—Tom Sawyer and Huckleberry Finn. They plied the Mississippi River, but Dan and his brother push their machines into a wild and savage land—Alaska. My boys loved it."

—John Mathews, father of two boys and a daughter.

Bicycling the Continental Divide: Slice of Heaven, Taste of Hell—
"This bicycle dream ride carries a bit of mountain man adventure. The author mixes hope with frustration, pain with courage and bicycling over the mountains. John Brown, a friend left behind to battle cancer, provides guts and heart for his two friends who ride

into the teeth of nature's fury. Along the way, you'll laugh, cry and gain new appreciation while pondering the meaning of life."

—Paul Jackson

Losing Your Best Friend: Vacancies of the Heart— "This is one heck of a powerful book. It's a must-read for anyone that has lost a friend or parent. It will give you answers that you may not have thought about. It will touch your heart and you will learn from their experiences. It also shows you what you can do if you suffer conflict with your friend's wife or girlfriend."

—Jonathan Runy

Rafting the Rolling Thunder: A Journey Through the Grand Canyon— "Fasten your raft-belts folks. You're in for the white-water rafting ride of your life. Wooldridge keeps readers on the edge of their seats on a wild excursion through the Grand Canyon. Along the way, he offers you an outlaw run by the intrepid legend "High Water Harry," a man who makes a bet with the devil and nearly loses his life. The raft bucks beneath you as Harry crashes through Class V rapids. And the Grand Canyon Dish Fairies, well, they take you on separate rides of laughter and miles of smiles. Enjoy this untamed excursion on a river through time."

—Jason Rogers

Misty's Long Ride: Across America on Horseback—by Howard Wooldridge (Frosty Wooldridge's brother). "As good as Howard was, sometimes there was nothing he could do about our situation in the burning inferno of Utah. In that agonizing desert, a man's mouth became so dry, he couldn't spit. I felt the heat cook my hooves at ground level where it felt like walking alone in the middle of a farrier's furnace. Above us, vultures soared in the skies searching for roadkill. Yet, Howard pulled down the brim of his hat and pushed forward. I followed this cowboy because he was a Long Rider, and I was his horse." For anyone who loves horses and high adventure, Howard's horse Misty tells one of the great adventure tales of the 21st century by galloping across America. You'll enjoy horse sense, horse humor, unique characters and ride across America."

How to Deal with 21st Century Women: Co-Creating a Successful Relationship—The chapters on the nine key points for creating a successful long-term relationship are the best suggestions for anyone considering marriage. Every woman should read them along with her man. This is the first male relationship book that honors the male perspective and aims for sensible collaboration. I highly recommend this book for men and women." Chelsea Robinson

How to Live a Life of Adventure: The Art of Exploring the World—"If you endeavor to live like you mean it, to aspire to show up with passion and purpose, and take your being to maximum heart rate in mind and body—please allow Frosty to coach, inspire and guide you. How to Live a Life of Adventure will rock your body and soul, and enliven within you your belief and practice of living like you mean it—with passion and purpose."

—James Rouse

America on the Brink: The Next Added 100 Million Americans—electrifying reading! This is a veritable cannonade of a book. Wooldridge targets the people and institutions, from the president of the USA on down, who refuse to look at the consequences of population growth in the modern era. His focus is on the United States, but his range is the world. He fearlessly addresses issues that politicians fear to mention, such as the effects of mass immigration on our population's future and social systems. He engages leaders to force population issues into our local and national political decisions. Lindsey Grant, former Deputy Assistant Secretary of State for Environment and Population.

Living Your Spectacular Life— "This book entertains, inspires and motivates. What I liked most about it: Wooldridge offers other motivational writers in each chapter to give you new ideas on living a spectacular life. He wants you to succeed for your sake. If that means you enjoy a greater affinity to another writer, he gives you plenty of choices. He's got six concepts and six practices that provide you with personal courage, self-confidence and empowerment. He offers you dozens of ordinary men and women living spectacular lives in various pursuits from world travel to growing a garden. He kept me reading through every chapter."

—Jake Hodges

Old Men Bicycling Across America: A Journey Beyond Old Age—"This book is a ton of fun. Five gray-haired, bald and grizzled old guys get together around a campfire along with one of them a guitarist, and they sing and tell stories. If you can imagine that all of them had been married once, twice and three times, well, their stories lifted into the treetops with outrageous laughter. More than that, they followed the Lewis & Clark Trail all the way to Bismarck, North Dakota on the northern tier bicycle route, the longest ride in America. This book will make you want to take the ride yourself."

—Rex Hamilton

Zen Between Two Bicycle Wheels: Eat, Pedal Sleep Subtitle: Baby Boomers Bicycling the West Coast—Take a fun ride down America's amazing West Coast from Canada to Mexico. Visit exciting historical locations like Fort Clatsop with Lewis & Clark. Enjoy the stunning Oregon Coastline. Ride through the redwoods of California. Pedal down world-famous Big Sur. Stop at the Hearst Castle. Ride across the Golden Gate Bridge. Share in the antics of endless beaches while riding toward the Mexican border. Additionally, you will find a complete guide on how to tour on a bicycle, locally, nationally and internationally.

America's Overpopulation Predicament: Blindsiding Future Generations—Discover America's biggest challenge of the 21st century—How to create a sustainable civilization. This book covers the consequences of water shortages, energy depletion and resource exhaustion. It covers the environmental consequences of plastic in the oceans, chemical destruction of the soils, air pollution and much more.

All books are available at: 1 888 519 5121, www.amazon.com, www.barnesandnoble.com, and also on Kindle.

Praise for The Kickstand Chronicles:

"Hang on to your handlebars and keep your eyes on the road! In the storied tradition of Meriwether Lewis, Ernest Shackleton, and Robert Service—Frosty Wooldridge takes you headlong on an irresistible and compelling adventure across America and five other continents. Decades of cycling and writing have forged Frosty's keen eye for characters and the details that bring them to life. The pure joy and simplicity of life on the road shine through in Frosty's prose, beckoning all of us to lay down our plow and join him in our quest for adventure."

—Sandy Colhoun, Explorer/Photojournalist

"Frosty's book is chockfull of incredible adventures. The best part is he drags you right into the middle of them. This is a remarkable book for veteran riders and armchair adventurers. You'll laugh your head off, cry and feel the spokes turning beneath you."

—Doug Armstrong, 7-continent long-distance touring rider

"Not since 'MILES FROM NOWHERE', has another long-distance touring rider come close to writing an epic and thoroughly entertaining world bicycle touring book as Wooldridge. Every chapter compels you to read into the next adventure. Before you can blink, it's 3:00 a.m. and you'll die at work if you don't put it down...but no, just one more crank of the pedals, one more amazing moment with your panniers packed and the open road before you."

—Bryan Delay, 5-continent touring rider

"I'm not kidding! You're going to be 'on' the bicycle seat in this book. You are going to be pounding those pedals and break out in a sweat. You're going to feel the headwinds. You'll suffer the climbs and shout as you fly downhill into these adventures. You'll freeze to death on 15,000-foot mountain passes in the Andes and fry like an egg in Death Valley. You'll face grizzlies in Alaska. Along the way, you're going to get arrested for having too much fun. This is one heck of a read."

—Paul Jenkins, casual rider

"What amazing adventures on a bicycle! Right from the start, you feel like you're riding with Frosty and his friends. You're living their struggles, sharing their laughter and triumphs. This book is the ultimate Zen and Art of Bicycle Adventure. If you love bicycling, read this book. You'll feel yourself shifting gears as you turn the pages.

—Mike Machuga, casual bicycle rider

"The real danger in reading Frosty's book is that you will have 'Been There, Done That' with none of the sweat and tears shed by the writer in his travels. For the non-bicycling reader... have fun with his stories and read dangerously! For veteran riders, read this book cover to cover. You won't be disappointed."

—Gary Hall, adventurer, and photographer

"You have thought about it, dreamed about it, wanted it, your entire life. But the job, house, kids, wife, and life came first. OK! But right

in front of you is this book of the journey of your dreams. Read it and feel the chain tighten on the freewheel as you climb a mighty mountain pass or ride into a howling rainstorm. You can even smell the campfire burning by a quiet lake somewhere in the world."

—Rex Jesse, Traveler

"In 1995, we met Frosty on our honeymoon while touring the West Coast on our way around the world. We were miserable until he stopped to fit our bikes into our bodies. He saved our marriage and our tour.

We finished the coast ride, to New Zealand, Australia and Europe. This book is as good as our world tour. His special section on long-distance touring will save your life."

—John and Mary Ann Hamilton, long-distance riders

"A friend sent me this book as a gift. I don't even ride a bicycle. But after reading the first chapter, I couldn't put it down. These are the kinds of stories told by men like Jack London, John Muir, and Edward Abbey. Those men lived in wilderness orbits. They threaded their way, not through life, but, instead, they took a club 'at' life. All of them could have died during their wilderness meanderings. Instead, they lived to tell the tales that enthralled generations of armchair adventurers and adventure-seekers. Wooldridge follows in their footsteps. He could have been killed countless times on the highways of the world, but instead, he lived to tell the tale. You're going to love this book for its humor, grand sweep of the planet, its history, its sublime moments, and above all, its humanity."

—John Stanton

Lightning Source UK Ltd.
Milton Keynes UK
UKHW010628160123
415428UK00001B/13

9 781957 208732